P9-DJL-546

"Breathtaking. . . . Fiction doesn't get any better than this."
—JEFFERY DEAVER

"A propulsive, high-stakes thriller rife with intrigue and suspense."
—USA TODAY

"If you're into mystery thrillers, then you're into Karin Slaughter."
—theSkimm

"[A] PULSE-POUNDING standalone."
—ENTERTAINMENT WEEKLY

"Slaughter's prodigious gifts of characterization make her stand out among thriller writers."
—WASHINGTON POST

"Simply one of the best thriller writers working today."
—GILLIAN FLYNN

"Enter the world of KARIN SLAUGHTER. Just be forewarned, there's no going back."
—LISA GARDNER

DEAR READER —

HAVE you ever looked at the person you know best in the world, and wondered what really lies below the surface? Whether what you see is _genuinely_ what you get? I've always been fascinated by the secrets and lies that underpin our lives, and so that's the question Pieces of her asks: CAN you ever know anybody completely?

I hope you enjoy it —

# PIECES OF HER

Also by Karin Slaughter

*Blindsighted*
*Kisscut*
*A Faint Cold Fear*
*Indelible*
*Faithless*
*Triptych*
*Beyond Reach*
*Fractured*
*Undone*
*Broken*
*Fallen*
*Criminal*
*Unseen*
*Cop Town*
*Pretty Girls*
*The Kept Woman*
*The Good Daughter*

EBOOK ORIGINALS
*Cold, Cold Heart*
*Blonde Hair, Blue Eyes*
*Last Breath*

NOVELLAS AND STORIES
*Like a Charm* (Editor)

# Karin Slaughter

# PIECES OF HER

*A Novel*

WILLIAM MORROW
*An Imprint of HarperCollinsPublishers*

This is a work of fiction. Names, characters, places, and incidents are products of the author's imagination or are used fictitiously and are not to be construed as real. Any resemblance to actual events, locales, organizations, or persons, living or dead, is entirely coincidental.

P.S.™ is a trademark of HarperCollins Publishers.

PIECES OF HER. Copyright © 2018 by Karin Slaughter. All rights reserved. Printed in the United States of America. No part of this book may be used or reproduced in any manner whatsoever without written permission except in the case of brief quotations embodied in critical articles and reviews. For information, address HarperCollins Publishers, 195 Broadway, New York, NY 10007.

HarperCollins books may be purchased for educational, business, or sales promotional use. For information, please email the Special Markets Department at SPsales@harpercollins.com.

A hardcover edition of this book was published in 2018 by William Morrow, an imprint of HarperCollins Publishers.

FIRST WILLIAM MORROW PAPERBACK EDITION PUBLISHED 2019.

The Library of Congress has catalogued a previous edition as follows:

Names: Slaughter, Karin, 1971- author.
Title: Pieces of her : a novel / Karin Slaughter.
Description: New York : William Morrow, 2018.
Identifiers: LCCN 2018032169 | ISBN 9780062430274 (hardback)
Subjects: LCSH: Mothers and daughters—Fiction. | Violence—Fiction. | Identity (Psychology)—Fiction. | Family secrets—Fiction. | BISAC: FICTION / Mystery & Detective / Police Procedural. | FICTION / Mystery & Detective / Women Sleuths. | FICTION / Suspense. | GSAFD: Mystery fiction. | Suspense fiction.
Classification: LCC PS3569.L275 P54 2018 | DDC 813/.54—dc23
LC record available at https://lccn.loc.gov/2018032169

ISBN 978-0-06-288309-4 (pbk.)

22 23  LSC  20 19 18 17 16 15 14 13

*For my GPP peeps*

*I'm Nobody! Who are you?*
*Are you—Nobody—Too?*
*Then there's a pair of us!*
*Don't tell! they'd advertise—you know!*

*How dreary—to be—Somebody!*
*How public—like a Frog—*
*To tell one's name—the livelong June—*
*To an admiring Bog!*

*—Emily Dickinson*

# PROLOGUE

For years, even while she'd loved him, part of her had hated him in that childish way that you hate something you can't control. He was headstrong, and stupid, and handsome, which gave him cover for a hell of a lot of the mistakes he continually made—the same mistakes, over and over again, because why try new ones when the old ones worked so well in his favor?

He was charming, too. That was the problem. He would charm her. He would make her furious. Then he would charm her back again so that she did not know if he was the snake or she was the snake and he was the handler.

So he sailed along on his charm, and his fury, and he hurt people, and he found new things that interested him more, and the old things were left broken in his wake.

Then, quite suddenly, his charm had stopped working. A trolley car off the tracks. A train without a conductor. The mistakes could not be forgiven, and eventually, the second same mistake would not be overlooked, and the third same mistake had dire consequences that had ended with a life being taken, a death sentence being passed, then—almost—resulted in the loss of another life, her life.

How could she still love someone who had tried to destroy her?

When she had been with him—and she was decidedly with

him during his long fall from grace—they had raged against the system: The group homes. The emergency departments. The loony bin. The mental hospital. The squalor. The staff who neglected their patients. The orderlies who ratcheted tight the straitjackets. The nurses who looked the other way. The doctors who doled out the pills. The urine on the floor. The feces on the walls. The inmates, the fellow prisoners, taunting, wanting, beating, biting.

The spark of rage, not the injustice, was what had excited him the most. The novelty of a new cause. The chance to annihilate. The dangerous game. The threat of violence. The promise of fame. Their names in lights. Their righteous deeds on the tongues of schoolchildren who were taught the lessons of change.

*A penny, a nickel, a dime, a quarter, a dollar bill . . .*

What she had kept hidden, the one sin that she could never confess to, was that she had ignited that first spark.

She had always believed—vehemently, with great conviction—that the only way to change the world was to destroy it.

August 20, 2018

# 1

"Andrea," her mother said. Then, in concession to a request made roughly one thousand times before, "Andy."

"Mom—"

"Let me speak, darling." Laura paused. "Please."

Andy nodded, preparing for a long-awaited lecture. She was officially thirty-one years old today. Her life was stagnating. She had to start making decisions rather than having life make decisions for her.

Laura said, "This is my fault."

Andy felt her chapped lips peel apart in surprise. "What's your fault?"

"Your being here. Trapped here."

Andy held out her arms, indicating the restaurant. "At the Rise-n-Dine?"

Her mother's eyes traveled the distance from the top of Andy's head to her hands, which fluttered nervously back to the table. Dirty brown hair thrown into a careless ponytail. Dark circles under her tired eyes. Nails bitten down to the quick. The bones of her wrists like the promontory of a ship. Her skin, normally pale, had taken on the pallor of hot dog water.

The catalog of flaws didn't even include her work outfit. The navy-blue uniform hung off Andy like a paper sack. The stitched silver badge on her breast pocket was stiff, the Belle Isle palm tree logo surrounded by the words POLICE DISPATCH DIVISION. Like a police officer, but not actually. Like an adult, but not really. Five nights a week, Andy sat in a dark, dank room with four other women answering 911 calls, running license plate and driver's license checks, and assigning case numbers. Then, around six in the morning, she slinked back to her mother's house and spent the majority of what should've been her waking hours asleep.

Laura said, "I never should have let you come back here."

Andy pressed together her lips. She stared down at the last bits of yellow eggs on her plate.

"My sweet girl." Laura reached across the table for her hand, waited for her to look up. "I pulled you away from your life. I was scared, and I was selfish." Tears rimmed her mother's eyes. "I shouldn't have needed you so much. I shouldn't have asked for so much."

Andy shook her head. She looked back down at her plate.

"Darling."

Andy kept shaking her head because the alternative was to speak, and if she spoke, she would have to tell the truth.

Her mother had not asked her to do anything.

Three years ago, Andy had been walking to her shitty Lower East Side fourth-floor walk-up, dreading the thought of another night in the one-bedroom hovel she shared with three other girls, none of whom she particularly liked, all of whom were younger, prettier and more accomplished, when Laura had called.

"Breast cancer," Laura had said, not whispering or hedging but coming straight out with it in her usual calm way. "Stage three. The surgeon will remove the tumor, then while I'm under, he'll biopsy the lymph nodes to evaluate—"

Laura had said more, detailing what was to come with a degree of detached, scientific specificity that was lost on Andy, whose language-processing skills had momentarily evaporated. She had heard the word "breast" more than "cancer," and thought instantly of her mother's generous bosom. Tucked beneath her modest one-piece swimsuit at the beach. Peeking over the neckline of her Regency dress for Andy's Netherfield-themed sixteenth birthday party. Strapped under the padded cups and gouging underwires of her LadyComfort Bras as she sat on the couch in her office and worked with her speech therapy patients.

Laura Oliver was not a bombshell, but she had always been what men called very well put together. Or maybe it was women who called it that, probably back in the last century. Laura wasn't the type for heavy make-up and pearls, but she never left the house without her short gray hair neatly styled, her linen pants crisply starched, her underwear clean and still elasticized.

Andy barely made it out of the apartment most days. She was constantly having to double back for something she had forgotten like her phone or her ID badge for work or, one time, her sneakers because she'd walked out of the building wearing her bedroom slippers.

Whenever people in New York asked Andy what her mother was like, she always thought of something Laura had said about her own mother: *She always knew where all the tops were to her Tupperware.*

Andy couldn't be bothered to close a Ziploc bag.

On the phone, eight hundred miles away, Laura's stuttered intake of breath was the only sign that this was difficult for her. "Andrea?"

Andy's ears, buzzing with New York sounds, had zeroed back in on her mother's voice.

*Cancer.*

Andy tried to grunt. She could not make the noise. This was shock. This was fear. This was unfettered terror because the world had suddenly stopped spinning and everything—the failures, the disappointments, the horror of Andy's New York existence for the last six years—receded like the drawback wave of a tsunami. Things that should've never been uncovered were suddenly out in the open.

Her mother had cancer.

She could be dying.

*She could die.*

Laura had said, "So, there's chemo, which will by all accounts be very difficult." She was used to filling Andy's protracted silences, had learned long ago that confronting her on them was more likely to end up in a fight than a resumption of civil conversation. "Then I'll take a pill every day, and that's that. The five-year survival rate is over seventy percent, so there's not a lot to worry about except for getting through it." A pause for breath, or maybe in hopes that Andy was ready to speak. "It's very treatable, darling. I don't want you to worry. Just stay where you are. There's nothing you can do."

A car horn had blared. Andy had looked up. She was standing statue-like in the middle of a crosswalk. She struggled to move. The phone was hot against her ear. It was past midnight. Sweat rolled down her back and leached from her armpits like melted butter. She could hear the canned laughter of a sitcom, bottles clinking, and an anonymous piercing scream for help, the likes of which she had learned to tune out her first month living in the city.

Too much silence on her end of the phone. Finally, her mother had prompted, "Andrea?"

Andy had opened her mouth without considering what words should come out.

"Darling?" her mother had said, still patient, still generously *nice* in the way that her mother was to everyone she met. "I can hear the street noises, otherwise I'd think we'd lost the connection." She paused again. "Andrea, I really need you to acknowledge what I'm telling you. It's important."

Her mouth was still hanging open. The sewer smell that was endemic to her neighborhood had stuck to the back of her nasal passages like a piece of overcooked spaghetti slapped onto a kitchen cabinet. Another car horn blared. Another woman screamed for help. Another ball of sweat rolled down Andy's back and pooled in the waistband of her underwear. The elastic was torn where her thumb went when she pulled them down.

Andy still could not recall how she'd managed to force herself out of her stupor, but she remembered the words she had finally said to her mother: "I'm coming home."

There had not been much to show for her six years in the city. Andy's three part-time jobs had all been resigned from by text. Her subway card was given to a homeless woman who had thanked her, then screeched that she was a fucking whore. Only the absolutely necessary things went into Andy's suitcase: favorite T-shirts, broken-in jeans, several books that had survived not just the trip from Belle Isle, but five different moves into progressively shittier apartments. Andy wouldn't need her gloves or her puffy winter coat or her earmuffs back home. She didn't bother to wash her sheets or even take them off the old Chesterfield sofa that was her bed. She had left for LaGuardia at the crack of dawn, less than six hours after her mother's phone call. In the blink of an eye, Andy's life in New York was over. The only thing the three younger, more accomplished room-mates had to remember her by was the half-eaten Filet-O-Fish sandwich Andy had left in the fridge and her part of the next month's rent.

That had been three years ago, almost half as many years as she had lived in the city. Andy didn't want to, but in low moments she checked in with her former cohabitants on Facebook. They were her yardstick. Her truncheon. One had reached middle management at a fashion blog. The other had started her own bespoke sneaker design company. The third had died after a cocaine binge on a rich man's yacht and still, some nights when Andy was answering calls and the person on the end of the line was a twelve-year-old who thought it was funny to call 911 and pretend he was being molested, she could not help but think that she remained the least accomplished of them all.

A yacht, for chrissakes.

A *yacht*.

"Darling?" her mother rapped the table for attention. The lunch crowd had thinned out. A man seated at the front gave her an angry look over his newspaper. "Where are you?"

Andy held out her arms again, indicating the restaurant, but the gesture felt forced. They knew exactly where she was: less than five miles from where she had started.

Andy had gone to New York City thinking she would find a way to shine and ended up emitting the equivalent amount of light you'd find in an old emergency flashlight left in a kitchen drawer. She hadn't wanted to be an actor or a model or any of the usual clichés. Stardom was never her dream. She had yearned to be star-adjacent: the personal assistant, the coffee fetcher, the prop wrangler, the scenery painter, the social media manager, the support staff that made the star's life possible. She wanted to bask in the glow. To be in the middle of things. To know people. To have connections.

Her professor at the Savannah College of Art and Design had seemed like a good connection. She had dazzled him with her passion for the arts, or at least that's what he'd claimed. That they were in bed when he'd said this only mattered to Andy after the fact. When she'd broken off the affair, the man had taken as a threat her idle chatter about wanting to focus on her career. Before Andy knew what was happening, before she could explain to her professor that she wasn't trying to leverage his gross inappropriateness into career advancement, he had pulled some strings to get her a job as an assistant to the assistant scenery designer in an off-Broadway show.

*Off-Broadway!*

Just down the street from *on Broadway!*

Andy was two semesters away from earning her degree in technical theater arts. She had packed her suitcase and barely did more than toss a wave over her shoulder as she headed to the airport.

Two months later, the show had closed under crushingly bad reviews.

Everyone on the crew had quickly found other jobs, joined other shows, except for Andy, who had settled into a real New York life. She was a waitress, a dog walker, a sign painter, a telephone debt collector, a delivery person, a fax machine monitor, a sandwich maker, a non-unionized copier paper feeder, and finally, the loser bitch who had left a half-eaten Filet-O-Fish in the fridge and one month's rent on the counter and run off to Buttfuck, Georgia, or wherever the hell it was that she was from.

Really, all Andy had brought home with her was one tiny shred of dignity, and now she was going to waste it on her mother.

She looked up from the eggs.

"Mom." She had to clear her throat before she could get out the confession. "I love you for saying that, but it's not your fault. You're right that I wanted to come home to see you. But I stayed for other reasons."

Laura frowned. "What other reasons? You loved New York."

*She had hated New York.*

"You were doing so well up there."

*She had been drowning.*

"That boy you were seeing was so into you."

*And every other vagina in his building.*

"You had so many friends."

*She had not heard from one of them since she'd left.*

"Well." Laura sighed. The list of encouragements had been short if not probing. As usual, she had read Andy like a book. "Baby, you've always wanted to be somebody different. Someone special. I mean in the sense of someone with a gift, an unusual talent. Of course you're special to me and Dad."

Andy's eyes strained to roll up in her head. "Thanks."

"You *are* talented. You're smart. You're better than smart. You're *clever*."

Andy ran her hands up and down her face as if she could erase herself from this conversation. She knew she was talented and smart. The problem was that in New York, everyone else had been talented and smart, too. Even the guy working the counter at the bodega was funnier, quicker, more clever than she was.

Laura insisted, "There's nothing wrong with being normal. Normal people have very meaningful lives. Look at me. It's not selling out to enjoy yourself."

Andy said, "I'm thirty-one years old, I haven't gone on a real date in three years, I have sixty-three thousand dollars in student debt for a degree I never finished and I live in a one-room apartment over my mother's garage." Air strained through Andy's nose as she tried to breathe. Verbalizing the long list had put a tight band around her chest. "The question isn't what else can I do. It's what else am I going to fuck up?"

"You're not fucking up."

"Mom—"

"You've fallen into the habit of feeling low. You can get used to anything, especially bad things. But the only direction now is up. You can't fall off the floor."

"Have you ever heard of basements?"

"Basements have floors, too."

"That's the ground."

"But *ground* is just another word for *floor*."

"Ground is like, six feet under."

"Why do you always have to be so morbid?"

Andy felt a sudden irritation honing her tongue into a razor. She swallowed it back down. They couldn't argue about curfew or make-up or tight jeans anymore, so these were the fights that she now had with her mother: That basements had floors. The proper direction from which toilet paper should come off the roll. Whether forks should be placed in the dishwasher tines up or tines down. If a grocery cart was called a cart or a buggy. That Laura was pronouncing it wrong when she called the cat "Mr. Perkins" because his name was actually Mr. Purrkins.

Laura said, "I was working with a patient the other day, and the strangest thing happened."

The cliffhanger-change-of-subject was one of their well-worn paths to truce.

"So strange," Laura baited.

Andy hesitated, then nodded for her to continue.

"He presented with Broca's Aphasia. Some right-side paralysis." Laura was a licensed speech pathologist living in a coastal retirement community. The majority of her patients had experienced some form of debilitating stroke. "He was an IT guy in his previous life, but I guess that doesn't matter."

"What happened that was strange?" Andy asked, doing her part.

Laura smiled. "He was telling me about his grandson's wedding, and I have no idea what he was trying to say, but it came out as 'blue suede shoes.' And I had this flash in my head, this sort of memory, to back when Elvis died."

"Elvis Presley?"

She nodded. "This was '77, so I would've been fourteen years old, more Rod Stewart than Elvis. But anyway. There were these very conservative, beehived ladies at our church, and they were bawling their eyes out that he was gone."

Andy grinned the way you grin when you know you're missing something.

Laura gave her the same grin back. Chemo brain, even this far out from her last treatment. She had forgotten the point of her story. "It's just a funny thing I remembered."

"I guess the beehive ladies were kind of hypocritical?" Andy tried to jog her memory. "I mean, Elvis was really sexy, right?"

"It doesn't matter." Laura patted her hand. "I'm so grateful for you. The strength you gave me while I was sick. The closeness we still have. I cherish that. It's a gift." Her mother's voice started to quiver. "But I'm better now. And I want you to live your life. I want you to be happy, or, failing that, I want you to find peace with yourself. And I don't think you can do it here, baby. As much as I want to make it easier for you, I know that it'll never take unless you do it all on your own."

Andy looked up at the ceiling. She looked out at the empty mall. She finally looked back at her mother.

Laura had tears in her eyes. She shook her head as if in awe. "You're magnificent. Do you know that?"

Andy forced out a laugh.

"You are magnificent because you are so uniquely you." Laura pressed her hand to her heart. "You are talented, and you are beautiful, and you'll find your way, my love, and it will be the right way, no matter what, because it's the path that you set out for yourself."

Andy felt a lump in her throat. Her eyes started to water. There was a stillness around them. She could hear the sound of her own blood swooshing through her veins.

"Well." Laura laughed, another well-worn tactic for lightening an emotional moment. "Gordon thinks I should give you a deadline to move out."

Gordon. Andy's father. He was a trusts and estates lawyer. His entire life was deadlines.

Laura said, "But I'm not going to give you a deadline, or an ultimatum."

Gordon loved ultimatums, too.

"I'm saying if this is your life"—she indicated the police-like, adult-ish uniform—"then embrace it. Accept it. And if you want to do something else"—she squeezed Andy's hand—"do something else. You're still young. You don't have a mortgage or even a car payment. You have your health. You're smart. You're free to do whatever you like."

"Not with my student loan debt."

"Andrea," Laura said, "I don't want to be a doomsayer, but if you continue listlessly spinning around, pretty soon you'll be forty and find yourself very tired of living inside of a cartwheel."

"Forty," Andy repeated, an age that seemed less decrepit every year it drew closer.

"Your father would say—"

"Shit or get off the pot." Gordon was always telling Andy to move, to make something of herself, to *do something*. For a long time, she had blamed him for her lethargy. When both of your parents were driven, accomplished people, it was a form of rebellion to be lazy, right? To stubbornly and consistently take the easy road when the hard road was just so . . . hard?

"Dr. Oliver?" an older woman said. That she was invading a quiet mother–daughter moment seemed to be lost on her. "I'm Betsy Barnard. You worked with my father last year. I just wanted to say thank you. You're a miracle worker."

Laura stood up to shake the woman's hand. "You're very sweet to say that, but he did the work himself." She slipped into what Andy thought of as her Healing Dr. Oliver Mode, asking open-ended questions about the woman's father, clearly not quite remembering who he was but making a passable effort so that the woman was just as clearly fooled.

Laura nodded toward Andy. "This is my daughter, Andrea."

Betsy duplicated the nod with a passing interest. She was beaming under Laura's attention. Everyone loved her mother, no matter what mode she was in: therapist, friend, business owner, cancer patient, mother. She had a sort of relentless kindness that was kept from being too sugary by her quick, sometimes acerbic wit.

Occasionally, usually after a few drinks, Andy could show these same qualities to strangers, but once they got to know her, they seldom stuck around. Maybe that was Laura's secret. She had dozens, even hundreds, of friends, but not one single person knew all of the pieces of her.

"Oh!" Betsy practically shouted. "I want you to meet my daughter, too. I'm sure Frank told you all about her."

"Frank sure did." Andy caught the relief on Laura's face; she really had forgotten the man's name. She winked at Andy, momentarily switching back into Mom Mode.

"Shelly!" Betsy frantically waved over her daughter. "Come meet the woman who helped save Pop-Pop's life."

A very pretty young blonde reluctantly shuffled over. She tugged self-consciously at the long sleeves of her red UGA T-shirt. The white bulldog on her chest was wearing a matching red shirt. She was obviously mortified, still at that age when you didn't want a mother unless you needed money or compassion. Andy could remember what that push-pull felt like. Most days, she wasn't as far removed from it as she wanted to be. It was a truth universally acknowledged that your mother was the only person in the world who could say, "Your hair looks nice," but what you heard was, "Your hair always looks awful except for this one, brief moment in time."

"Shelly, this is Dr. Oliver." Betsy Barnard looped a possessive arm through her daughter's. "Shelly's about to start UGA in the fall. Isn't that right, sweetie?"

Laura said, "I went to UGA, too. Of course, this was back when we took notes on stone tablets."

Shelly's mortification amped up a few degrees as her mother laughed a little too loudly at the stale joke. Laura tried to smooth things over, politely questioning the girl on her major, her dreams, her aspirations. This was the type of prying you took as a personal affront when you were young, but as an adult, you realized these were the only types of questions adults knew how to ask you.

Andy looked down at her half-filled coffee cup. She felt unreasonably tired. Night shifts. She couldn't get used to them, only handled them by stringing together naps, which meant that she ended up stealing toilet paper and peanut butter from her mother's pantry because she never made time to go to the grocery store. That was probably why Laura had insisted they have a birthday lunch today instead of a birthday breakfast, which would've allowed Andy to return to her cave over the garage and fall asleep in front of the TV.

She drank the last of her coffee, which was so cold it hit the back of her throat like crushed ice. She looked for the waitress. The girl had her nose buried in her phone. Her shoulders were slouched. She was smacking gum.

Andy suppressed the wave of bitchiness as she stood up from the table. The older she got, the harder it was to resist the urge to become her mother. Though, in retrospect, Laura had often had good advice: Stand up straight or your back will hurt when you're thirty. Wear better shoes or you'll pay for it when you're thirty. Establish sensible habits or you'll pay for it when you're thirty.

Andy was thirty-one. She was paying so much that she was practically bankrupt.

"You a cop?" The waitress finally looked up from her phone.

"Theater major."

The girl wrinkled her nose. "I don't know what that means."
"You and me both."

Andy helped herself to more coffee. The waitress kept giving her sideways glances. Maybe it was the police-like uniform. The girl looked like the type who would have some Molly or at least a bag of weed stashed in her purse. Andy was wary of the uniform, too. Gordon had gotten her the job. She figured he was hoping she would eventually join the force. At first, Andy had been repulsed by the idea because she'd had it in her head that cops were bad guys. Then she had met some actual cops and realized they were mostly decent human beings trying to do a really shitty job. Then she had worked dispatch for a year and started to hate the entire world, because two thirds of the calls were just stupid people who didn't understand what an emergency was.

Laura was still talking with Betsy and Shelly Barnard. Andy had seen this same scene play out countless times. They didn't quite know how to gracefully exit and Laura was too polite to move them along. Instead of returning to the table, Andy walked over to the plate glass window. The diner was in a prime location inside the Mall of Belle Isle, a corner unit on the bottom floor. Past the boardwalk, the Atlantic Ocean roiled from a coming storm. People were walking their dogs or riding their bikes along the flat stretch of packed sand.

Belle Isle was neither belle nor, technically, an isle. It was basically a man-made peninsula created when the Army Corps of Engineers had dredged the port of Savannah back in the eighties. They had intended the new landmass to be an uninhabited, natural barrier against hurricanes, but the state had seen dollar signs on the new beachfront. Within five years of the dredging, more than half the surface area was covered in concrete: beach villas, townhouses, condos, shopping malls. The rest was tennis courts and golf courses. Retired Northerners played in the sun all day, drank martinis at sunset and called 911 when their neighbors left their trash cans by the street too long.

"Jesus," somebody whispered, low and mean, but with a tinge of surprise, all at the same time.

The air had changed. That was the only way to describe it. The fine hairs on the back of Andy's neck stood up. A chill went down her spine. Her nostrils flared. Her mouth went dry. Her eyes watered.

There was a sound like a jar popping open.

Andy turned.

The handle of the coffee cup slipped from her fingers. Her eyes followed its path to the floor. White ceramic shards bounced off the white tiles.

There had been an eerie silence before, but now there was chaos. Screaming. Crying. People running, ducked down, hands covering their heads.

Bullets.

*Pop-pop.*

Shelly Barnard was lying on the floor. On her back. Arms splayed. Legs twisted. Eyes wide open. Her red T-shirt looked wet, stuck to her chest. Blood dribbled from her nose. Andy watched the thin red line slide down her cheek and into her ear.

She was wearing tiny Bulldog earrings.

"No!" Betsy Barnard wailed. "N—"

*Pop.*

Andy saw the back of the woman's throat vomit out in a spray of blood.

*Pop.*

The side of Betsy's skull snapped open like a plastic bag.

She fell sideways onto the floor. On top of her daughter. Onto her dead daughter.

*Dead.*

"Mom," Andy whispered, but Laura was already there. She was running toward Andy with her arms out, knees bent low. Her mouth was open. Her eyes were wide with fear. Red dots peppered her face like freckles.

The back of Andy's head slammed into the window as she

was tackled to the ground. She felt the rush of air from her mother's mouth as the wind was knocked out of her. Andy's vision blurred. She could hear a cracking sound. She looked up. The glass above her had started to spiderweb.

"Please!" Laura screamed. She had rolled over, was on her knees, then her feet. "Please, stop."

Andy blinked. She rubbed her fists into her eyes. Grit cut into her eyelids. Dirt? Glass? Blood?

"Please!" Laura shouted.

Andy blinked again.

Then again.

A man was pointing a gun at her mother's chest. Not a cop's gun, but the kind with a cylinder like in the Old West. He was dressed the part—black jeans, black shirt with pearl buttons, black leather vest and black cowboy hat. Gunbelt hanging low on his hips. One holster for the gun, a long leather sheath for a hunting knife.

Handsome.

His face was young, unlined. He was Shelly's age, maybe a little older.

But Shelly was dead now. She would not be going to UGA. She would never be mortified by her mother again because her mother was dead, too.

And now the man who had murdered them both was pointing a gun at her mother's chest.

Andy sat up.

Laura only had one breast, the left one, over her heart. The surgeon had taken the right one and she hadn't gotten reconstructive surgery yet because she couldn't stand the thought of going to yet another doctor, having another procedure, and now this murderer standing in front of her was going to put a bullet in it.

"Mm—" The word got caught in Andy's throat. She could only think it—

*Mom.*

"It's all right." Laura's voice was calm, controlled. She had her hands out in front of her like they could catch the bullets. She told the man, "You can leave now."

"Fuck you." His eyes darted to Andy. "Where's your gun, you fucking pig?"

Andy's whole body cringed. She felt herself tightening into a ball.

"She doesn't have a gun," Laura said, her voice still composed. "She's a secretary at the police station. She's not a cop."

"Get up!" he screamed at Andy. "I see your badge! Get up, pig! Do your job!"

Laura said, "It's not a badge. It's an emblem. Just stay calm." She patted her hands down the same way she used to tuck Andy into bed at night. "Andy, listen to me."

"Listen to *me*, you fucking bitches!" Saliva flew from the man's mouth. He shook the gun in the air. "Stand up, pig. You're next."

"No." Laura blocked his way. "I'm next."

His eyes turreted back to Laura.

"Shoot me." Laura spoke with unmistakable certainty. "I want you to shoot me."

Confusion broke the mask of anger that was his face. He hadn't planned for this. People were supposed to be terrified, not volunteer.

"Shoot me," she repeated.

He peered over Laura's shoulder at Andy, then looked back.

"Do it," Laura said. "You only have one bullet left. You know that. There are only six bullets in the gun." She held up her hands showing four fingers on her left hand, one on her right. "It's why you haven't pulled the trigger yet. There's only one bullet left."

"You don't know—"

"Only one more." She waved her thumb, indicating the sixth bullet. "When you shoot me, my daughter will run out of here. Right, Andy?"

*What?*

"Andy," her mother said. "I need you to run, darling."

*What?*

"He can't reload fast enough to hurt you."

"Fuck!" the man screamed, trying to get his rage back. "Be still! Both of you."

"Andy." Laura took a step toward the gunman. She was limping. A tear in her linen pants was weeping blood. Something white stuck out like bone. "Listen to me, sweetheart."

"I said don't move!"

"Go through the kitchen door." Laura's voice remained steady. "There's an exit in the back."

*What?*

"Stop there, bitch. Both of you."

"You need to trust me," Laura said. "He can't reload in time."

*Mom.*

"Get up." Laura took another step forward. "I said, get up."

*Mom, no.*

"Andrea Eloise." She was using her Mother voice, not her Mom voice. "Get up. Now."

Andy's body worked of its own volition. Left foot flat, right heel up, fingers touching the ground, a runner at the block.

"Stop it!" The man jerked the gun toward Andy, but Laura moved with it. He jerked it back and she followed the path, blocking Andy with her body. Shielding her from the last bullet in the gun.

"Shoot me," Laura told the man. "Go ahead."

"Fuck this."

Andy heard a *snap*.

The trigger pulling back? The hammer hitting the bullet?

Her eyes had squeezed closed, hands flew to cover her head.

But there was nothing.

No bullet fired. No cry of pain.

No sound of her mother falling dead to the ground.

*Floor. Ground. Six feet under.*

Andy cringed as she looked back up.

The man had unsnapped the sheath on the hunting knife.

He was slowly drawing it out.

Six inches of steel. Serrated on one side. Sharp on the other.

He holstered the gun, tossed the knife into his dominant hand. He didn't have the blade pointing up the way you'd hold a steak knife but down, the way you'd stab somebody.

Laura asked, "What are you going to do with that?"

He didn't answer. He showed her.

Two steps forward.

The knife arced up, then slashed down toward her mother's heart.

Andy was paralyzed, too terrified to ball herself up, too shocked to do anything but watch her mother die.

Laura stuck out her hand as if she could block the knife. The blade sliced straight into the center of her palm. Instead of collapsing, or screaming, Laura's fingers wrapped around the hilt of the knife.

There was no struggle. The murderer was too surprised.

Laura wrenched the knife away from his grip even as the long blade was still sticking out of her hand.

He stumbled back.

He looked at the knife jutting out of her hand.

*One second.*

*Two seconds.*

*Three.*

He seemed to remember the gun on his hip. His right hand reached down. His fingers wrapped around the handle. The silver flashed on the muzzle. His left hand swung around to cup the weapon as he prepared to fire the last bullet into her mother's heart.

Silently, Laura swung her arm, backhanding the blade into the side of his neck.

*Crunch*, like a butcher cutting a side of beef.

The sound had an echo that bounced off the corners of the room.

The man gasped. His mouth fished open. His eyes widened.

The back of Laura's hand was still pinned to his neck, caught between the handle and the blade.

Andy saw her fingers move.

There was a clicking sound. The gun shaking as he tried to raise it.

Laura spoke, more growl than words.

He kept lifting the gun. Tried to aim.

Laura raked the blade out through the front of his throat.

Blood, sinew, cartilage.

No spray or mist like before. Everything gushed out of his open neck like a dam breaking open.

His black shirt turned blacker. The pearl buttons showed different shades of pink.

The gun dropped first.

Then his knees hit the floor. Then his chest. Then his head.

Andy watched his eyes as he fell.

He was dead before he hit the ground.

# 2

When Andy was in the ninth grade, she'd had a crush on a boy named Cletus Laraby, who went by Cleet, but in an ironic way. He had floppy brown hair and he knew how to play the guitar and he was the smartest guy in their chemistry class, so Andy tried to learn how to play the guitar and pretended to be interested in chemistry, too.

This was how she ended up entering the school's science fair: Cleet signed up, so Andy did, too.

She had never spoken a word to him in her life.

No one questioned the wisdom of giving a drama club kid who barely passed earth sciences access to ammonium nitrate and ignition switches, but in retrospect, Dr. Finney was probably so pleased Andy was interested in something other than mime arts that she had looked the other way.

Andy's father, too, was elated by the news. Gordon took Andy to the library where they checked out books on engineering and rocket design. He filled out a form for a loyalty card from the local hobby shop. Over the dinner table, he would read aloud from pamphlets from the American Association for Rocketry.

Whenever Andy was staying at her dad's house, Gordon worked in the garage with his sanding blocks, shaping the fins and nose cone shoulders, while Andy sat at his workbench and sketched out designs for the tube.

Andy knew that Cleet liked the Goo Goo Dolls because he had a sticker on his backpack, so she started out thinking the tube of the rocket would look like a steampunk telescope from the video for "Iris," then she thought about putting wings on it because "Iris" was from the movie *City of Angels*, then she decided that she would put Nicolas Cage's face on the side, in profile, because he was the angel in the movie, then she decided that she should paint Meg Ryan instead because this was for Cleet and he would probably think that Meg Ryan was a lot more interesting than Nicolas Cage.

A week before the fair, Andy had to turn in all of her notes and photographs to Dr. Finney to prove that she had actually done all of the work herself. She was laying out the dubious evidence on the teacher's desk when Cleet Laraby walked in. Andy had to clasp together her hands to keep them from trembling when Cleet stopped to look at the photos.

"Meg Ryan," Cleet said. "I dig it. Blow up the bitch, right?"

Andy felt a cold slice of air cut open her lips.

"My girlfriend loves that stupid movie. The one with the angels?" Cleet showed her the sticker on his backpack. "They wrote that shitty song for the soundtrack, man. That's why I keep this here, to remind me never to sell out my art like those faggots."

Andy didn't move. She couldn't speak.

*Girlfriend. Stupid. Shitty. Man. Faggots.*

Andy had left Dr. Finney's classroom without her notes or her books or even her purse. She'd walked through the cafeteria, then out the exit door that was always propped open so the lunch ladies could smoke cigarettes behind the Dumpster.

Gordon lived two miles away from the school. It was June. In Georgia. On the coast. By the time she reached his house, Andy was badly sunburned and soaked in her own sweat and tears. She took the Meg Ryan rocket and the two Nicolas Cage test rockets and threw them in the outdoor trash can. Then she soaked them with lighter fluid. Then she threw a match into the can. Then she woke up on her back in Gordon's driveway because a neighbor was squirting her down with the garden hose.

The *whoosh* of fire had singed off Andy's eyebrows, eyelashes, bangs and nose hairs. The sound of the explosion was so intense that Andy's ears had started to bleed. The neighbor started screaming in her face. His wife, a nurse, came over and was clearly trying to tell Andy something, but the only thing she could hear was a sharp tone, like when her chorus teacher blew a single note on her pitch pipe—

*Eeeeeeeeeee . . .*

Andy heard The Sound, and nothing but The Sound, for four whole days.

Waking. Trying to sleep. Bathing. Walking to the kitchen. Sitting in front of the television. Reading notes her mother and father furiously scratched out on a dry erase board.

*We don't know what's wrong.*

*Probably temporary.*

*Don't cry.*

*Eeeeeeeeeee . . .*

That had been almost twenty years ago. Andy hadn't thought much about the explosion until now, and that was only because The Sound was back. When it returned, or when she became aware of the return, she was standing in the diner by her mother, who was seated in a chair. There were three dead people on the floor. On the ground. The murderer, his black shirt even blacker. Shelly Barnard, her red shirt even redder. Betsy Barnard, the bottom part of her face hanging by strands of muscle and sinew.

Andy had looked up from the bodies. People were standing outside the restaurant. Mall shoppers with Abercrombie and Juicy bags and Starbucks coffees and Icees. Some of them had been crying. Some of them had been taking pictures.

Andy had felt pressure on her arm. Laura was struggling to turn the chair away from the gawkers. Every movement had a stuttering motion to Andy's eye, like she was watching a stop-action movie. Laura's hand shook as she tried to wrap a tablecloth around her bleeding leg. The white thing sticking out was not a bone but a shard of broken china. Laura was right-handed, but the knife jutting from her left hand made wrapping her leg impossible. She was talking to Andy, likely asking for help, but all Andy could hear was The Sound.

"Andy," Laura had said.

*Eeeeeeeeeeee . . .*

"Andrea."

Andy stared at her mother's mouth, wondering if she was hearing the word or reading the word on her lips—so familiar that her brain processed it as heard rather than seen.

"Andy," Laura repeated. "Help me."

That had come through, a muffled request like her mother was speaking through a long tube.

"Andy," Laura had grabbed both of Andy's hands in her own. Her mother was bent over in the chair, obviously in pain. Andy had knelt down. She'd started knotting the tablecloth.

*Tie it tight—*

That's what Andy would have said to a panicked caller on the dispatch line: *Don't worry about hurting her. Tie the cloth as tight as you can to stop the bleeding.*

It was different when your hands were the ones tying the cloth. Different when the pain you saw was registered on your own mother's face.

"Andy." Laura had waited for her to look up.

Andy's eyes had trouble focusing. She wanted to pay attention. She needed to pay attention.

Her mother had grabbed Andy by the chin, given her a hard shake to knock her out of her stupor.

She had said, "Don't talk to the police. Don't sign a statement. Tell them you can't remember anything."

*What?*

"Promise me," Laura had insisted. "Don't talk to the police."

Four hours later, Andy still hadn't talked to the police, but that was more because the police had not talked to her. Not at the diner, not in the ambulance and not now.

Andy was waiting outside the closed doors to the surgical suite while the doctors operated on Laura. She was slumped in a hard plastic chair. She had refused to lie down, refused to take the nurse up on the offer of a bed, because nothing was wrong with her. Laura needed the help. And Shelly. And Shelly's mother, whose name Andy could not now remember.

Who was Mrs. Barnard, really, if not a mother to her child?

Andy sat back in the chair. She had to turn a certain way to keep the bruise on her head from throbbing. The plate glass window overlooking the boardwalk. Andy remembered her mother tackling her to the ground. The pounding at the back of her head as her skull cracked against the window. The spider-webbing glass. The way Laura quickly scrambled to stand. The way she had looked and sounded so calm.

The way she had held up her fingers—four on the left hand, one on the right—as she explained to the shooter that he only had one bullet left out of the six he had started with.

Andy rubbed her face with her hands. She did not look at the clock, because looking up at the clock every time she wanted to would make the hours stretch out interminably. She ran her tongue along her fillings. The metal ones had been drilled out and replaced with composite, but she could still remember how The Sound had made them almost vibrate inside her molars. Into her jaw. Up into her skull. A vise-like noise that made her brain feel as if it was going to implode.

*Eeeeeeeeeeee . . .*

Andy squeezed her eyes shut. Immediately, the images started scrolling like one of Gordon's vacation slide shows.

Laura holding up her hand.

The long blade slicing into her palm.

Wrenching the knife away.

Backhanding the blade into the man's neck.

Blood.

So much blood.

Jonah Helsinger. That was the murderer's name. Andy knew it—she wasn't sure how. Was it on the dispatch radio when she rode in the ambulance with her mother? Was it on the news blaring from the TV when Andy was led into the triage waiting room? Was it on the nurses' lips as they led her up to the surgical wing?

"*Jonah Helsinger*," someone had whispered, the way you'd whisper that someone had cancer. "*The killer's name is Jonah Helsinger.*"

"Ma'am?" A Savannah police officer was standing in front of Andy.

"I don't—" Andy tried to recall what her mother had told her to say. "I can't remember."

"Ma'am," the officer repeated, which was weird because she was older than Andy. "I'm sorry to bother you, but there's a man. He says he's your father, but—"

Andy looked up the hall.

Gordon was standing by the elevators.

She was up and running before she could think about it. Gordon met her halfway, grabbing her in a bear hug, holding her so close that she could feel his heart pounding in his chest. She pressed her face into his starched white shirt. He had been at work, dressed in his usual three-piece suit. His reading glasses were still on top of his head. His Montblanc pen was tucked into his shirt pocket. The metal was cold against the tip of her ear.

Andy had been losing her shit in little pieces since the shooting began, but in her father's arms, finally safe, she completely lost it. She started to cry so hard that she couldn't support her own weight. Gordon half lifted, half dragged her to a set of chairs against the wall. He held onto her so tightly that she had to take shallow breaths to breathe.

"I'm here," he told her, again and again. "I'm here, baby. I'm here."

"Daddy," she said, the word coming out around a sob.

"It's okay." Gordon stroked back her hair. "You're safe now. Everybody's safe."

Andy kept crying. She cried so long that she began to feel self-conscious, like it was too much. Laura was alive. Bad things had happened, but Laura was going to be okay. Andy was going to be okay. She *had* to be okay.

"It's okay," Gordon murmured. "Just let it all out."

Andy sniffed back her tears. She tried to regain her composure. And tried. Every time she thought she might be all right, she remembered another detail—the sound of the first gunshot, like a jar popping open, the *thwack* as her mother lodged the knife into flesh and bone—and the tears started to fall again.

"It's all right," Gordon said, patiently stroking her head. "Everybody's okay, sweetheart."

Andy wiped her nose. She took a shaky breath. Gordon leaned up in the chair, still holding onto her, and pulled out his handkerchief.

Andy blotted away her tears, blew her nose. "I'm sorry."

"You have nothing to apologize for." Gordon pushed her hair back out of her eyes. "Were you hurt?"

She shook her head. Blew her nose again until her ears popped.

The Sound was gone.

She closed her eyes, relief taking hold.

"All right?" Gordon asked. His hand was warm against her back. She felt anchored again. "You okay?"

Andy opened her eyes. Her nerves still felt raw, but she had to tell her father what had happened. "Mom—she had a knife, and this guy, she mur—"

"Shhh," he hushed, pressing his fingers to her lips. "Mom's okay. We're all okay."

"But—"

He put his finger back to her lips to keep her quiet. "I talked to the doctor. Mom's in recovery. Her hand is going to be fine. Her leg is fine. It's all fine." He raised an eyebrow, tilted his head slightly to the right where the cop was standing. The woman was on the phone, but she was clearly listening.

Gordon asked Andy, "You sure you're okay? Did they check you out?"

She nodded.

"You're just tired, baby. You were up all night working. You saw something horrible happen. Your life was in danger. Your mother's life was in danger. It's understandable you're in shock. You need some rest, give your memories some time to piece themselves together." His tone was measured. Andy realized that Gordon was coaching her. "All right?"

She nodded because he was nodding. Why was he telling her what to say? Had he talked to Laura? Was her mother in trouble?

She had killed a man. Of course she was in trouble.

The police officer said, "Ma'am, do you mind giving me some basic information? Full name, address, birthdate, that kind of thing."

"I'll provide that, Officer." Gordon waited for the woman to pull out her pen and notebook before he complied.

Andy tucked herself back underneath his protective arm. She swallowed so hard that her throat clicked.

And then she made herself look at the situation as a human being out in the world rather than a terrified spectator.

This wasn't one drug dealer shooting another drug dealer in the streets, or an abusive spouse finally crossing the last line. A white kid had shot two white women, then was killed by another white woman, in one of the most affluent malls in the state.

News trucks would probably come down from Atlanta and Charleston. Lawyers would intervene for the families, the victims, the mall management, the city, the county, maybe even the feds. An array of police forces would descend: Belle Isle, Savannah, Chatham County, the Georgia Bureau of Investigation. Witness statements. Forensics. Photographs. Autopsies. Evidence collection.

Part of Andy's job in radio dispatch was to assign case numbers for crimes on a far smaller scale, and she often tracked their progress over the months, sometimes years, it took for a case to go to trial. She of all people should have known that her mother's actions would be scrutinized at every single level of the criminal justice system.

As if on cue, there was a loud ding from the elevator. The cop's leather gunbelt made a squeaking noise as she adjusted it on her hips. The doors slid open. A man and a woman walked into the hallway. Both in wrinkled suits. Both with tired looks on their faces. The guy was bald and bloated with patches of peeling sunburn on his nose. The woman was around Andy's height, at least ten years older, with olive skin and dark hair.

Andy started to stand, but Gordon kept her in the chair.

"Ms. Oliver." The woman took out her badge and showed it to Andy. "I'm Detective Sergeant Lisa Palazzolo. This is Detective Brant Wilkes. We're with the Savannah Police Department. We're assisting Belle Isle with the investigation." She tucked her badge back into her jacket pocket. "We need to talk to you about what happened this morning."

Andy's mouth opened, but again, she couldn't remember what her mother had told her to say, or what Gordon had coached her to say, so she reverted to her default response which was to close her mouth and stare blankly at the person who had asked the question.

Gordon said, "This isn't a good time, Detectives. My daughter is in shock. She's not yet ready to give her statement."

Wilkes huffed a disapproving grunt. "You're her father?"

Andy always forgot Gordon was black and she was white until someone else pointed it out to her.

"Yes, Detective. I'm her father." Gordon's tone was patient. He was used to this. Over the years, he'd smoothed the nerves of anxious teachers, concerned store clerks, and aggressively racist store security. "I'm Gordon Oliver, Laura's ex-husband. Andrea's adoptive father."

Wilkes twisted his mouth to the side as he silently scrutinized the story.

Palazzolo said, "We're real sorry about what happened, Mr. Oliver, but we need to ask Andrea some questions."

Gordon repeated, "As I said, she isn't prepared at the moment to discuss the incident." He crossed his legs, casual, as if this was all a formality. "Andrea is a dispatch operator, which I'm sure you can tell from her uniform. She worked a night shift. She's bone-tired. She witnessed a terrible tragedy. She's not in any shape to give a statement."

"It *was* a terrible tragedy," Palazzolo agreed. "Three people are dead."

"And my daughter could've been the fourth." Gordon kept a protective arm around Andy's shoulders. "We'd be happy to make an appointment to come to the station tomorrow."

"This is an active murder investigation."

"The suspect is dead," Gordon reminded her. "There's no clock on this, Detective. One more day won't make a difference."

Wilkes grunted again. "How old are you?"

Andy realized he was talking to her.

Gordon said, "She's thirty-one. Her birthday is today."

Andy suddenly remembered Gordon's voicemail this morning, an off-key version of "Happy Birthday" in his deep baritone.

Wilkes said, "She's a little old to let her *daddy* talk for her."

Palazzolo rolled her eyes, but said, "Ms. Oliver, we'd really like it if you helped us get the chain of events down on paper. You're the only witness who hasn't given a statement."

Andy knew that wasn't true, because Laura was still coming round from the anesthesia.

Gordon said, "Detectives, if—"

"You her daddy or her fucking lawyer?" Wilkes demanded. "Because we can remove you from—"

Gordon stood up. He was at least a foot taller than Wilkes. "I happen to be a lawyer, Mr. Wilkes, and I can either school you on my daughter's constitutional right to refuse this interrogation or I can file a formal complaint with your superiors."

Andy could see the man's eyes shifting back and forth, his mouth itching to put Gordon in his place.

Palazzolo said, "Brant, take a walk."

Wilkes didn't move.

"Brant, come on. Meet me in the cafeteria. Get something to eat."

Wilkes glared at Gordon like an unneutered pitbull before stomping away.

Palazzolo said, "Mr. Oliver, I understand your daughter's been through a lot today, but even though Savannah's not what you'd call a sleepy town, we're unaccustomed to triple homicides. We really need to get your daughter's statement down. We need to know what happened."

Gordon corrected, "Double homicide."

"Right." There was a moment of hesitation before Palazzolo spoke again. "Can we do this sitting down?" She offered Andy a conciliatory smile. "I work the night shift, too. I've been up eighteen hours straight with no end in sight." She was dragging over a chair before Gordon could stop her. "Look, I'll tell you what I know, and then if Andrea feels like it, she can tell me what she knows. Or not. Either way, you get to see our side of this thing." She indicated the other chairs. "That's a good deal, Mr. Oliver. I hope you'll consider taking it."

Andy looked up at her father. Triple homicide? Two people wounded? Why did it feel like the detective was not counting Laura among the injured?

"Mr. Oliver?" Palazzolo tapped the back of her chair, but didn't sit. "What about it?"

Gordon looked down at Andy.

She had seen that look a thousand times before: *Remember what I told you.*

Andy nodded. She was, if anything, extraordinarily good at keeping her mouth shut.

"Great." Palazzolo sat down with a sharp groan.

Gordon nudged Andy down so that he would be the one who was directly across from Palazzolo.

"Okay." Palazzolo took out her notebook, but not her pen. She flipped through the pages. "The shooter's name is Jonah Lee Helsinger. Eighteen years old. High school senior. Early acceptance into Florida State University. The young girl was Shelly Anne Barnard. She was at the diner with her mother, Elizabeth Leona Bernard; Betsy. Jonah Lee Helsinger is—was—the ex-boyfriend of Shelly. Her father says Shelly broke up with Helsinger two weeks ago. Wanted to do it before going to college next month. Helsinger didn't take it well."

Gordon cleared his throat. "That's quite an understatement."

She nodded, ignoring the sarcasm. "Unfortunately, law enforcement has had a lot of these cases to study over the years. We know that spree killings aren't usually spur of the moment. They're well-planned, well-executed operations that tend to get worked over in the back of the killer's mind until something—an event like a break-up or an impending life change like going off to college—jumpstarts the plan. The first victim is generally a close female, which is why we were relieved to find Helsinger's mother was out of town this morning. Business in Charleston. But the way Helsinger was dressed—the black hat, the vest and gunbelt he bought on Amazon six months ago—all that tells us that he put a lot of thought into how this was going to go down. The spark came when Shelly broke up with him, but the idea of it, the planning, was in his head for months."

*Spree killings.*

The two words bounced around inside Andy's head.

Gordon asked, "His victims were all women?"

"There was a man sitting in the restaurant. He was struck in the eye by shrapnel. Not sure if he'll lose it or not. The eye." She went back to Jonah Helsinger. "What we also know about spree killers is, they tend to plant explosive devices in their homes for maximum casualties. That's why we got the state bomb squad to clear Helsinger's bedroom before we went in. He had a pipe bomb wired to the doorknob. Faulty set-up. Probably got it off the internet. Nothing went boom, thank God."

Andy opened her mouth so she could breathe. She had come face-to-face with this guy. He had almost killed Laura. Almost killed Andy. Murdered people. Tried to blow them up.

He had probably attended Belle Isle High School, the same as Andy.

"Helsinger," Gordon said. "That name sounds familiar."

"Yeah, the family's pretty well known up in Bibb County. Anyway—"

"Well known," Gordon repeated, but the two words were weighted in a way that Andy could not decipher.

Palazzolo obviously got their meaning. She held Gordon's gaze for a moment before she continued, "Anyway—Jonah Helsinger left some school notebooks on his bed. Most of them were filled with drawings. Disturbing images, weird stuff. He had four more handguns, an AR-15 and a shotgun, so he chose to take the six-shooter and the knife for a reason. We think we know the reason. There was a file on his laptop called 'Death Plan' that contained two documents and a PDF."

Andy felt a shudder work its way through her body. While she was getting ready for work last night, Jonah Helsinger was probably lying in bed, psyching himself up for his killing spree.

Palazzolo continued, "The PDF was a schematic of the diner, sort of like what you'd see an architect draw. One of the docs was a timeline, like a bullet point: wake up at this time, shower at this time, clean gun here, fill up car with gas there. The other doc was sort of like a diary entry where Helsinger wrote about how and why this was going to go down." She referred to her notebook again. "His first targets were going to be Shelly and her mother. Apparently, they had a standing lunch date every Monday at the Rise-n-Dine. Shelly wrote about it on Facebook, Snapchatted her food or whatever. Mr. Barnard told us the lunches are something his wife and daughter decided to do together over the summer before college."

"*Were* something they decided to do," Gordon mumbled, because everything in the two women's lives was past tense now.

"Were. Yeah," Palazzolo said. "Helsinger planned to kill both of them. He blamed the mother for the break-up. He said in his diary that it was Betsy's fault, that she was always pushing Shelly, blah blah blah. Crazy talk. It doesn't matter, because we all know it's Jonah Helsinger's fault, right?"

"Right," Gordon said, his voice firm.

Palazzolo held his gaze in that meaningful way again before she referred back to her notes. "This was his plan: after he killed Betsy and Shelly, Helsinger was going to take hostage whoever was left in the diner. He had a time noted—1:16, not the actual time but a notation of timing." She looked up at Andy, then

Gordon. "See, we think that he did a dry run. Last week, at approximately the same time as the shooting today, somebody threw a rock through the plate glass window that faces the boardwalk. We're waiting for the security feed. The incident was filed with burglary division. It took the first mall cop about one minute, sixteen seconds, to get to the diner."

The mall cops weren't the usual rent-a-cops, but off-duty police officers hired to protect the high-end stores. Andy had seen the guns on their hips and never given it a second thought.

Palazzolo told them, "In Helsinger's predicted timeline of the shooting, he allowed that he would have to kill at least one other bystander to let the cops know that he was serious. Then he was going to let the cops kill him. Helsinger must have thought his plan was fast-forwarded when he saw your uniform and assumed that you were law enforcement." Palazzolo was talking directly to Andy now. "We gather from the other witnesses that he wanted you to shoot him. Suicide by cop."

Except Andy was not a cop.

*Get up! Do your job!*

That's what Helsinger had screamed at Andy.

Then Andy's mother had said, "*Shoot me.*"

"He's a really bad guy. Was a bad guy. This Helsinger kid." Palazzolo was still focused on Andy. "We've got it all in his notes. He planned this out meticulously. He knew he was going to murder people. He hoped that he would murder even more people when somebody opened his bedroom door. He packed screws and nails into that pipe bomb. If the wiring hadn't been switched on the doorknob end, the whole house would be gone, along with whoever happened to be inside. We would've found nails two blocks away buried in God knows who or what."

Andy wanted to nod but she felt immobilized. Screws and nails flying through the air. What did it take to build such a device, to pack in all those projectiles in hopes that they would maim or kill people?

"You're lucky," Palazzolo told Andy. "If your mom hadn't

been there, he would've killed you. He was just a really bad guy."

Andy felt the woman looking at her, but she kept her eyes directed toward the floor.

*Bad guy.*

Palazzolo kept repeating the phrase, like it was okay that Helsinger was dead. Like he had gotten what he deserved. Like whatever Laura had done was completely justified because Jonah Lee Helsinger was a *bad guy*.

Andy worked at a police station. Most of the people who got murdered would fall into the bad guy category, yet she had never heard any of the detectives harp on the fact that the victim was a *bad guy*.

"Mr. Oliver," Palazzolo had turned to Gordon. "Has your wife had any military training?"

Gordon did not answer.

Palazzolo said, "Her background is pretty bland." Again, she flipped through the pages in her notebook. "Born in Providence, Rhode Island. Attended the University of Rhode Island. Master's and PhD from UGA. She's lived in Belle Isle for twenty-eight years. House is paid off, which, congratulations. She could sell it for a bag of money—but, I get it, where would she go? One marriage, one divorce. No large outstanding debts. Pays her bills on time. Never left the country. Got a parking ticket three years ago that she paid online. She must've been one of the first people to buy here." Palazzolo turned back toward Andy. "You were raised here, right?"

Andy stared at the woman. She had a mole near her ear, just under her jawline.

"You went to school on the Isle, then SCAD for college?"

Andy had spent the first two years of her life in Athens while Laura was finishing her doctorate, but the only thing she remembered about UGA was being scared of the neighbor's parakeet.

"Ms. Oliver." Palazzolo's voice sounded strained. She was apparently used to having her questions answered. "Did your mother ever take any self-defense classes?"

Andy studied the mole. There were some short hairs sticking out of it.

"Yoga? Pilates? Tai chi?" Palazzolo waited. And waited. Then she closed her notebook. She put it back into her pocket. She reached into her other pocket. She pulled out her phone. She tapped at the screen. "I'm showing you this because it's already on the news." She swiped at the screen. "One of the patrons in the diner decided that it was more important to record what was happening on his cell phone than to call 911 or run for his life."

She turned the phone around. The image was paused. Jonah Helsinger stood at the entrance to the restaurant. The lower half of his body was obscured by a trash can. The mall was empty behind him. From the angle, Andy knew the waitress standing in the back had not taken the video. She wondered if it was the man with the newspaper. The phone had been tilted just over the salt and pepper shakers, like he was trying to hide the fact that he was recording the weird kid who was dressed like the villain from a John Wayne movie.

Objectively, the hat was ridiculous; too large for Helsinger's head, stiff on the top and curled up almost comically.

Andy might have filmed him, too.

Palazzolo said, "This is pretty graphic. They're blurring the images on the news. Are you okay to see this?" She was talking to Gordon because, obviously, Andy had already seen it.

Gordon smoothed down his mustache with his finger and thumb as he considered the question. Andy knew he could handle it. He was asking himself if he really wanted to see it.

He finally decided. "Yes."

Palazzolo snaked her finger around the edge of the phone and tapped the screen.

At first, Andy wondered if the touch had registered because Jonah Helsinger was not moving. For several seconds, he just stood there behind the trash can, staring blankly into the restaurant, his ten-gallon hat high on his shiny-looking forehead.

Two older women, mall walkers, strutted behind him. One

39

of them clocked the western attire, elbowed the other, and they both laughed.

Muzak played in the background. Madonna's "Dress You Up."

Someone coughed. The tinny sound vibrated into Andy's ears, and she wondered if she had registered any of these noises when they happened, when she was in the restaurant telling the waitress she was a theater major, when she was staring out the window at the waves cresting in the distance.

On the screen, Helsinger's head moved to the right, then the left, as if he was scanning the restaurant. Andy knew there was not much to see. The place was half-empty, a handful of patrons enjoying a last cup of coffee or glass of tea before they did errands or played golf or, in Andy's case, went to sleep.

Helsinger stepped away from the garbage can.

A man's voice said, "Jesus."

Andy remembered that word, the lowness and meanness to it, the hint of surprise.

The gun went up. A puff of smoke from the muzzle. A loud *pop*.

Shelly was shot in the back of the head. She sank to the floor like a paper doll.

Betsy Barnard started screaming.

The second bullet missed Betsy, but a loud cry said that it had hit someone else.

The third bullet came sharp on the heels of the second.

A cup on the table exploded into a million pieces. Shards flew through the air.

Laura was turning away from the shooter when one of the pieces lodged into her leg. The wound did not register in her mother's expression. She started to run, but not away. She was closer to the mall entrance than to the back of the restaurant. She could've ducked under a table. She could've escaped.

Instead, she ran toward Andy.

Andy saw herself standing with her back now turned toward the window. Video-Andy dropped her coffee mug. The ceramic splintered. In the foreground, Betsy Barnard was being murdered. Bullet four was fired into her mouth, the fifth into her head. She fell on top of her daughter.

Then Laura tackled Andy to the ground.

There was a blink of stillness before Laura jumped up.

She patted her hands down the same way she used to tuck Andy into bed at night. The man in black, Jonah Lee Helsinger, had a gun pointed at Laura's chest. In the distance, Andy could see herself. She was curled into a ball. The glass behind her was spiderwebbing. Chunks were falling down.

Sitting in the chair beside Gordon, Andy reached up and touched her hair. She pulled out a piece of glass from the tangles.

When she looked back down at Detective Palazzolo's phone, the angle of the video had changed. The image was shaky, taken from behind the shooter. Whoever had made the recording was lying on the ground, just beyond an overturned table. The position afforded Andy a completely different perspective. Instead of facing the shooter, she was behind him now. Instead of watching her mother's back, she could see Laura's face. Her hands holding up six digits to indicate the total number of bullets. Her thumb wagging to show the one live round left in the chamber.

*Shoot me.*

That's what Laura had told the kid who had already murdered two people—*shoot me.* She had said it repeatedly. Andy's brain echoed the words each time Laura said them on the video.

*Shoot me, I want you to shoot me, shoot me, when you shoot me, my daughter will run—*

When the killing spree had first started, every living person in the restaurant had screamed or ducked or run away or all three.

Laura had started counting the number of bullets.

"What?" Gordon mumbled. "What's he doing?"

*Snap.*

41

On the screen, Helsinger was unsnapping the sheath hanging from his gunbelt.

"That's a knife," Gordon said. "I thought he used a gun."

The gun was holstered. The knife was gripped in Helsinger's fist, blade angled down for maximum carnage.

Andy wanted to close her eyes, but just as badly, she wanted to see it again, to watch her mother's face, because right now, at this moment on the video when Helsinger was holding the menacing-looking hunting knife, Laura's expression was almost placid, like a switch inside of her had been turned off.

The knife arced up.

Gordon sucked in air between his teeth.

The knife arced down.

Laura lifted her left hand. The blade sliced straight through the center of her palm. Her fingers wrapped around the handle. She wrenched it from his grasp, then, the knife still embedded in her hand, backhanded the blade into the side of his neck.

*Thunk.*

Helsinger's eyes went wide.

Laura's left hand was pinned to the left side of his neck like a message tacked to a bulletin board.

There was a slight pause, no more than a few milliseconds.

Laura's mouth moved. One or two words, her lips barely parting.

Then she crossed her right arm underneath her trapped left.

She braced the heel of her right hand near Helsinger's right shoulder.

Her right hand pushed his shoulder.

Her left hand jerked the knife blade straight out of the front of his throat.

Blood.

Everywhere.

Gordon's mouth gaped open.

Andy's tongue turned into cotton.

Right hand pushing, left hand pulling.

From the video, it looked like Laura had willfully pulled the knife out of Helsinger's throat.

Not just killing him.

*Murdering* him.

"She just—" Gordon saw it, too. "She—"

His hand went to his mouth.

On the video, Helsinger's knees hit the floor. His chest. His face.

Andy saw herself in the distance. The whites of her eyes were almost perfect circles.

In the foreground, Laura's expression remained placid. She looked down at the knife that pierced her hand straight through, turning it to see—first the palm, then the back—as if she had found a splinter.

That's where Palazzolo chose to pause the video.

She waited a beat, then asked, "Do you want to see it again?"

Gordon swallowed so hard that Andy saw his Adam's apple bob.

"Mr. Oliver?"

He shook his head, looked down the hallway.

Palazzolo clicked off the screen. She returned the phone to her pocket. Without Andy noticing, she had angled her chair away from Gordon. Palazzolo leaned forward, hands resting on her legs. There was only two inches of space between her knees and Andy's. She said, "It's pretty horrific. It must be hard seeing it again."

Gordon shook his head. He thought the detective was still talking to him.

Palazzolo said, "Take all the time you need, Ms. Oliver. I know this is hard. Right?" She was talking to Andy again, leaning in closer; so close that it was making Andy feel uncomfortable.

One hand pushing, one hand pulling.

Pushing his shoulder. Pulling the knife through his neck.

The calm expression on Laura's face.

*I'll tell you what I know, and then if Andrea feels like it, she can tell me what she knows.*

The detective had not told them anything, or shown them anything, that probably was not already on the news. And now she was crowding Andy without seeming to crowd her, taking up a section of her personal space. Andy knew this was an interview technique because she had read some of the training textbooks during slow times at work.

*Horton's Annotations on the Police Interview: Witness Statements, Hostile Witness Interrogations and Confessions.*

You were supposed to make the subject feel uncomfortable without them knowing why they were feeling uncomfortable.

And the reason Palazzolo was trying to make Andy uncomfortable was because she was not taking a statement. She was interrogating her.

Palazzolo said, "You're lucky your mom was there to save you. Some people would call her a hero."

*Some people.*

Palazzolo asked, "What did your mother say to Jonah before he died?"

Andy watched the space between them narrow. Two inches turned into one.

"Ms. Oliver?"

Laura had seemed too calm. That was the problem. She had been too calm and methodical the whole time, especially when she'd raised her right hand and placed it near Jonah's right shoulder.

One hand pushing, one hand pulling.

Not scared for her life.

*Deliberate.*

"Ms. Oliver?" Palazzolo repeated. "What did your mother say?"

The detective's unspoken question filled that tiny inch of uncomfortable space between them: If Laura really was that calm, if she really was that methodical, why hadn't she used the same hand to take away Helsinger's gun?

"Andrea?" Palazzolo rested her elbows on her knees. Andy could smell coffee on the detective's breath. "I know this is a difficult time for you, but we can clear this up really fast if you just tell me what your mom said before Helsinger died." She waited a beat. "The phone didn't pick it up. I guess we could send the video to the state lab, but it would be easier if you just told—"

"The father," Gordon said. "We should pray for the father."

Palazzolo didn't look at him, but Andy did. Gordon was not the praying kind.

"I can't imagine . . ." he paused. "I can't imagine what it feels like, to lose your family like that." He had snapped his fingers together on the last word, but close to his face, as if to wake himself from the trance that the video had put him in. "I'm so glad your mother was there to protect you, Andrea. And herself."

Andy nodded. For once, she was a few steps ahead of her father.

"Look, guys," Palazzolo finally sat back in her chair. "I know you're thinking I'm not on your side, but there are no sides here. Jonah Helsinger was a bad guy. He had a plan. He wanted to murder people, and that's exactly what he did. And you're right, Mr. Oliver. Your wife and daughter could've been his third and fourth victims. But I'm a cop, and it's my job to ask questions about what really happened in that diner this afternoon. All I'm after is the truth."

"Detective Palazzolo." Gordon finally sounded like himself again. "We've both been on this earth long enough to know that the truth is open to interpretation."

"That's true, Mr. Oliver. That's very true." She looked at Andy. "You know, I've just realized that you haven't said one word this whole time." Her hand went to Andy's knee with almost sisterly affection. "It's all right, honey. Don't be afraid. You can talk to me."

Andy stared at the mole on the woman's jawline because it was too hard to look her in the eye. She wasn't afraid. She was confused.

Was Jonah Helsinger still a threat when Laura had killed him? Because you could legally kill someone who was threatening you, but if they weren't threatening you and you killed them, that meant you weren't defending yourself anymore.

You were just killing them.

Andy tried to think back to this morning, to fill in the blanks with the video. Could Laura have left the knife in Jonah Helsinger's throat, taken away his gun, and then . . . *what?*

The police would've come. Dispatch would've radioed in an ambulance, not a coroner, because the fact was that, even with a knife sticking Herman Munster–like from the side of his neck, Jonah Helsinger had not been dead. No blood had coughed from his mouth or sneezed from his nose. He had still been capable of moving his arms and legs, which meant his carotid, his jugular, were likely intact. Which meant he had the chance to remain alive until Laura had killed him.

So, what would've happened next?

The EMTs could've stabilized him for the ride to the hospital and the surgeons could've worked to safely remove the knife, but none of that had happened because Laura had braced her right hand near Jonah Helsinger's right shoulder and ended his life.

"Ms. Oliver," Palazzolo said. "I find the lack of communication on your part very troubling. If nothing's wrong, then why aren't you talking to me?"

Andy made herself look the detective in the eye. She had to speak. This was her time to say that Laura had no other choice. *My mother was acting in self-defense. You weren't there but I was and I will swear on a stack of Bibles in front of any jury that my mother had no other choice but to kill Jonah Lee Helsinger.*

"Laura?" Gordon said.

Andy turned, finally breaking out of Palazzolo's vortex. She had expected to see her mother lying in yet another hospital bed, but Laura was sitting up in a wheelchair.

"I'm all right," Laura said, but her face was contorted in pain. She was dressed in a white gown. Her arm was strapped to her waist in a Velcro sling. Her fingers were held stiff by something that looked like a biker's glove with the tips cut off. "I need to change, then I'm ready to go home."

Gordon opened his mouth to protest, but Laura cut him off. "Please," she said. "I've already told the doctor I'm going to sign myself out. She's getting together the paperwork. Can you pull up the car?" She looked annoyed, especially when Gordon didn't move. "Gordon, can you please pull up your car?"

"Dr. Oliver," Palazzolo said. "Your surgeon told me you would need to stay overnight, maybe longer."

Laura didn't ask the woman who she was or why she was talking to the surgeon. "Gordon, I want to go home."

"Ma'am," Palazzolo tried again. "I'm Detective Lisa Palazzolo with the Savannah—"

"I don't want to talk to you." She looked up at Gordon. "I want to go home."

"Ma'am—"

"Are you hard of hearing?" Laura asked. "This man is a lawyer. He can advise you of my legal rights if you're unfamiliar with them."

Palazzolo frowned. "Yeah, we've already do-si-doed that two-step, but I want to get this straight with you, on the record: you're refusing to be interviewed?"

"For now," Gordon intervened, because nothing made him stand more firmly by Laura's side than to have a stranger challenge her. "My office will call you to schedule an appointment."

"I could detain her as a material witness."

"You could," Gordon agreed. "But then she could stay here under doctor's orders and you'd be denied access to her anyway."

Laura tried, "I was under anesthesia. I'm not competent to—"

"You're making this worse. You realize that, right?" Palazzolo had let the helpful, we're-on-the-same-team façade drop. She was clearly pissed off. "The only people who are quiet are the ones who have something to hide."

Gordon said, "My office will be in touch when she's ready to talk."

The hinge of Palazzolo's jaw stuck out like a bolt on the side of her face as she gritted her teeth. She gave a curt nod, then walked off, her jacket swinging as she made her way toward the elevator.

Gordon told Laura, "You should stay in the hospital. She won't bother you. I'll get a restraining order if I—"

"Home," Laura said. "Either get your car or I'll call a taxi."

Gordon looked to the orderly behind the wheelchair for help.

The man shrugged. "She's right, bro. Once she signs that paperwork, we can't keep her here if she doesn't wanna stay."

Gordon knelt down in front of the chair. "Honey, I don't think—"

"Andrea." Laura squeezed Andy's hand so hard that the bones moved. "I don't want to be here. I can't be in a hospital again. Not overnight. Do you understand?"

Andy nodded, because that much, at least, she understood. Laura had spent almost a year in and out of the hospital because of complications from her surgery, two bouts of pneumonia and a case of *C. difficile* that was persistent enough to start shutting down her kidneys.

Andy said, "Dad, she wants to go home."

Gordon muttered something under his breath. He stood up. He tucked his hand into his pocket. His keys jangled. "You're sure?" He shook his head, because Laura wasn't given to making statements she wasn't sure about. "Get changed. Sign your paperwork. I'll be out front."

Andy watched her father leave. She felt a familiar guilt ebb into her chest because she had chosen her mother's demands over her father's wishes.

"Thank you." Laura loosened her grip on Andy's hand. She asked the orderly, "Could you find a T-shirt or something for me to change into?"

He bowed out with a nod.

"Andrea." Laura kept her voice low. "Did you say anything to that detective?"

Andy shook her head.

"You were talking to her when I was being wheeled up the hall."

"I wasn't—" Andy wondered at her mother's sharp tone. "She asked questions. I didn't tell her anything." Andy added, "I didn't speak. At all."

"Okay." Laura tried to shift in the chair but, judging by the wince on her face, the pain was too much. "What we were discussing before, in the diner. I need you to move out. Tonight. You have to go."

*What?*

"I know I said I wasn't going to give you a deadline, but I am, and it's now." Laura tried to shift in the chair again. "You're an adult, Andrea. You need to start acting like one. I want you to find an apartment and move out. Today."

Andy felt her stomach go into free fall.

"Your father agrees with me," Laura said, as if that carried more weight. "I want you out of the house. The garage. Just get out, okay? You can't sleep there tonight."

"Mom—"

Laura hissed in air between her teeth as she tried again to find a comfortable position. "Andrea, please don't argue with me. I need to be alone tonight. And tomorrow, and—you just need to go. I've looked after you for thirty-one years. I've earned the right to be alone."

"But—" Andy didn't know what the *but* was.

But people are dead.

But you could've died.

But you killed somebody when you didn't have to.

*Didn't you?*

Laura said, "My mind is made up. Go downstairs and make sure your father knows the right entrance to pull up to."

Gordon had picked them up at the hospital before. "Mom—"

"Andrea! Can't you just for once do something I tell you to do?"

Andy wanted to cover her ears. She had never in her life felt this much coldness from her mother. There was a giant, frozen gulf between them.

Laura's teeth were clenched. "Go."

Andy turned on her heel and walked away from her mother. Tears streamed down her face. She had heard that same edge to her mother's voice twice today, and each time, her body had responded before her mind could shut her down.

Gordon was nowhere in sight, but Detective Palazzolo was waiting for the elevator. The woman opened her mouth to speak. Andy kept walking. She took the stairs. Her feet stumbled over the treads. She was numb. Her head was spinning. Tears rolled like rain.

Move out? Tonight?

As in now? As in forever?

Andy bit her lip so that she would stop crying. She had to keep it together at least until she saw her dad. Gordon would fix this. He would make it better. He would have a plan. He would be able to explain what the hell had happened to her kind, caring mother.

Andy picked up the pace, practically flinging herself down the stairs. The anvil on her chest lifted the tiniest bit. There had to be a reason Laura was acting like this. Stress. Anesthesia. Grief. Fear. Pain. Any one of these things could bring out the worst in a person. All of them wrapped together could make them go crazy.

That was it.

Laura just needed time.

Andy felt her breathing start to calm. She rounded the stairs at the next landing. Her sweaty hand slipped on the railing. One foot hit sideways on the tread, the other foot slipped out from under her and she found herself flat on her ass.

*Fuck.*

Andy put her head in her hands. Something wet slid down the back of her fingers that was too thick to be sweat.

*Fuck!*

Her knuckle was bleeding. She put it in her mouth. She could feel her hands trembling. Her brain was spinning inside her head. Something weird was happening with her heartbeat.

Above her, a door opened, then closed, then there were scuffling footsteps on the stairs.

Andy tested her ankle, which, remarkably, was fine. Her knee felt wonky but nothing was sprained or broken. She stood up, ready to head down to the ground floor, but a wave of nausea spun up her throat.

Above her, the footsteps were getting closer.

It was bad enough to vomit in a public place. The only thing worse was having a witness. Andy had to find a bathroom. At the next landing, she pushed open the door and sprinted down another hallway until she found the toilets.

She had to run to make it to the stall in time. She opened her mouth and waited to throw up but now that she was here, squatting in front of the toilet bowl, the only thing that came up was bile.

Andy horked out as much as she could before flushing the toilet. She sat down on the closed lid. She used the back of her hand to wipe her mouth. Sweat dripped down her neck. She was breathing like she'd run a marathon.

"Andrea?"

*Fuck.*

Her legs retracted like a roller shade, heels hooked onto the edge of the toilet bowl, as if drawing herself into a ball would make her invisible.

"Andrea?" Palazzolo's chunky police-issue shoes thumped across the tiles. She stopped directly in front of Andy's stall.

Andy stared at the door. A faucet was dripping. She counted off six drops before—

"Andrea, I know you're in there."

Andy rolled her eyes at the stupidity of the situation.

"I gather you don't like to talk," Palazzolo said. "So maybe you could just listen?"

Andy waited.

"Your mom might be in a lot of trouble." Palazzolo waited another beat. "Or not."

Andy's heart leapt at the possibility of the *not*.

"What she did—I get that. She was protecting her daughter. I've got a kid. I would do anything for the little guy. He's my baby."

Andy bit her bottom lip.

"I can help you with this. Help you both get out of this."

Andy waited again.

"I'm going to leave my card here on the counter."

Andy kept waiting.

"You call me, anytime, day or night, and together, you and I can figure out what you need to say to make this problem go away." She paused. "I'm offering to help your mom, Andrea. That's all I want to do—help."

Andy rolled her eyes again. She had learned a long time ago that one of the prices of prolonged silence was people assumed that you were simple-minded or outright stupid.

"But here's the thing: if you really want to help your mom," Palazzolo tried. "First you have to tell me the truth. About what happened."

Andy almost laughed.

"Then we'll go from there. All right?" Another weighted pause. "Right?"

*Right.*

"Card's on the counter, doll. Day or night."

Andy listened to the drips from the faucet.

*One drip . . . two drips . . . three . . . four . . . five . . . six . . .*

"You wanna make a gesture, like flush the toilet to let me know you heard me?"

Andy held up her middle finger to the back of the stall door.

"All right," Palazzolo said. "Well, I'm just going to assume you heard. The thing is, sooner rather than later, okay? We don't wanna have to drag your mom down to the station, open a formal interview, all that stuff. Especially since she's been hurt. Right?"

Andy had this flash in her head, the image of herself standing from the toilet, kicking open the stall, and telling the woman to go fuck herself.

Then she realized that the stall door opened in, not out, so she couldn't really kick it open, so she waited on the toilet, hands wrapped around her legs, head buried between her knees, until the detective went away.

# 3

Andy waited on the toilet so long that her knee popped when she finally uncurled from her perch. Her hamstrings jangled like ukulele strings. She pulled open the stall door. She walked to the sink. She ignored the detective's card with its shiny gold shield as she washed her face with cold water. The blood on her knuckle ran fresh. She wrapped a paper towel around her finger, then tentatively opened the bathroom door.

She checked the hallway. No Detective Palazzolo. Andy started to leave, but at the last minute, she grabbed the detective's card off the counter. She would give it to her father. She would tell him what had happened. The cops were not supposed to question you when you had a lawyer. Anybody who watched *Law & Order* knew that.

There was a crowd in front of the elevator. Again, no Detective Palazzolo, but Andy used the stairs anyway. She walked carefully this time. Her knuckle had stopped bleeding. She threw the napkin into a trash can outside the stairwell. The air in the hospital's main waiting room was tinged with chemicals and vomit. Andy hoped that the vomit smell wasn't coming from her. She looked down at her shirt to check.

"My Lord," someone muttered. "My good Lord."

The TV.

A sudden understanding hit Andy like a punch to the face.

Every single person in the waiting room, at least twenty people, was watching the diner video play on CNN.

"Holy crap," someone else said.

On the television, Laura's hands were showing five fingers and a thumb for six bullets.

Helsinger was standing in front of her. Cowboy hat. Leather vest. Gun still out.

A banner rolled across the bottom of the TV warning people that they were about to see graphic content.

A woman asked, "What's he doing?"

Helsinger was drawing his knife from the sheath on his hip.

"What the—"

"Oh, shit!"

The crowd went silent as they watched what came next.

There were gasps, a shocked scream, like they were inside a movie theater instead of a hospital waiting room.

Andy was as transfixed as everyone else. The more she watched it, the more she was able to see it happening outside of herself. Who was that woman on the television? What had Laura become while Andy was cowering against the broken window pane?

Someone joked, "Like some kinda ninja granny."

"Grambo."

There was uncomfortable laughter.

Andy couldn't listen to it. She couldn't be in this room, in this hospital, in this emotional turmoil where the tether that had always linked her back to her mother had been broken.

She turned around and slammed right into a man who was standing too close behind her.

"Sorry." He tipped his Alabama baseball cap at her.

Andy wasn't in the mood for chivalry. She stepped to the left as he stepped to the right. The opposite happened when she stepped to the right.

He laughed.

She glared at him.

"My apologies." Alabama took off his hat and made a sweeping gesture, indicating that she could pass.

Andy walked so quickly that the sliding doors didn't have time to fully open. She slapped her hand against the frame.

"Bad day?" Alabama had followed her outside. He stood at a respectful distance, but even that felt too close. "You all right?"

Andy glared at him again. Had he not just seen what was on television? Did he not understand that Andy was the useless girl whose mother had faced down a cold-blooded murderer?

And then turned into a murderer herself?

"Is something wrong, Officer?" Alabama kept smiling at Andy.

She looked down at her police-like uniform. The stupid silver badge that was stitched on like a Girl Scout patch—but with far less meaning, because Girl Scouts had to at least do something for those patches. All Andy did was answer phones and walk terrified people through performing CPR or turning off their car engines after a crash.

Jonah Lee Helsinger had thought that she was a cop.

He had thought that she would kill him. Murder him. In cold blood.

Andy looked down at her own hands. They would not stop shaking. She was going to start crying again. Why did she keep crying?

"Here." Alabama offered her a handkerchief.

Andy stared at the folded white cloth. She thought Gordon was the only man who still carried a handkerchief.

"Just trying to help a lady in need," he grinned, still holding out the cloth.

Andy did not take it. For the first time, she really looked at the man. He was tall and fit, probably close to forty. Jeans and sneakers. His white button-down shirt was open at the collar, long sleeves neatly rolled up. He looked like he had forgotten to shave this morning, or maybe that was part of his look.

A thought occurred to her that was so startling she blurted it out. "Are you a reporter?"

He laughed and shook his head. "I make my living the honest way."

"You're a cop?" she tried. "Detective?" When he did not immediately answer, she told him, "Please leave me alone."

"Whoa, porcupine." He held up both his hands in surrender. "I was just making small talk."

Andy did not want to talk. She scanned the drive for Gordon's white BMW.

*Where was her father?*

Andy took out her cell phone. The home screen was filled with text alerts and missed calls. *Mindy Logan. Sarah Ives. Alice Blaedel. Danny Kwon.* In the last few hours, the smattering of band, chorus and drama geeks Andy had been friends with in high school had all suddenly remembered her phone number.

She dismissed the notices, then pulled up DAD and texted: *hurry.*

Alabama finally seemed to realize that she wasn't open to small talk. He tucked his handkerchief back into his jeans pocket. He walked over to one of the benches and sat down. He pulled out his phone. His thumbs worked across the screen.

Andy glanced behind her, wondering what was taking Laura so long. Then she scanned the front parking area for Gordon. Her father was probably in the parking deck, which meant he would be at least twenty minutes because the woman working the booth had to talk to every single person who handed her a ticket to get out.

All she could do was sit down on a bench three down from Alabama. Every muscle in Andy's body felt like an overstretched rubber band. Her head throbbed. Her stomach was sour. She checked her phone to see if Gordon had texted back, but he would never look at his phone while he was driving because it was dangerous.

The sliding doors opened. Andy felt relief, then trepidation, upon seeing her mother. The orderly pushed the wheelchair to a stop beside the curb. Laura was wearing a cotton candy pink Belle Isle Medical Center T-shirt that was too big for her slender frame. She was clearly in pain. Her face was the color of notebook paper. Her good hand was wrapped around the arm of the chair in a death grip.

Andy asked, "Didn't they give you anything?"

Laura said nothing, so the orderly volunteered, "The surgery meds are wearing off. The doc offered her a script but she wouldn't take it."

"Mom—" Andy didn't know what to say. Laura wouldn't even look at her. "Mother."

"I'm fine," Laura insisted, though her teeth were gritted. She asked the orderly, "Do you have a cigarette?"

"You don't smoke," Andy said, just as her mother reached for a Marlboro from the pack that the orderly pulled from his shirt pocket.

The man cupped his hand as he flicked the lighter.

Andy stepped away from the smell.

Laura didn't seem to notice. She took a deep drag, then coughed out white puffs of smoke. She held the cigarette awkwardly, pinched between her thumb and forefinger the way a junkie would.

"I'm all right," Laura said, her voice a raspy whisper. "I just need some space."

Andy took her at her word. She stepped farther away, putting distance between herself and her mother. She looked at the parking deck, willing Gordon to hurry. She started to cry again, but quietly. She didn't know what to do. None of this made any sense.

Laura said, "There are some boxes at your father's house."

Andy's lips trembled. Silence eluded her. She had to have answers. "What did I do wrong?"

"You didn't do anything wrong." Laura smoked the cigarette. "I just need to stop coddling you. You need to learn to stand on your own two feet."

"By moving in with Dad?" She needed this to make sense. Laura always made sense. "Mom, please—"

Laura took a last hit from the cigarette, then handed it to the orderly to finish. She told Andy, "Pack what you need for the night. Your dad won't let you stay with him forever. You'll work out a budget. You'll see what you can afford. You could move to Atlanta, or even back to New York." She looked up at Andy from her chair. "You have to go, Andrea. I want to be alone now. I've earned the right to be alone."

"I didn't . . ." the words got tangled in Andy's mouth. "I never—"

"Stop," Laura said. She had never talked to Andy this way. It was as if she hated her. "Just stop."

*Why?*

"Thank God," Laura muttered as Gordon's BMW glided to a stop in front of the wheelchair ramp.

"Help me up." Laura held out her hand for the orderly, but the guy in the Alabama hat was suddenly at her side.

He said, "Happy to be of service, ma'am."

If Andy hadn't been watching closely, she would've missed the look that flashed across her mother's face. Panic? Fear? Disgust?

He said, "Up you go."

"Thank you." Laura let him lift her to standing.

Gordon came around the car and opened the door. He told Alabama, "I've got it from here."

"No problem, big guy." Alabama didn't relinquish his hold. He guided Laura down to the front seat, then gently lifted her legs as she turned to face the front. "Take care, now."

Gordon said, "Thank you."

"My pleasure." Alabama offered Gordon his hand. "I'm sorry for the situation your wife and daughter are in."

"Uh—yes." Gordon was too polite to correct him about his marital status, let alone refuse to shake his hand. "Thank you."

Alabama tipped his hat at Andy as she got into the back of the car. He shut the door before she could slam it in his face.

Gordon got behind the wheel. He sniffed the air with visible distaste. "Have you been smoking?"

"Gordon, just drive."

He waited for her to look at him. She did not. He put the car in gear. He drove away from the portico, past the entrance to the parking garage, then pulled over and parked the car. He turned to Laura. His mouth opened. Nothing came out.

"No," she said. "Not here. Not now."

He shook his head slowly back and forth.

"Andy doesn't need to hear this."

Gordon didn't seem to care. "The kid's father was Bobby Helsinger. Did you know that?"

Laura's lips pursed. Andy could tell she knew.

Gordon said, "He was the sheriff of Bibb County before a bank robber blew off his head with a shotgun. This was six months ago, around the same time the detective says Jonah Helsinger started weaponizing."

*The vest and gunbelt.*

Palazzolo had told them that Jonah bought it off Amazon six months ago.

Gordon said, "I looked up the obituary on my phone. Jonah's got three uncles who are cops, two cousins who are in the military. His mother used to work at the district attorney's office in Beaufort before she went private. The family's practically law enforcement royalty." He waited for Laura to say something. "Did you hear me? Do you understand what I'm saying to you?"

Laura took a sharp breath before speaking. "His family royalty does not negate the fact that he murdered two people."

"He didn't just murder them. He planned it. He knew exactly what he was doing. He had maps and—" Gordon shook his head, like he could not believe how stupid she was. "Do you think the family's going to believe their little boy is a sadistic murderer, or do you think they're going to say he had some kind of mental problem because his hero daddy was murdered by a bank robber and all of this was a cry for help?"

"They can say what they want."

"That's the first thing you've said that makes any fucking sense," Gordon snapped. "The Helsingers are going to say *exactly* what they want—that yeah, this poor, heart-broken, dead cop's son deserved to go to prison for what he did, but he didn't deserve to be viciously murdered."

"That's not—"

"They're going to take you down harder than him, Laura. You did that kid a favor. This is all going to be about what *you* did, not what *he* did."

Laura kept silent.

Andy stopped breathing.

Gordon asked, "Do you know there's a video?"

Laura did not answer, though she must have seen the TV when the orderly wheeled her through the waiting room.

"That detective showed—" Gordon had to stop to swallow. "The look on your face when you killed him, Laura. The serenity. The everyday-ness. How do you think that's going to stack up against a mentally troubled, fatherless teenage boy?"

Laura turned her head and looked out the window.

"Do you know what that detective kept asking? Over and over again?"

"The pigs always ask a lot of questions."

"Stop fucking around, Laura. What did you say before you killed him?" Gordon waited, but she did not respond. "What did you say to Helsinger?"

Laura continued to stare out the window.

"Whatever you said—that's motivation. That's the difference between maybe—just maybe—being able to argue justifiable homicide and the death penalty."

Andy felt her heart stop.

"Laura?" He banged his hand on the steering wheel. "God dammit! Answer me. Answer me or—"

"I am not a fool, Gordon." Laura's tone was cold enough to burn. "Why do you think I refused to be interviewed? Why do you think I told Andrea to keep her mouth shut?"

"You want our daughter to lie to a police detective? To perjure herself in court?"

"I want her to do what she always does and keep her mouth

shut." Her tone was quiet but her anger was so palpable that Andy felt like the air was vibrating with rage.

*Why wasn't her mother arguing that Gordon was wrong? Why wasn't she saying that she didn't have a choice? That she was saving Andy? That it was self-defense? That she was horrified by what she had done? That she had panicked or just reacted or was terrified and she was sorry—so sorry—that she had killed that troubled kid?*

Andy slid her hand into her pocket. The detective's card was still wet from the bathroom counter.

*Palazzolo tried to talk to me again. She wanted me to turn on you. She gave me her card.*

Gordon said, "Laura, this is deadly serious."

She fake-laughed. "That's an interesting choice of words."

"Cops protect their own. Don't you know that? They stick together no matter what. That brotherhood bullshit is not just some urban legend you hear on TV." Gordon was so angry that his voice broke. "This whole thing will turn into a crusade just by virtue of the kid's last name."

Laura inhaled, then slowly shushed it out. "I just—I need a moment, Gordon. All right? I need time alone to think this through."

"You need a criminal litigator to do the thinking for you."

"And you need to stop telling me what to do!" She was so furious that she screeched out the words. Laura covered her eyes with her hand. "Has hectoring me ever worked? Has it?" She wasn't looking for an answer. She turned to Gordon, roaring at him, "This is why I left you! I had to get away from you, to get you out of my life, because you have no idea who I am. You never have and you never will."

Each word was like a slap across her father's face.

"Jesus." Laura grabbed the handle above the door, tried to shift her weight off her injured leg. "Will you drive the fucking car?"

Andy waited for her father to say Laura was welcome to walk

home, but he didn't. He faced forward. He pushed the gear into drive. He glanced over his shoulder before hitting the gas.

The car lurched toward the main road.

Andy didn't know why, but she found herself turning to look out the back window.

Alabama was still standing under the portico. He tipped his hat one last time.

The look on her mother's face—panic? Fear? Disgust?

*Is something wrong, Officer?*

Alabama stood rooted in place as Gordon took a left out of the hospital drive. He was still standing there, head turning to follow their progress, when they drove down the street.

Andy watched him watching the car until he was just a speck in the distance.

*I'm sorry for the situation your wife and daughter are in.*

How had he known that Gordon was her father?

Andy stood under the shower until the hot water ran out. Manic thoughts kept flitting around inside of her head like a swarm of mosquitos. She could not blink without remembering a stray detail from the diner, from the video, from the police interview, the car.

None of it made sense. Her mother was a fifty-five-year-old speech therapist. She played bridge, for chrissakes. She didn't kill people and smoke cigarettes and rail against the pigs.

Andy avoided her reflection in the bathroom mirror as she dried her hair. Her skin felt like sandpaper. There were tiny shards of glass embedded in her scalp. Her chapped lips had started bleeding at the corner. Her nerves were still shaky. At least she thought it was her nerves. Maybe it was lack of sleep that was making her feel so jumpy, or the absence of adrenaline, or the desperation she felt every time she replayed the last thing that Laura had said to Andy before she went into the house—

*I'm not going to change my mind. You need to leave tonight.*

Andy's heart felt so raw that a feather could've splayed it open.

She rummaged through the clean clothes pile and found a pair of lined running shorts and a navy-blue work shirt. She dressed quickly, walking to the window as she did up the buttons. The garage was detached from the house. The apartment was her cave. Gray walls. Gray carpet. Light-blocking shades. The ceiling sloped with the roofline, only made livable by two tiny dormers.

Andy stood at the narrow window and looked down at her mother's house. She could not hear her parents arguing, but she knew what was happening the same way that you knew you had managed to give yourself food poisoning. She was seized by that awful, clammy feeling that something just wasn't right.

The death penalty.

Where had her mother even learned to catch a knife like that? Laura had never been in the military. As far as Andy knew, she hadn't taken any self-defense classes.

Almost every day of her mother's life for the last three years had been spent either trying not to die from cancer or enduring all the horrible indignities that cancer treatment brought with it. There had not been a hell of a lot of free time to train for hand-to-hand combat. Andy was surprised her mother had been able to raise her arm so quickly. Laura struggled to lift a grocery bag, even with her good hand. The breast cancer had invaded her chest wall. The surgeon had removed part of her pectoral muscle.

*Adrenaline.*

Maybe that was the answer. There were all kinds of stories about mothers lifting cars off their trapped babies or performing other tremendous physical feats in order to protect their children. Sure, it wasn't common, but it happened.

But that still didn't explain the look on Laura's face when she pulled the knife through. Blank. Almost workman-like. Not panicked. Not afraid. She could've just as easily been sitting at her desk reviewing a patient's chart.

Andy shivered.

Thunder rumbled in the distance. The sun would not go down for another hour, but the clouds were dark and heavy with the promise of rain. Andy could hear waves throwing themselves onto the beach. Seagulls hashing out dinner plans. She looked down at her mother's tidy bungalow. Most of the lights were on. Gordon was pacing back and forth in front of the kitchen window. Her mother was seated at the table, but all that Andy could make out was her hand, the one that wasn't strapped to her waist, resting on a placemat. Laura's fingers occasionally tapped, but otherwise she was still.

Andy saw Gordon throw his hands into the air. He walked toward the kitchen door.

Andy stepped back into the shadows. She heard the door slam closed. She chanced another look outside the window.

Gordon walked down the porch stairs. The motion detector flipped on the floodlights. He looked up at them, shielding his eyes with his hand. Instead of heading toward her apartment, he stopped on the bottom riser and sat down. He rested his forehead on the heels of his hands.

Her first thought was that he was crying, but then she realized that he was probably trying to regain his composure so that Andy wouldn't be even more worried when she saw him.

She had seen Gordon cry once, and only once, before. It was at the beginning of her parents' divorce. He hadn't let go and sobbed or anything. What he had done was so much worse. Tears had rolled down his cheeks, one long drip after another, like condensation on the side of a glass. He'd kept sniffing, wiping his eyes with the back of his hand. He had left for work one morning assuming his fourteen-year marriage was solid, then before lunchtime had been served with divorce papers.

"*I don't understand,*" he had told Andy between sniffles. "*I just don't understand.*"

Andy couldn't remember the man who was her real father, and even thinking the words *real father* felt like a betrayal to Gordon. *Sperm donor* felt too overtly feminist. Not that Andy wasn't a feminist, but she didn't want to be the kind of feminist that men hated.

Her *birth father*—which sounded strange but kind of made sense because adopted kids said birth mother—was an optometrist whom Laura had met at a Sandals resort. Which was weird, because her mother hated to travel anywhere. Andy thought they'd met in the Bahamas, but she was told the story so long ago that a lot of details were lost.

These were the things she knew: That her birth parents had never married. That Andy was born the first year they were together. That her birth father, Jerry Randall, had died in a car accident while on a trip home to Chicago when Andy was eighteen months old.

Unlike Laura's parents, who had both died before Andy was born, Andy still had grandparents on her birth father's side—Laverne and Phil Randall. She had an old photo somewhere of herself, no more than two, sitting in their laps, balanced between each of their knees. There was a painting of the beach on the wood-paneled wall behind them. The couch looked scruffy. They seemed like kind people, and maybe they were in some ways, but they had completely cut off both Laura and Andy when Gordon had entered their lives.

Gordon—of all people. A Phi Beta Sigma who had graduated Georgetown Law while working as a volunteer coordinator at Habitat for Humanity. A man who played golf, loved classical music, was the president of his local wine-tasting society and had chosen for his vocation one of the most boring areas of the law, helping wealthy people figure out how their money would be spent after they died.

That Andy's birth grandparents had balked at the dorkiest, most uptight black man walking the planet simply because of the color of his skin was enough to make Andy glad she didn't have any contact with them.

The kitchen door opened. Andy watched Gordon stand up. He tripped the floodlights again. Laura handed him a plate of food. Gordon said something Andy could not hear. Laura slammed the door in lieu of response.

Through the kitchen window, she saw her mother making her way back to the table, gripping the counter, the doorjamb, the back of a chair—anything she could find to take the pressure off of her leg.

Andy could've helped her. She could've been down there making her mother tea or helping her wash off the hospital smell the way she'd done so many times before.

*I've earned the right to be alone.*

The TV by Andy's bed caught her attention. The set was small, formerly taking up space on her mother's kitchen counter. By habit, Andy had turned it on when she walked through the door. The sound was muted. CNN was showing the diner video again.

Andy closed her eyes, because she knew what the video showed.

She breathed in.

Out.

The air conditioner hummed in her ears. The ceiling fan *wah-wahed* overhead. She felt cold air curl around her neck and face. She was so tired. Her brain was filled with slow-rolling marbles. She wanted to sleep, but she knew she could not sleep here. She would have to stay at Gordon's tonight and then, first thing tomorrow morning, her father would require she make some kind of a plan. Gordon always wanted a plan.

A car door opened and closed. Andy knew it was her father because the McMansions along her mother's street, all of them so huge that they literally blocked out the sun, were always vacant during the most extreme heat of the summer.

She heard scuffling feet across the driveway. Then Gordon's heavy footsteps were on the metal stairs to the apartment.

Andy grabbed a trashbag out of the box. She was supposed to be packing. She opened the top drawer of her dresser and dumped her underwear into the bag.

"Andrea?" Gordon knocked on the door, then opened it.

He glanced around the room. It was hard to tell whether Andy had been robbed or a tornado had hit. Dirty clothes carpeted the floor. Shoes were piled on top of a flat box that contained two unassembled Ikea shoe racks. The bathroom door hung open. Her period panties from a week ago hung stiffly from the towel rod.

"Here." Gordon offered the plate that Laura had given him. PB&J, chips and a pickle. "Your mom said to make sure you eat something."

*What else did she say?*

"I asked for a bottle of wine, but got this." He reached into his jacket pocket and pulled out a pint-sized bottle of Knob Creek. "Did you know your mother keeps bourbon in the house?"

Andy had known about her mother's stash since she was fourteen.

"Anyway, I thought this might help tamp down some nerves. Take the edge off." He broke the seal on the top. "What are the chances that you have some clean glasses in this mess?"

Andy put the plate on the floor. She felt underneath the sofa bed and found an open pack of Solo cups.

Gordon scowled. "I guess that's better than passing the bottle back and forth like a couple of hobos."

*What did Mom say?*

He poured two fingers of bourbon into the deep cup. "Eat something before you have a drink. Your stomach's empty and you're tired."

Belle Isle Andy hadn't had a drink since she'd returned home. She wasn't sure whether or not she wanted to break the streak. Still, she took a cup and sat cross-legged on the floor so that her dad could sit in the chair.

He sniffed at the chair. "Did you get a dog?"

Andy sucked down a mouthful of bourbon. The 100 proof made her eyes water.

He said, "We should toast your birthday."

She pressed together her lips.

He held up the cup. "To my beautiful daughter."

Andy held up her drink, too. Then she took another sip.

Gordon didn't imbibe. He dug into his suit pocket and retrieved a white mailing envelope. "I got you these. I'm sorry I didn't have time to wrap them in something pretty."

Andy took the envelope. She already knew what was inside. Gordon always bought her gift cards because he knew the stores she liked, but he had no idea what she liked from those stores. She dumped the contents onto the floor. Two $25 gas cards for the station down the street. Two $25 iTunes cards. Two $25 Target gift cards. One $50 gift card to Dick Blick for art supplies. She picked up a piece of paper. He had printed out a coupon for a free sandwich at Subway when you bought one of equal or lesser value.

He said, "I know you like sandwiches. I thought we could go together. Unless you want to take someone else."

"These are great, Dad. Thank you."

He swished around the bourbon but still did not drink. "You should eat."

Andy bit into the sandwich. She looked up at Gordon. He was touching his mustache again, smoothing it down the same way he stroked Mr. Purrkins' shoulders.

He said, "I have no idea what's going through your mother's mind."

Andy's jaw made a grinding noise as she chewed. She might as well have been eating paste and cardboard.

He said, "She told me to let you know that she's going to pay off your student loans."

Andy choked on the bite.

"That was my response, too." Her student loans were a sore point with Gordon. He had offered to refinance the debt in order to help Andy get out from under $800's worth of interest a month, but for reasons known only to her id, she had passed his deadline for gathering all the paperwork.

He said, "Your mother wants you to move back to New York

City. To pursue your dreams. She said she'd help you with the move. Financially, I mean. Suddenly, she's very free with her money."

Andy worked peanut butter off the roof of her mouth with her tongue.

"You can stay with me tonight. We'll work out something tomorrow. A plan. I—I don't want you going back to New York, sweetheart. You never seemed happy up there. I felt like it took a piece of you; took away some of your Andy-ness."

Andy's throat made a gulping sound as she swallowed.

"When you moved back home, you were so good taking care of Mom. So good. But maybe that was asking too much. Maybe I should've helped more or . . . I don't know. It was a lot for you to take on. A lot of pressure. A lot of stress." His voice was thick with guilt, like it was his fault that Laura got cancer. "Mom's right that you need to start your life. To have a career and maybe, I don't know, maybe one day a family." He held up his hand to stop her protest. "Okay, I know I'm getting ahead of myself, but whatever the problem is, I just don't think going back to New York is the answer."

Gordon's head turned toward the television. Something had caught his eye. "That's—from high school. What's her—"

*Motherfucker.*

CNN had identified Alice Blaedel, one of Andy's friends from high school, as a *Close Friend of the Family.*

Andy found the remote and unmuted the sound.

"—always the cool mom," Alice, who had not spoken to Andy in over a decade, was telling the reporter. "You could, you know, talk to her about your problems and she'd, like, she wouldn't judge, you know?" Alice kept shrugging her shoulder every other word, as if she was being electrocuted. "I dunno, it's weird to watch her on the video because, you're like, wow, that's Mrs. Oliver, but it's like in *Kill Bill* where the mom is all normal in front of her kid but she's secretly a killing machine."

Andy's mouth was still thick with peanut butter, but she managed to push out the words, "Killing machine?"

Gordon took the remote from Andy. He muted the sound. He stared at Alice Blaedel, whose mouth was still moving despite not knowing a goddamn thing.

Andy poured more bourbon into her empty cup. Alice had walked out on *Kill Bill* because she'd said it was stupid and now she was using it as a cultural touchstone.

Gordon tried, "I'm sure she'll regret her choice of words."

*Like she'd regretted getting genital warts from Adam Humphrey.*

He tried again. "I didn't realize you had reconnected with Alice."

"I haven't. She's a self-serving bitch." Andy swallowed the bourbon in one go. She coughed at the sudden heat in her throat, then poured herself some more.

"Maybe you should—"

"They lift cars," Andy said, which wasn't exactly what she meant. "Mothers, I mean. Like, the adrenaline, when they see that their kids are trapped." She raised her hands to indicate the act of picking up an overturned automobile.

Gordon stroked his mustache with his fingers.

"She was so calm," Andy said. "In the diner."

Gordon sat back in the chair.

Andy said, "People were screaming. It was terrifying. I didn't see him shoot—I didn't see the first one. The second one, I saw that." She rubbed her jaw with her hand. "You know that phrase people say in the movies, 'I'm gonna blow your head off'? That happens. It literally happens."

Gordon crossed his arms.

"Mom came running toward me." Andy saw it all happening again in her head. The tiny red dots of blood freckling Laura's face. Her arms reaching out to tackle Andy to the ground. "She looked scared, Dad. With everything that happened, that's the only time I ever saw her look scared."

He waited.

"You watched the video. You saw what I did. Didn't do. I was panicked. Useless. Is that why . . ." She struggled to give voice to her fear. "Is that why Mom's mad at me? Because I was a coward?"

"Absolutely not." He shook his head, vehement. "There's no such thing as a coward in that kind of situation."

Andy wondered if he was right, and more importantly, if her mother agreed with him.

"Andrea—"

"Mom killed him." Saying the words put a burning lump of coal in her stomach. "She could've taken the gun out of his hand. She had time to do that, to reach down, but instead she reached up and—"

Gordon let her speak.

"I mean—did she have time? Is it right to assume she was capable of making rational choices?" Andy did not expect an answer. "She looked calm in the video. Serene, that's what you said. Or maybe we're both wrong, because, really, she didn't have an expression. Nothing, right? You saw her face. Everydayness."

He nodded, but let her continue.

"When it was happening, I didn't see it from the front. I mean, I was behind her, right? When it was happening. And then I saw the video from the front and it—it looked different." Andy tried to keep her muddled brain on track. She ate a couple of potato chips, hoping the starch would absorb the alcohol.

She told her father, "I remember when the knife was in Jonah's neck and he was raising the gun—I remember being really clear that he could've shot somebody. Shot me. It doesn't take much to pull a trigger, right?"

Gordon nodded.

"But from the front—you see Mom's face, and you wonder if she did the right thing. If she was thinking that, yes, she could take away the gun, but she wasn't going to do that. She was going to kill the guy. And it wasn't out of fear or self-preservation but it was like . . . a conscious choice. Like a killing machine." Andy couldn't believe she had used Alice Blaedel's spiteful words to describe her mother. "I don't get it,

Daddy. Why didn't Mom talk to the police? Why didn't she tell them it was self-defense?"

*Why was she letting everyone believe that she had deliberately committed murder?*

"I don't get it," Andy repeated. "I just don't understand."

Gordon stroked his mustache again. It was becoming a nervous habit. He didn't answer her at first. He was used to carefully considering his words. Everything felt especially dangerous right now. Neither one of them wanted to say something that could not be taken back.

*Your mother is a murderer. Yes, she had a choice. She chose to kill that boy.*

Eventually, Gordon said, "I have no idea how your mother was able to do what she did. Her thought process. The choices she made. Why she behaved the way she did toward the police." He shrugged, his hands out in the air. "One could hazard that her refusal to talk about it, her anger, is post-traumatic stress, or perhaps it triggered something from her childhood that we don't know about. She's never been one to discuss the past."

He stopped again to gather his thoughts.

"What your mother said in the car—she's right. I don't know her. I can't comprehend her motivations. I mean, yes, I do get that she had the instinct to protect you. I'm very glad that she did. So grateful. But *how* she did it . . ." He let his gaze travel back to the television. More talking heads. Someone was pointing to a diagram of the Mall of Belle Isle, explaining the route Jonah Helsinger had taken to the diner. "Andrea, I just don't know." Gordon said it again: "I just don't know."

Andy had finished her drink. Under her father's watchful eye, she poured another one.

He said, "That's a lot of alcohol on an empty stomach."

Andy shoved the rest of the sandwich into her mouth. She chewed on one side so she could ask, "Did you know that guy at the hospital?"

"Which guy?"

"The one in the Alabama hat who helped Mom into the car."

He shook his head. "Why?"

"It seemed like Mom knew him. Or maybe was scared of him. Or—" Andy stopped to swallow. "He knew you were my dad, which most people don't assume."

Gordon touched the ends of his mustache. He was clearly trying to recall the exchange. "Your mother knows a lot of people in town. She has a lot of friends. Which, hopefully, will help her."

"You mean legally?"

He did not answer the question. "I put in a call to a criminal defense lawyer I've used before. He's aggressive, but that's what your mother needs right now."

Andy sipped the bourbon. Gordon was right: the edge was coming off. She felt her eyes wanting to close.

He said, "When I first met your mom, I thought she was a puzzle. A fascinating, beautiful, complex puzzle. But then I realized that no matter how close I got to her, no matter what combination I tried, she would never really open up to me." He finally drank some bourbon. Instead of gulping it like Andy, he let it roll down his throat.

He told her, "I've said too much. I'm sorry, sweetheart. It's been a troubling day, and I haven't done much to help the situation." He indicated a box filled with art supplies. "I assume you want this to go tonight?"

"I'll get it tomorrow."

Gordon gave her a careful look. As a kid, she would freak out whenever her art supplies were not close at hand.

Andy said, "I'm too tired to do anything but sleep." She did not tell him that she had not held a charcoal pencil or a sketchpad in her hands since her first year in New York. "Daddy, should I talk to her? Not to ask her if I can stay, but to ask her why."

"I don't feel equipped to offer you advice."

Which probably meant she shouldn't.

"Sweetheart." Gordon sensed her melancholy. He leaned over and put his hands on her shoulders. "Everything will work itself out. We'll discuss your future at the end of the month, all right? That gives us eleven days to formulate a plan."

Andy chewed her lip. Gordon would formulate a plan. Andy would pretend like she had a lot of time to think about it until the tenth day, then she would panic.

He said. "For tonight, we'll take your toothbrush, your comb, whatever you absolutely need, then we'll pack everything else tomorrow. And get your car. I assume it's still at the mall?"

Andy nodded. She had forgotten all about her car. Laura's Honda was there, too. They were probably both clamped or towed by now.

Gordon stood up. He closed her art supply box and put it on the floor out of the way. "I think your mother just needs some time alone. She used to take her drives, remember?"

Andy remembered.

On weekends, Andy and Gordon would be doing a project, or Gordon would be doing the project and Andy would be nearby reading a book, and suddenly Laura would burst in, keys in her hand, and announce, "I'm going to be gone for the day."

Oftentimes she would bring back chocolate for Andy or a nice bottle of wine for Gordon. Once, she'd brought a snowglobe from the Tubman Museum in Macon, which was two and a half hours away. Whenever they asked Laura where she had gone and why, she would say, "Oh, you know, just needed to be somewhere besides here."

Andy looked around the cramped, cluttered room. Suddenly, it felt less like a cave and more like a hovel.

Before Gordon could say it, she told him, "We should go."

"We should. But I'm leaving this on your mother's porch." Gordon pocketed the bourbon. He hesitated, then added, "You know you can always talk to me, sweetie. I just wish you didn't have to get tipsy to do it."

"Tipsy." Andy laughed at the silly-sounding word because the alternative was to cry, and she was sick of crying. "Dad, I think—I think I want some time alone, too."

"O-kay," he drew out the word.

"Not, like, forever. I just think maybe it would be good if I walked to your house." She would need another shower, but something about being enveloped by the sweltering, humid night was appealing. "Is that okay?"

"Of course it's okay. I'll tell Mr. Purrkins to warm your bed for you." Gordon kissed the top of her head, then grabbed the plastic garbage bag she had filled with underwear. "Don't dawdle too long. The app on my phone says it's going to start raining in half an hour."

"No dawdling," she promised.

He opened the door but did not leave. "Next year will be better, Andrea. Time puts everything into perspective. We'll get through what happened today. Mom will be herself again. You'll be standing on your own two feet. Your life will be back on track."

She held up her crossed fingers.

"It'll be better," Gordon repeated. "I promise."

He closed the door behind him.

Andy heard his heavy footsteps on the metal stairs.

She didn't believe him.

# 4

Andy rolled over in bed. She brushed something away from her face. In her sleeping brain, she told herself it was Mr. Purrkins, but her half-awake brain told her that the item was way too malleable to be Gordon's chubby calico. And that she couldn't be at her father's house because she had no recollection of walking there.

She sat up too fast and fell back from dizziness.

An involuntary groan came out of Andy's mouth. She pressed her fingers into her eyes. She could not tell if she was tipsy from the bourbon or had crossed into legit hungover, but the headache she'd had since the shooting was like a bear's teeth gnawing at her skull.

*The shooting.*

It had a name now, an *after* that calved her life away from the *before*.

Andy let her hand fall away. She blinked her eyes, willing them to adjust to the darkness. Lowlight from a soundless television. The *wah-wah* noise of a ceiling fan. She was still in her apartment, splayed out on the pile of clean clothes that she stored on the sofa bed. The last thing she remembered was searching for a clean pair of socks.

Rain pelted the roof. Lightning zigzagged outside the tiny dormer windows.

*Crap.*

She had dawdled after promising her father that she would not dawdle, and now her choices were to either beg him to pick her up or walk through what sounded like a monsoon.

With great care, she slowly sat back up. The television pulled Andy's attention. CNN was showing a photo of Laura from two years ago. Bald head covered in a pink scarf. Tired smile on her face. The Breast Cancer Awareness Walk in Charleston. Andy had been cropped out of the image, but her hand was visible on Laura's shoulder. Someone—maybe a friend, maybe a stranger—had taken that private, candid moment and exploited it for a photo credit.

Laura's details appeared on one side of the screen, a résumé of sorts:

—55-Year-Old Divorcee.
—One Adult Child.
—Speech Pathologist.
—No Formal Combat Training.

The image changed. The diner video started to play, the ubiquitous scroll warning that some viewers might find it graphic.

*They're going to take you down harder than him, Laura. This is all going to be about what* you *did, not what* he *did.*

Andy couldn't bear to watch it again; didn't really need to because she could blink and see it all happening live in her head. She stumbled out of bed. She found her phone in the bathroom. 1:18 a.m. She'd been asleep for over six hours. Gordon hadn't texted, which was some kind of miracle. He was probably as wiped out as Andy. Or maybe he thought that Laura and Andy had made amends.

If only.

She tapped on the text icon and selected DAD. Her eyes watered. The light from the screen was like a straight razor. Andy's brain was still oscillating in her skull. She dashed off an apology in case her father woke up, found her bed empty and freaked: *fell asleep almost there don't worry I've got an umbrella.*

The part about the umbrella was a lie. Also the part about

being almost there. And that he shouldn't worry, because she could very well get struck by lightning.

Actually, considering how her day had gone, the odds that Andy would be electrocuted seemed enormously high.

She looked out the dormer window. Her mother's house was dark but for the light in her office window. It seemed very unlikely that Laura was working. During her various illnesses, she had slept in the recliner in the living room. Maybe Laura had accidentally left the light on and couldn't bring herself to limp across the foyer to turn it off.

Andy turned away from the window. The television pulled her back in. Laura backhanding the knife into Jonah Helsinger's neck.

*Thwack.*

Andy had to get out of here.

There was a floor lamp by the chair but the bulb had blown weeks ago. The overhead lights would be like a beacon in the night. Andy used the flashlight app on her phone to search for an old pair of sneakers that could get ruined in the rain and a poncho she'd bought at a convenience store because it seemed like an adult thing to have in case of an emergency.

Which is why she had left it in the glove box of her car, because why would she go out in the rain unless she got caught without an umbrella in her car?

Lightning illuminated every corner of the room.

*Crap.*

Andy pulled a trashbag from the box. Of course she didn't have any scissors. She used her teeth to rip out a hole approximately the circumference of her head. She held up the phone to gauge her progress.

The screen flickered, then died.

The last thing Andy saw were the words LO BAT.

She found the charger stuck in an outlet. The cable was in her car. Her car was two and a half miles away parked in front of the Zegna menswear store.

Unless it had already been towed.

"Fuck!" She said the word with heartfelt conviction. She pushed her head through the trashbag hole and stepped outside. Rain slid down her back. Within seconds, her clothes were soaked so that the homemade poncho turned into cling wrap.

Andy kept walking.

The rain had somehow amplified the day's heat. She felt hot needles stabbing into her face as she turned onto the road. Streetlights did not exist in this part of the city. People bought houses on Belle Isle because they wanted an authentic, old-fashioned, southern coastal town experience. At least as old-fashioned as you could get when the cheapest mansion off the beach ran north of two million dollars.

Nearly three decades ago, Laura had paid $118,000 for her beachside bungalow. The closest grocery store had been the Piggly Wiggly outside of Savannah. The gas station sold live bait and pickled pigs' feet in large jars by the cash register. Now, Laura's house was one of only six original bungalows left in Belle Isle. The land itself was worth literally twenty times the house.

A bolt of lightning licked down from the sky. Andy's arms flew up as if she could stop it. The rain had intensified. Visibility was around five feet. She stopped in the middle of the road. Another flash of lightning stuttered the raindrops. She couldn't decide whether or not to turn around and wait for a lull in the storm or keep heading toward her father's.

Standing in the street like an idiot seemed like the worst of her options.

Andy jumped over the curb onto the sidewalk. Her sneakers made a satisfying splash. She made another splash. She picked up her feet and lengthened her strides. Soon, Andy had pushed herself into a light jog. Then she went faster. And faster.

Running was the only thing that Andy ever felt she did well. It was hard to continually throw one foot after the other. Sweating. Heart pounding. Blood racing through your ears. A lot of people couldn't do it. A lot of people didn't want to, especially in the summer when there were heat advisories warning people not to go outside because they could literally die.

Andy could hear the rhythmic slap of her sneakers over the shushing rain. She detoured away from the road that led to Gordon's, not ready to stop. The boardwalk was thirty yards ahead. The beach just beyond. Her eyes started to sting from the salt air. She couldn't hear the waves, but she somehow absorbed their velocity, the relentless persistence to keep pushing forward no matter how hard gravity pulled at your back.

She took a left onto the boardwalk, fighting an inelegant battle between the wind and the trashbag before she managed to tear off the plastic and slam it into the nearest recycling bin. Her shoes *thudded* on the wooden planks. Hot rain drilled open her pores. She wasn't wearing socks. A blister rubbed on her heel. Her shorts were bunched up. Her shirt was glued down. Her hair was like resin. She sucked in a great big gulp of wet air and coughed it back out.

The spray of blood coming from Betsy Barnard's mouth.

Shelly already dead on the floor.

Laura with the knife in her hand.

*Thwack.*

Her mother's face.

*Her face.*

Andy shook her head. Water flew like a dog sloughing off the sea. Her fingernails were cutting into her palms. She loosened her hands out of the tight fists they'd clawed into. She swiped hair away from her eyes. She imagined her thoughts receding like the low tide. She pulled air into her lungs. She ran harder, legs pumping, tendon and muscle working in tandem to keep her upright during what was nothing more than a series of controlled falls.

Something clicked inside of her head. Andy had never achieved a runner's high, not even back when she kept to something like a schedule. She just got to a place where her body didn't hurt so much that she wanted to stop, but her brain was occupied enough by that pain to keep her thoughts floating along the surface rather than diving down into the darkness.

Left foot. Right foot.

Breathe in. Breathe out.

Left. Right. Left.

*Breathe.*

Tension slowly drained from her shoulders. Her jaw unclenched. The bear-teeth headache turned from a gnawing to a more manageable nibble. Andy's thoughts started to wander. She listened to the rain, watched the drops fall in front of her face. What would it feel like to open her box of art supplies? To take out her pencil and sketchbook? To draw something like a puddle splattering up from her ruined sneakers? Andy visualized lines and light and shadows, the impact of her sneaker inside a puddle, the jerk of her shoestring caught mid-step.

Laura had almost died during her cancer treatments. It wasn't just the toxic mixture of drugs, but the other problems that treatment brought with it. The infections. The *C. difficile*. Pneumonia. Double pneumonia. Staph infections. A collapsed lung.

And now they could add to the list: Jonah Helsinger. Detective Palazzolo. Needing Gordon to butt out of her life. Needing space from her only daughter.

They were going to survive Laura's coldness the same way they had survived the cancer.

Gordon was right about time putting things in perspective. Andy knew all about waiting—for the surgeon to come out, for the films to be read for the biopsy to be cultured for the chemo and the antibiotics and the pain meds and the anti-nausea shot and the clean sheets and the fresh pillows and finally, blissfully, for the cautious smile on the doctor's face when she had told Laura and Andy that the scan was clear.

All that Andy had to do now was wait for her mother to come back around. Laura would fight her way out of the dark place she was in until eventually, finally, in a month or six months or by Andy's next birthday, she would be looking back at what had happened yesterday as if through a telescope rather than through a magnifying glass.

The boardwalk ran out sooner than Andy had expected. She

jumped back onto the one-way road that skirted the beachfront mansions. The asphalt felt solid beneath her feet. The roar of the sea began to fade behind the giant houses. The shore along this stretch bent around the tip of the Isle. Her mother's bungalow was another half mile away. Andy hadn't meant to go back home. She started to turn around but then remembered—

Her bicycle.

Andy saw the bike hanging from the ceiling every time she went into the garage. The trip back to Gordon's would be faster on two wheels. Considering the lightning, having a set of rubber tires between herself and the asphalt seemed like a good idea.

She slowed down to a jog, then a brisk walk. The intensity of the rain dialed back. Fat water drops slapped against the top of her head, made divots in her skin. Andy slowed her walk when she saw the faint glow of light from Laura's office. The house was at least fifty yards away, but this time of year, all the McMansions in the vicinity were unoccupied. Belle Isle was mostly a snowbird town, a respite for Northerners during the harsh winter months. The other homeowners were chased away by the August heat.

Andy glanced into Laura's office window as she walked down the driveway. Empty, at least as far as she could tell. She used the side entrance to the garage. The glass panes rattled in the door as she closed it. The shushing sound of the rain was amplified in the open space. Andy reached for the garage door opener to turn on the light, but caught herself at the last minute because the light only came on when the door rolled up and the rackety sound could wake the dead. Fortunately, the glow from Laura's office reached through the glass in the side door. Andy had just enough light to squint by.

She walked to the back, leaving a Pig-Pen–like trail of rain puddles in her wake. Her bike hung upside down from two hooks Gordon had screwed into the ceiling. Andy's shoulders screamed with pain as she tried to lift the Schwinn's tires from the hooks. Once. Twice. Then the bike was falling and she almost toppled backward trying to turn it right side up before it hit the ground.

*Which was why she hadn't wanted to hang the fucking thing from the ceiling in the first place*, Andy would never, ever say to her father.

One of the pedals had scraped her shin. Andy didn't worry about the trickle of blood. She checked the tread, expecting dry rot, but found the tires were so new they still had the little alveoli poking out of the sides. Andy sensed her father's handiwork. Over the summer, Gordon had repeatedly suggested they resume their weekend bike rides. It was just like him to make sure everything would be ready on the off-chance that Andy said yes.

She started to lift her leg, but stopped mid-air. There was a distinct, jangly noise from above. Andy cocked her head like a retriever. All she could make out was the white noise of the rain. She was trying to think of a Jacob Marley joke when the jangle happened again. She strained to listen, but there was nothing more than the constant *shush* of water falling.

Great. She was a proven coward. She literally did not know when to come in out of the rain, and now, apparently, she was paranoid.

Andy shook her head. She had to get moving again. She sat on the bike and wrapped her fingers around the handlebars.

Her heart jumped into her throat.

*A man.*

Standing outside the door. White. Beady eyes. Dark hoodie clinging to his face.

Andy froze.

He cupped his hands to the glass.

She should scream. She should be quiet. She should look for a weapon. She should walk the bike back. She should hide in the shadows.

The man leaned closer, peering into the garage. He looked left, then right, then straight ahead.

Andy flinched, drawing in her shoulders like she could fold herself into obscurity.

He was staring right at her.

She held her breath. Waited. Trembled. He could see her. She was certain that he could see her.

Slowly, his head turned away, scanning left, then right, again. He took one last look directly at Andy, then disappeared.

She opened her mouth. She drew in a thimbleful of air. She leaned over the handlebars and tried not to throw up.

The man at the hospital—the one in the Alabama hat. Had he followed them home? Had he been lying in wait until he thought the coast was clear?

No. Alabama had been tall and slim. The guy at the garage door, Hoodie, was stocky, muscle-bound, about Andy's height but three times as wide.

The jangling noise had been Hoodie walking down the metal stairs.

He had checked to make sure the apartment was vacant.

He had checked to make sure the garage was empty.

And now he was probably going to break into her mother's house.

Andy furiously patted her pockets, even as she realized that her phone was upstairs, dead where she had left it. Laura had gotten rid of the landline last year. The mansions on either side probably didn't have phones, either. The bike ride back to Gordon's would take ten minutes at least and by then her mother could be—

Andy's heart jerked to a stop.

Her bladder wanted to release. Her stomach was filled with thumbtacks. She carefully stepped off the bike. She leaned it against the wall. The rain was a steady snare drum now. All that she could hear over the *shush-shush-shush* was her teeth chattering.

She made herself walk to the door. She reached out, wrapped her hand around the doorknob. Her fingers felt cold. Was Hoodie waiting on the other side of the door, back pressed to the garage, arms raised with a bat or a gun or just his giant hands that could strangle the life out of her?

Andy tasted vomit in her mouth. The water on her skin felt frozen. She told herself that the man was cutting through to the beach, but nobody cut through to the beach here. Especially in the rain. And lightning.

Andy opened the door. She bent her knees low, then peered out into the driveway. The light was still on in Laura's office. Andy saw no one—no shadows, no tripped floodlights, no man in a hoodie waiting with a knife beside the garage or looking through the windows to the house.

Her mother could take care of herself. She *had* taken care of herself. But that was with both hands. Now, one arm was strapped to her waist and Laura could barely walk across the kitchen on her injured leg without grabbing onto the counter for support.

Andy gently closed the garage door. She cupped her hands to the glass, the same as Hoodie. She looked into the dark space. Again, she could see nothing—not her bike, not the shelves of emergency food and water.

Her relief was only slight, because Hoodie had not walked up the driveway when he'd left. He had turned toward the house.

Andy brushed her fingers across her forehead. She was sweating underneath all the rain. Maybe the guy hadn't gone inside the bungalow. Why would a burglar choose the smallest house on the street, one of the smallest in the entire city? The surrounding mansions were filled with high-end electronics. Every Friday night, dispatch got at least one call from someone who had driven down from Atlanta expecting to enjoy a relaxing weekend and found instead that their TVs were gone.

Hoodie had been upstairs in the apartment. He had looked in the garage.

He hadn't taken anything. He was looking for something.

*Someone.*

Andy walked along the side of the house. The motion detector was not working. The floodlights were supposed to trip. She felt glass crunch under her sneaker. Broken lightbulbs? Broken motion detector? She stood on tiptoe, peered through the kitchen window. To the right, the office door was ajar, but just slightly. The narrow opening cast a triangle of white light onto the kitchen floor.

Andy waited for movement, for shadows. There were none. She stepped back. The porch steps were to her left. She could enter the kitchen. She could turn on the lights. She could surprise Hoodie so that he turned around and shot her or stabbed her the same way that Jonah Helsinger had tried to do.

The two things had to be connected. That was the only thing that made sense. This was Belle Isle, not Atlantic City. Guys in hoodies didn't case bungalows in the pouring rain.

Andy walked to the back of the house. She shivered in the stiff breeze coming off the ocean. She carefully opened the door to the screened porch. The squeak of the hinge was drowned out by the rain. She found the key inside the saucer under the pansies.

Two French doors opened onto her mother's bedroom. Again, Andy cupped her hand to glass. Unlike the garage, she could see clear to the corners of the room. The nightlight was on in the bathroom. Laura's bed was made. A book was on the nightstand. The room was empty.

Andy pressed her ear to the glass. She closed her eyes, tried to focus all of her senses on picking up sounds from inside—feet creaking across the floor, her mother's voice calling for help, glass breaking, a struggle.

All she heard were the rocking chairs swaying in the wind.

Over the weekend, Andy had joined her mother on the porch to watch the sun rise.

"Andrea Eloise." Laura had smiled over her cup of tea. "Did you know that when you were born, I wanted to name you Heloise, but the nurse misunderstood me and she wrote down 'Eloise,' and your father thought it was so beautiful that I didn't have the heart to tell him she'd spelled it wrong?"

Yes, Andy knew. She had heard the story before. Every year, on or around her birthday, her mother contrived a reason to tell her that the *H* had been dropped.

Andy listened at the glass for another moment before forcing herself to move. Her fingers felt so thick she could barely slide the key into the lock. Tears filled her eyes. She was so scared. She had never been this terrified. Not even at the diner, because during the shooting spree, there was no time to think. Andy was reacting, not contemplating. Now, she had plenty of time to consider her actions and the scenarios reeling through her mind were all horrifying.

Hoodie could injure her mother—again. He could be inside, waiting for Andy. He could be killing Laura right now. He could rape Andy. He could kill her in front of her mother. He could rape them both and make one watch or he could kill them then rape them or—

Andy's knees nearly buckled as she walked into the bedroom. She pulled the door closed, cringing when the latch clicked. Rainwater puddled onto the carpet. She slipped out of her sneakers. Pushed back her wet hair.

She listened.

There was a murmuring sound from the other side of the house.

Conversational. Not threatening, or screaming, or begging for help. More like Andy used to hear from her parents after she went to bed.

"*Diana Krall's going to be at the Fox next weekend.*"

"*Oh, Gordon, you know jazz makes me nervous.*"

Andy felt her eyelids flutter like she was going to pass out. Everything was shaking. Inside her head, the sound of her heartbeat was like a gymnasium full of bouncing basketballs. She had to press her palm to the back of her leg to make herself walk.

The house was basically a square with a hallway that horseshoed around the interior. Laura's office was where the dining room had been, off the front of the kitchen. Andy walked up the opposite side of the hallway. She passed her old bedroom, now a guest room, ignored all of the family photos and school drawings hanging on the walls.

"—do anything," Laura said, her tone firm and clear.

Andy stood in the living room. Only the foyer separated her from Laura's office. The pocket doors had been pulled wide open. The layout of the room was as familiar to Andy as her garage apartment. Couch, chair, glass coffee table with a bowl of potpourri, desk, desk chair, bookcase, filing cabinet, reproduction of the *Birth of Venus* on the wall beside two framed pages taken from a textbook called *Physiology and Anatomy for Speech-Language Pathology*.

A framed snapshot of Andy on the desk. A bright green leather blotter. A single pen. A laptop computer.

"Well?" Laura said.

Her mother was sitting on the couch. Andy could see part of her chin, the tip of her nose, her legs uncrossed, one hand resting on her thigh while the other was strapped to her waist. Laura's face was tilted slightly upward, looking at the person sitting in the leather chair.

Hoodie.

His jeans were soaked. A puddle spread out on the rug at his feet.

He said, "Let's think about our options here." His voice was deep. Andy could feel his words rattle inside her chest. "I could talk to Paula Koontz."

Laura was silent, then said, "I hear she's in Seattle."

"Austin." He waited a moment. "But good try."

There was silence, long and protracted.

Then Laura said, "Hurting me won't get you what you need."

"I'm not going to hurt you. I'm just going to scare the shit out of you."

Andy felt her eyelids start to flutter again. It was the way he said it—with conviction, almost with glee.

"Is that so?" Laura forced out a fake-sounding laugh. "You think I can be scared?"

"Depends on how much you love your daughter."

Suddenly, Andy was standing in the middle of her old bedroom. Teeth chattering. Eyes weeping. She couldn't remember how she had gotten there. Her breath was huffing out of her lungs. Her heart had stopped beating, or maybe it was beating so fast that she couldn't feel it anymore.

Her mother's phone would be in the kitchen. She always left it to charge overnight.

*Leave the house. Run for help. Don't put yourself in danger.*

Andy's legs were shaky as she walked down the hall toward the back of the house. Involuntarily, her hand reached out, grabbed onto the doorjamb to Laura's bedroom, but Andy compelled herself to continue toward the kitchen.

Laura's phone was at the end of the counter, the section that was closest to her office, the part that was catching a triangle of light from the partially open door.

They had stopped talking. Why had they stopped talking?

*Depends on how much you love your daughter.*

Andy swung around, expecting to see Hoodie, finding nothing but the open doorway to her mother's bedroom.

She could run. She could justify leaving because her mother would want her to leave, to be safe, to get away. That's all Laura had wanted in the diner. That's all that she would want now.

Andy turned back toward the kitchen. She was inside of her body but somehow outside of it at the same time. She saw herself walking toward the phone at the end of the counter. The cold tile cupped her bare feet. Water was on the floor by the side entrance, probably from Hoodie. Andy's vision tunneled on her mother's cell phone. She gritted her teeth to keep them from clicking. If Hoodie was still sitting in the chair, all that separated him from Andy was three feet and a thin wooden door. She reached for the phone. Gently pulled out the charging cord. Slowly walked backward into the shadows.

"Tell me," Hoodie said, his voice carrying into the kitchen. "Have you ever had one of those dreams where you're being buried alive?" He waited. "Like you're suffocating?"

Andy's mouth was spitless. The pneumonia. The collapsed lung. The horrible wheezing sounds. The panicked attempts to breathe. Her mother had been terrified of suffocating. She was so obsessed with the fear of choking to death on the fluids from her lungs that the doctors had to give her Valium to make her sleep.

Hoodie said, "What I'm going to do is, I'm going to put this bag over your head for twenty seconds. You're going to feel like you're dying, but you're not." He added, "Yet."

Andy's finger trembled as she pressed the *home* button on her mother's phone. Both of their fingerprints were stored. Touching the button was supposed to unlock the screen, but nothing happened.

Hoodie said, "It's like dry waterboarding. Very effective."

"Please . . ." Laura choked on the word. "You don't have to do this."

Andy wiped her finger on the wall, trying to dry it.

"Stop!" her mother shouted so loudly that Andy almost dropped the phone. "Just listen to me. Just for a moment. Just listen to me."

Andy pressed *home* again.

Hoodie said, "I'm listening."

The screen unlocked.

"You don't have to do this. We can work something out. I have money."

"Money's not what I want from you."

"You'll never get it out of me. What you're looking for. I'll never—"

"We'll see."

Andy tapped the text icon. Belle Isle dispatch had adopted the Text-to-911 system six months ago. The alerts flashed at the top of their monitors.

"Twenty seconds," the man said. "You want me to count them for you?"

Andy's fingers worked furiously across the keyboard:
*419 Seaborne Ave armed man imminent danger pls hurry*

"The street's deserted," Hoodie said. "You can scream as loud as you need to."

Andy tapped the arrow to send.

91

"Stop—" Laura's voice rose in panic. "Please." She had started to cry. Her sobs were muffled like she was holding something to her mouth. "Please," she begged. "Oh, God, plea—"

Silence.

Andy strained to hear.

Nothing.

Not a cry or a gasp or even more pleading.

The quiet was deafening.

"One," Hoodie counted. "Two." He paused. "Three."

*Clank.* The heavy glass on the coffee table. Her mother was obviously kicking. Something *thumped* onto the carpet. Laura only had one hand free. She could barely lift a shopping bag.

"Four," Hoodie said. "Try not to wet yourself."

Andy opened her mouth wide, as if she could breathe for her mother.

"Five." Hoodie was clearly enjoying this. "Six. Almost halfway there."

Andy heard a desperate, high-pitched wheezing, the exact same sound her mother had made in the hospital when the pneumonia had collapsed her lung.

She grabbed the first heavy object she could find. The cast iron frying pan made a loud screech as she lifted it off the stove. There was no chance of surprising Hoodie now, no going back. Andy kicked open the door. Hoodie was standing over Laura. His hands were wrapped around her neck. He wasn't choking her. His fingers were sealing the clear plastic bag that encased her mother's head.

Hoodie turned, startled.

Andy swung the frying pan like a bat.

In the cartoons, the flat bottom of the pan always hit the coyote's head like the clapper on a bell, rendering him stunned.

In real life, Andy had the pan turned sideways. The cast iron edge wedged into the man's skull with a nauseatingly loud crack.

Not a ringing, but like the sound a tree limb makes when it breaks off.

The reverberations were so strong that Andy couldn't hold onto the handle.

The frying pan banged to the floor.

At first, Hoodie didn't respond. He didn't fall. He didn't rage. He didn't strike out. He just looked at Andy, seemingly confused.

She looked back.

Blood slowly flushed into the white of his left eye, moving through the capillaries like smoke, curling around the cornea. His lips moved wordlessly. His hand was steady as he reached up to touch his head. The temple was crushed at a sharp angle, a perfect match to the edge of the frying pan. He looked at his fingers.

No blood.

Andy's hand went to her throat. She felt like she had swallowed glass.

Was he okay? Was he going to be okay? Enough to hurt her? Enough to suffocate her mother? To rape them? To kill them both? To—

A trilling noise came from his throat. His mouth fell open. His eyes started to roll up. He reached for the chair, knees bent, trying to sit down, but he missed and fell to the floor.

Andy jumped back like she might get scalded.

He had fallen on his side, legs twisted, hands clutching his stomach.

Andy could not stop staring, waiting, trembling, panicking.

Laura said, "Andrea."

Andy's heart flickered like a candle. Her muscles were stone. She was fixed in position, cast like a statue.

Laura screamed, "Andrea!"

Andy was jolted out of her trance. She blinked. She looked at her mother.

Laura was trying to lean up on the couch. The whites of her eyes were dotted with broken blood vessels. Her lips were blue. More broken blood vessels pinpricked her cheeks. The plastic bag was still tied around her neck. Deep gouge marks ringed her skin. She had clawed the bag open with her fingers the same way Andy had chewed through the poncho trashbag.

"Hurry." Laura's voice was hoarse. "See if he's breathing."

Andy's vision telescoped. She felt dizzy. She heard a whistling sound as she tried to draw air into her lungs. She was starting to hyperventilate.

"Andrea," Laura said. "He has my gun in the waist of his jeans. Give it to me. Before he wakes up."

*What?*

"Andrea, snap out of it." Laura slid off the couch onto the floor. Her leg was bleeding again. She used her good arm to edge across the carpet. "We need to get the gun. Before he comes round."

Hoodie's hands moved.

"Mom!" Andy fell back against the wall. "Mom!"

Laura said, "It's okay, he's—"

Hoodie gave a sudden, violent jerk that knocked over the leather chair. His hands started moving in circles, then the circles turned into tremors that quaked into his shoulders, then head. His torso. His legs. Within seconds, his entire body convulsed into a full-blown seizure.

Andy heard a wail come out of her mouth. He was dying. He was going to die.

"Andrea," Laura said, calm, controlled. "Go into the kitchen."

"Mom!" Andy cried. The man's back arched into a half-circle. His feet kicked into the air. What had she done? What had she done?

"Andrea," Laura repeated. "Go into the kitchen."

He started to make a grunting noise. Andy covered her ears, but nothing could block the sound. She watched in horror as his fingers curved away from his hands. His mouth foamed. His eyes rolled wildly.

"Go into the—"

"He's dying!" Andy wailed.

The grunting intensified. His eyes had rolled up so far in his head that it looked like cotton had been stuffed into the sockets.

Urine spread out from the crotch of his jeans. His shoe flew off. His hands scratched at the air.

"Do something!" Andy screamed. "Mom!"

Laura grabbed the frying pan. She lifted it over her head.

"No!" Andy leapt across the room. She wrenched the frying pan away from her mother. Laura's arm snaked around her waist before Andy could get away. She pulled her close, pressed her mouth to Andy's head. "Don't look, baby. Don't look."

"What did I do?" Andy keened. "What did I do?"

"You saved me," Laura said. "You saved me."

"I d-d-d . . ." Andy couldn't get out the words. "Mom . . . he's . . . I c-can't . . ."

"Don't look." Laura tried to cover Andy's eyes, but she pushed her mother's hand away.

There was total silence.

Even the rain had stopped tapping against the window.

Hoodie had gone still. The muscles in his face were relaxed. One eye stared up at the ceiling. The other looked toward the window. His pupils were solid black dimes.

Andy felt her heart tumble back down her throat.

The waist of the man's hoodie had slipped up. Above the white waistband of his underwear, Andy could see a tattoo of a smiling dolphin. It was cresting out of the water. The word *Maria* was written in an ornate script underneath.

"Is he—" Andy couldn't say the words. "Mom, is he—"

Laura did not equivocate. "He's dead."

"I k-k-k . . ." Andy couldn't get the word out. "K-kill . . . k-kill—"

"Andy?" Laura's tone had changed. "Do you hear sirens?" She turned to look out the window. "Did you call the police?"

Andy could only stare at the tattoo. Was Maria his girlfriend? His wife? Had she killed someone's dad?

"Andy?" Laura pushed herself back along the carpet. She reached under the couch with her hand. She was searching for something. "Darling, quickly. Get his wallet out of his pants."

Andy stared at her mother.

"Get his wallet. Now."

Andy did not move.

"Look under the couch, then. Come here. Now." Laura snapped her fingers. "Andy, come here. Do as I say."

Andy crawled toward the couch, not sure what she was supposed to do.

"Back corner," Laura told her. "Inside the batting on top of the spring. Reach up. There's a make-up bag."

Andy leaned down on her elbow so she could reach into the innards of the couch. She found a vinyl make-up bag, black with a brass zipper. It was heavy, packed tight.

*How had it gotten here?*

"Listen to me." Laura had the man's wallet. She pulled out the cash. "Take this. All of it. There's a town called Carrollton in West Georgia. It's on the state line. Are you listening to me?"

Andy had unzipped the bag. Inside was a flip phone with a charging cable, a thick stack of twenty-dollar bills, and a white, unlabeled keycard like you'd use to get into a hotel room.

"Andy," Laura was reaching for the framed photo on her desk. "You want the Get-Em-Go storage facility. Can you remember? G-e-t-e-m-g-o."

*What?*

"Take his wallet. Throw it in the bay."

Andy looked down at the leather wallet that her mother had tossed onto the floor. The driver's license showed through a plastic sleeve. Her eyes were so swollen from crying that she couldn't see the words.

Laura said, "Don't use the credit cards, all right? Just use the cash. Close your eyes." She broke the picture frame against the side of her desk. Glass splintered. She picked away the photo. There was a small key inside, the kind you'd use to open a padlock. "You'll need this, okay? Andy, are you listening? Take this. Take it."

Andy took the key. She dropped it into the open bag.

"This, too." Laura wedged the wallet into the make-up bag alongside the cash. "Unit one-twenty. That's what you need to remember: One-twenty. Get-Em-Go in Carrollton." She searched the man's pockets, found his keys. "This is for a Ford. He probably parked in the cul-de-sac at the end of Beachview. Take it."

Andy took the keys, but her mind would not register what she was holding.

"Unit one-twenty. There's a car inside. Take that one, leave his Ford. Unhook the battery cables. That's very important, Andy. You need to cut the power to the GPS. Can you remember that, baby? Unhook the battery cables. Dad showed you what the battery looks like. Remember?"

Andy slowly nodded. She remembered Gordon showing her the parts of a car.

"The unit number is your birthday. One-twenty. Say it."

"One-twenty," Andy managed.

"The sirens are getting closer. You have to leave," Laura said. "I need you to leave. Now."

Andy was incapacitated. It was too much. Way too much.

"Darling." Laura cupped Andy's chin with her hand. "Listen to me. I need you to run. Now. Go out the back. Find the man's Ford. If you can't find it, then take Daddy's car. I'll explain it to him later. I need you to head northwest. Okay?" She gripped Andy's shoulder as she struggled to stand. "Andy, please. Are you listening?"

"Northwest," Andy whispered.

"Try to make it to Macon first, then buy a map, an actual paper map, and find Carrollton. Get-Em-Go is near the Walmart." Laura pulled Andy up by the arm. "You need to leave your phone here. Don't take anything with you." She shook Andy again. "Listen to me. Don't call Daddy. Don't make him lie for you."

"Lie for—"

"They're going to arrest me for this." She put her finger to Andy's lips to stop her protest. "It's okay, darling. I'll be okay. But you have to leave. You can't let Daddy know where you are. Do you understand? If you contact him, they'll know. They'll trace it back and find you. Telephone calls, email, anything.

Don't reach out to him. Don't try to call me. Don't call any of your friends, or anyone you've ever had contact with, okay? Do you understand me? Do you hear what I'm saying?"

Andy nodded because that's what her mother wanted her to do.

"Keep heading northwest after Carrollton." Laura walked her through the kitchen, her arm tight around Andy's waist. "Somewhere far away, like Idaho. When it's safe, I'll call you on the phone that's in the bag."

*Safe?*

"You're so strong, Andrea. Stronger than you know." Laura was breathing hard. She was clearly trying not to cry. "I'll call you on that phone. Don't come home until you hear from me, okay? Only respond to my voice, my actual voice, saying these exact words: 'It's safe to come home.' Do you understand? Andy?"

The sirens were getting closer. Andy could hear them now. At least three cruisers. There was a dead man in the house. Andy had killed him. She had murdered a man and the cops were almost here.

"Andrea?"

"Okay," Andy breathed. "Okay."

"Get-Em-Go. One-twenty. Right?"

Andy nodded.

"Out the back. You need to run." Laura tried to push her toward the door.

"Mom." Andy couldn't leave without knowing. "Are you—are you a spy?"

"A what?" Laura looked bewildered.

"Or an assassin, or government agent, or—"

"Oh, Andy, no," Laura sounded as if she wanted to laugh. "I'm your mother. All I've ever been is your mother." She pressed her palm to the side of Andy's face. "I'm so proud of you, my angel. The last thirty-one years have been a gift. You are the reason I am alive. I would've never made it without you. Do you understand me? You are my heart. You are every ounce of blood in my body."

The sirens were close, maybe two streets over.

"I'm so sorry." Laura could no longer hold back her tears. Yesterday, she had killed a man. She had been stabbed, cut, almost suffocated. She had pushed away her family and not a tear had dropped from her eyes until this moment. "My angel. Please forgive me. Everything I've ever done is for you, my Andrea Heloise. Everything."

The sirens were out front. Tires screeched against pavement.

"Run," Laura begged. "Andy, please, my darling, please—run."

# 5

Wet sand caked into the insides of Andy's sneakers as she ran along the shore. She had the make-up bag clutched to her chest, fingers holding together the top because she dared not take the time to zip it. There was no moon, no light from the McMansions, nothing but mist in her face and the sounds of sirens at her back.

She looked over her shoulder. Flashlights were skipping around the outside of her mother's house. Shouting traveled down the beach.

"Clear on the left!"

"Clear in the back!"

Sometimes, when Andy stayed on a 911 call, she would hear the cops in the background saying those same words.

"It's okay to hang up now," she would tell the caller. "The police will take care of you."

Laura wouldn't tell the cops anything. She would probably be sitting at the kitchen table, mouth firmly closed, when they found her. Detective Palazzolo wouldn't be making any deals after tonight. Laura would be arrested. She would go to jail. She would appear in front of a judge and jury. She would go to prison.

Andy ran harder, like she could get away from the thought of her mother behind bars. She bit her lip until she tasted the metallic tang of blood. The wet sand had turned into concrete inside her shoe. There was a tiny bit of karmic retribution about the pain.

Hoodie was dead. She had killed him. She had murdered a man. Andy was a murderer.

She shook her head so hard that her neck popped. She tried to get her bearings. Seaborne extended three tenths of a mile before it dead-ended into Beachview. If she missed the turn-off, she would find herself in a more inhabited area of the Isle where someone might glance out the window and call the police.

Andy tried to count her footsteps, pacing off two hundred yards, then three hundred, then finally veering left away from the ocean. All of the McMansions had security gates to keep strangers from wandering in off the beach. City code forbade any permanent fences in front of the sand dunes, so people had erected flimsy wooden slats hanging from barbed wire to serve as a deterrent. Only some of the gates were alarmed, but all of them were marked with warnings that a siren would go off if they were opened.

Andy stopped at the first gate she came to. She ran her hand along the sides. Her fingers brushed against a plastic box with a wire coming out of it.

Alarmed.

She ran to the next gate and went through the same check.

Alarmed.

Andy cursed, knowing the fastest way to the street would be to climb over the dunes. She gingerly pushed the wooden slats with her foot. The wire bowed. Some unseen anchor slipped from the sand so that the fence fell low enough to step over. She lifted her leg, careful not to snag her shorts on the barbed wire. Sea oats crushed under her feet as she traversed the steep slope. She cringed at the destruction she was causing. By the time she made it to a stone path, she was limping.

Andy leaned her hand against the wall, stopped to take a breath. Her throat was so dry that she went into a coughing attack. She covered her mouth, waiting it out. Her eyes watered. Her lungs ached. When the coughing had finally passed, she let her hand drop. She took a step that might as well have been on glass. The sand in her sneakers had the consistency of clumping cat litter. Andy took them off, tried to shake them out. The synthetic mesh had turned into a cheese grater. Still, she tried to cram her feet back into the sneakers. The pain was too much. She was already bleeding.

Andy walked barefoot up the path. She thought about all of the clues that Detective Palazzolo would find when she arrived at the bungalow: Laura's face, especially her bloodshot eyes, still showing signs of suffocation. The plastic bag around her neck with the dead man's fingerprints on it. The dead man lying in the office by the overturned coffee table. The side of his head caved in. Urine soaking his pants. Foam drying on his lips. His eyes pointing in two different directions. Blood from Laura's leg streaked across the carpet. Andy's fingerprints on the handle of the frying pan.

In the driveway: broken glass from the floodlights. The lock on the kitchen door probably jimmied. The puddles on the kitchen tiles showing the path Hoodie had taken. More water showing Andy's route from the bedroom to the hall to the guest room to the living room and back again.

On the beach: Andy's footprints carved into the wet sand. Her destructive path up the dunes. Her blood, her DNA, on the stone path where she now stood.

Andy clamped her teeth closed and groaned into the sky. Her neck strained from the effort. She leaned over, elbows on her knees, bowed over by the impact of her horrible actions. None of this was right. Nothing made sense.

What was she supposed to do?

What *could* she do?

She needed to talk to her father.

Andy started to walk toward the road. She would go to Gordon's house. She would ask him what to do. He would help her do the right thing.

Andy stopped walking.

She knew what her father would do. Gordon would let Laura

take the blame. He would not allow Andy to turn herself in. He would not risk the possibility that she could go to prison for the rest of her life.

But then Palazzolo would find Andy's wet footprints inside Laura's house, more footprints in the sand, her DNA between the McMansions, and she would charge Gordon with lying to a police officer and accomplice to murder after the fact.

Her father could go to prison. He could lose his license to practice.

*Don't make him lie for you.*

Andy remembered the tears in her mother's eyes, her insistence that everything she'd done was for Andy. At a basic level, Andy had to trust that Laura was telling her to do the right thing. She continued up the driveway. Laura had guessed that the man's Ford would be in the Beachview Drive cul-de-sac. She had also said to run, so Andy started to run again, holding her sneakers in one hand and the make-up bag in the other.

She was rounding the corner when a bright light hit her face. Andy ducked back onto the stone path. Her first thought was that a police cruiser had hit her with the spotlight. Then she chanced a look up and realized she had triggered the motion detector on the floodlights.

Andy ran up the driveway. She kept to the middle of the street away from the motion detectors on the houses. She did not look back, but her peripheral vision had caught the distant rolling of the red and blue lights. It looked like every Belle Isle police cruiser had responded to the emergency text. Andy probably had minutes, possibly seconds, before someone in charge told them to fan out and search the area.

She got to the end of the one-way street. Beachview Drive dead-ended into Seaborne Avenue. There was a little dog-leg at the other end that served as beach access for emergency vehicles. Laura had guessed that the dead man's car would be there.

There was no Ford in sight.

*Shit.*

A pair of headlights approached from Beachview. Andy

panicked, running left, then right, then circling back and diving behind a palm tree as a black Suburban drove by. There was a giant, springy antenna on the bumper that told Andy the car belonged to law enforcement.

Andy looked back up Beachview Drive. There was an unpaved driveway halfway up, weeds and bushes overgrown at the entrance. One of the six remaining bungalows on Belle Isle was owned by the Hazeltons, a Pennsylvania couple who'd stopped coming down years ago.

Andy could hide there, try to figure out what to do next.

She checked Seaborne in case any cars were driving up the wrong way. She scanned Beachview for headlights. Then she jogged up the road, her bare feet slapping the asphalt, until she reached the Hazeltons' long, sandy driveway.

There was something off.

The overgrown tangle of bushes had been tamped down.

Someone had recently driven up to the house.

Andy skirted the bushes, heading into the yard instead of down the driveway. Her feet were bleeding so badly that the sand created a second layer of sole. She kept moving forward, crouching down to make herself less visible. No lights were on inside the Hazelton house. Andy realized she could sort of see in the darkness. It was later—or earlier—than she'd thought. Not exactly sunrise, but Andy recalled there was a sciencey explanation about how the rays bounced against the ocean surface and brought the light to the beach before you could see the sun.

Whatever the phenomenon, it allowed her to make out the Ford truck parked in the driveway. The tires were bigger than normal. Black bumpers. Tinted windows. Florida license plate.

There was another truck parked beside it—smaller; a white Chevy, probably ten years old but otherwise nondescript. The license plate was from South Carolina, which wasn't unusual this close to Charleston, but as far as Andy knew, the Hazeltons were still based in Pennsylvania.

Andy carefully approached the Chevy, crouching to look

inside. The windows were rolled down. She saw the key was in the ignition. There was a giant lucky rabbit's foot dangling from the keychain. Fuzzy dice hung from the mirror. Andy had no idea whether or not the truck belonged to the Hazeltons, but leaving the keys inside seemed like something the older couple would do. And the dice and giant rabbit's foot keychain was right up their grandson's alley.

Andy considered her options.

No GPS in the Chevy. No one to report it stolen. Should she take this instead? Should she leave the dead man's truck behind?

Andy let Laura do the thinking for her. Her mother had said to take the dead man's truck so she was going to take the dead man's truck.

Andy approached the Ford cautiously. The dark windows were rolled tight. The doors were locked. She found Hoodie's keys in the make-up bag. The ring had a can opener and the Ford key. No house keys, but maybe they were inside the truck.

Instead of pressing the remote, Andy used the actual key to unlock the door. Inside, she smelled a musky cologne mingled with leather. She tossed the make-up bag onto the passenger's seat. She had to brace her hands on the sides of the cab to pull herself up into the driver's seat.

The door gave a solid *thunk* when she closed it.

Andy stuck the key into the ignition. She turned it slowly, like the truck would blow up or self-destruct with the wrong move. The engine gave a deep purr. She put her hand on the gear. She stopped, because something was wrong.

There should have been light coming from the dash, but there was nothing. Andy pressed her fingers to the console. Construction paper, or something that felt like it, was taped over the display. She turned her head. The dome light had not come on, either.

Andy thought about Hoodie sitting in the truck blacking out all the light then parking it at the Hazeltons.

And then she thought about the light in her mother's office. The only light Laura had left on in the house. Andy had assumed her mother had forgotten to turn it off, but maybe Laura had not been sleeping in the recliner. Maybe she had been sitting on the couch in her office waiting for someone like Hoodie to break in.

*He has my gun in the waistband of his jeans.*

Not *a* gun, but *my* gun.

Andy felt her mouth go dry.

*When had her mother bought a gun?*

A siren whooped behind her. Andy cringed, but the cruiser rolled past rather than turning down the driveway. She moved the gear around, slowly letting her foot off the brake, testing each notch until she found reverse.

There was no seeing out the dark windows as she backed out of the driveway. Tree limbs and thorny bushes scraped at the truck. She hit Beachview Drive sideways, the truck wheels bumping off the hard edge of the curb.

Andy performed the same trick with the gear until she found drive. The headlights were off. In the pre-dawn darkness, she had no way of finding the dial to turn them on. She kept both hands tight on the wheel. Her shoulders were up around her ears. She felt like she was about to roll off a cliff.

She drove past the road to Gordon's house. The flashing lights of a police cruiser were at the end of his street. Andy accelerated before she could be seen. And then she realized that she could not be seen because all of the lights were off, not just the interior lights and the headlights. She glanced into the rearview mirror as she tapped the brakes. The taillights did not come on, either.

This was not good.

It was one thing to cover all of your lights when you were on the way to doing something bad, but when you were leaving the bad thing, when the road was crawling with police officers, driving without your lights was tantamount to writing the word GUILTY on your forehead.

There was one bridge in and out of Belle Isle. The Savannah police would be streaking down one side while Andy, illuminated by the sun reflecting off the water, would be trying to sneak out of town on the other.

She pulled into the parking lot of what happened to be the Mall of Belle Isle. She jumped out of the truck and walked around to the back. Some kind of thick black tape covered the taillights. She picked at the edge and found that it wasn't tape, but a large magnetic sheet. The other light had the same.

The corners were rounded off. The sheets were the exact size needed to cover both the brake lights and the back-up lights.

Andy's brain lacked the ability to process why this mattered. She tossed the magnets into the back of the truck and got behind the wheel. She peeled away the construction paper on the console. Like the magnets, the paper was cut to the exact size. More black paper covered the radio and lighted buttons on the console.

She found the knob for the headlights. She drove away from the mall. Her heart was thumping against the side of her neck as she approached the bridge. She held her breath. She crossed the bridge. No other cars were on the road. No other cars were on the turn-off.

As she accelerated toward the highway, she caught a glimpse of three Savannah cruisers rushing toward the bridge, lights rolling, sirens off.

Andy let out the breath she'd been holding.

There was a sign by the road:

MACON 170

ATLANTA 248

Andy checked the gas gauge. The tank was full. She would try to make the over four-hour trip to Atlanta without stopping, then buy a map at the first gas station she found. Andy had no idea how far Carrollton was from there, or how she'd find the Get-Em-Go storage facility near the Walmart.

*The unit number is your birthday. One-twenty. Say it.*

"One-twenty," Andy spoke the numbers aloud, suddenly confused.

Her birthday was yesterday, August twentieth.

Why had Laura said that she was born in January?

# 6

Andy drove up and down what seemed like the city of Carrollton's main drag. She had easily found the Walmart, but unlike the Walmart, the Get-Em-Go storage facility did not have a gigantic, glowing sign that you could see from the interstate.

The bypass into Atlanta had been tedious and—worse—unnecessary. Andy had been tempted to use the truck's navigation system, but in the end decided to follow Laura's orders. She'd bought a folding map of Georgia once she was inside the Atlanta city limits. The drive from Belle Isle to Carrollton should have been around four and a half hours. Because Andy had driven straight through Atlanta during morning rush hour, six hours had passed before she'd finally reached the Walmart. Her eyelids had been so heavy that she'd been forced to take a two-hour nap in the parking lot.

How did people locate businesses before they had the internet?

The white pages seemed like an obvious source, but there were no phone booths in sight. Andy had already asked a Walmart security guard for directions. She sensed it was too dangerous to keep asking around. Someone might get suspicious. Someone might call a cop. She did not have her driver's license or proof of insurance. Her rain-soaked hair had dried in crazy, unkempt swirls. She was driving a stolen truck with Florida plates and dressed like a teenager who had woken up in the wrong bed during spring break.

Andy had been in such a panicked hurry to get to Carrollton that she hadn't bothered to wonder why her mother was sending her here in the first place. What was inside the storage facility? Why did Laura have a hidden key and a flip phone and money and what was Andy going to find if she ever located the Get-Em-Go?

The questions seemed pointless after over an hour of searching. Carrollton wasn't a Podunk town, but it wasn't a buzzing metropolis, either. Andy had figured her best bet was to aimlessly drive around in search of her destination, but now she was worried that she would never find it.

The library.

Andy felt the idea hit her like an anvil. She had passed the building at least five times, but she was just now making the connection. Libraries had computers and, more importantly, anonymous access to the internet. At the very least, she would be able to locate the Get-Em-Go.

Andy swerved a massive U-turn and got into the turning lane for the library. The big tires bumped over the sidewalk. She had her choice of parking spaces, so she drove to the far end. There were only two other cars, both old clunkers. She assumed they belonged to the library staff. The branch was small, probably the size of Laura's bungalow. The plaque beside the front door said the building opened at 9 a.m.

Eight minutes.

She stared at the squat building, the crisp edges of the red brick, the grainy pores in the mortar. Her vision was oddly sharp. Her mouth was still dry, but her hands had stopped shaking and her heart no longer felt like it was going to explode. The stress and exhaustion from the last few days had peaked around Macon. Andy was numb to almost everything now.

She felt no remorse.

Even when she thought about the horrible last few seconds of Hoodie's life, she could not summon an ounce of pity for the man who had tortured her mother.

What Andy did feel was guilt over her lack of remorse.

She remembered years ago one of her college friends proclaiming that everyone was capable of murder. At the time, Andy had silently bristled at the generalization, because if everyone were truly capable of murder, there would be no such thing as rape. It was the kind of stupid *what if* question that came up at college parties—what if you had to defend yourself? Could you kill someone? Would you be able to do it? Guys always said yes because guys were hardwired to say yes to everything. Girls tended to equivocate, maybe because statistically they were a billion times more likely to be attacked. When the question invariably came round to Andy, she had always joked that she would do exactly what she'd ended up doing at the diner: cower and wait to die.

Andy hadn't cowered in her mother's kitchen. Maybe it was different when someone you loved was being threatened. Maybe it was genetic.

Suicides ran in families. Was it the same with killing?

What Andy really wanted to know was what had her face looked like. In that moment, as she kicked open the office door and swung the pan, she had been thoughtless, as in, there was not a single thought in her mind. Her brain was filled with the equivalent of white noise. There was a complete disconnect between her head and her body. She was not considering her own safety. She was not thinking about her mother's life or death. She was just acting.

*A killing machine.*

Hoodie had a name. Andy had looked at his driver's license before she'd thrown the wallet into the bay.

Samuel Godfrey Beckett, resident of Neptune Beach, Florida, born October 10, 1981.

The Samuel Beckett part had thrown her off, because Hoodie's existence outside Laura's office had taken shape with the name. He'd had a parent who was a fan of Irish avant-garde poetry. That somehow made his life more vivid than the *Maria* tattoo. Andy could picture Hoodie's mother sitting on her back porch watching the sunrise, asking her son, "Do you know who I named you after?" the same way that Laura always told Andy the story about how the *H* got dropped from her middle name.

Andy pushed away the image.

She had to remind herself that Samuel Godfrey Beckett was, in Detective Palazzolo's parlance, a *bad guy*. There were likely a lot of bad things Samuel or Sam or Sammy had done in his lifetime. You didn't darken all the interior lights in your truck and cover your taillights on a whim. You did these things deliberately, with malice aforethought.

And someone probably paid you for your expertise.

Nine a.m. A librarian unlocked the door and waved Andy in.

Andy waved back, then waited until the woman went inside before retrieving the black make-up bag from under the seat. She opened the brass zip. She checked the phone to make sure the battery was full. No calls registered on the screen. She closed the phone and shoved it back into the bag alongside the keycard, the padlock key, the thick bundle of twenties.

She had counted the stash in Atlanta. There was only $1,061 to get Andy through however many days she needed to get through before the phone rang and her mother said it was safe to come home.

Andy felt stricken by the thought that she would have to devise some kind of budget. A Gordon budget. Not an Andy budget, which consisted of praying that cash would appear from the ether. She had no way of making more money. She couldn't get a job without using her social security number and even then, she had no idea how long she'd need the job for. And she especially did not know what kind of job she could possibly be qualified to do in Idaho.

*Keep heading northwest after Carrollton . . . Somewhere far away, like Idaho.*

Where the hell had her mother gotten that idea? Andy had only ever been to Georgia, New York, Florida and the Carolinas. She knew nothing about Idaho except that there was probably a lot of snow and undoubtedly a lot of potatoes.

$1,061.

Gas, meals, hotel rooms.

Andy zipped the bag closed. She got out of the truck. She pulled down the ridiculously small T-shirt, which was as flattering as Saran Wrap on a waffle fry. Her shorts were stiff from the salt air. Her feet hurt so badly that she was limping. There was a cut on her shin that she did not remember getting. She needed a shower. She needed Band-Aids, better shoes, long pants, shirts, underwear . . . that thousand bucks and change would probably not last more than a few days.

She tried to do the math in her head as she walked toward the library. She knew from one of her former roommates that the driving distance between New York City and Los Angeles was almost three thousand miles. Idaho was somewhere in the upper left part of the United States—Andy sucked at geography—but it was definitely northwest.

If she had to guess, Andy would assume the driving time was about the same from Georgia to Idaho as from New York to California. The trip from Belle Isle to Macon was right under two hundred miles, which took about two and a half hours to drive, so basically she was looking at around twelve days of driving, eleven nights in cheap motels, three meals a day, gas to get there, whatever supplies she needed in the immediate . . .

Andy shook her head. Would it take twelve days to get to Idaho?

She really sucked at math, too.

"Good morning," the librarian said. "Coffee's ready in the corner."

"Thanks," Andy mumbled, feeling guilty because she wasn't a local taxpayer and shouldn't technically be able to use all of this stuff for free. Still, she poured herself a cup of coffee and sat down at a computer.

The glowing screen made her feel oddly at ease. She had been without her phone or iPad all night. Andy had not realized how much time she wasted listening to Spotify or checking Instagram and Snapchat and reading blogs and doing Hogwarts house sorting quizzes until she lacked the means to access them.

She stared at the computer screen. She drank her coffee. She thought about emailing her father. Or calling him. Or sending him a letter.

*If you contact him, they'll know. They'll trace it back and find you.*

Andy put down her cup. She typed *Get-Em-Go Carrollton GA* into the browser, then clicked on the map.

She almost laughed.

The storage facility was just over one hundred yards behind the library. She knew this because the high school's football field separated the two. Andy could've walked to it. She checked the hours on the Get-Em-Go website. The banner across the top said that the facilities were open twenty-four hours, but then it also said that the office was open from 10 a.m. to 6 p.m.

Andy looked at the clock. She had fifty minutes.

She opened MapQuest on the computer and pulled up driving directions from Georgia to Idaho. Two thousand three hundred miles. Thirty hours of driving, not twelve days, which was why Andy had been forced to take Algebra twice. She had selected PRINT before her brain could tell her not to. Andy clicked CANCEL. The library charged ten cents a page, but money wasn't the issue. She would have to walk up to the counter and ask for the pages, which meant the librarian would see that she was driving to Idaho.

Which meant if somebody else, maybe a guy like Hoodie who had magnets on his taillights and construction paper on his dashboard, asked the librarian where Andy was heading, then the librarian would know.

*They'll trace it back and find you. Telephone calls, email, anything.*

Andy silently mulled over Laura's warning in her head. Obviously, *they* were the ones who'd hired Hoodie, aka Samuel Godfrey Beckett. But what exactly had *they* hired him to do? Hoodie had told Laura that he wasn't going to kill her. At least not instantly. He'd said that he was going to scare the shit out of her by suffocating her with the plastic bag. Andy's knowledge of torture came mostly from Netflix. If you weren't a torturer in a sadistic, *Saw* kind of way, then you were a torturer in the badass *Jack Reacher* way, which meant you wanted information.

What information did a fifty-five-year-old divorced speech pathologist have that was worth hiring a goon to torture it out of her?

Better yet, during what period of her life had Laura accumulated this torturable information?

Everything Detective Palazzolo had said about Laura's past, from being born in Rhode Island to attending UGA to buying the house on Belle Isle tracked with what Andy knew to be true. There was no unexplained gap in Laura's history. She had never been out of the country. She never even took vacations because she already lived right on the beach.

So what did Laura know that *they* wanted to torture out of her?

And what was so important that Laura would endure torture rather than give it up?

Andy fluttered out air between her lips. She could spend the rest of her life circling down this rabbit hole.

She located the scratch paper and pencils beside the computer. She took several sheets and began to transcribe the directions to Idaho: *75S to 84E to 80E, NE2E, 1-29S, I70E . . .*

Andy stared at the jumble of numbers and letters. She would need to buy another map. There would be a rest stop at the Georgia/Alabama border. First, she would go to the storage facility, change out the truck for the car Laura had said would be there, then head northwest.

She fluttered her lips again.

She was taking a hell of a lot on her mother's word. Then again, following her own instincts would've meant that Andy would be at the funeral home right now sobbing on Gordon's shoulder while he worked out burial arrangements for her mother.

Andy's fingers returned to the keyboard. She looked over her shoulder. The librarians had disappeared, probably to log in the returned books or practice shushing people.

Andy clicked on PREFERENCES under the Google tab. She set the browser to Incognito Mode to mask her browsing history. She probably should've done this first thing. Or maybe it was overkill. Or maybe she should stop berating herself for acting paranoid and just accept the fact that she *was* paranoid for a very damn good reason.

The first site she went to was the *Belle Isle Review*.

The front page was devoted to Laura Oliver, local speech pathologist and killing machine. They didn't actually call her a killing machine, but they'd quoted Alice Blaedel in the first paragraph, which was the same as.

Andy scanned the article. There was no mention of a man in a hoodie found with a frying-pan-shaped indentation in his head. There wasn't even a stolen vehicle report on the black truck. She clicked through the other stories and gave them a quick read.

Nothing.

She sat back in her chair, perplexed.

Behind her, the door opened. An old man shuffled in, heading straight for the coffee as he launched into a political tirade.

Andy didn't know who the tirade was for, but she tuned out the rant and pulled up CNN.com. The site led with the *Killing Machine* quote in the headline. Gordon was right about a lot of things, but Andy knew her father would not be pleased to be proven correct about the focus of the news stories. The patheticness of Jonah Lee Helsinger's life was highlighted in the second paragraph:

*Six months ago, Helsinger's sheriff father, a war veteran and local hero, was tragically killed in a stand-off with a gunman, around the same time police believe young Helsinger's thoughts turned to murder.*

Andy checked FoxNews.com, the *Savannah Reporter*, the *Atlanta Journal-Constitution*.

All of the stories were focused on Laura Oliver and what she had done at the Rise-n-Dine. There was no mention of Samuel Godfrey Beckett, or even an unidentified murder victim in a hoodie.

Had Laura managed to move the body? That didn't seem possible. Andy supposed her mother could've refused the police entry into the house, but the 911 text sent from Laura's phone was probable cause for entry. Even if Laura managed to turn away the Belle Isle cops, the person in that unmarked black Suburban would not have taken no for an answer.

Andy tapped her finger on the mouse as she tried to think it through.

Someone with a lot of connections was keeping a tight lid on the story.

*They?*

The same people who had sent Hoodie? The same people Laura was terrified would track down Andy?

She felt her heart bang against the base of her throat. Half the police force would have been outside Laura's bungalow. Probably Palazzolo, maybe even the Georgia Bureau of Investigation. That would mean *they* had some kind of pull with the governor, maybe even the feds.

Andy checked behind her.

The old man was leaning on the check-in desk, trying to engage one of the librarians in a political discussion.

Andy looked at the time on the computer again, watched the seconds turn into minutes.

*The unit number is your birthday. One-twenty.*

Andy put down the coffee. She typed in January 20, 1987.

*January 20, 1987, was a Tuesday. People born on this day are Aquarius. Ronald Reagan was president. "Walk Like an Egyptian" by the Bangles was on the radio.* Critical Condition *starring Richard Pryor topped the box office. Tom Clancy's* Red Storm Rising *was #1 on the* New York Times *bestseller list.*

Andy counted back nine months in her head and entered *April 1986 news* into the search. Instead of a month-specific timeline, she got a general overview of the year:

*US bombs Libya. Iran–Contra. Chernobyl nuclear disaster. Perestroika. Halley's Comet. Challenger explosion. Swedish Prime Minister murdered. Oslo G-FAB assassination. Pan-Am 73 hijacked. Explosion on TWA jet over Greece. Mercantile bombing. FBI Miami bank shoot-out.* Oprah Winfrey Show *debuts. 38,401 cases of AIDS worldwide.*

Andy stared at the words, only some of which seemed familiar. She could spend all day backtracking the events, but the fact was, you couldn't find something if you didn't know what you were looking for.

*Paula Koontz.*

The name had been edging around Andy's thoughts for the last few hours. She had never, ever heard her mother mention a woman named Paula. As far as Andy knew, all of Laura's friends were in Belle Isle. She never talked to anyone else on the phone. She wasn't even on Facebook because she claimed there was no one back in Rhode Island she wanted to keep in touch with.

*I could talk to Paula Koontz.*

*I hear she's in Seattle.*

*Austin. But good try.*

Laura had tried to fake out Hoodie. Or maybe she was testing him? But testing him for what?

Andy searched for *Paula Koontz Austin TX.*

Nothing Austin-specific came back, but apparently, Paula Koontz was a popular name for real estate agents in the northeast.

"Koontz," Andy whispered the word aloud. It didn't sound right to her ears. She had been thinking more like Dean Koontz when Hoodie had said it more like "koontz-ah."

She tried *koontze, koontzee, khoontzah . . .*

Google asked: *do you mean koontah?*

Andy clicked the suggested search. Nothing, but Google offered *khoontey* as an alternative. She kept clicking through the *do you means.* Several iterations later brought up a faculty directory for the University of Texas at Austin.

Paula Kunde was currently teaching *Introduction to Irish Women's Poetry and Feminist Thought* on Mondays, Wednesdays and Fridays. She was head of the women's studies department.

Her book, *The Madonna and Madonna: Like a Virgin from Jesus Christ to Ronald Reagan*, was available in paperback from IndieBound.

Andy enlarged the woman's photo, which had been taken in an unflattering side profile. Black and white, but that didn't help matters. It was hard to tell how old Paula was because she'd obviously spent way too much time in the sun. Her face was worn and craggly. She was at least Laura's age, but she did not look like any of her mother's usual friends, who wore Eileen Fisher and sunscreen every time they left the house.

Paula Kunde was basically a washed-out old hippie. Her hair was a mixture of blonde and gray with an unnatural-looking dark streak in the bangs. Her shirt, or dress, or whatever she was wearing, had a Native American pattern.

The sunken look to her cheeks reminded Andy of Laura during chemo.

Andy scrolled through Kunde's credentials. Publications in *Feminist Theory and Exposition*, several keynote speaker slots at feminist conferences. Kunde had earned her undergrad at the University of California, Berkeley, and her master's at Stanford, which explained the hippie vibe. Her doctorate came from a state college in western Connecticut, which seemed weird because Bryn Mawr or Vassar would've better suited her field of study, especially with a Stanford master's, which was to Andy's unfinished technical theater arts degree as diamonds were to dog shit.

More importantly, there was nothing in Paula Kunde's résumé that indicated she would ever cross paths with Laura. Feminist theory did not overlap with speech therapy in any way that Andy could think of. Laura was more likely to ridicule an old hippie than befriend one. So why had her mother recognized this woman's name smack in the middle of being tortured?

"Hey, hon." The librarian smiled down at Andy. "Sorry, but we're gonna have to ask you not to drink coffee around the computers." She nodded toward the old guy, who was glaring at Andy over his own steaming cup of coffee. "Rules have to apply to everybody."

"I'm sorry," Andy said, because it was her nature to apologize for everything in her orbit. "I was leaving anyway."

"Oh, you don't have to—" the woman tried, but Andy was already getting up.

"I'm sorry." Andy stuffed the scribbled directions to Idaho into her pocket. She tried to smile at the old man as she left. He did not return the gesture.

Outside, the intense sunlight made her eyes water. Andy had to find some sunglasses before she went blind. She guessed Walmart would be the best place to go. She would also need to purchase some essentials like underwear and jeans and another T-shirt, plus maybe a jacket in case Idaho was cold this time of year.

Andy stopped walking. Her knees went wobbly.

Someone was looking inside the truck. Not just glancing as he walked by but looking with his hands pressed to the glass the same way Hoodie had peered through the garage door a few hours ago. The man was wearing a blue baseball cap, jeans and a white T-shirt. His face was cast in shadow under the brim of his hat.

Andy felt a scream get caught up in her throat. Her heart boxed at her ribs as she walked backward, which was stupid because the guy could turn around any minute and see her. But he did not, even as Andy darted around the back of the building, her throat straining from the scream that she could not let out.

She ran into the woods, frantically trying to summon up the Google Earth view, the high school behind the library, the squat storage facility with its rows of metal buildings. The relief she felt when she saw the high fence around the football field was only dampened by the fear that she was being followed. With every step, Andy tried to talk herself out of her paranoia. The guy in the hat hadn't seen her. Or maybe it didn't matter if he had. The black truck was nice. Maybe the guy was looking to buy one. Or maybe he was looking to see how to break in. Or maybe he was looking for Andy.

*You think I can be scared?*

*Depends on how much you love your daughter.*

The Get-Em-Go office lights were off. A sign on the door read CLOSED. A chain-link fence, even taller than the one at the high school, ringed around the storage units. The low one-story buildings with metal roll-up doors looked like something you'd see in a *Mad Max* movie. There was a gate across the driveway. A keypad was at car-window height, but it didn't have numbers, just a black plastic square with a red light.

She unzipped the make-up bag. She found the white, unlabeled keycard. She pressed it to the black square. The red light turned green. The gate screeched as it moved back on rubber tires.

Andy closed her eyes. She tried to calm herself. She had a right to be here. She had a keycard. She had a unit number. She had a key.

Still, her legs felt shaky as she walked into the compound. There would be answers inside the storage unit. Andy would find out something about her mother. Maybe something that she did not want to know. That Laura did not want her to know—not until now, because *they* were after her.

Andy wiped sweat from the back of her neck. She checked behind her to make sure she was not being followed. There was no way of knowing whether or not she was safe. The complex was huge. She counted at least ten buildings, all of them about fifty feet long with rolled doors like dirty teeth. Andy checked the signs until she found building one hundred. She paced down the aisle and stopped in front of unit one-twenty.

Her birthday.

Not the one she'd had all of her life, but the one Laura told her was real.

"Christ," Andy hissed.

She wasn't sure what was real anymore.

The padlock looked new, or at least it wasn't rusted like the other ones. Andy reached into the make-up bag and retrieved the tiny key. She could not keep the tremble out of her hands as she opened the padlock.

The smell was the first thing she noticed: clean, almost sanitized. The concrete floor looked like it had been poured last week. There were no cobwebs in the corners. No scuffs or fingerprints on the walls. Empty particleboard shelves lined the back. A tiny metal desk with a lamp was shoved into the corner.

A dark blue station wagon was parked in the middle of the space.

Andy found the light switch. She closed the rolling door behind her. Instantly, the heat started to swelter, but she thought about the man looking inside the truck—not her truck, but the dead man's truck—and figured she had no choice.

The first thing she checked out was the car, which was so boxy it looked like something Fred Flintstone would drive. The paint was pristine. The tires had to be brand new. A sticker on the windshield said the oil had been changed four months ago. As with everything else inside the unit, there was no dust, no grime. The car could have been sitting on a showroom floor.

Andy peered inside the open driver's side window. There were rolly things, like actual cranks that you had to turn to open and close the windows. The seats were dark blue vinyl, one long bench, no center console. The radio had thick white punch-buttons. There were big silver knobs and slider controls. The gearshift was on the steering wheel. The dash had stickers on the flat parts to simulate woodgrain. The odometer showed only 22,184 miles.

Andy didn't recognize the logo on the steering wheel, a pentagon with a star inside, but there were raised metal letters on the outside of the car that read RELIANT K FRONT WHEEL DRIVE.

She went around to the other side and reached in to open the glove box. Andy reeled back. A gun had fallen out; a revolver, the same type that Jonah Helsinger had pointed at Laura's chest. There were scratch marks on the side where the serial number had been shaved off. Andy stared at the nasty-looking weapon sitting on the floorboard, waiting, like it might suddenly twitch.

It did not.

She found the owner's manual.

1989 Plymouth Reliant SE Wagon.

She flipped through the pages. The graphics were old, the illustrations clearly placed by hand. A twenty-nine-year-old car with barely any miles on it. Two years younger than Andy. Stored in a place that Andy did not know about in a town that she had never heard of before her mother told her to go there.

*So many questions.*

Andy started to walk around the back of the car, but stopped. She turned around and stood by the closed door. She listened to make sure a car hadn't pulled up, or a man wasn't standing on the other side. Just to be extra paranoid, she lay down on her stomach. She looked under the crack to the door.

Nothing.

Andy pushed herself up. She wiped her hands on her shorts. She continued her walk around the station wagon to check the license plate.

Canada. The plate design was as boxy as the car; blue on white with a crown between the letters and numbers, the words *Yours To Discover* at the bottom. The emissions sticker read 18 DEC, which meant that the registration was current.

Andy knew from her work at dispatch that the NCIC, the National Crime Information Center, shared information with Canada. The thing was, the system only checked for stolen vehicles. If a cop pulled over this car, all they'd be able to verify was that the registered owner's name matched the driver's license.

Which meant that for the last twenty-nine years, her mother had kept a secret, untraceable car hidden from the world.

From Andy.

She opened the wagon's hatch. The springs worked silently. She rolled back the vinyl cover obscuring the cargo area. Navy-blue sleeping bag, a pillow, an empty cooler, a box of Slim Jims, a case of water, a white beach tote filled with paperbacks, batteries, a flashlight, a first aid kit.

Underneath it was a light blue Samsonite suitcase. Fake leather. Gold zippers. Carry-on size. Not the kind with wheels but the kind you had to carry. The bag had a top and a bottom clam-shell design. Andy opened the top first. She found three of everything: jeans, white silk panties, matching white bras, socks, white button-up shirts with polo ponies on the front, and a tan Members Only jacket.

None of the clothes looked like anything her mother would wear. Maybe that was the point. Andy slipped off her shorts and pulled on the underwear. She preferred cotton, but anything was better than the shorts. The jeans were loose at the waist, but again, she was in no position to complain. She removed the twenties from the make-up bag and shoved them into the back pocket. She changed out of her shirt but kept her bra because Laura was two cups bigger. At least she used to be.

Which meant that her mother had packed this bag before the cancer diagnosis three years ago.

Andy turned the suitcase over. She unzipped the other side.

*Holy shit.*

Stacks of money. Twenties again, each bundle wrapped with a lavender strap that said $2,000. The bill design looked like the old kind before all the new security features had been added. Andy counted the stacks. Ten across, three wide, four deep.

Two hundred and forty thousand dollars.

She zipped up the bag, pulled the vinyl cargo cover over everything, then closed the hatch.

Andy leaned against the car for a moment, her mind reeling. Was it worth it to wonder where her mother had gotten all of this money? She would be better served wondering how many unicorns were left in the forest.

The shelves behind the car were empty but for two jugs of bleach, a scrub brush and a folded pile of white cleaning rags. An upside down mop and broom were in the corner. Andy ran her hand along the particleboard shelves. No dust. Her mother, who was not a neat freak, had scrubbed this place top to bottom.

*Why?*

Andy sat down at the desk in the corner. She turned on the lamp. She checked the drawers. A box of pens. Two pencils. A legal pad. A leather folio. The keys to the Plymouth. The file drawer was packed with empty hanging files. Andy pushed them aside. She reached into the back and found a small shoebox with the lid taped on.

Andy put the box on the desk.

She opened the leather folio. Two pockets. One held a car registration receipt from the Province of Ontario for a blue 1989 Plymouth Reliant. The owner's name was listed as Daniela Barbara Cooper. The original registration date was August 20, the day Andy had always thought was her birthday, but two years from her birth, 1989. The annual car tag receipt was clipped to the corner. The printout listed the date it was processed as May 12, 2017.

Last year.

There was no calendar to confirm, but the date had to be around Mother's Day. Andy tried to think back. Had she picked up her mother from the airport before taking her to lunch? Or was that the year before? Laura didn't often leave Belle Isle, but at least once a year, she attended a professional conference. This had been going on since Andy's childhood and she'd never bothered to look up the events because why would she?

What she did know was that the annual pilgrimage was very important to her mother. Even when Laura was sick from the chemo treatments, she had made Andy drive her to the Savannah airport so she could attend a speech pathologist thing in Houston.

Had she really gone to Houston? Or had she skipped over to Austin to see her old friend Professor Paula Kunde?

Once Andy dropped her off at the airport, she had no idea where Laura went.

Andy dug around inside the other folio pocket. Two laminated cards. The first was a light blue Ontario, Canada, enhanced driver's license.

The *enhanced* part meant the license could be used for sea and land US border crossings. So, no taking an airplane to Canada, but a car could get through.

The photo on the license showed Laura before the cancer had taken some of the roundness from her cheeks. The expiration date was in 2024. Her mother was listed by the same name as the owner of the Reliant, Daniela Barbara Cooper, born December 15, 1964, which was wrong because Laura's birthdate was April 9, 1963, but what the hell did that matter because her mother, as far as Andy knew, was not currently residing in apartment 20 at 22 Adelaide Street West in Toronto, Ontario.

D.B. Cooper.

Andy wondered if the name was some kind of joke, but given where she was sitting, maybe it wasn't crazy to wonder if Laura was the famous hijacker who'd parachuted out of a plane with millions of dollars and never been heard from again.

Except Cooper was a man, and in the seventies Laura was still a teenager.

*This was '77, so I would've been fourteen years old, more Rod Stewart than Elvis.*

Andy pulled out the other card. Also from Ontario, also with Daniela Cooper's name and birthdate. This one said HEALTH • SANTE. Andy had taken Spanish in high school. She had no idea what *sante* meant, but she wondered why the hell her mother hadn't used Canada's national insurance program instead of depleting most of her retirement savings to pay for her cancer treatments in the United States.

Which brought her to the shoebox. Taped closed, hidden in a desk drawer inside a locked, secret storage facility. The logo on the outside was from Thom McAn. The box was small, definitely not for adult-sized shoes. When Andy was little, Laura always took her to the Charleston mall to buy shoes before school started.

Whatever was inside was lightweight, but felt like a bomb.

Or maybe it was more like Pandora's box, containing all the evils of Laura's world. Andy knew the rest of the myth, that once you let out the evil, all that was left was hope, but she doubted very seriously that anything inside the box would give her hope.

Andy picked at the tape. The tacky side had turned to dust. She had no problem slipping off the lid.

Photographs—not many, some in black and white, some in faded color.

A bundle of Polaroids was held together by an old rubber band. Andy chose those first because she had never seen her mother look so young.

The rubber band broke off in her hands.

Laura must have been in her early twenties when the pictures were taken. The 1980s were on full display, from her blue eyeshadow to her pink lipstick to the blush strafing up her cheeks like a bird's wings. Her normally dark brown hair was shockingly blonde and over-permed. Giant shoulder pads squared off her short-sleeved white sweater. She could've been about to tell everybody who shot J.R. Ewing.

The only reason Andy wasn't smiling was that it was clear from the photo that someone had repeatedly punched her mother in the face.

Laura's left eye was swollen shut. Her nose was askew. There were deep bruises around her neck. She stared into the camera, expressionless. She was somewhere else, being someone else, while her injuries were documented.

Andy knew that look.

She shuffled to the next Polaroid. The white sweater was lifted to show bruises on Laura's abdomen. The next photo showed a gash on the inside of her thigh.

Andy had seen the horrible-looking scar during one of her mother's hospital stays. Three inches long, pink and jagged even after all of this time. Andy had actually gasped at the sight of it.

"*Ice skating*," Laura had said, rolling her eyes like those two words explained everything.

Andy picked up the next stack of pictures, which were jarring, but only in their differentness. Not Polaroids, but regular printed snapshots of a toddler dressed in pink winter clothing. The date stamped on the back was January 4, 1989. The series captured the little girl rolling around in the snow, throwing snowballs, making angels, then a snowman, then destroying the snowman. Sometimes there was an adult in the photo—a disembodied hand hanging down or a leg sticking out below a heavy wool coat.

Andy recognized the toddler as herself. She had always had the same distinctive almond shape to her eyes, a feature she had inherited from her mother.

Going by the date on the back, toddler Andy would've been almost two years old when the series of photos was taken. That was the same time period that Andy and Laura had lived at UGA while Laura finished her PhD.

That kind of snow did not happen in Athens and especially not in Belle Isle. Andy had no recollection from her youth of ever taking a trip up north. Nor had Laura ever told her about one. Actually, when Andy revealed her plans to move to New York City, the first thing Laura had said was, "*Oh, darling, you've never been that far away from home before.*"

The last two photos in the box were paperclipped together.

Phil and Laverne Randall, her birth father's parents, were sitting on a couch. A painting of the beach hung on the wood-paneled wall behind them. There was something very familiar about the expressions on their faces, how they were sitting, even the shadow of a floor lamp that was cast along the back of the couch.

Andy slid away the paperclip to reveal the second photo.

Same people, same expressions, same postures, same shadows—but this time Andy, maybe six months old, was sitting in the Randalls' laps, balanced on one knee each.

She traced her finger along the thick outline of her baby self.

In school, Andy had learned to use Photoshop to, among other things, superimpose one image onto another. She had forgotten that, before computers, people had to alter images by hand. What you did was take an X-Acto knife and carefully cut someone out of a photo, then you sprayed the back with mounting adhesive, then positioned the cut-out piece onto a different photo.

Once you were happy with the result, you had to take another photograph of the overlaid images, and even then it didn't always turn out right. Shadows were wrong. The positioning looked unnatural. The whole process was painstakingly delicate.

Which made Laura's skill that much more impressive.

During Andy's early teens, she had often stared longingly at the photo of her Randall grandparents. Usually, she was mad at Laura, or worse, at Gordon. Sometimes, she would search the Randalls' features, trying to divine why their hatred and bigotry were more important to them than having contact with their dead son's only child.

Andy had never really focused on the section of the photo that her baby self was in. Which was too bad. If she'd made even a cursory study, she would have noticed that she was not actually sitting in the Randalls' lap.

Hovering would be a better word to describe it.

The racist Randalls were a difficult subject that Andy did not bring up to her mother, the same way she did not bring up Laura's own parents, Anne and Bob Mitchell, who had died before Andy was born. Nor did she ask about Jerry Randall, her father, who had been killed in a car accident long before Andy could establish any memories of him. They had never visited his grave in Chicago. They had never visited anyone's grave.

"*We should meet in Providence,*" Andy had told Laura her first year in New York. "*You can show me where you grew up.*"

"*Oh, darling,*" Laura had sighed. "*Nobody* wants *to go to Rhode Island. Besides, it was so long ago I'm sure I can't remember.*"

There were all kinds of photographs at home—an abundance of photos. From hiking trips and Disney World vacations and beach picnics and first days of schools. Only a handful showed

Laura alone because she hated having her picture taken. There was nothing from the time before Andy was born. Laura had just one picture of Jerry Randall, the same photo Andy had found online in the *Chicago Sun Times* obituary archives.

*Jerome Phillip Randall, 28 yrs old; optometrist and avid Bears fan; survived by a daughter, Andrea, and parents Phillip and Laverne.*

Andy had seen other documents, too: her father's birth certificate and death certificate, both issued in Cook County, Illinois. Laura's various diplomas, her birth certificate from Rhode Island, her social security card, her driver's license. Andrea Eloise Mitchell's record of live birth dated August 20, 1987. The deed to the Belle Isle house. Immunization records. Marriage license. Divorce decree. Car titles. Insurance cards. Bank statements. Credit card statements.

Daniela Barbara Cooper's driver's license. The Ontario car registration. The HEALTH card. The Plymouth station wagon with a gun in the glove box and supplies and money in the trunk that was waiting in a storage facility in an anonymous town.

The make-up bag hidden inside the couch in Laura's office. The padlock key taped behind the framed photo of Andy.

*Everything I've ever done is for you, my Andrea Heloise. Everything.*

Andy spread out the Polaroids of her mother on the desk. The gash in her leg. The black eye. The bruised neck. The pummeled abdomen. The broken nose.

Pieces of a woman she had never known.

# July 26, 1986

*They tried to bury us.*
*They didn't know we were seeds.*
                                        —Mexican Proverb

# 7

Martin Queller's children were spoiled in that quintessential American way. Too much money. Too much education. Too much travel. Too much too much, so that the abundance of things had left them empty.

Laura Juneau found the girl in particular painful to watch. Her eyes furtively darting around the room. The nervous way she kept twitching her fingers as if they were floating across invisible keys. Her need to connect was reminiscent of an octopus blindly extending its tendrils in search of nourishment.

As for the boy—well, he had charm, and a lot could be forgiven of a charming man.

"Excuse me, madam?" The *politi* was lean and tall. The rifle hanging from his neck reminded Laura of her youngest son's favorite toy. "Have you misplaced your conference badge?"

Laura gave him an apologetic look as she leaned into her walking cane. "I had planned to check in before my panel."

"Shall I escort you?"

She had no choice but to follow. The additional security was neither unexpected nor without cause. Protestors were picketing outside the Oslo conference center—the usual mix of anarchists, anti-fascists, skinheads and trouble-makers alongside some of Norway's Pakistani immigrants, who were angry about recent immigration policy. The unrest had found its way inside, where there were lingering suspicions around Arne Treholt's trial the previous year. The former labor party politician was serving a twenty-year term for high treason. There were those who believed the Russians had more spies planted within the Norwegian government. There were still more who feared that the KGB was spreading Hydra-like into the rest of Scandinavia.

The *politi* turned to ensure Laura was following. The cane was a hindrance, but she was forty-three, not ninety-three. Still, he cut a channel for her through the crowd of stodgy old men in boxy suits, all wearing badges that identified them by name, nationality, and field of expertise. There were the expected scions from top universities—MIT, Harvard, Princeton, Cal Tech, Stanford—alongside the usual suspects: Exxon, Tenneco, Eastman Kodak, Raytheon, DuPont and, in a nod to keynote speaker Lee Iacocca, a healthy smattering of senior executives from the Chrysler Motor Company.

The check-in table was beneath a large banner reading WELCOME TO G-FAB. As with everything else at the Global Finance and Business Consortium, the words were written in English, French, German and, in deference to the conference hosts, Norwegian.

"Thank you," Laura told the officer, but the man would not be dismissed. She smiled at the woman sitting behind the table, and delivered the well-practiced lie: "I'm Dr. Alex Maplecroft with the University of California at Berkeley."

The woman thumbed through a card catalog and pulled the appropriate credentials. Laura had a moment of relief when she thought that the woman would simply hand over the badge, but she said, "Your identification, please, madam."

Laura rested her cane against the table. She unzipped her purse. She reached for her wallet. She willed the tremble out of her fingers.

She had practiced for this, too; not formally, but in her mind, Laura had walked herself through the steps of approaching the check-in table, pulling out her wallet and showing the fake ID that identified her as Alexandra Maplecroft, Professor of Economics.

*I'm very sorry but could you hurry? My panel starts in a few minutes.*

"Madam." The woman behind the table looked not at Laura's eyes, but at her hair. "Could you kindly remove your identification from your wallet?"

Another layer of scrutiny Laura had not anticipated. She again found her hands trembling as she tried to work the card from beneath the plastic sleeve. According to the forger in Toronto, the ID was perfect, but then the man's vocation was deception. What if the girl behind the table found a flaw? What if a photo of the real Alex Maplecroft had somehow been scrounged? Would the *politi* drag Laura away in handcuffs? Would the last six months of careful planning fall apart for want of a simple plastic card?

"Dr. Maplecroft!"

They all turned to locate the source of the yelling.

"Andrew, come meet Dr. Maplecroft!"

Laura had always known Nicholas Harp to be breathtakingly handsome. In fact, the woman behind the table inhaled sharply as he approached.

"Dr. Maplecroft, how lovely to see you again." Nick shook her hand with both of his. The wink he offered was clearly meant to reassure her, but Laura would find no reassurance from this point forward. He said, "I was in your econ 401 at Berkeley. Racial and Gender Disparities in Western Economies. I can't believe I finally remembered."

"Yes." Laura was always taken aback by the ease with which Nick lied. "How lovely to see you again, Mister—"

"Harp. Nicholas Harp. Andrew!" He waved over another young man, handsome but less so, similarly dressed in chinos and a button-down, light blue polo. Future captains of industry, these young men. Their sun-bleached hair just so. Skin tanned a healthy bronze. Stiff collars upturned. No socks. Pennies stuck into the slots on the top of their loafers.

Nick said, "Andy, be quick. Dr. Maplecroft doesn't have all day."

Andrew Queller seemed flustered. Laura could understand why. The plan had dictated that they all stay anonymous and separate from one another. Andrew glanced at the girl behind the table, and in that moment, seemed to understand why Nick had risked breaking cover. "Dr. Maplecroft, you're on Father's two p.m. panel, I believe? 'Socio-Political Ramifications of the Queller Correction.'"

"Yes, that's right." Laura tried to force some naturalness into her tone. "You're Andrew, Martin's middle child?"

"Guilty." Andrew smiled at the girl. "Is there a problem, miss?"

His sense of entitlement was communicable. The woman handed Laura the badge for Dr. Alex Maplecroft, and like that, Laura was legitimized.

"Thank you," Nick told the girl, who beamed under his attention.

"Yes, thank you." Laura's hands were considerably more steady as she pinned the badge to the breast of her navy-blue blazer.

"Madam." The *politi* took his leave.

Laura found her cane. She wanted to get away from the table.

"Not so fast, Dr. Maplecroft." Nick, ever the showman, clapped together his hands. "Shall we buy you a drink?"

"It's very early," Laura said, though in fact she could use something to calm her nerves. "I'm not sure what time it is."

"Just shy of one," Andrew provided. He was using a hand-kerchief to wipe his already red nose. "Sorry, I caught a stinking cold on the flight."

She tried to keep the sadness out of her smile. Laura had wanted to mother him from the beginning. "You should find some soup."

"I should." He tucked the handkerchief back into his pocket. "We'll see you in an hour, then? Your panel will be in the Raufoss ballroom. Father was told to get there ten minutes ahead of time."

"You might want to freshen up before that." Nick nodded toward the ladies room. He was giddy with the deception. "It's a wonder they even bothered to open it, Dr. Maplecroft. The wives have all gone on a shopping excursion to Storo. It appears you're the only woman slated to speak at the conference."

"Nick," Andrew cautioned. "'It's such a fine line between stupid and clever.'"

"Ouch, old boy. I know it's time to go when you start quoting *Spinal Tap*." Nick gave Laura another wink before allowing Andrew to lead him away. The river of suited old men turned as the two young bucks, so full of life and possibility, rode in their wake.

Laura pursed her lips and drew in a shallow breath. She feigned interest in locating an item inside of her handbag as she tried to regain her equilibrium.

As was often the case when she was around Nick and Andrew, Laura was reminded of her eldest son. On the day he was murdered, David Juneau was sixteen years old. The fuzz along his jaw had started to form into the semblance of a beard. His father had already shown him at the bathroom mirror how much shaving cream to use, how to draw the blade down his cheek and up his neck. Laura could still recall that crisp fall morning, their last morning, how the sun had teased its fingers through the fine hairs on David's chin as she had poured orange juice into his glass.

"Dr. Maplecroft?" The voice was hesitant, the vowels rounded in that distinctively Scandinavian way. "Dr. Alex Maplecroft?"

Laura furtively glanced for Nick to save her again.

"Dr. Maplecroft?" The Scandinavian had persuaded himself that he had the right person. There was nothing more validatory than a plastic conference badge. "Professor Jacob Brundstad, *Norges Handelshøyskole*. I was eager to discuss—"

"It's my pleasure to meet you, Professor Brundstad." Laura gave his hand a firm shake. "Shall we speak after my panel? It's in less than an hour and I need to collect my notes. I hope you understand."

He was too polite to argue. "Of course."

"I look forward to it." Laura stabbed her cane into the floor as she turned away.

She inserted herself into the crowd of white-haired men with pipes and cigarettes and briefcases and rolled sheaths of paper in their hands. That she was being stared at was undeniable. She propelled herself forward, head held high. She had studied Dr. Alex Maplecroft enough to understand that the woman's arrogance was legend. Laura had watched from the back of packed classes as Maplecroft eviscerated the slower students; overheard her chastising colleagues for not reaching the point quickly enough.

Or maybe it wasn't arrogance so much as the wall Maplecroft had built in order to protect herself from the stares of angry men. Nick was correct when he said that the renowned economics professor was the only woman slated to speak at the conference. The accusatory looks—*Why isn't that waitress wearing a uniform? Why isn't she emptying our ashtrays?*—were doubly warranted.

Laura hesitated. She was walking straight into nothing; a blank wall with a poster advertising Eastern Airline's Moonlight Special flights. Under such withering examination, she felt she could not reverse course. She took a sharp right and found herself standing at the closed glass door leading into the bar.

Blessedly, Laura found the door unlocked.

Stale smoke with an undertone of expensive bourbon shrouded the bar. There was a wooden dance floor with a darkened disco ball. The booths were low to the floor. Darkened mirrors hung from the ceiling. Laura's watch was turned to Toronto time, but she gathered from the empty room that it was still too early to have a proper drink.

After today, Dr. Maplecroft's reputation would be the least of her worries.

Laura could hear the tinkling of keys on the piano as she took her place at the end of the bar. She rested her cane against the wall. Her hand was reliably steady as she found the pack of Marlboros in her purse. There was a box of matches on top of the glass ashtray. The flash of nicotine catching fire soothed her jangling nerves.

The bartender came through the swinging door. He was stout and starched with a white apron wrapped around his thick waist. "Madam?"

"Gin and tonic," she said, her voice soft, because the cacophonous notes from the piano had turned into a familiar melody; not Rossini or even, given the locale, Edvard Grieg, but a slow tune that escalated into a familiar verve.

Laura smiled as she blew out a plume of smoke.

She recognized the song from the radio. A-ha, the Norwegian singing group with the funny cartoon video. "Take On Me" or "Take Me On" or some variation of those words repeated *ad nauseam* over a relentlessly chirpy electric keyboard.

When Laura's daughter was still alive, the same type of candy synthpop had recurrently blared from Lila's record player or Walkman or even her mouth while she was in the shower. Every car trip, no matter how short, began with her daughter tuning the radio dial to The Quake. Laura was not shy with her daughter when she explained why the silly songs grated on her nerves. The Beatles. The Stones. James Brown. Stevie Wonder. *Those* were artists.

Laura had never felt so old as when Lila had made her watch a Madonna video on MTV. The only semi-positive comment Laura could muster was, "What a bold choice to wear her underwear on the outside."

Laura retrieved a pack of tissues from her purse and wiped her eyes.

"Madam." The bartender pronounced the word as an apology, gently placing her drink on a cocktail napkin.

"May I join you?"

Laura was stunned to find Jane Queller suddenly at her elbow. Andrew's sister was a complete stranger and meant to stay that way. Laura struggled to keep the recognition out of her expression. She had only ever seen the girl in photographs or from a great distance. Up close, she looked younger than her twenty-three years. Her voice, too, was deeper than Laura had imagined.

Jane said, "Please forgive the interruption." She had seen Laura's tears. "I was just sitting over there wondering if it's too early to drink alone."

Laura quickly recovered. "I think it is. Won't you join me?"

Jane hesitated. "You're sure?"

"I insist."

Jane sat, nodding for the same from the bartender. "I'm Jane Queller. I think I saw you talking to my brother, Andrew."

"Alex Maplecroft." For the first time in this entire enterprise, Laura regretted a lie. "I'm on a panel with your father in"—she checked the clock on the wall—"forty-five minutes."

Jane worked artlessly to mask her reaction to the news. Her eyes, as was so often the case, went to Laura's hairline. "Your photo wasn't in the conference directory."

"I'm not much for photographs." Laura had heard Alex Maplecroft say the same thing at a lecture in San Francisco. Along with shortening her first name, the doctor felt hiding the fact of her womanhood was the only way to make sure that her work was taken seriously.

Jane asked, "Has Father ever met you in person?"

Laura found the phrasing odd—not asking if she'd met Martin Queller, but whether or not Martin Queller had met her. "No, not that I can recall."

"I think I'll actually enjoy attending one of the old man's panels, then." Jane picked up her glass as soon as the bartender set it down. "I'm sure you're aware of his reputation."

"I am." Laura raised her own glass in a toast. "Any advice?"

Jane's nose wrinkled in thought. "Don't listen to the first five words he says to you, because none of them will make you feel good about yourself."

"Is that a general rule?"

"It's carved into the family coat of arms."

"Is that before or after the '*arbeit macht frei*'?"

Jane choked out a laugh, spitting gin and tonic onto the bar. She used the cocktail napkin to wipe up the mess. Her long, elegant fingers looked incongruous to the task. "Could I bum one off you?"

She meant the cigarettes. Laura slid the pack over, but warned, "They'll kill you."

"Yes, that's what Dr. Koop tells us." Jane held the cigarette between her lips. She picked open the box of matches, but ended up scattering them across the bar. "God. I'm so sorry." Jane looked like a self-conscious child as she gathered the matches. "Clumsy Jinx strikes again."

The phrase had a practiced tone. Laura could imagine Martin Queller had found unique and precise ways to remind his children that they would never be perfect.

"Madam?" The bartender had appeared with a light.

"Thank you." Rather than cup her hands to his, Jane leaned toward the match. She inhaled deeply, her eyes closed like a cat enjoying a sunbeam. When she found Laura watching, she laughed out puffs of smoke. "Sorry, I've been in Europe for three months. It's good to have an American cigarette."

"I thought all of you young expats enjoyed smoking Gauloises and arguing about Camus and the tragedy of the human condition?"

"If only." Jane coughed out another cloud of dark smoke.

Laura felt a sudden maternal rush toward the girl. She wanted to snatch the cigarette from her hand, but she knew the gesture would be pointless. At twenty-three, Laura had been desperate for the years to come more quickly, to firmly step into her adulthood, to establish herself, to become someone. She had not yet felt the desire to claw back time as you would a piece of wet muslin clinging to your face; that one day her back might ache as she climbed the stairs, that her stomach could sag from childbirth, that her spine might become misshapen from a cancerous tumor.

"Disagree with him." Jane held the cigarette between her thumb and forefinger, the same way as her brother. "That's my advice to you on Father. He can't stomach people contradicting him."

"I've staked my reputation on contradicting him."

"I hope you're prepared for battle." She indicated the conference buzzing outside the barroom door. "Was it Jonah or Daniel who was in the lion's den?"

"Jonah was in the belly of a whale. Daniel was in the lions' den."

"Yes, of course. God sent an angel to close the lions' mouths."

"Is your father really that bad?" Laura realized too late the pointedness of her question. All three Queller children had found their own particular way to live in their father's shadow.

Jane said, "I'm sure you can hold your own against the Mighty Martin. You weren't invited here on a whim. Just keep in mind that once he's locked onto something, he won't back down. All or none is the Queller way." She didn't seem to expect a reply. Her eyes kept finding the mirror behind the bar as she scanned the empty room. Here was the octopus from the lobby, the one who was desperately in search of something, anything, that would render her whole.

Laura asked, "You're Martin's youngest?"

"Yes, then Andrew, then there's our older brother, Jasper. He's given up glory in the Air Force to join the family business."

"Economic advisory?"

"Oh, God, no. The money-making side. We're all terribly proud of him."

Laura disregarded the sarcasm. She knew full well the details of Jasper Queller's ascendancy. "Was that you just now on the piano?"

Jane offered a self-deprecating eye-roll. "Grieg seemed too aphoristic."

"I saw you play once." The shock of truthfulness brought an image to Laura's mind: Jinx Queller at the piano, the entire audience held rapt as her hands floated across the keyboard. Squaring that remarkably confident performer with the anxious young girl beside her—the nails bitten to the quick, the furtive glances at the mirror—was an unwieldy task.

Laura asked, "You don't go by Jinx anymore?"

Another eye-roll. "An unfortunate cross I bore from my childhood."

Laura knew from Andrew that Jane abhorred the family nickname. It felt wrong to know so much about the girl when she knew nothing of Laura, but this was how the game had to be played. "Jane suits you more, I think."

"I like to think so." She silently tapped ash off of her cigarette. The fact that Laura had seen her perform was clearly bothersome. Had Jane been rendered in paint, lines of anxiety would have radiated from her body. She finally asked, "Where did you see me play?"

"The Hollywood Bowl."

"Last year?"

"Eighty-four." Laura worked to keep the melancholy out of her tone. The concert had been a last-minute invitation from her husband. They had eaten dinner at their favorite Italian restaurant. Laura had drunk too much chianti. She could remember leaning into her husband as they walked to the parking lot. The feel of his hand on her waist. The smell of his cologne.

Jane said, "That was part of the Jazz Bowl before the Olympics. I sat in with the Richie Reedie Orchestra. There was a Harry James tribute and"—she squinted her eyes in memory—"I fell out of time during 'Two O'Clock Jump.' Thank God the horns came in early."

Laura hadn't noticed any slips, just that the crowd had been on its feet by the end. "Do you only remember your performances by their mistakes?"

She shook her head, but there was more to the story. Jane Queller had been a world-class pianist. She had sacrificed her youth to music. She had given up classical for jazz, then jazz for studio work. Between them all, she had performed in some of the most venerated halls and venues.

And then she had walked away.

"I read your paper on punitive taxation." Jane lifted her chin toward the bartender, silently requesting another drink. "If you're wondering, Father expects us to keep up with his professional life. Even from nearly six thousand miles away."

"How edifying."

"I'd say it's more alarming than edifying. He sneaks his clippings into my mother's letters to save postage. 'Dear Daughter, we attended supper with the Flannigans this weekend and please be prepared to answer questions pertaining to the enclosed abstract on macroeconomic variables in Nicaragua.'" Jane watched the gin fall from the bottle. The bartender was being more generous with the alcohol than he'd been with Laura, but beautiful young women always got more.

Jane said, "Your passage about the weaponization of financial policy against minorities really made me think about government in a different way. Though, to hear my father tell it, your type of social engineering will ruin the world."

"Only for men like him."

"Be careful." This was a serious warning. "My father does not like to be contradicted. Especially by women." She met Laura's gaze. "Especially by women who look like you."

Laura remembered something her mother had told her a long time ago. "Men never have to be uncomfortable around women. Women have to be uncomfortable around men all of the time."

Jane gave a rueful laugh as she stubbed her cigarette into the ashtray.

Laura motioned for another gin and tonic, though the first one sat sourly in her stomach. She needed her hands to stop shaking, her heart to stop pattering like a frightened rabbit.

The clock gave her only thirty minutes to prepare herself.

In the best of circumstances, Laura had never been a comfortable public speaker. She was a watcher by nature, preferring to blend with the crowd. Behind Iacocca's keynote, the Queller panel was expected to be the most well-attended of the conference. The ticket supply had been exhausted within a day of the announcement. There were two other men who would join them, a German analyst from the RAND Corporation, and a Belgian executive from Royal Dutch Shell, but the focus of the eight hundred attendees would be squarely on the two Americans.

Even Laura had to admit that Martin Queller's C.V. could draw a crowd: former president of Queller Healthcare, professor emeritus at the Queller School of Economics, Long Beach, former advisor to the governor of California, current member of the President's Council on Economic Development, at the top of the shortlist to replace James Baker as Secretary of the Treasury, and, most importantly, progenitor of the Queller Correction.

It was the Correction that had brought them all here. While Alex Maplecroft had managed to distinguish herself first at Harvard, then Stanford and Berkeley, she would have likely lived in academic obscurity but for her writings and publications accomplishing something that no man dared: vehemently questioning the morality of not just the Queller Correction, but Martin Queller himself.

Given Martin's standing in the economic and business community, this was tantamount to nailing the Ninety-Five Theses on the church doors.

Laura gladly counted herself among Maplecroft's converts.

In a nutshell, the Queller Correction posited that economic expansion has historically been underpinned by an undesirable minority or immigrant working class that is kept in check by nativistic corrections.

The progress of many on the backs of an *other*.

Irish immigrants erecting New York's bridges and skyscrapers. Chinese laborers building the transcontinental railroad. Italian workers fueling the textile industry. Here was the so-called nativistic correction: Alien Land Laws. No Irish, No Blacks, No Dogs. The Emergency Quota Act. The Literacy Act. *Dred Scott v. Sandford*. The Chinese Exclusion Act. Jim Crow. *Plessy v. Ferguson*. The Bracero Programs. Poll taxes. Operation Wetback.

The research behind Martin's theory was well substantiated. One might even call it a summation of facts rather than an actual theory. The problem—at least according to Alex Maplecroft—was that the Queller Correction was being used

145

not as an academic term to describe a historical phenomenon but as a justification for setting current monetary and social policy. A sort of "history repeats itself," but without the usual irony.

Here were some of the more recent Queller Corrections: less AIDS funding to thin out the homosexual population, harsher sentences for African American crack users, regressive penalties for post-conviction felons, mandatory life sentences for repeat offenders, the for-profit privatization of prisons and mental health facilities.

In a *Los Angeles Times* op-ed, Alex Maplecroft derided the thinking that went into the Queller Correction with this inflammatory line: "*One wonders if Hermann Göring swallowed that cyanide capsule after all.*"

"Doctor?" Jane pulled Laura out of her thoughts. "Do you mind if—"

The girl wanted another cigarette. Laura shook two out of the pack.

This time, the bartender had a light for both of them.

Laura held in the smoke. She watched Jane watching the mirror. She asked, "Why did you give up performing?"

At first, Jane did not answer. She must have been asked the same question dozens of times. Maybe she was preparing to give Laura the same pat answer, but something altered in her expression as she turned in her seat. "Do you know how many famous women pianists there are?"

Laura was no musical expert—that had been her husband's hobby—but she had the tickling of a memory. "There's a Brazilian woman, Maria Arruda, or . . . ?"

"Martha Argerich, from Argentina, but well done." Jane smiled without humor. "Name another."

Laura shrugged. She had not technically named one.

Jane said, "I was backstage at Carnegie, and I looked around and realized I was the only woman there. Which had happened before, many times, but this was the first time that I had really noticed. And that people noticed *me*." She rolled the ash off of her cigarette. "So then my teacher dropped me." The sudden appearance of tears at the corners of her eyes indicated the girl was still stung by the loss. "I'd trained with Pechenikov from the age of eight, but he told me that he had taken me as far as I could go."

Laura felt the need to ask, "Can you not find another teacher?"

"No one will take me on." She puffed the cigarette. "Pechenikov was the best, so I went to the second best. Then the third. By the time I worked my way down to the junior high band directors, I realized that they were using the same code." She held Laura's gaze with a knowing expression. "When they said, 'I don't have time to take on a new student,' what they meant was, 'I'm not going to waste my talent and effort on a silly girl who's going to give it all up once she falls in love.'"

"Ah," Laura said, because that was really all she could say.

"It's easier in some ways, I suppose. I've been devoting three or four hours a day, every day of my life, to practicing. Classical is so exact. You have to play every note as written. Your dynamics matter almost more than touch. With jazz, there's a melodic expression you can bring to the piece. And rock—do you know The Doors?"

Laura had to shift her thinking in a different direction. "Jim Morrison?"

Jane tapped her fingers on the bar top. At first, Laura only heard a frantic rapping, but then, remarkably—

"'Love Me Two Times.'" Laura laughed at the neat trick.

Jane said, "Manzarek played both the keyboard part and the bass part at the same time. It's amazing how he pulled it off, as if each hand worked completely independent of the other. A split personality, almost, but people don't concentrate on the technical aspects. They just love the sound." She kept tapping out the song as she spoke. "If I can't play music that people appreciate, then I want to play music that people love."

"Good for you." Laura let the beats play in the silence for a moment before asking, "You've been in Europe for the last three months, you said?"

"Berlin." Jane's hands finally wound down. "I was filling in as a session pianist at Hansa Tonstudio."

Laura shook her head. She had never heard of it.

"It's a recording studio by the Wall. They have a space, the Meistersaal, which has the most beautiful acoustics for every type of music—classical, chamber, pop, rock. Bowie recorded there. Iggy Pop. Depeche Mode."

"Sounds like you've met some famous people."

"Oh, no. My part's done by the time they roll in. That's the beauty of it. It's just me and my performance in isolation. No one knows who's behind the keyboard. No one cares if you're a woman, or a man, or a French poodle. They just want you to feel the music, and that's what I'm good at—feeling where the notes go." A glow of excitement enhanced her natural beauty. "If you love music—really, truly, love music—then you play it for yourself."

Laura felt herself nodding. She had no musical point of reference, but she understood that the pure love of something could not only give you strength but propel you forward.

Still, she said, "It's a lot to give up."

"Is it?" Jane seemed genuinely curious. "How can I give up something that was never really offered to me because of what's between my legs?" She gave a hard laugh. "Or *not* between my legs, or what might come out from between my legs at some point in the future."

"Men can always reinvent themselves," Laura said. "For women, once you're a mother, you're always a mother."

"That's not terribly feminist of you, Dr. Maplecroft."

"No, but you understand this because you're a chameleon like me. If you can't play the music people appreciate, then you play the music that they love." Laura hoped that one day that might change. Then again, she hoped every morning when she woke up that she would hear Lila's awful music on the radio, watch Peter run around the living room looking for his shoes, and find David talking low into the telephone because he did not want his mother to know that he had a girlfriend.

"You should go." Jane pointed to the clock. The forty-five minutes were almost up.

Laura wanted to keep talking, but she knew she had no choice. She reached into her purse for her wallet.

"It's on me," Jane offered.

"I couldn't—"

"I should say it's on the Queller family tab."

"All right," Laura agreed. She slid from the stool, stifling a wince from the pain as she put weight back on her leg. Her cane was where she had left it. She gripped the silver knob in her hand. She looked at Jane and wondered if this was the last person she would have a normal conversation with. If that turned out to be the case, she was glad.

She told the girl, "It's been a pleasure talking to you."

"You, too." Jane offered, "I'll be on the front row if you need a friendly face."

Laura felt enormously sad at the news. Uncharacteristically, she reached out and covered Jane's hand with her own. She could feel the coolness of the girl's skin. Laura wondered how long it had been since she had touched another human being for comfort.

She blurted out the words, "You are a magnificent person."

"Gosh." Jane blushed.

"It's not because you're talented, or beautiful, though you certainly are both. It's because you're so uniquely you." Laura said the words that she wished she'd had time to tell her own daughter: "Everything about you is amazing."

The blush reddened as Jane struggled for a pithy response.

"No." Laura would not let the girl's sarcasm ruin the moment. "You'll find your way, Jane, and it will be the right way, no matter what, because it's the path that you set out for yourself." She squeezed the girl's hand one last time. "That's my advice."

Laura felt Jane's eyes follow her progress as she slowly walked across the room. She had sat at the bar too long. Her foot was numb. The bullet lodged inside of her back felt as if it was a living, breathing thing. She cursed the shard of metal, no larger than the nail on her pinky finger, that sat dangerously close to her spinal cord.

Just this once, this last time, she wanted to move quickly, to recapture some of her former agility, and complete the task before Jane could find her seat on the front row.

The lobby had emptied of important men, but their cigarette and pipe smoke lingered. Laura pushed open the door to the ladies room.

Empty, as Nick had predicted.

She walked to the last stall. She opened and closed the door. She struggled with the lock. The sliding bolt would not fit into the slot. She banged it twice, the metal singing against metal, then finally got it to stay closed.

Laura was overcome by a sudden dizziness. She pressed her hands to the walls. She took a few moments to stabilize. The two drinks on top of her jet lag had been a mistake, but she could be forgiven her fatalistic choices on today of all days.

The toilet was old-fashioned, the tank mounted high on the wall. She reached behind it. Her heart fluttered as she blindly searched. She felt the tape first. Her panic ebbed only slightly as her fingers traced their way up to the paper bag.

The door opened.

"*Hej-hej*?" a man said.

Laura froze, heart stopped.

"Hello?" The man was dragging something heavy across the floor. "Cleaner here. Hello?"

"Just a moment," Laura called back, the words choking in her throat.

"Cleaner," he repeated.

"*Nej*," she said, more stridently. "Occupied."

He gave a vexed sigh.

She waited.

Another sigh.

Another moment.

Finally, he dragged whatever he had brought into the toilets back across the floor. He closed the door so hard that the stall door slipped its flimsy lock and creaked open.

Laura felt the sliding bolt press its finger into the small of her back.

Improbably, a laugh tickled the back of her throat. She could only imagine what she looked like, skirt rucked up, standing with a leg on either side of the toilet bowl, her hand up the back of the tank.

All that was missing was the sound of a passing train and Michael Corleone.

Laura pulled down the paper bag. She shoved it into her purse. She went to the sink. She checked her hair and lipstick in the mirror. She studied her reflection as she washed her trembling hands.

The eyeshadow was jarring. She had never really worn make-up in her normal life. Her hair was normally worn back off her face. She normally wore jeans and one of her husband's shirts and a pair of her son's sneakers that he normally left by the door.

Normally, she had a camera swung around her neck.

Normally, she was frantically running around, trying to book sessions, working sessions, planning recitals and rehearsals and practice and meals and time to cook and time to read and time to love.

But normal wasn't normal anymore.

Laura dried her hands on a paper towel. She put on fresh lipstick. She bared her white teeth to the mirror.

The cleaner was waiting outside the ladies room. He was smoking, leaning against a large trash can that had spray bottles looped around the sides.

Laura suppressed the urge to apologize. She checked the paper bag in her purse. She pulled closed the zipper. The dizziness returned, but she managed to shake it. There was nothing to do about the churning in her stomach. Her heart was a metronome at the base of her throat. She could feel the blood pulsing through her veins. Her vision sharpened to the point of a tack.

"Dr. Maplecroft?" A flustered young woman in a floral dress

approached from nowhere. "Follow me, please. Your panel will start soon."

Laura tried to keep up with the girl's brisk, almost panicked walk. They were halfway down the hall when Laura realized she was getting winded. She slowed down, letting her hand rest longer on the cane. She had to remain calm. What she was about to do could not be rushed.

"Madam," the young girl pleaded, motioning for Laura to hurry.

"They won't start without me," Laura said, though she wasn't certain, given Martin Queller's reputation, that the man would wait. She found the pack of tissues in her purse. She wiped the sweat from her forehead.

A door flew open.

"Young lady." Martin Queller was snapping his fingers as if to call a dog. "Where is Maplecroft?" He glanced at Laura. "Coffee, two sugars."

The girl tried, "Doctor—"

"Coffee," Martin repeated, visibly annoyed. "Are you deaf?"

"I'm Dr. Maplecroft."

He did a double-take. Twice. "*Alex* Maplecroft?"

"Alexandra." She offered her hand. "I'm glad for this opportunity to meet in person."

A group of colleagues had congregated behind him. Martin had no choice but to shake her hand. His eyes, as was the case with so many before him, went to her hair. That's what gave it away. Laura's skin tone was closer to her white mother's, but she had the distinctive, kinky hair of her black father.

Martin said, "I understand you now. You've let your anecdotal experiences color your research."

Laura gazed down at the stark white hand she was holding. "Color is such an interesting choice of words, Martin."

He corrected her, "It's Dr. Queller."

"Yes, I heard about you while I was at Harvard." Laura turned toward the man on Martin's right; the German, judging by the sharp gray suit and thin navy tie. "Dr. Richter?"

"Friedrich, please. It is my pleasure." The man could hardly be bothered to hide his smile. He pulled over another man, gray-haired but wearing a fashionable, teal-colored jacket. "May I introduce you to our fellow panelist, Herr Dr. Maes?"

"So good to meet you." Laura shook the Belgian's hand, feeding off Martin's obvious disdain. She turned to the young woman. "Are we ready to begin?"

"Certainly, madam." The girl escorted them across the hall to the stage entrance.

The introductions had already begun. The lights were darkened in the wings. The girl used a flashlight to show the way. Laura could hear the rumble of male voices from the audience. Another man, the announcer, was speaking into a microphone. His French was too rapid for Laura to follow. She was grateful when he switched to English.

"And now, enough of my babbling, hey? Without further ado, we must welcome our four panelists."

The applause shook the floor beneath Laura's feet. Butterflies flipped inside her stomach. Eight hundred people. The house lights had gone up. Just past the curtain, she could see the right side of the auditorium. The audience, most all of them men, was standing, their hands clapping, waiting for the show to begin.

"Doctor?" Friedrich Richter murmured.

Her fellow panelists were waiting for Laura to lead the way. Even Martin Queller had the basic manners to not walk out ahead of a woman. This was the moment Laura had waited for. This was what had forced her out of her hospital bed, pushed her to complete the excruciating therapies, propelled her onto the four airplanes she'd taken to get here.

And yet, Laura felt herself frozen in place, momentarily lost in what she was about to do.

"For Godsakes." Martin quickly grew impatient. He strode onto the stage.

The crowd roared at his appearance. Feet were stamped. Hands were waved. Fists were pumped.

Friedrich and Maes performed a Laurel and Hardy-like panto-mime of who would have the honor of letting Laura precede them.

She had to go. She had to do this.

Now.

The air grew suffocatingly close as she walked onto the stage. Despite the howl of cheers and applause, Laura was conscious of the hard tap of her cane across the wooden boards. She felt her shoulders roll in. Her head bowed. The urge to make herself smaller was overpowering.

She looked up.

More lights. A fugue of cigarette smoke hung in the rafters.

She turned toward the audience—not to see the crowd, but to find Jane. She was in the front row, as promised. Andrew was to her left, Nick to her right, but it was Jane who held Laura's attention. They exchanged private smiles before Laura turned back to the stage.

She had to start this so that she could end it.

Microphones pointed rifle-like at four chairs that were separated by small side tables. Laura had not been part of any discussion regarding seating, so she stopped at the first chair. Beads of sweat broke out onto her upper lip. The harsh lights might as well have been lasers. She realized too late that this was the part she should have practiced. The chair was typical Scandinavian design: beautiful to look at, but low to the ground with not much support in the back. Worse yet, it appeared to swivel.

"Doctor?" Maes grabbed the back of the adjacent chair, holding it still for her. So, Laura was meant to go in the middle. She lowered herself into the low chair, the muscles in her shoulders and legs spasming with pain.

"Yes?" Maes offered to lay her cane on the floor.

"Yes." Laura clutched her purse in her lap. "Thank you."

Maes took the chair on her left. Friedrich walked to the far end, leaving the chair beside Laura empty.

She looked past the pointed end of the microphones into the

crowd. The clapping was tapering off. People were starting to take their seats.

Martin Queller was not quite ready to let them settle. He stood with his hand high in the air as he saluted the audience. Poor optics, given Maplecroft's line about Göring. As was the slight bow he gave before finally taking the chair center stage.

Now the audience began to settle. The last of the stray claps died down. The house lights lowered. The stage lights came up.

Laura blinked, momentarily blinded. She waited for the inevitable, which was for Martin Queller to adjust the microphone to his satisfaction and begin speaking.

He said, "On behalf of my fellow panelists, I'd like to thank you for your attendance. It is my fervent hope that our discourse remain lively and civil and, most importantly, that it lives up to your expectations." He looked to his left, then right, as he reached into his breast pocket and pulled out a stack of index cards. "Let's begin with what Comrade General Secretary Gorbachev has dubbed the 'Era of Stagnation.'"

There was laughter from the crowd.

"Dr. Maes, let's let you take this one." Martin Queller was, it must be said, a man who could command a room. He was clearly putting on a show, teasing around the edges of the topic they had all come to see debated. In his youth, he'd likely been considered attractive in that way that money makes a boring man suddenly interesting. Age had agreed with him. Laura knew he was sixty-three, but his dark hair was only slightly peppered with gray. The aquiline nose was less pronounced than in his photographs, which had likely been chosen for their ability to garner respect rather than physical admiration. People often mistook personality for character.

"What of Chernenko, Herr Richter?" Martin's voice boomed without the aid of a microphone. "Is it likely we'll see the full implementation of Andropov's arguably modest reforms?"

"Well," Friedrich began. "As perhaps the Russians would tell us, 'When money speaks, the truth keeps silent.'"

There was another smattering of laughter.

Laura shifted in the chair as she tried to relieve the pain radiating down her leg. Her sciatic nerve sang like the strings of a harp. Instead of listening to Friedrich's densely academic answer, she stared off to the side of the audience. There was a bank of lights hanging from a metal pole. A man stood on a raised platform working a shoulder-mounted Beta Movie video camera. His hand manually twisted around the lens. The lighting had likely thrown off the auto-focus.

Laura looked down at her own hand. The thumb and two of her fingers were still calloused from years of adjusting the focus ring on her Hasselblad.

The month before Lila had died, she'd told Laura that she wanted to take photography lessons, just not from her mother. Laura had been hurt. She was, after all, a professional photographer. But then a friend had reminded Laura that teenage girls were finished learning from their mothers until they had children of their own, and Laura had decided to bide her time.

And then time had run out.

All because of Martin Queller.

"—the juxtaposition of social policy and economics," Martin was saying. "So, Dr. Maplecroft, while you might disagree with what you call the 'atavistic tone' of the Queller Correction, I merely sought to put a name to a statistically occurring phenomenon."

Laura saw his chest rise as he took a breath to continue, so she jumped in. "I wonder, Dr. Queller, if you understand that your policies have real-world implications."

"They are not policies, dear. They are theories assigned to what you yourself have described as tribal morality."

"But, Doctor—"

"If you find my conclusions cold, then I would warn you that statistics are, in fact, a cold mistress." He seemed to enjoy the turn of phrase. It had appeared in many of his editorials and essays. "Using emotion or hysterics to interpret the datum opens up the entire field to ridicule. You might as well ask a janitor to explain how the volcanic eruption at Beerenberg will influence weather patterns in Guam."

He seemed very smug about the pronouncement. Laura yearned to be the one who slapped that self-satisfied grin off of his face. She said, "You say that your theories are not policies, but in fact, your economic theories have been used to affect policy."

"You flatter me," he said, though in a way that indicated the flattery was warranted.

"Your work influenced the Lanterman-Petris-Short Act in '67."

Martin scowled at the comment, but then turned to the audience and said, "For the benefit of the Europeans, you should explain that the Patients' Bill of Rights was a landmark piece of legislation in the state of California. Among other things, it helped end the practice of institutionalizing people in mental hospitals against their will."

"Didn't the bill also cut funding to state mental hospitals?"

The smirk on his lips said he knew where this was going. "The funding cuts were temporary. Then-governor Reagan re-instated the funds the following year."

"To previous levels?"

"You've spent your life in front of a chalkboard, Maplecroft. It's different in the real world. The turning of government policy is as the turning of a battleship. You need a lot of room to make corrections."

"Some would call them mistakes rather than corrections." Laura held up her hand to stop his retort. "And another *correction* was that the following year, the criminal justice system saw twice as many mentally ill people entering into, and staying in, the criminal justice system."

"Well—"

"The overcrowding of the California penal system has given rise to violent gangs, led to the re-incarceration of thousands and helped incubate an explosion of HIV cases." Laura turned to the audience. "Churchill told us that 'those who fail to learn from history are doomed to repeat it.' My colleague seems to be saying, 'Repeating our history is the only way we can stay in power.'"

"Patients!" He said the word so loudly that it echoed against the back wall.

In the ensuing silence, Laura asked, "Sir?"

"Doctor." Martin smoothed down his tie. He visibly worked to control his temper. "This law that you're talking about was rightly called a Patients' Bill of Rights. Those who left state mental hospitals were either moved into group homes or received out-patient treatment so that they could become useful members of society."

"Were they capable of being useful?"

"Of course they were. This is the problem with socialists. You believe the government's job is to coddle man from cradle to grave. That's the very type of faulty reasoning that has turned half of America into a welfare state." He leaned forward, addressing the audience. "I believe—and most Americans believe—every man deserves a chance to stand on his own two feet. It's called the American Dream, and it's available to anyone who's willing to work for it."

Laura indicated her cane. "What if they can't stand on their own two feet?"

"For God's sake, woman. It's a figure of speech." He turned back to the audience. "The group home setting allows—"

"What group homes? The ones run by Queller Healthcare Services?"

That threw him off, but only for a moment. "The company is privately held in a blind trust. I have no say over any of the decisions made."

"Are you not aware that Queller Healthcare derives upwards of thirty percent of its annual profits from the management of group homes for the mentally ill?" She held up her hands in an open shrug. "What a wonderful coincidence that your position as an economic advisor to the state allowed you to advocate that government money should be diverted into the private, for-profit healthcare industry which has been the source of so much of your family's wealth."

Martin sighed. He gave a dramatic shake of his head.

"Your company is about to go public, is it not? You took on some very high-level investors going into the offering to make sure your numbers were up." This was the reason behind the *now* of it all, why there was no turning back. "Your family's fortune will grow considerably when the Queller model is expanded to the rest of the United States. Isn't that right?"

Martin sighed again, shook his head again. He glanced at the crowd as if to pull them to his side. "I feel you have hijacked this panel with your own agenda, Maplecroft. It matters not one lick what I say. You seem to have your mind made up. I'm an evil man. Capitalism is an evil system. We'd all be better off if we picked flowers and braided them into our hair."

Laura said the words she had lied for, stolen for, kidnapped for and finally flown nearly six thousand miles to say to Martin Queller's face: "Robert David Juneau."

Again, Martin was caught off guard, but he made an adroit recovery, once more addressing the audience. "For those of you who do not read the newspapers in northern California, Robert David Juneau was a black construction worker who—"

"Engineer," Laura interrupted.

He turned, seemingly stunned that she had corrected him.

"Juneau was an engineer. He studied at Cal Tech. He was not a construction worker, though he was black, if that's the point you're making."

He started to wag his finger at her. "Let's remember that you're the one who keeps bringing race into this."

She said, "Robert Juneau was injured while visiting a construction site in downtown San Francisco." Laura turned to the crowd. She tried to keep the quiver out of her voice when she told the story. "One of the workers made a mistake. It happens. But Juneau was in the wrong place at the wrong time. A steel beam struck his head here—" She pointed to her own head, and for a moment, her fingers could feel the rough scar on Robert's scalp. "His brain started to swell. He experienced a series of strokes during the surgery to relieve the swelling. The doctors were unsure of his recovery, but he managed to walk again, to speak, to recognize his children and his wife."

"Yes," Martin snapped. "There's no need to over-dramatize the story. There was severe damage in the frontal lobe. The man's personality was permanently altered by the accident. Some call it Jekyll and Hyde Syndrome. Juneau was a competent family man before the injury. Afterward, he became violent."

"You like to draw straight lines across a crooked world, don't you?" Laura was repulsed by his cavalier assessment. She finally let her gaze find Jane in the front row. Laura spoke to the girl because she wanted her to know the truth. "Robert Juneau was a good man before he got hurt. He fought for his country in Vietnam. He earned his degree on the GI Bill. He paid taxes. He saved his money, bought a house, paid his bills, took care of his family, reached out with both hands for the American Dream, and . . ." Laura had to pause to swallow. "And when he couldn't stand on his own two feet anymore, when it came time for his country to take care of him—" She turned back to Martin. "Men like you said no."

Martin heaved a pained sigh. "That's a tragic tale, Maplecroft, but who's going to write a check for twenty-four-hour, supervised medical care? That's three doctors on call, at least five nursing staff, the facilities, the infrastructure, the insurance billing, the secretaries, the janitors, the cafeteria staff, the bleach, the Mop & Glo, multiplied by however many seriously mentally ill people there are in America. Do you want to pay eighty percent of your income in taxes as they do in our host country? If your answer is yes, feel free to move. If the answer is no, then tell me, where do we get the money?"

"We are the richest country in the—"

"Because we don't squander—"

"From you!" she yelled. There was a stillness in the audience that transferred to the stage. She said, "How about we get the money from you?"

He snorted by way of answer.

"Robert Juneau was kicked out of six different group homes managed by Queller Healthcare. Each time he returned, they contrived a different reason to send him away."

"I had nothing to do with—"

"Do you know how much money it costs to bury three children?" Laura could still see her babies on that crisp fall day. David whispering to some girl on the phone. Lila upstairs listening to the radio as she dressed for school. Peter running around the living room looking for his shoes.

*Pow.*

A single shot to the head brought down her youngest son.

*Pow-pow.*

Two bullets tore open David's chest.

*Pow-pow.*

Lila had slipped as she was running down the stairs. Two bullets went into the top of her head. One of them exited out of her foot.

The other was still lodged in Laura's spine.

She'd hit her head on the fireplace as she fell to the ground. There were six shots in the revolver. Robert had brought it back from his tunnel-rat duty in Vietnam.

The last thing Laura had seen that day was her husband pressing the muzzle of the gun underneath his chin and pulling the trigger.

She asked Martin Queller, "How much do you think those funerals cost? Coffins, clothes, shoes—you have to put them in shoes—Kleenex, burial space at the cemetery, headstones, hearse rental, pallbearers, and a preacher to bless a dead sixteen-year-old boy, a dead fourteen-year-old girl, and a dead five-year-old little boy?" She knew that she was the only person in this room who could answer that question because she had written the check. "What were their lives worth, Martin? Were they worth more to society than the cost of keeping a sick man hospitalized? Were those three babies nothing more than a goddamn *correction*?"

Martin seemed at a loss for words.

"Well?" she waited. Everyone was waiting.

Martin said, "He served. The Veterans' Hospital—"

"Was overcrowded and underfunded," she told him. "Robert was on a yearlong waiting list at the VA. There was no state mental hospital to go to because there was no state funding. The regular hospital had barred him. He'd already attacked a nurse and hurt an orderly. They knew he was violent, but they moved him to a group home because there was nowhere else to warehouse him." She added, "A Queller Healthcare–managed group home."

"You," Martin said, because the well-respected thinker had finally figured her out. "You're not Alex Maplecroft."

"No." She reached into her purse. She found the paper bag. Dye packs.

That was what was supposed to be inside the bag.

Back in California, they had all agreed on the red dye packs, flat and slim, less than the size and thickness of a pager. Banks hid the exploding dye inside stacks of paper money so that would-be bank robbers would be indelibly stained when they tried to count their loot.

The plan was to see Martin Queller humiliated on the world stage, stained by the proverbial blood of his victims.

Laura had lost faith in proverbs when her children were murdered by their father.

She took a deep breath. She located Jane again.

The girl was crying. She shook her head, silently mouthed the words her father would never say: *I'm sorry.*

Laura smiled. She hoped that Jane remembered what Laura had told her in the bar. She *was* magnificent. She *would* find her own path.

The next part went quickly, perhaps because Laura had watched it play out so many times in her head—that is, when she wasn't trying to conjure memories of her children; the way David's feet had smelled when he was a baby, the soft whistle that Peter's lips made when he colored with his crayons, the wrinkle in Lila's brow when she studied how to frame a photograph. Even Robert sometimes haunted her thoughts. The man before the accident who had danced to Jinx Queller on the piano at the Hollywood Bowl. The patient who had wanted so desperately to get well. The violent inmate at the hospital. The trouble-maker who'd been kicked out of so many group homes. The homeless man who'd been arrested time and time again for theft, assault, public intoxication, aggressive panhandling, public nuisance, loitering, suicidal tendencies, making terroristic threats, willfully threatening to commit bodily harm.

"*In some ways you were lucky,*" Laura's oncologist had told her after the shooting. "*If the bullet had entered your back three centimeters lower, the scan would've never found the cancer.*"

Laura reached into the paper bag.

She had known the moment she pulled it from behind the toilet tank that she was not holding the agreed-upon dye packs, but something better.

A six-shot revolver, just like the one her husband had used.

First, she shot Martin Queller in the head.

Then she pressed the muzzle of the gun beneath her chin and killed herself.

August 21, 2018

# 8

Andy felt numb as she drove through Alabama in her mother's secret Reliant K station wagon filled with secret money toward a destination that Laura had seemed to pull from thin air. Or maybe she hadn't. Maybe her mother knew exactly what she was doing, because you didn't have a covert storage facility filled with everything you needed to completely restart your life unless you had a hell of a lot of things to hide.

The fake IDs. The revolver with the serial number shaved off. The photos of Andy in snow that she could not ever recall seeing, holding the hand of a person she could not remember.

The Polaroids.

Andy had shoved them into the beach tote in the back of the Reliant. She could've spent the rest of her day staring at them, trying to pick apart the terrible things that had happened to the young woman in the pictures. Beaten. Punched. Bitten—that was what the gash on her leg looked like, as if an animal had taken a bite of her flesh.

That young woman had been her mother.

Who had done all of those awful things to Laura? Was it the *they* who had sent Hoodie? Was it the *they* who were probably tracking Andy?

Andy wasn't doing a great job of eluding them. She had made it as far as Birmingham before she remembered that she hadn't unhooked the battery cables in the dead man's truck. Laura had told her that she had to make sure the GPS wasn't working. Did GPS work without the engine running? Coordinating with a satellite seemed like something the on-board computer would do, which meant the computer had to be awake, which meant the car had to be on.

*Right?*

The LoJack vehicle recovery system had its own battery. Andy knew this from working stolen car reports through dispatch. She also knew Ford had a Sync system, but you had to register for the real-time monitoring service, and Andy didn't think that a guy who went to the trouble of blocking out all the lights on his vehicle would give up his anonymity just so he could use voice commands to locate the nearest Mexican restaurant.

*Right?*

What would happen if the truck was found? Andy played out the investigation in her mind, the same as she had while running away from her mother's house.

First up, the police would have to ID Hoodie, aka Samuel Godfrey Beckett. Considering the guy's vocation, he was more than likely in the system, so a fingerprint scan was all it would take to get his name. Once they had his name, they would find the truck registration, then they would put out an APB on the wire, which would create an alert that would show up on the screen of every squad car in the tri-state area.

Of course, this assumed that what was supposed to happen was what actually happened. There were tons of APBs all the time. Even the high-priority ones were missed by a lot of the patrol officers, who had maybe a billion things to do on their shifts, including trying not to get shot, and stopping to read an alert was often not a high priority.

That did not necessarily mean Andy was in the clear. If the cops didn't find the truck, the librarians, or more likely the grumpy old guy with the political rants, would probably report the abandoned vehicle. Then the cops would roll up. The officer would run the plates and VIN, see there was an APB, notify

Savannah, then the forensic techs would find Andy's shoes and work shirt and her fingerprints and DNA all over the interior.

Andy felt her stomach pitch.

Her fingerprints on the frying pan could be explained away—Andy cooked eggs in her mother's kitchen all of the time—but stealing the dead man's truck and crossing state lines put her squarely in special circumstances territory, meaning if Palazzolo charged Andy with the murder of Hoodie, the prosecutor could seek the death penalty.

*The death penalty.*

She opened her mouth to breathe as a wave of dizziness took hold. Her hands were shaking again. Big, fat tears rolled down her face. The trees blurred outside the car windows. Andy should turn herself in. She shouldn't be running away. She had dropped her mother in a pile of shit. It didn't matter that Laura had told Andy to leave. She should've stayed. At least that way Andy wouldn't be so alone right now.

The truth brought a sob to her mouth.

"Get it together," she coaxed herself. "Stop this."

Andy gripped the steering wheel. She blinked away her tears. Laura had told her to go to Idaho. She needed to go to Idaho. Once Andy was there, once she crossed the state line, she could break down and cry every single day until the phone rang and Laura told her it was safe to come home. Following Laura's orders was the only way she would get through this.

Laura had also told her to unhook the Ford's battery.

"Fuck," Andy muttered, then, channeling Gordon, Andy told herself, "What's done is done." The finality of the proclamation loosened the tight bands around Andy's chest. There was also the benefit of it being true. Whether or not the Ford was found or what the cops did with it was completely out of Andy's control.

This was the question she needed to worry about: during her computer searches at the library, at what point exactly had she turned on the Google Incognito Mode? Because once the cops found the truck, they would talk to the librarians, and the librarians would tell them that Andy had used the computer. While she felt certain that the librarians would put up a fight—as a group, they were mostly First Amendment badasses—a warrant to search the computer would take maybe an hour and then a tech would need five seconds to find Andy's search history.

She was certain the Incognito Mode was on before she looked up Paula Kunde of Austin, Texas, but was it on before or after she searched for directions to Idaho?

Andy could not recall.

Second worrisome thing: what if it wasn't the cops who asked the librarians these questions? What if Laura's omniscient *they* found someone to look for Hoodie's truck, and *they* talked to the librarians, and *they* searched the computer?

Andy wiped her nose with her arm. She backed down on the speed because the Reliant started to shake like a bag of cat treats if she went over fifty-five.

Had she put other people's lives at risk by abandoning the truck? Had she put her own life at risk by looking up the directions to Idaho? Andy tried again to mentally walk through the morning. Entering the library. Pouring the coffee. Sitting down at the computer. She had looked up the *Belle Isle Review* first, right? And then clicked to private browsing?

She was giving Google Incognito Mode a lot of credit. It seemed very unlikely that something so standard could fool a forensic computer whiz. Andy probably should've cleared out the cache and wiped the history and erased all the cookies the way she had learned to do after that horrible time Gordon had accidentally seen the loop of erotic *Outlander* scenes Andy had accessed from his laptop.

Andy wiped her nose again. Her cheeks felt hot. She saw a road sign.

FLORENCE 5 MI

Andy guessed she was heading in the right direction, which was somewhere in the upper left corner of Alabama. She hadn't stopped to buy a new map to plot the route to Idaho. Once she'd left the storage unit, her only goal was to get as far away from Carrollton as possible. She had her highway and interstate scribbles from the library, but she was mostly relying on the back of the Georgia map, which had ads for other maps. There was a small rendering of *The Contiguous United States of America* available for $5.99 plus postage and handling. Andy had grown up looking at similar maps, which was why she was in her twenties before she'd understood how Canada and New York State could share Niagara Falls.

This was her plan: after Alabama, she'd cut through a corner of Tennessee, a corner of Arkansas, Missouri, a tiny piece of Kansas, left at Nebraska, then Wyoming, then she would literally fucking kill herself if she wasn't in Idaho by then.

Andy leaned forward, resting her chin on the shaky steering wheel. The vertebrae in her lower back had turned into prickly pears. The trees started to blur again. She wasn't crying anymore, just exhausted. Her eyelids kept fluttering. She felt like they were weighted down with paste.

She made herself sit up straight. She punched the thick white buttons on the radio. She twisted the dial back and forth. All she found were sermons and farm reports and country music, but not the good kind; the kind that made you want to stab a pencil into your ear.

Andy opened her mouth and screamed as loud as she could. It felt good, but she couldn't scream for the rest of her life.

At some point, she would have to get some sleep. The five-and-a-half-hour drive from Belle Isle had been draining enough. So far, the drive from Carrollton had added another four and a half hours because of traffic, which Andy seemed pre-ordained to find no matter which route she took. It was almost three p.m. Except for zonking out for a few hours in her apartment and the catnap in the Walmart parking lot, she hadn't really slept since she got up for her dispatch shift two days ago. During that time, Andy had survived a shooting, watched her mother get injured, agonized outside of the surgical suite, freaked out over a police interrogation and killed a man, so as these things went, it was no wonder that she felt like she wanted to vomit and yell and cry at the same time.

Not to mention that her bladder was a hot-water bottle sitting inside of her body. She had stopped only once since leaving the storage unit, pulling onto the shoulder of the highway, hiding between the open front and back car doors, waiting for traffic to clear, then squatting down to relieve herself in the grass because she was terrified to leave the Reliant unattended.

$240,000

Andy couldn't leave that kind of cash in the car while she ran into Burger King, and taking the suitcase inside would be like carrying a neon sign for somebody to rob her. What the hell was Laura doing with that kind of cash? How long had it taken for her to save it?

Was she a bank robber?

The question was only a little crazy. Being a bank robber would explain the money, and it jibed with the D.B. Cooper joke on the Canada ID and maybe even the gun in the glove box.

Andy's heart pinged at the thought of the gun.

Here was the problem: bank robbers seldom got away with their crimes. It was a very high risk for a very low reward, because the FBI was in charge of all investigations that had to do with federally insured funds. Andy thought the law's origins had something to do with Bonnie and Clyde or John Dillinger or the government just basically making sure that people knew their money was safe.

Anyway, she couldn't see her mother pulling on a ski mask and robbing a bank.

Then again, before the shooting at the diner, she couldn't see her mom knifing a kid in the neck.

Then again—again—Andy could not see her reliable, sensible mother doing a lot of the crazy shit that Laura had done in the last thirty-six hours. The hidden make-up bag, the key behind the photograph, the storage unit, the Thom McAn box.

Which brought Andy to the photo of toddler Andy in the snow.

Here was the Lifetime Movie question: Had Andy been kidnapped as a child? Had Laura seen a baby left alone in a shopping cart or unattended on a playground and decided to take her home?

Andy glanced in the rearview mirror. The shape of her eyes, the same shape as Laura's, told her that Laura was her mother.

The Polaroids showed Laura so badly beaten that her bottom lip was split open. Maybe Jerry Randall was an awful man. Maybe back in 1989, he was beating Laura, and she snapped and took Andy on the run with her, and Jerry had been looking for them ever since.

Which was a Julia Roberts movie. Or a Jennifer Lopez movie. Or Kathy Bates. Or Ashley Judd, Keri Russell, Ellen Page . . .

Andy snorted.

There were a lot of movies about women getting pissed off about men beating the shit out of them.

But the Polaroids showed that her mother had in fact had the shit beaten out of her, so maybe that wasn't so far off base.

Andy found herself shaking her head.

Laura hadn't said *he* can trace you. She'd said *they*.

Going by the movies, *they* generally meant evil corporations, corrupt presidents or power-hungry tech billionaires with unlimited funds. Andy tried to play out each scenario with her mother at the center of some vast conspiracy. And then she decided she should probably stop using Netflix as a crime sourcebook.

The Florence exit was up. Andy couldn't squat on the highway again. She hadn't had lunch because she couldn't bear to eat another hamburger in another car. The part of her brain that was still capable of thinking told her that she could not make the thirty-hour drive straight through to Idaho without sleep. Eventually, she would have to stop at a hotel.

Which meant that, eventually, she would have to figure out what to do with the money.

Her hand had pushed down the blinker before she could stop it. She glided off the Florence exit. Adrenaline had kept Andy going for so long that there was hardly anything left to move

her. There were signs off the exit for six different hotels. She
took a right at the light because it was easier. She coasted to
the first motel because it was the first motel. Worrying about
safety and cleanliness were luxuries from her former life.

Still, her heart started pounding as she got out of the Reliant.
The motel was two stories, a squat, concrete design from the
seventies with an ornate balcony railing around the top floor.
Andy had backed crookedly into the parking space so that the
rear of the station wagon never left her sight. She clutched the
make-up bag in her hand as she walked into the lobby. She
checked the flip phone. Laura had not called. Andy had depleted
the battery by half from constantly checking the screen.

There was an older woman at the front desk. High hair. Tight
perm. She smiled at Andy. Andy glanced back at the car. There
were huge windows all around the lobby. The Reliant was where
she had left it, unmolested. She didn't know if she looked weird
or normal swiveling her head back and forth, but at this point,
Andy didn't care about anything but falling into a bed.

"Hey there," the woman said. "We got some rooms on the
top floor if you want."

Andy felt the vestiges of her waking brain start to slip away.
She'd heard what the woman had said, but there was no sense
in it.

"Unless you want something on the bottom floor?" The
woman sounded dubious.

Andy was incapable of making a decision. "Uh—" Her throat
was so dry that she could barely speak. "Okay."

The woman took a key from a hook on the wall. She told
Andy, "Forty bucks for two hours. Sixty for the night."

Andy reached into the make-up bag. She peeled off a few
twenties.

"Overnight, then." The woman handed back one of the bills.
She slid the guestbook across the counter. "Name, license plate,
make and model." She was looking over Andy's shoulder at the
car. "Boy, haven't seen one of those in a long time. They make
those new in Canada? Looks like you just drove it off the lot."

Andy wrote down the car's information. She had to look at the license plate three times before she got the correct combination of numbers and letters.

"You okay, sweetheart?"

Andy smelled French fries. Her stomach grumbled. There was a diner connected to the motel. Red vinyl booths, lots of chrome. Her stomach grumbled again.

What was more important, eating or sleeping?

"Hon?"

Andy turned back around. She was clearly expected to say something.

The woman leaned across the counter. "You okay, sugar?"

Andy struggled to swallow. She couldn't be weird right now. She didn't need to make herself memorable. "Thank you," was the first thing that came out. "Just tired. I came from . . ." She tried to think of a place that was far from Belle Isle. She settled on, "I've been driving all day. To visit my parents. In I-Iowa."

She laughed. "Honey, I think you overshot Iowa by about six hundred miles."

*Shit.*

Andy tried again. "It's my grandmother's car." She searched her brain for a compelling lie. "I mean, I was at the beach. The Alabama beach. Gulf. In a town called Mystic Falls." Christ, she was crazy-sounding. Mystic Falls was from the *Vampire Diaries*. She said, "My grandmother's a snowbird. You know, people who—"

"I know what a snowbird is." She glanced down at the name Andy had written in the guestbook. "Daniela Cooper. That's pretty."

Andy stared, unblinking. Why had she written down that name?

"Sweetheart, maybe you should get some rest." She pushed the key across the counter. "Top floor, corner. I think you'll feel safer there."

"Thank you," Andy managed. She was in tears again by the time she climbed behind the wheel of the Reliant. The diner was so close. She should get something to eat. Her stomach was doing that thing where it hurt so bad she couldn't tell if it was from being hungry or being sick.

Andy got back out of the car. She held the make-up bag in both hands as she walked the twenty feet to the diner. The sun beat down on the top of her head. The heat brought out a thick layer of sweat. She stopped at the door. She looked back at her car. Should she get the suitcase? How would that look? She could take it to her room, but then how could she leave the suitcase in her room when—

The diner was empty when she walked in, a lone waitress reading a newspaper at the bar. Andy went to the ladies room first because her bladder gave her no other choice. She was in such a hurry that she didn't wash her hands. The car was still there when she came out of the bathroom. No one in a blue baseball cap and blue jeans was peering into the windows. No one was running away with a 1989 Samsonite suitcase in their hand.

She found a booth by the window overlooking the parking lot. She kept the make-up bag between her legs. The menu was giant, filled with everything from tacos to fried chicken. Her eyes saw the words but by the time they made it into her consciousness, she was stymied. She would never be able to make a choice. She could order a bunch of things, but that would only draw even more attention. She should probably leave, drive up another few exits and find a different motel where she didn't act like an idiot. Or she could just put her head in her hands and stay here, in the air-conditioning, for a few minutes while she tried to get her thoughts in order.

"Honey?"

Andy jerked up from the table, disoriented.

"You're beat, ain't you?" the woman from the motel said. "Poor thing. I told them to let you sleep."

Andy felt her stomach drop. She had fallen asleep again. In public—again. She looked down. The make-up bag was still between her legs. There was drool on the table. She used a napkin to wipe it up. She used her hand to wipe her mouth. Everything was vibrating. Her brain felt like it was being squished onto the point of a juice grinder.

"Hon?" the woman said. "You should probably go to your room now. It's getting a little busy in here."

The restaurant had been empty when Andy walked in, but now it was filling with people.

"I'm sorry," she said.

"It's all right." The woman patted Andy's shoulder. "I asked Darla to put a plate aside for you. You want it here or do you wanna take it to your room?"

Andy stared at her.

"Take it to your room," the woman said. "That way you can go right back to sleep when you're finished."

Andy nodded, grateful that someone was telling her what to do.

Then she remembered the money.

Her neck strained as she turned to look for the car. The blue Reliant was still parked in front of the motel office. Had someone opened the trunk? Was the suitcase still there?

"Your car is fine." The woman handed her a Styrofoam box. "Take your food. Your room's the last one on the top floor. I don't like to put young women on the ground floor. Old gals like me, we'd welcome a strange man knocking at our door, but you . . ." She gave a husky chuckle. "Just keep to yourself and you'll be fine."

Andy took the box, which weighed the equivalent of a cement block. She put the make-up bag on top. Her legs were wobbly when she stood. Her stomach rumbled. She ignored the people staring at her as she walked back into the parking lot. She fumbled with the keys to open the hatch. She couldn't decide what to take inside, so she loaded herself up like a pack mule, slinging the tote bag over her shoulder, tucking the sleeping bag into her armpit, grabbing the handle of the suitcase and balancing the make-up bag/take-out Jenga with her free hand.

Andy made it as far as the stairway landing before she had to stop to readjust her load. Her shoulders felt boneless. Either she was still exhausted or she'd lost all of her muscle mass from sitting in the car for almost ten hours.

She scanned the numbers as she walked along the narrow balcony on the top floor. There were burned-out hibachi grills and empty beer cans and greasy pizza boxes in front of some of the doors. The smell of cigarettes was strong. It brought back the memory of Laura bumming a smoke off the orderly in front of the hospital.

Andy longed for the time when her biggest concern was that her mother held a cigarette between her finger and thumb like a junkie.

Behind her, a door opened. A disembodied hand dropped an empty pizza box on the concrete balcony. The door slammed shut.

Andy tried to calm her heart, which had detonated inside her throat when the door opened. She took a deep breath and let it go. She readjusted the sleeping bag under her arm. She mentally summoned her father and tried to make a list of things she would need to stop doing. One, stop panicking every time she heard a noise. Two, stop falling asleep in public places. That seemed a hell of a lot easier than it was proving to be. Three, figure out what to do with all of the money. Four, locate another library so she could read the *Belle Isle Review*. Five, stop being weird, because right now, if the cops happened to follow her trail, the first person any of the potential witnesses would think of was Andy.

Then they'd get Daniela Cooper's name, and the car details, and that would be it.

Andy looked out at the road. There was a bar across the street. Neon signs filled the windows. The parking lot was packed with trucks. She could hear the faint clink of honky-tonk music. In that moment, she wanted a drink so badly that her body strained toward the bar like a plant reaching up to the sun.

She put down the suitcase and used the key to open the door

to her room. It was the kind of cheap place Laura used to book for vacations when Andy was little. The single window looked out at the parking lot. The air conditioner rattled below. There were two queen-sized beds with sticky-looking bedspreads and a plastic dining table with two chairs. Andy gladly put the heavy take-out box on the table. The chest of drawers had a place for a suitcase. She lugged the Samsonite on top. She dropped the tote bag and make-up bag and the sleeping bag on the bed. She lowered the blind on the window and dragged closed the flimsy blackout curtain. Or at least tried to. The curtain rod stopped an inch before the window did. Light bled in around the edge.

A flat-screen television was mounted on the wall. The cords hung down like tendrils. Out of habit, Andy found the remote and turned on the TV.

CNN. The weatherman was standing in front of a map. Andy had never been so relieved to see a hurricane warning.

She muted the sound. She sat down at the table. She opened the Styrofoam box.

Fried chicken, mashed potatoes, green beans, a cornbread muffin. She should've been disgusted, but her stomach sent up a noise like the Hallelujah Chorus.

There was no silverware, but Andy was no stranger to this dilemma. She used the chicken leg to eat the mashed potatoes, then she ate the chicken, then she used her fingers to go after the green beans, then she used the cornbread like a sponge to clean up any edible pieces of fried chicken skin or green bean juice that she had missed. It wasn't until she closed the empty box that she considered how filthy her hands were. The last time they'd been washed was in the shower of her apartment. The cleanest thing she'd touched since then was probably the desk in Laura's secret storage unit.

She looked up at the television. As if on cue, the story had switched from the hurricane to her mother. The diner video was paused on Laura holding up her hands to show Jonah Helsinger the number of bullets.

So weird, the way she was doing it—four fingers on the left

179

hand, one on her right. Why not hold up just one hand to show five fingers for five bullets?

Suddenly, the image switched to a photograph. Andy felt her heart do a weird flip at the sight of Laura. She was wearing her standard going-out-to-parties outfit of a simple black dress with a colorful silk scarf. Andy knelt in front of the TV so she could study the details. Laura's chest was flat on one side. Her hair was short. There was a lighted star behind her, the topper on a Christmas tree. The hand on her waist must have belonged to Gordon, though he'd been cropped out of the image. The photo was probably from Gordon's most recent office Christmas party, which Laura had never missed, even when they'd wanted to kill each other. She smiled at the camera, her expression slightly guarded in what Andy always thought of as her mother's Gordon's Wife Mode.

She unmuted the sound.

". . . on the off-chance that it might happen. Ashleigh?"

Andy had missed the story. The camera cut to Ashleigh Banfield, who said, "Thanks, Chandra. We have breaking news about a shooting in Green County, Oregon."

Andy pressed the mute button again. She sat on the edge of the bed. She watched Ashleigh Banfield's face go into a split scene beside a run-down looking house that was surrounded by a SWAT team. The banner said: *Man kills own mother, two kids, holding injured wife hostage, demanding pizza and beer.*

Another shooting.

Andy flipped the channels. She wanted to see the photo of Laura again, or even to glimpse Gordon's hand. MSNBC. Fox. The local news stations. All of them were showing the live stand-off with the man who wanted pizza after murdering most of his family.

Was that a good or bad thing—not the man killing people, but the news stations covering it live? Did that mean they'd moved on from covering Laura? Would there be another *killing machine* to profile?

Andy's head was shaking even before she asked herself the

obvious question: where was the story about the body of Samuel Godfrey Beckett being found in Laura Oliver's beachside bungalow? That was big news. The victim had been felled by a frying pan, ostensibly by a woman who had hours before killed a police officer's son.

And yet, the scroll at the bottom of the screen contained the usual headlines: another senator resigning, probably because of sexual harassment, another gunman shot by cops, interest rates going up, healthcare costs on the rise, stock market drops.

Nothing about Hoodie.

Andy felt her eyebrows furrow. None of this made sense. Had Laura somehow managed to keep the police out of the house? How would she even do that? The 911 text Andy had sent provided legal cause for them to break down the door. So why wasn't *Killing Machine Strikes Again* being shouted about all over the news? Even with the SWAT stand-off happening in Oregon, the last photo of Laura should have been her mugshot or, worse, video of her entering the jail in handcuffs, not a photo from a Christmas celebration.

Andy's brain was overloaded with all the *whats* and *whys*.

She let herself fall back onto the bed. She closed her eyes. When she opened them again, there was no light coming from around the closed curtain. She looked at the clock: nine thirty in the evening.

She should go back to sleep, but her eyes refused to stay closed. She stared at the brown spots on the popcorn-textured ceiling. What was her mother doing right now? Was she at home? Was she talking to Gordon on a jail phone with a thick piece of glass between them? Andy turned her head to look at the television. Still the SWAT story, even this many hours later. Her nostrils flared. The bedspread smelled like a bear had slept on it. Andy sniffed under her arms.

*Ugh.*

She was the bear.

She checked the lock on the door. She closed the hotel latch. She wedged one of the chairs underneath the doorknob.

Someone could still break the large window to get in, but if someone broke the window to get in, she was fucked anyway. Andy peeled off the jeans and polo shirt and underwear. Her bra was disgusting. The underwire had rubbed the skin raw underneath her armpit. She threw it into the sink and turned on the cold water.

The hotel soap was the size of a pebble and smelled like the last vestiges of a dying bouquet of flowers. She took it into the shower and between the soap and the shampoo, the tiny bathroom took on the scent of a whore house. At least what Andy thought a whore house might smell like.

She turned off the shower. She dried herself with the hotel towel, which had the consistency of notebook paper. The soap came apart in her hands as she tried to clean the stink out of her bra. She spread the crappy hotel lotion on her body as she walked into the bedroom. Then she wiped her hands on the towel to get the lotion off, then she washed her hands at the sink to remove the fuzz from the towel.

She unrolled the sleeping bag on the bed. She unzipped the side. The material was thick, filled with some kind of synthetic down, and with a nylon, waterproof outer layer. Flannel liner. Not the kind of thing you'd ever need in Belle Isle, so maybe Laura hadn't pulled Idaho out of thin air after all.

Andy opened the suitcase and picked off the top row of twenties. Ten across, three wide, times $2,000 was . . . a lot of money to hide inside of a sleeping bag.

She laid the stacks out in a flat row along the bottom of the bag. She smoothed down the nylon and pulled up the zipper. She started to roll the sleeping bag from the bottom, but the money bunched into a lump. Andy took a deep breath. She unrolled the bag again. She reached into the bottom and pulled the stacks to the center. She rolled the bag carefully from the top, secured it with the Velcro strap, then stood back to judge her work.

It looked like a sleeping bag.

Andy hefted the weight. Heavier than a sleeping bag, but not so that you'd become alarmed and think there was a small fortune inside.

She turned back to the suitcase. A third of the money was left. Bad guys in movies always ended up in train stations, which had lockers, which made it easy for them to hide money. Andy doubted there were any train stations in Florence, Alabama.

The best solution was to split it up. She should probably hide some of it in the car. There would be space inside the spare tire well under the trunk. That way, if she got separated from the sleeping bag, she could jump in the car and still have some cash. For the same reason, she could put some of the cash in her purse. Except that her purse was back in her apartment.

Andy found the hotel notepad. She wrote *purse* at the top, then *soap, lotion, bra*.

She dumped out the white tote bag. Flashlight. Batteries. Three paperbacks, unread, the titles popular approximately eleven billion years ago. The plastic first aid kit had some Band-Aids. Andy covered the scrape on her shin, which she suddenly remembered was caused by the pedal on her bike. She used the alcohol wipes to clean her blisters. It would take more than Band-Aids to get her feet into something more than Crocs. There was a cut on the side of her foot that looked pretty bad. She slapped on another Band-Aid and prayed for the best.

The Ace bandage gave her an idea. She could wrap some of the cash around her waist and secure it with the bandage. Driving would be uncomfortable, but it wasn't a bad idea to keep some of the money as close to her as possible.

Or was it? Andy remembered an NPR story about cops in rural areas pulling people over and confiscating their cash. Civil forfeiture. The Canada license plate would make her the proverbial sitting duck.

Andy unzipped the make-up bag. She opened the phone. No calls.

She pulled the Daniela Cooper driver's license from the black vinyl bag. Andy had taken the Canadian ID, health insurance card and car registration with her when she left the storage unit.

She studied her mother's photograph. They had always looked like mother and daughter. Even strangers had commented on it. The eyes were a dead giveaway, but their faces were both heart-shaped and their hair was the same color brown. Andy had forgotten how dark her mother used to keep her hair. Post-cancer treatments, it had grown out in a shockingly beautiful gray. Laura wore it fashionably short now, but the Laura in the driver's license photo wore her hair down to her shoulders. Andy's hair was the same length, but she always kept it in a ponytail because she was too lazy to style it.

She looked at the mirror across from the bed. Her face was ragged. Dark circles were under her eyes. Mirror Andy looked older than her thirty-one years, that was for damn sure, but could she pass for the woman in the photo? Andy held up the driver's license. She let her eyes go back and forth. She scrunched her wet hair. She pulled down the bangs. Did that help or hinder Andy's ability to look twenty-four years older than she actually was?

There was one way to get an honest appraisal.

Andy rinsed her bra in the sink. The hotel soap had made it smell like Miss Havisham's asshole, but that was actually an improvement. Patting it dry with the towel transferred white fuzz onto the material. She used the hairdryer until the bra was only slightly damp. Then she dried her hair messier than usual, pulling it forward, styling it close to the way Laura wore hers in the Canada license photo. She put on another pair of jeans, another white polo shirt. Andy cringed as her feet slid into the Crocs again. She needed socks and real shoes. And she needed an actual written list to keep track of everything.

She grabbed a $2,000 brick of twenties, split it in two and shoved one half into each of her back pockets. The jeans were old, from a time when manufacturers actually sewed usable pockets into women's wear. Still, the bills stuck out like large cell phones. She transferred some layers into her front pocket. She looked at herself in the mirror. It worked.

Andy scooped up more handfuls of strapped twenties and

hid some between the mattress and boxspring. Others got folded into her wet towel, which she artfully arranged on the bathroom floor. The rest lined the bottom of the tote bag. She put the paperbacks on top along with the first aid kit and make-up bag.

All of her machinations had left one row of bills on the bottom of the suitcase. Ten across, three wide, times $2,000 was . . . a lot of money to have in a suitcase. There was nothing to do but zip it closed and leave it out in the open. If someone broke into the room, they hopefully would be excited enough by the cash in the Samsonite to not look for the rest of the money.

Andy slung the tote bag over her shoulder as she walked out of the room. The night air slapped her face like the sudden blast of heat from an oven door. She scanned the parking lot as she walked down the stairs. There were a few Serv-Pro vans, a red truck with a Trump sticker on one side and a Confederate flag on the other, and a Mustang from the 1990s that had the front bumper held on with duct tape.

The diner was closed. The motel office lights were still on. Andy guessed it was about ten in the evening. The clerk behind the desk had his nose in his phone.

She got behind the wheel of the Reliant and moved the car to the far end of the parking lot. There were security lights on the building, but several bulbs were out. Andy walked to the back of the station wagon and opened the hatch. She checked to make sure no one was watching, then pried open the bottom of the cargo area.

*Jesus.*

More money, this time hundreds, stacked all around the spare tire.

Andy quickly pressed the floor cover back into place. She closed the hatch. She kept her hand pressed to the back of the car. Her heart was jackrabbiting against her ribs.

Should she feel good that her mother had split up the money the same way Andy had intended to, or should she be freaked the hell out that Laura had so carefully thought out an escape plan that there was over half a million bucks stashed in the trunk of her untraceable car?

This was the part where Andy wondered where she would've fit into Laura's disappearance, because everything Andy had found so far pointed to only one person being on the lam.

So Andy had to wonder: which Laura was her real mother—the one who'd told Andy to leave her alone or the one who'd said that everything she'd done in her life was for Andy?

"Okay," Andy mumbled, acknowledging the question had finally been asked, but fully prepared not to do any more thinking about it.

The new Andy who did math and planned driving routes and considered consequences and dealt with money problems was wearing the hell out of the old Andy, who desperately needed a drink.

She carried the tote like a purse as she walked toward the bar across the road from the motel. Half a dozen pick-up trucks were in the parking lot. All of them had signs on their sides—Joe's Plumbing, Bubba's Locksmith Services, Knepper's Knippers. Andy took a closer look at the last one, which apparently belonged to a gardener. The logo on the side, a mustachioed grasshopper holding a pair of shears, promised, *We'll knip your lawn into shape!*

Every set of eyes inside the place looked up when Andy walked through the front door. She tried to pretend like she belonged, but it was hard, considering she was the only woman. A television was blaring in the corner. Some kind of sports show. Most of the guys were sitting one or two to a booth. Two men were standing around the pool table. They had both stopped, pool sticks in the air, to watch her progress through the room.

There was only one customer sitting at the bar, but his attention was squarely focused on the television. Andy took a seat as far away from him as possible, her ass hanging off the stool, the tote bag wedged between her arm and the wall.

The bartender ambled over, throwing a white towel over his shoulder. "Whatcha want, babydoll?"

*Not to be called babydoll.*

"Vodka rocks," she requested, because for the first time since college, her student loan debt didn't dictate her drinking habits.

"Gottan ID?"

She found Laura's license in the make-up bag and slid it over.

He gave it a quick glance. "Vodka rocks, eh?"

Andy stared at him.

He mixed the drink in front of her, using a lot more ice than Andy would've liked.

She picked one of the twenties off the brick in her back pocket. She waited for him to leave, then tried not to set on the vodka like a wildebeest. "Personality shots," her roommates used to call the first drinks of the night. Liquid courage. Whatever you called it, the point was to turn off the voice in your head that reminded you of everything wrong in your life.

Andy tossed back the drink. The fiery sensation of the alcohol sliding down her throat made the muscles of her shoulders relax for the first time in what felt like decades.

The bartender was back with her change. She left it on the bar, nodded toward the glass. He poured another, then leaned against the bar to watch TV. Some half-bald guy in a suit was talking about the possibility of a football coach getting fired.

"Bullshit," the man at the end of the bar mumbled. He rubbed his jaw, which was rough with stubble. For some reason, Andy's gaze found his hand. The fingers were long and lean, like the rest of him. "I can't believe what that moron just said."

The bartender asked, "Want me to turn it?"

"Well, hell yeah. Why would I want to keep listening to that crap?" The guy took off his burgundy-colored baseball cap and threw it onto the bar. He ran his fingers through his thick hair. He turned to Andy and her jaw dropped open in shock.

Alabama.

From the hospital.

She was certain of it.

"I know you." His finger was pointing at her. "Right? Don't I know you?"

Fear snapped her jaw shut.

*What was he doing here? Had he followed her?*

"You were at the—" He stood up. He was taller than she remembered, leaner. "Are you following me?" He swiped his hat off the bar as he walked down to her end of the bar.

She looked at the door. He was in her way. He was getting closer. He was standing right in front of her.

"You're the same gal, right?" He waited for an answer that Andy could not give. "From the hospital?"

Andy's back was to the wall. She had nowhere else to go.

His expression changed from annoyed to concerned. "You okay?"

Andy could not answer.

"Hey, buddy," Alabama called to the bartender. "What'd you give her?"

The bartender looked insulted. "What the hell are you—"

"Sorry." Alabama held up his hand, but his eyes stayed on Andy. "What are you doing here?"

She couldn't swallow, let alone speak.

"Seriously, lady. Did you follow me?"

The bartender was listening now. "She's from Canada," he said, like that might help clear things up.

"Canada?" Alabama had his arms crossed. He looked uneasy. "This is some kind of weird freaking coincidence." He told the bartender, "I saw this same gal yesterday down in Savannah. I told you my granny was poorly. Had to drive down to see her. And now here's this lady right in front of me that I saw outside of the hospital the day I left. Weird, right?"

The bartender nodded. "Weird."

Alabama asked Andy, "Are you going to talk to me or what?"

"Yeah," the bartender echoed. "What's up, little bit? You stalking this guy?" He told Alabama, "You could be stalked by worse, bro."

"Not funny, man." Alabama told Andy, "Explain yourself, porcupine. Or should I call the cops?"

"I—" Andy couldn't let him call the police. "I don't know."

She realized that wasn't enough. "I was visiting," she said. "My mother. And—" *Fuck, fuck, fuck.* What could she say? How could she turn this around?

Her mental Gordon offered the solution: she could turn it around.

Andy tried to make her voice strong. "What are *you* doing here?"

"Me?"

She tried to sound indignant. "I was just passing through. Why are *you* following *me*?"

"What?" he seemed taken aback by the question.

"You," she said, because his presence made about as much sense as hers did. "I'm on my way back from visiting my parents. That's why I'm here." She squared her shoulders. "What's your reason? Why are *you* here?"

"Why am I here?" He reached behind his back.

Andy braced herself for a police badge or, worse, a gun.

But he took out his wallet. There was no badge, just his Alabama driver's license. He held it up to her face. "I live here."

Andy scanned the name.

Michael Benjamin Knepper.

He introduced himself. "Mike Knepper. The *K* is silent."

"Mi'e?" The joke came out before she could stop it.

He gave a startled laugh. His face broke out into a grin. "Holy shit, I can't believe I've gone thirty-eight years with nobody ever making that joke."

The bartender was laughing, too. They clearly knew each other, which made sense because they were roughly the same age. In a town this small, they'd probably gone to school together.

Andy felt some of the tension leave her chest. So, this was a coincidence.

*Was it?*

She hadn't looked closely at the photo on his license. She hadn't looked to see what town he was from.

"You're a funny lady." Mike was already tucking his wallet back into his pocket. "What're you drinking?"

The bartender said, "Vodka."

Mike held out two fingers as he sat down on the stool beside her. "How's your mom doing?"

"My—" Andy suddenly felt tipsy from the alcohol. This didn't feel completely right. She probably shouldn't drink anything else.

"Hello?" Mike said. "You still in there?"

Andy said, "My mother is fine. Just needs rest."

"I bet." He was scratching his jaw again. She tried not to look at his fingers. He looked like a man, was the thing that kept drawing her attention. Andy had only ever dated guys who looked like guys. Her last sort-of almost boyfriend had shaved once a week and needed a trigger warning anytime Andy talked about calls that came in through dispatch.

"Here ya go." The bartender placed a Sam Adams in front of Mike and a new glass of vodka in front of Andy. This one had less ice and more alcohol. He gave Mike a salute before walking to the far end of the bar.

"To coincidences." Mike raised his beer.

Andy tapped her glass against his bottle. She kept her gaze away from his hands. She took a drink before she remembered not to.

Mike said, "You cleaned up nice."

Andy felt a blush work its way up her neck.

"Seriously," Mike said. "What are you doing in Muscle Shoals?"

She sipped some vodka to give herself time to think. "I thought this was Florence?"

"Same difference." His smile was crooked. There were flecks of umber in his brown eyes. Was he flirting with her? He couldn't be flirting with her. He was too good-looking and Andy had always looked too much like somebody's kid sister.

He said, "You gonna tell me why you're here or do I have to guess?"

Andy could have cried with relief. "Guess."

He squinted at her like she was a crystal ball. "People either come here for the book warehouse or the music, but you got a rock-n-roll thing going with your hair, so I'm gonna say music."

She liked the hair compliment, though she was completely clueless about his guess. "Music is right."

"You gotta book appointments to tour the studios." He kept looking at her mouth in a very obvious way. Or maybe it wasn't obvious. Maybe she was imagining the sparkle in his beautiful eyes, because in her long history of being Andy, no man had ever openly flirted with her like this.

Mike said, "Nobody really plays on weeknights, but there's a bar over near the river—"

"Tuscumbia," the bartender volunteered.

"Right, anyway, a lot of musicians, they'll go out to the clubs and work on new material. You can check online to see who's gonna be where." He took his phone out of his back pocket. She watched him dial in the code, which was all 3s. He said, "My mom's got this story. Back when she was a kid, she saw George Michael working a live set trying out that song, 'Careless Whisper.' You know it?"

Andy shook her head. He was just being nice. He wasn't flirting. She was the only woman here, and he was the best-looking guy, so it followed that he'd be the one talking with her.

But should she be talking back? He had been at the hospital. Now he was here. That couldn't be right. Andy should go. But she didn't want to go.

Every time the pendulum of doubt swung her away, he managed to charm it back in his direction.

"Here we go." Mike put his phone on the bar so she could see the screen. He'd pulled up a website that listed a bunch of names she had never heard of alongside clubs she would never go to.

To be polite, Andy pretended to read the list. Then she wondered if he was waiting for her to suggest they go to a club together, then she wondered how embarrassing it would be if she asked Mike to go and he said no, then she was finishing her drink in one gulp and motioning for another.

Mike asked, "So, where're you heading to from here?"

Andy almost told him, but she still had a bit of sanity underneath the all-consuming flattery of his attention. "What happened to your head?" She hadn't noticed before, but he had those weird clear strips holding together a not insignificant cut on his temple.

"Weedeater kicked a rock in my face. Does it look bad?"

Nothing could make him look bad. "How did you know he was my father?"

The crooked grin was back. "The weedeater?"

"The guy with us. Driving the car. At the hospital yester—The day before, or whenever." Andy had lost track. "You told my dad you were sorry his family was going through this. How did you know he was my father?"

Mike rubbed his jaw again. "I'm kind of nosey." He spoke with a mixture of embarrassment and pride. "I blame my three older sisters. They were always keeping things from me, so I just kind of got nosey as a way of self-preservation."

"I haven't drunk so much that I didn't notice that you didn't answer the question." Andy never articulated her thoughts this way, which should have been a warning, but she was sick of feeling terrified all of the time. "How did you know he was my dad?"

"Your cell phone," he admitted. "I saw you pull up the text messages and it said DAD at the top, and you texted 'hurry.'" He pointed to his eyes. "They just go where they want to go." As if to prove the point, he looked down at her mouth again.

Andy used her last bit of common sense to turn back toward the bar. She rolled her glass between her hands. She had to stop being stupid with this man. Mike was flirting with her when nobody ever flirted with her. He had been at the hospital and now he was hundreds of miles away in a town whose name Andy had never even heard of before she saw it on the exit sign. Setting aside her criminal enterprises, it was just damn creepy that he was here. Not just *here*, but smiling at her, looking at her mouth, making her feel sexy, buying her drinks.

But Mike lived here. The bartender knew him. And his explanations made sense, especially about Gordon. She remembered Mike hovering at her elbow in front of the hospital while she wrote the text. She remembered the glare that sent him to the bench on the opposite side of the doors.

She asked, "Why did you stay?"

"Stay where?"

"Outside the hospital." She watched his face, because she wanted to see if he was lying. "You backed off, but you didn't go back inside. You sat down on the bench outside."

"Ah." He drank a swig of beer. "Well, I told you that my granny was sick. She's not a nice person. Which is hard, because, well, as my granny herself used to say, when somebody dies, you forget they're an asshole. But at that point when you saw me outside, she wasn't dead yet. She was still alive and disapproving of me and my sisters—especially my sisters—so I just needed a break." He took another drink. He gave her a sideways glance. "Okay, that's not completely truthful."

Andy felt like an idiot, because she had bought the entire story until he'd told her not to.

Mike said, "I saw the news and . . ." He lowered his voice. "I don't know, it's kind of weird, but I saw you in the waiting room and I recognized you from the video, and I just wanted to talk to you."

Andy had no words.

"I'm not a creep." He laughed. "I understand that's what a creep would say, but this thing happened when I was a kid, and . . ." He was leaning closer to her, his voice lower. "This guy broke into our house, and my dad shot him."

Andy felt her hand go to her throat.

"Yeah, it was pretty bad. I mean, shit, I was a kid, so I didn't realize how bad it really was. Plus it turned out to be the guy he shot was dating one of my sisters, but she had broken up with him, and he had all this shit on him like handcuffs and a gag and a knife, and, anyway—" he waved all of that off. "After it happened, I had this sick feeling in my gut all of the time. Like, on the one hand, this guy was going to kidnap my sister and probably hurt her really bad. On the other hand, my dad had killed somebody." He shrugged. "I saw you and I thought, well, hey, there's somebody who knows what it feels like. For, like, the first time in my life."

Andy tilted the vodka to her lips but she did not drink. The story was too good. Somewhere in the back of her head, she could hear warning bells clanging. This was too much of a coincidence. He had been at the hospital. He was here. He had a story that was similar to her own.

But he had the driver's license. And the truck outside. And this was obviously his local bar, and coincidences happened, otherwise there wouldn't be a word called *coincidences*.

Andy stared at the clear liquid in her glass. She needed to get out of here. It was too risky.

"—doesn't make sense," Mike was saying. "If you look at the part where—"

"What?"

"Here, let me show you." He stood up. He turned Andy's barstool so that she was facing him. "So, I'm the bad guy with the knife in his neck, right?"

Andy nodded, only now realizing that he was talking about the video from the Rise-n-Dine.

"Put the back of your left hand here at the left side of my neck like your mom." He had already picked up her left hand and placed it in position. His skin was hot against the back of her hand. "So, she's got her left hand trapped at his neck, and she crosses her other arm underneath and puts her right hand here." He picked up Andy's right hand and placed it just below his right shoulder. "Does that make sense, crossing all the way underneath to put your hand there?"

Andy considered the position of her hands. It was awkward. One arm was twisted under the other. The heel of her palm barely reached into the meaty part of his shoulder.

One hand pushing, one hand pulling.

The calm expression on Laura's face.

"Okay," Mike said. "Keep your left hand where it is, pinned to my neck. Push me with your right hand."

She pushed, but not hard, because her right arm was mostly already extended. His right shoulder barely twinged back. The rest of his body did not move. Her left hand, the one at his neck, had stayed firmly at his neck.

"Now here." He moved her right hand to the center of his chest. "Push."

It was easier to push hard this time. Mike took a step back. If she'd had a knife sticking through the back of her left hand, it would've come straight out of his neck.

Mike said, "Right?"

Andy mentally ran through the motions, saw Laura with the knife, pushing and pulling—but maybe not.

Mike said, "No offense, but we both know your mom knew what she was doing. You don't catch a knife like that, then your next move is to tweak the guy on the shoulder. If you're gonna kill him, you're gonna shove him hard, center mass."

Andy nodded. She was starting to see it now. Laura had not been pushing Jonah away. Her right hand had reached for his shoulder. She was trying to grab onto it.

Mike asked, "Have you looked at her feet in the video?"

"Her feet?"

"You'd step forward, right? If you were planning on yanking out that knife, you'd counterbalance the movement with one foot in front, the other in back. Basic Einstein. But that's not what she does."

"What does she do?"

"She steps her foot out to the side, like this." He slid his feet shoulder-width apart, like a boxer, or like someone who does not want to lose their balance because they are trying to keep another person from moving.

Mike said, "It's Helsinger who starts to step back. Watch the video again. You can see him lift his foot, clear as day."

Andy hadn't noticed any of this. She had assumed that her mother was some kind of cold-blooded killing machine when in fact, her right hand had gone to Jonah Helsinger's shoulder to keep him from moving, not aid in his violent murder.

She asked, "You're sure he was stepping back on his own? Not stepping back to catch himself?"

"That's what it looks like to me."

Andy replayed the familiar sequence in her head. Had Jonah really stepped back? He'd written a suicide note. He'd clearly had a death wish. But was an eighteen-year-old kid really capable of stepping back from the knife, knowing what a horrific death he would be giving himself?

Mike asked, "She said something, right?"

Andy almost answered.

Mike shrugged it off. "The geeks will figure it out. But what I'm saying is, everybody's been watching the faces in the video when they should've been watching the feet."

Andy's head was reeling as she tried to process it in her mind's eye. Was he right? Or was he some kind of Belle Isle truther trying to spread conspiracy theories, and Andy believed him because she so desperately wanted another explanation?

Mike said, "Hey, listen, I gotta go see a man about a dog."

Andy nodded. She wanted time to think about this. She needed to see the video again.

Mike joked, "Don't follow me this time."

Andy didn't laugh. She watched him head to the back of the bar and disappear down a hallway. The men's room door squeaked open and banged closed.

Andy rubbed her face with her hands. She was more than tipsy after all of those stupid gulps from the glass. She needed to think about what Mike had said about the diner video. And consider her own guilt, because she had assumed that her mother was a killer. No one, not Andy, not Gordon, had thought for a moment that Laura was trying to do the right thing.

So why hadn't Laura told that to the cops? Why had she

acted so guilty? And where the hell had Hoodie come from? What about the storage unit?

Every time Andy thought something made sense, the world went sideways again.

Andy started to reach for her drink.

Mike had left his phone on the bar.

She had seen his passcode. Six 3s.

The bartender was watching television. The pool players were arguing about a shot. The long hallway was still empty. She would hear the door when Mike came out of the bathroom. She had heard it when he went in.

Andy picked up the phone. She dialed in the 3s. The home screen had a photo of a cat behind it, and weirdly, she thought a man who had his cat on his phone could not be that bad. Andy tapped Safari. She pulled up the *Belle Isle Review*. The front page had the new photo of Laura at the party, the one she'd seen on CNN. Gordon was not cropped out this time. Andy scanned the story, which was basically the same one that had been there the day before.

She scrolled down for other news. She was more relieved than startled when she saw the headline:

BODY FOUND UNDER YAMACRAW BRIDGE

Andy skimmed the details. Head injury. No ID. Jeans and a black hoodie. Dolphin tattoo on his hip. Found by fishermen. No foul play suspected. Police asking people to come forward with information.

She heard the bathroom door open. Andy closed the browser page. She tapped back to the home screen. She clicked the phone off and had it back on the bar by the time Mike appeared in the hallway.

Andy sipped the vodka.

Unidentified body?

Head injury?

*No foul play?*

Mike groaned as he sat back on the stool. "Had to lift about sixteen thousand pounds of boulders today."

Andy murmured in sympathy, but the new story was her focus now. The Yamacraw Bridge spanned the Tugaloo River. How had Hoodie's body gotten there? Laura couldn't have taken him herself. Even without the police watching, she only had one good arm and one good leg.

What the hell was going on?

"Hello?" Mike was rapping his knuckles on the bar again, this time for Andy's attention. "Past my bedtime. I gotta big job to start tomorrow. Want me to walk you to your car?"

Andy didn't think it was a good idea to stay in the bar alone. She looked around for the bartender.

"He'll put it on my tab." Mike tucked his phone into his pocket. He indicated Andy should go ahead of him. He kept his distance until she got to the door, then he reached ahead to hold it open.

Outside, the heat was only slightly less awful than before. Andy would take another shower before she went to bed. Maybe she would crank down the a/c and climb into the sleeping bag. Or maybe she would climb into the Reliant because wasn't it still weird that she had met Mike here, of all places? And that he was telling her things that she wanted to hear? And that he had walked her out of the bar, which meant he would know where she was going next?

Knepper Knippers. There was lawn equipment in the back of the truck—a weedeater, a leaf blower, some rakes and a shovel. Streaks of dirt and grass were on the side panels. Mike had been in the bar when she got there, not the other way around. His truck was clearly used for lawncare purposes. He had a driver's license with his name on it. He had a tab at the bar, for the love of God. Either he was a clairvoyant psychopath or Andy was losing her mind.

He patted the truck. "This is me."

She said, "I like the grasshopper."

"You're beautiful."

Andy was taken off guard.

He laughed. "That was weird, right? I just met you. I mean,

really met you. And we flirted with each other in a bar and it was nice but it's still kind of strange that we're both here at the same time, right?"

"You keep saying things that I'm thinking in my head, but you say them like they're normal instead of something I should be worried about." Andy wanted to clap her hands over her mouth. She had not meant to say any of that out loud. "I should go."

"All right."

She didn't go. Why had he called her beautiful?

"You've got—" he reached to pick something out of her hair. A piece of fuzz from the cheap motel towel.

Andy wrapped her hand around his, because apparently, Hand-fetish Andy was also a hell of a lot bolder than normal Andy.

"You really are so damn beautiful." He said it like he was in awe. Like he meant it.

Andy leaned her head into his hand. His palm was rough against her cheek. The neon lights from the bar caught the umber in his eyes. She wanted to melt into him. It felt so damn good to be looked at, to be touched, by somebody. By this body. By this weird, attractive man.

And then he kissed her.

Mike was tentative at first but then her fingers were in his hair and the kissing got deeper and suddenly all of Andy's nerves went collectively insane. Her feet left the ground. He backed her into the truck, pressed hard against her. His mouth was on her neck, her breasts. Every single inch of Andy's body wanted him. She had never been so overcome with lust. She reached down to stroke him with her hand, and—

"Keychain," he said.

He was laughing, so Andy laughed, too. She'd felt up the keychain in his front pocket.

Her feet went back to the ground. They were both breathing hard.

She leaned in to kiss him again, but Mike turned away.

He said, "I'm sorry."

*Oh, God.*

"I'm just—" His voice was rough. "I—"

Andy wanted to disappear into the ether. "I should—"

He pressed his fingers to her mouth to stop her. "You really are so beautiful. All I could think about in there was kissing you." His thumb traced across her lips. He looked like he was going to kiss her again, but he took a step back and tucked his hand into his pocket instead. "I'm really attracted to you. I mean, obviously, I'm attracted to you, but—"

"Please don't."

"I need to say this," he told her, because his feelings were the most important thing right now. "I'm not that guy. You know, the one who picks up women in bars and takes them to the parking lot and—"

"I wasn't going to," Andy said, but that was a lie because she'd been about to. "I didn't—"

"Could you—"

Andy waited.

Mike didn't finish his sentence. He just shrugged and said, "I should go."

She kept waiting for more because she was stupid.

"Anyway." He pulled his keys out of his pocket and looped the keychain around his fingers. And then he laughed.

*Please don't make a joke about me giving your keychain a handjob.*

He said, "I could—I mean, I should walk you to—"

Andy left. Her face was on fire as she crossed the road. He was watching her leave again the same way he had watched her leave outside of the hospital. "Idiot, idiot, idiot," Andy whispered, then, "What the fuck? What the *fuck*?"

She felt disgusted with herself as she climbed the stairs to the motel. Mike's truck was pulling onto the road. He was looking up at her as she walked across the balcony. Andy wished for a bazooka to blow him away. Or a gun to kill herself with. She had never hooked up with a stranger. Not even in college. What the hell was wrong with her? Why was she making such stupid decisions? She was a criminal on the run. No one could be trusted. So what if Mike had an Alabama driver's license? Laura had one from Ontario, for fucksakes. She had a fake car. Mike could have a fake truck. The sign with the grasshopper was magnetized, not permanently stuck on. The bartender could've been friendly with Mike because bartenders are always friendly with their customers.

Andy jammed the key in the lock and threw open the door to her room. She was so upset that she barely noted the suitcase and sleeping bag were where she'd left them.

She sat on the bed, head in her hands, and tried not to burst into tears.

Had Mike played her? For what purpose? Was he some freak who was interested in Andy because he saw her on the diner video? He'd sure as hell spent a lot of time figuring out what had happened between Laura and Jonah Helsinger. At least what he thought had happened. He probably had a conspiracy blog. He probably listened to those crazy shows on the radio.

But he had called her beautiful. And he was right about being excited. Unless somehow between opening the front door of the bar and walking to his truck he'd shoved a can of Coke down his pants.

"Christ!"

That stupid keychain.

Andy stood up. She had to pace. She had to go through every single fucking stupid thing she had done. Kissed him too deeply? Too much saliva? Not enough tongue? Maybe her breasts were too small. Or, God, no—

She smelled her bra, which carried the scent of the disgusting hotel soap.

Did guys care about that kind of thing?

Andy covered her eyes with her hands. She sank back to the bed.

The memory of her fingers stroking that stupid keychain in his pocket made her cheeks radiate with heat. He had probably been insulted. Or maybe he hadn't wanted to take advantage of someone who was so painfully inept. What kind of idiot thought a rabbit's foot keychain was a man's penis?

But what kind of grown-ass man kept a giant rabbit's foot in his pocket?

*That guy.*

What the hell did that even mean—*that guy?*

Andy dropped her hands from her face.

She felt her mouth gape open.

The truck.

Not Mike's grasshopper truck or the dead man's truck, but the beat-up old Chevy she had seen parked in the Hazeltons' driveway early this morning.

This morning—

After Andy had killed a man. After she had run down the beach looking for the dead man's Ford because Laura had told her to.

There had been two trucks parked in the Hazeltons' driveway, not one.

The windows had been rolled down. Andy had looked inside the cab. She had considered stealing the old Chevy instead of taking the Ford. It would've been easy, because the key was in the ignition. She had seen it clearly in the pre-dawn light.

It was attached to a rabbit's foot keychain, just like the one that Mike Knepper had taken out of his pocket and looped around his fingers.

# July 31, 1986

## FIVE DAYS AFTER THE OSLO SHOOTING

# 9

Jane Queller woke in a cold sweat. She had been crying in her sleep again. Her nose was raw. Her body ached. She started shaking uncontrollably. Panic made her heart shiver inside of her chest. In the semi-darkness, she thought she was back in Berlin, then in the Oslo hotel room, then she realized that she was in her childhood bedroom inside the Presidio Heights house. Pink wallpaper. Satin pink duvet and pillows. More pink in the rug, on the couch, the desk chair. Posters and stuffed animals and dolls.

Her mother had decorated the room because Jane did not have time to do it herself. From the age of six, almost every waking moment of Jane's life had been spent in front of the piano. Tinkering. Practicing. Playing. Learning. Performing. Touring. Judging. Failing. Recovering. Coaxing. Succeeding. Mastering.

In the early days, Martin would stand behind Jane while she played, his eyes following the notes, his hands on her shoulders, gently pressing when she made a mistake. Pechenikov had requested Martin abandon his post as a condition of taking on Jane as a student, but the tension of Martin's presence had shadowed her career. Her life. Her triumphs. Her failures. Whether she was in Tokyo or Sydney or New York, or even during her three months of isolation in Berlin, Jane could always feel an invisible Martin hovering behind her.

Jane shivered again. She glanced behind her, as if Martin might be there. She sat up and pressed her back against the headboard. She pulled the sheets around her.

*What had they done?*

Nick would argue that they hadn't done anything. Laura Juneau was the one who'd pulled the trigger. The woman had been visibly at peace with the decision. She could've walked away at any time. That she had murdered Martin, then herself, was an act of bravery, and also an act that she had committed alone.

But for the first time in the six years that Jane had known Nicholas Harp, she found herself incapable of believing him.

They had all put Laura on that stage with Martin—Jane, Andrew, Nick, the other cells in the other cities. By Nick's design, they were each a cog in a decentralized machine. A mysterious man on the inside had helped Chicago infiltrate the company that produced the red dye packs that were supposed to be inside the brown paper bag. New York had worked with the document forger in Toronto. San Francisco had paid for airline tickets, hotel rooms, taxi rides and meals. Like Martin's shadow behind Jane, they had all stood invisible behind Laura Juneau as she pulled the revolver from her purse and twice squeezed the trigger.

Was this crazy?

Were they all insane?

Every morning for the last eighteen months Jane had found herself waking up with doubt on her mind. Her emotions would violently swing like the clapper inside a bell. One moment, she would think that they were acting like lunatics—running drills, practicing escapes and learning how to use weapons. Wasn't that ridiculous? Why did Jane have to learn hand-to-hand combat? Why did she need to memorize safe house locations and understand diagrams of false panels and secret compartments? They were just a handful of people, all of them under the age of thirty, believing that they had the wherewithal, the power, to pull off extraordinary acts of opposition.

Wasn't that the very definition of delusional?

But then the next moment, Nick would start speaking and Jane would be convinced beyond a shadow of a doubt that everything they were doing made perfect sense.

Jane put her head in her hands.

She had helped a woman murder her own father. She had planned for his death. She had known it was going to happen and said nothing.

Oslo had taken away the ridiculousness. The skepticism. Everything was real now. All of it was happening.

Jane was losing her mind.

"There you are." Nick came into the room with a mug in one hand and a newspaper in the other. He was wearing his boxer shorts and nothing else. "Drink all of this."

Jane took the mug. Hot tea and bourbon. The last time she'd had a drink was with Laura Juneau in the bar. Jane's heart had been pounding then as it pounded now. Laura had called Jane a chameleon. And she had been right. The woman had no idea that Jane was part of the group. They had talked like strangers, then intimates, then Laura was gone.

*You are a magnificent person*, she had told Jane before leaving. *You are magnificent because you are so uniquely you.*

"More G-men just pulled up." Nick was at the window looking down on the motorcourt. "I'm guessing FBI by the shitty car." He flashed Jane a crooked grin, as if the presence of more feds on top of the CIA, NSA, Interpol, Revenue Agents and Secret Service men they'd already spoken to was a trifle. "You be Bonnie and I'll be Clyde."

Jane gulped the tea. She barely tasted the hot liquid as it scorched into her stomach. Martin had been murdered five days ago. His funeral was tomorrow. Nick seemed to be feeding off the stress, almost giddy during the interviews that more and more felt like interrogations. Jane wanted to scream at him that this was real, that they had murdered someone, that what they were planning next could land them all in prison for the rest of their lives—or worse.

Instead, she whispered, "I'm scared, Nicky."

"Darling." He was on the bed, holding her, before she could ask. His lips were at her ear. "You'll be okay. Trust me. I've been through a hell of a lot worse than this. It makes you stronger. It reminds you why we're doing this."

Jane closed her eyes as she tried to absorb his words. She had lost the point of doing this. Why was she grieving her father? For so many years, she'd truly believed that any love she'd had for Martin had been beaten out of her. So why was Jane so racked with guilt? Why did it hurt every time she remembered that Martin was gone?

"Stop." Nick could always tell when she was troubled. He told her, "Think of something else. Something good."

Jane shook her head. She did not have Nick's talent of compartmentalization. She couldn't even close her eyes without seeing Martin's head exploding. He'd been shot in the temple. Brain and tissue and bone had splattered Friedrich Richter like mud from a car wheel. Then Laura had pulled the trigger again and the top of her head had sprayed up into the ceiling.

*I'm sorry*, Jane had mouthed to the woman seconds before.

Had Laura even known why Jane was apologizing?

"Come on," Nick said, giving Jane a squeeze on the shoulder to bring her back to the present. "Do you remember the first time I met you?"

Jane shook her head again, but only to try to clear the violent images from her mind. The gun. The explosions. The splatter and spray.

"Come on, Jinx," Nick coaxed. "Have you forgotten about the first time we met? It'll be six years in December. Did you know that?"

Jane wiped her nose. Of course she knew. The moment she first saw Nick was etched into every fiber of her being: Andrew and Nick home from college, pushing and shoving each other like schoolboys in the front hall. Jane had stormed out of the parlor to complain about the racket. Nick had smiled at her, and she'd felt her heart fill like a hot-air balloon that threatened to float out of her chest.

"Jinx?"

She knew that he wouldn't give up unless she played along, so she played along, saying, "You barely noticed me."

"You were barely legal."

"I was seventeen." She hated when he treated her like she was a child. Like Andrew, he was only three years her senior. "And you ignored me the entire weekend because you and Andy were chasing after those trashy girls from North Beach."

He laughed. "You would've never given me a chance if I'd fallen all over myself like the other fools."

There were no other fools. No one had ever fallen all over themselves for Jane. Men had looked at her with either awe or boredom, as if she was a doll inside of a glass case. Nick was the first of Andrew's friends who had seen her as a woman.

He stroked back her hair. His mouth went to her ear. He always whispered when he told her the important things. "I didn't ignore you the *entire* weekend."

Jane could not stop her heart from doing the floaty thing again. Even now in this horrible moment, she could still remember the thrill of Nick surprising her in the kitchen. She was reading a magazine when he'd wandered in. Jane had said something flinty to make him go away, and he'd kissed her, wordlessly, before backing out of the room and closing the door.

Nick said, "I was practically an orphan when I met you. I didn't have anybody. I was completely alone. And then I had you." His hand held the back of her neck. He was suddenly serious. "Tell me you're still with me. I have to know."

"Of course." He'd done this in Oslo, then again on the plane home, then their first night back in San Francisco. He seemed terrified that the three months they'd spent apart had somehow weakened her resolve. "I'm with you, Nick. Always."

He searched her eyes for a sign, some indication that she was lying to him the way that everyone else had in his life.

"I am yours," she repeated, firmly. "Every part of me is yours."

"Good girl." His smile was hesitant. He had been hurt by so many people before.

Jane wanted to hold him, but he hated when she got clingy. Instead, she tilted up her face so that he would kiss her. Nick obliged, and for the first time in days, Jane could breathe again.

"My darling," he whispered into her ear. His hands slid under her camisole. His mouth moved to her breasts. Jane was finally able to wrap her arms around him. She didn't want sex, but she knew telling him no again would hurt his feelings. What she craved most was the after. When he held her. When he told her that he loved her. When he made her feel like everything was going to be okay.

That would be the moment to tell him.

As Nick laid her back on the bed, Jane felt all the words she had silently practiced over the last month rush to her lips—*I'm sorry, terrified, ecstatic, overjoyed, anxious, panicky, elated, so scared that you'll leave me because—*

*I'm pregnant.*

"Hello?"

They both sat back up. Jane gripped the sheets around her neck.

"You guys awake?" Andrew knocked on the door before peering into the room. "Everyone decent?"

"Never," Nick said. He still held one of her breasts underneath the sheet. Jane tried to pull away, but Nick snaked his arm around her waist so that she could not. He stroked the small of her back, his eyes on Andrew.

Nick said, "Two more agents pulled into the front drive."

"I saw." Andrew wiped his nose with his sleeve. He was still fighting off the cold from Norway. He told Nick what Jane dared not. "Don't be aggressive with them, Nicky. Please."

They all looked at each other. Nick's hand stroked lower down Jane's back. She felt a flush of heat work its way up her neck and into her face. She hated when he did this sort of thing in front of Andrew.

Nick said, "I feel like we should be touching the sides of our noses like they did in *The Sting*."

"This is real life." Andrew's tone was strident. They were all terrified that the house was bugged. The last few days had been like tiptoeing around the sharp end of a needle. "Our father has been murdered. A woman has been kidnapped. You need to take this seriously."

"I'll at least take it cleanly." Nick bit Jane's shoulder before marching into the bathroom.

Jane pulled the sheets tighter around her neck. She stared at the closed bathroom door. She wanted to go after him, to beg him to listen to Andrew, but she had always lacked the ability to tell Nick that he was wrong about anything.

Andrew said, "Jane—"

She motioned for him to turn around so she could get dressed. He obliged, saying, "Mother was asking for you."

Jane rolled on a pair of pantyhose. The waist felt tight when she stood. "Was that Ellis-Anne you were on the phone with this morning?"

Andrew did not answer. The subject of his ex-girlfriend was somehow off limits now.

Still, she tried, "You were together for two years. She's just—"

"Jane," Andrew repeated, his voice low. He'd been trying to talk to her about Martin since they got home, but Jane was too afraid that speaking to him would open something inside of her that could not be closed.

She told him, "You should go to the doctor." Her fingers fumbled with the tiny pearl buttons on her blouse. She yanked a pair of slacks off the hanger.

"I feel—" His head slowly moved from side to side. "I feel like something is missing inside of me. Like an organ has been taken away. Is that strange?"

Jane tried to zip up the side of her slacks. Her fingers felt clumsy. She had to wipe the sweat off her hands. The pants were tight. Everything was tight because she was pregnant and they had killed their father and they were probably going to kill more people by the time this was over.

"Andy, I can't—" her words were cut off by a sob.

*I can't talk to you. I can't listen to you. I can't be around you because you're going to say what I've been thinking and it will end up tearing us to shreds.*

How had Laura Juneau done it?

Not the physical act—Jane had been there, she had witnessed every single detail of the actual murder and suicide—but how had Laura flipped that switch inside of herself that turned her into a cold-blooded killer? How could the kind, interesting woman whom Jane had smoked with in the conference center bar be the same woman who had taken a gun from her purse and murdered a man, then herself?

Jane kept coming back to the expression of absolute serenity on Laura Juneau's face. It was the slight smile on the woman's lips that had given her away. Clearly, Laura had been totally at peace with her actions. There was no hesitation. Not a moment of second thought or doubt. When Laura's hand had reached into her purse to find the revolver, she might as well have been looking for a pack of chewing gum.

"Jinx?" Andrew had turned back around. There were tears in his eyes, which made Jane cry even harder. "Let me help with this."

She watched him tug up the zipper on the side of her slacks. His breath had a sickly smell. His skin looked clammy. She said, "You've lost weight."

"Here it is." He playfully pinched the new roll of fat ringing her waist. "Nick said we'll get through this, right? And Nick's always right, isn't he?"

They smiled, but neither one of them laughed out loud, because they didn't know whether or not Nick was listening on the other side of the door.

"We should try to pull ourselves together." Jane found some tissue. She handed it to Andrew, then took some for herself.

They both blew their noses. Andrew coughed. The rattle in his chest was like marbles clicking together.

She put her hand to his forehead. "You need to go to the doctor."

He shrugged, asking, "When?"

The bathroom door opened. Nick came out, naked, toweling his hair dry. "What'd I miss?"

Andrew offered, "I'll go downstairs before Jasper comes looking for us."

"You go, too," Nick told Jane. "Wear the boots. They're more intimidating."

Jane found a pair of black socks in the drawer. She slipped them on over her pantyhose. She held up a few pairs of boots before Nick nodded that she'd found the right ones. She was leaning over to do up the buckles when she felt Nick pressing behind her. He talked to Andrew as his hands rubbed her lower back. "Jane's right. You should make time to go to the doctor. We can't have you sick for the—the funeral."

Jane felt bile slide up her throat as she finished buckling her riding boots. She didn't know if it was the awful morning sickness or the fear. From the beginning, Nick had been playing these unnecessary verbal games. Jane knew he got a thrill out of picturing an FBI agent sitting in a surveillance van down the street, hanging on his every word.

He put his mouth to her ear again. "Knock them out, my darling."

She nodded, telling Andrew, "Ready."

Nick slapped her ass as she left the room. Jane felt the same deep flush of embarrassment from before. It was pointless to ask him to stop because begging only made him worse.

Andrew let Jane precede him down the front stairs. She worked to cool the heat in her face. She knew that Nick had grown up unloved, that it was important to him that people understood he belonged, but she hated when he treated her like a hunting trophy.

"Okay?" Andrew asked.

Jane realized she'd put her hand to her stomach. She had not told Andrew or anyone else about the baby. At first, she'd persuaded herself that it was because she wanted Nick to be the first to know, but as the weeks had passed, she'd realized that she was terrified that he would not want the baby and she would have to explain to everyone why she was no longer pregnant.

*Next time*, he'd told her the last time. *We'll keep it next time.*

"Miss Queller?" a man was waiting for them in the front hallway. He had his wallet open to a gold shield. "I'm Agent Barlow with the FBI. This is Agent Danberry."

Danberry was standing inside the parlor with his hands clasped behind his back. He looked like a lesser version of Barlow: less hair, less confidence, less teeth, even, because he appeared to be missing an upper cuspid. He had been talking to Jasper, who was dressed in his Air Force Reserve uniform. Medals and colorful bars lined her brother's chest. Jasper was twelve years older than Jane, the over-protective brother who had always been her anchor. He had attended her concerts and asked about her schoolwork and taken her to the prom when no one else would. Jane had always seen him as a miniature adult, a heroic figure who played with his toy soldiers and read military history books but could reliably be depended upon to scare the hell out of any boy who dared hurt her feelings or to give her cash so she could buy lipstick.

"Miss Queller?" Agent Barlow repeated.

"I'm sorry," Jane apologized, taking a tissue from the box on the coffee table.

Barlow seemed chastened. "My condolences on your loss."

Jane wiped her eyes as she looked in the mirror behind the couch. Her skin felt raw. Her eyes were swollen. Her nose was bright red. She had been crying for almost five days straight.

"Take your time," Barlow offered, but he seemed anxious to begin.

Jane blew her nose as quietly as she could.

Nick had made them practice their statements for hours, but nothing could prepare Jane for the stress of being interviewed. The first time, she had sobbed uncontrollably, panicked that she would say the wrong thing. In subsequent interviews, Jane had realized that the tears were a godsend, because crying was what was expected of her. Andrew, too, seemed to have figured out a strategy. When a tough question was put to him, he would sniff and wipe his eyes and turn his head away while he considered his answer.

It was Nick who made them nervous—not just Jane and Andrew, but anyone who happened to be in the room. He seemed to get a perverse pleasure from taunting the agents, going right up to the line, then inventing an innocent explanation that pulled them back from the brink.

Watching him with the Secret Service agents yesterday, Jane had wondered if he was suicidal.

"Jinx?" Jasper said.

They were all waiting for her to sit down. She perched on the edge of the couch. Andrew sat beside her. Barlow sat on the couch opposite with his hands on his knees. Only Jasper and Danberry remained standing, one to pace and the other, seemingly, to inspect the room. Instead of asking a question, Danberry opened an onyx box on one of the bookshelves and peered inside.

Across from her, Barlow took a notebook out of his breast pocket and thumbed through the pages. His eyes moved back and forth as he silently read through the notes.

Jane looked at Andrew, then Jasper, who shrugged.

This was new. The other agents had started with small talk, asked about the house, the decorations. It was Andrew who usually gave them the rundown. The parlor, like the rest of the house, was a gothic-beaux-arts mishmash, with spindly furniture and velvet wallpaper between the dark mahogany panels. The twin chandeliers had belonged to some ancient Queller who'd worked with Mr. Tiffany on the design. The coffee table was from sequoias felled by her mother's side of the family. A grown man could stand comfortably inside the fireplace. Rumor had it that the rug was gotten off a Japanese family who'd been sent to an internment camp during the war.

Andrew shifted on the couch. Jasper resumed pacing.

Barlow turned a page in his notebook. The noise was like sandpaper in the silence. Danberry had tilted his head to the side so he could read the titles on the spines of books.

Jane had to do something with her hands. She found a pack of cigarettes on the coffee table. Andrew struck a match for her. He was staying only partially still beside her. He kept randomly tapping his foot. Jane wondered how it would look if she reached over to still his leg. Or if she asked Barlow to please begin. Or if she screamed as loud as she could until everyone left and she could go back upstairs and find Nick.

This was a manipulation tactic, obviously. Barlow and Danberry were ramping up everyone's nerves so that they would make stupid mistakes.

Silently, Jane went through the questions that all the other agents had asked.

*Have you ever met the real Alexandra Maplecroft? What did Laura Juneau say to you at the conference? Why didn't you know she was an imposter? Where do you think the real Dr. Alexandra Maplecroft is?*

Kidnapped.

The answer to the last question was common knowledge. The ransom note had been printed on the front page of yesterday's *San Francisco Chronicle*—

*We have Dr. Alexandra Maplecroft, a tool of the fascist regime . . .*

"Miss Queller?" Barlow was finally looking up from his notebook. "I'm just going to sum up what we already know from the other interviews you've given."

Jane could barely manage a nod. Her body had gone rigid with tension. Something was different about these two men. With their wrinkled suits and stained ties and missing teeth and bad haircuts, they looked like TV parodies of G-men, but they would not be here if they were second or third string.

"Here we go," Barlow said. "You'd never met Laura Juneau before the conference. You might've recognized her name from before, when her husband killed their children, because the story was in the newspapers. You were in Berlin to fill in for a friend at a studio for two months. You—"

"Three," Jasper corrected.

"Right, three months. Thank you, Major Queller." Barlow kept his focus on Jane as he continued, "You've never met Dr. Alexandra Maplecroft before and you've only heard her name in relation to your father, because she was a rival who—"

"No," Jasper said. "In order to be rivals, you have to be equals. Maplecroft was a nuisance."

"Thank you again, Major." Barlow clearly wanted Jasper to shut up, but instead, he continued, "Miss Queller, first, I'd like to talk about your discussion with Mrs. Juneau at the bar."

Jane blinked, and she could see the delighted look on Laura's face when she recognized Jane tapping out "Love Me Two Times" on the bar top.

Barlow asked, "Did you approach Mrs. Juneau or did she approach you?"

Jane's throat felt so tight that she had to cough before she could speak. "I did. I was on the piano, playing the piano, when she walked in. I assumed she was American because of—"

"The way she was dressed," Barlow finished. "You wanted to speak to an American after being in Germany for so long."

Jane felt a sick kind of dizziness. Why had he finished the sentence for her? Was he trying to prove that he'd talked to the other agents, that they'd all compared notes, or was he just trying to get her to move along?

Or, most terrifying of all, had Nick made them practice too much? Were their word choices, their gestures, their comments, so rehearsed that they'd managed to throw up flags?

Jane parted her lips. She tried to pull air into her lungs.

Barlow asked, "What did you and Mrs. Juneau talk about?"

Jane felt a pressing weight on her chest. The room suddenly felt stifling. She put the cigarette in the ashtray, worked to line it up in the groove. Her hand was trembling again. She didn't know what to do, so she told them the truth. "She'd seen me play a few years back. We talked about the performance. And about music in general."

"So, Bach, Beethoven, Mozart?" Barlow seemed to be plucking names from thin air. "Chopin? Chacopsky?"

*Tchaikovsky*, Jane almost corrected, but she caught herself at the last moment because—was it a trick? Had she told another agent something else?

Andrew coughed again. He picked up the cigarette that Jane had left smoldering in the ashtray.

Barlow prompted, "Miss Queller?"

Jane found the tissues and blew her nose. She willed the panic back down.

*Stick to the truth*, Nick had coached them. *Just make sure it's not the whole truth.*

"Well . . ." Jane tried not to rush her words. "We spoke about Edvard Grieg, because he's Norwegian. A-ha, the pop music group, also Norwegian. Martha Argerich, from Argentina. I'm not sure why she came up, but she did."

"Did you see Juneau go into the bathroom?" Barlow studied Jane closely as she shook her head. "Were you in the bathroom at any point before the shooting?"

"It was a long conference. I'm sure I was." Jane was aware that her voice was shaking. Was that a good thing? Did it make her story sound more believable? She looked at Danberry. He'd been circling the room like a shark. Why wasn't he asking any questions?

Barlow said, "There was tape residue behind one of the toilet tanks. We think the gun was hidden there."

"Fantastic," Jasper said. "Then you'll have fingerprints. Case closed."

"They wore gloves." Barlow asked Jane, "So, what we've been

told is, before the murder, you'd heard about Laura and Robert Juneau. What about Maplecroft?"

"Juneau and Maplecroft in the front parlor," Nick bellowed, choosing this moment to make his appearance. "Good God, they sound like characters from the Canadian version of Clue. Which one had the candlestick?"

Everyone had turned to look at Nick standing in the entryway. He had somehow managed to take all of the air out of the room. Jane had seen him do this countless times before. He could bring the tone up or down like a deejay turning the knob on a record player.

"Mr. Harp," Barlow said. "Nice that you can join us."

"My pleasure." Nick walked into the room with a self-satisfied grin on his face. Jane kept her eyes on Barlow, who was taking in Nick's fine features. The agent's expression was neutral, but she could feel his distaste. Nick's good looks and charm either worked for him or against him. There was never any in between.

"Now, gentlemen." Nick put a proprietary arm behind Jane as he wedged himself between Jane and Andrew on the couch. "I'm assuming you've already been told that none of us knew either Maplecroft or Juneau before Martin was murdered?" His fingers combed through the back of Jane's hair. "Poor girl has been broken up about it. I don't see how anyone could have that many tears inside of them."

Barlow held Nick's gaze for just a moment before turning to Andrew, asking, "Why weren't you and Mr. Harp on the same flight out of San Francisco?"

"Nick left a day ahead of me." Andrew took out his handkerchief and wiped his nose. "He had business in New York, I believe."

"What kind of business?"

Andrew looked puzzled, because Barlow wasn't asking Nick these questions.

"Major Queller." Barlow made a point of turning his head toward Jasper. "How is it that your family knows Mr. Harp?"

"Nick's been with us for years." Jasper's tone was even, which was surprising because he had never cared for Nick. "We've taken him on vacations, spent holidays together. That sort of thing."

Andrew added, "His family lives on the East Coast. Nick was sort of orphaned out here. Mother and Father welcomed him as one of the family."

Barlow asked, "He was sent out here at the age of fifteen, wasn't he?" He waited, but no one spoke. "Got into some trouble with the police back home? Mother shipped him across the country to live with his granny?"

"Nick told us all about it." Andrew glanced nervously at Nick. "It was a tough road, but he still managed to get into Stanford."

"Right." Barlow looked back at his notes. They were doing the silent thing again.

Nick affected indifference. He brushed imaginary lint from his trousers. He gave Jane a quick wink. Only she could feel the tension inside his body. His arm behind her shoulders had gone taut. She could feel his fingers digging into her skin.

*Was he mad at her? Should she be defending him? Should she tell the agents that Nick was a good man, that he'd managed to pull himself up from the gutter, that they had no right to treat him this way because he was—*

Losing.

Nick didn't see it now, but he had lost the game the minute he'd walked into the room. He had been making fun of the government agents for days, railing against their stupidity, bragging about his own cleverness. He had not realized that they were just as capable of putting on an act as he was.

Jane took a stuttered breath. She had started to cry again. Nothing was more terrifying than watching him try to punch his way out of a tight spot.

"Mr. Queller." Barlow looked up at Andrew. "Did Mr. Harp mention to you that he attended one of Dr. Maplecroft's lectures?"

Andrew shot Jane a frightened look that mirrored her own feelings: *What should they say? What did Nick want?*

"I can answer that one," Nick offered. "If you'd like me to?"

"Why not?" Barlow sat back on the couch.

Behind him, Danberry opened and closed another box.

Nick made them wait.

He reached for the cigarette in the ashtray. He inhaled audibly, then blew out a stream of smoke. He tapped off some ash. He lined the cigarette up with the groove in the marble ashtray. He leaned back against the couch. His arm went behind Jane.

Finally, he looked up, pretending to be surprised that they were all waiting on him. "Oh, you want my answer now?"

Danberry crossed his arms.

Jane swallowed back a flood of bile that rushed up her throat.

Nick asked Barlow, "Do you have a record of my attendance at this lecture?"

"According to her assistant, Dr. Maplecroft didn't believe in keeping attendance."

"Pity."

"We'll be talking to other students this week."

"That must be quite an undertaking," Nick said. "How many kids are at Berkeley now? Thirty, forty thousand?"

Barlow gave a heavy sigh. He opened his notebook again. He resumed the game, directing his words toward Andrew. "At the conference, when Mr. Harp approached Laura Juneau, who was at that time posing as Dr. Maplecroft, Mr. Harp mentioned attending one of Dr. Maplecroft's lectures. The police officer and the girl working the check-in table both heard him say the same thing."

Andrew said, "I wasn't there for that part of the conversation, but I'm sure Nick can—"

"Are you aware that Mr. Harp has a drug conviction?"

Nick snapped, "Are you aware that Mr. Queller does?"

"Christ," Jasper muttered.

"Just making sure they have the facts," Nick said. "It's a felony to lie to an FBI agent. Isn't that correct, Mr. Danberry?"

Danberry kept silent, but Jane could tell he'd picked up on

the fact that Nick had not been here when the agents had introduced themselves. Jane could've told him that he was likely listening at the top of the stairs. She had learned the hard way that Nick was a stealthy eavesdropper.

Andrew volunteered, "Two years ago, I was convicted for possession of cocaine. I performed community service in exchange for my record being expunged."

Nick added, "That kind of thing doesn't stay a secret in times like these, does it?"

Barlow quipped, "It does not."

Jane tried not to wince as Nick ran his fingers roughly through her hair. He told Barlow, "I met Laura Juneau in the KLM lounge at Schiphol. We were both en route to Oslo. She approached me. She asked if the seat next to me was taken. I said no. She introduced herself as Dr. Alexandra Maplecroft. She said she recognized me from one of her lectures, which could be true, but honestly, gentlemen, I was stoned out of my mind during most of my classes, so I'm hardly a reliable witness."

"Hardly," Barlow echoed.

Danberry still said nothing. He'd made it to the Bösendorfer Imperial Concert Grand on the other side of the room. Jane tried not to bristle when he soundlessly glided his fingers over the extra bass keys.

Barlow said, "So, Mr. Harp, as far as you can recall, you met Dr. Maplecroft for the first time at the Amsterdam airport, then you met her for the second time in Oslo?"

"That's right," Nick agreed. Jane could have cried with relief when he returned to the script. "In order to be polite, I pretended to recognize the woman whom I thought was Dr. Maplecroft. Then I saw her again at the conference and again pretended in order to be polite." His shoulder went up in a shrug. "I think the operative word here is 'pretend,' gentlemen. She pretended to know me. I pretended to know her. Only one of us had darker intentions."

Barlow made a mark in his notepad.

Andrew picked up his part. "At the conference, Nick introduced me to the Juneau woman as Dr. Maplecroft. I recognized the name, if not the face. There aren't many photographs of Maplecroft in circulation, as I'm sure you've realized now that you're searching for her. I believe I said something to the fake Maplecroft about being on Father's panel. She didn't have a badge, so I asked if there was a problem with the check-in." He shrugged the exact same way that Nick had shrugged. "That was the extent of my interaction with the woman. The next time I saw her, she was murdering my father."

Jane flinched. She couldn't help it.

Barlow said, "That's a very tidy explanation."

Nick said, "Most explanations are. The ones that are complicated are the ones I'd look out for." He smoothed out the leg of his trousers. "But you know, gentlemen, it seems to me that I've already told this to your compatriots. We all have, endlessly. So, I think I'll make my exit."

Neither agent moved to stop him.

Nick hesitated only slightly before he kissed Jane on the mouth, then crossed the room in long strides. Jane felt her heart drop when he took a left instead of a right. He wasn't going upstairs to wait for her.

*He was leaving.*

The front door opened and closed. She felt the sound reverberate like a knife to her heart. She had to part her lips again to take in breath. She was torn between relief to have him gone and fear that she would never see him again.

"I'm sorry Nick is such an ass," Jasper told Barlow. "But he does have a point. We can't keep doing this. The answers are not going to change."

Barlow said, "This is an active investigation. The people who orchestrated the Oslo assassination still have Dr. Maplecroft."

"Which is a tragedy," Jasper said. "However, there's nothing my family can do about it."

Barlow said, "The ransom note for Dr. Maplecroft asked for an admission of guilt from your father's company. They blame him for Robert Juneau's murderous spree."

"It's the family's company." Jasper had been sensitive about this since taking over last year. "The kidnappers also asked for one million dollars, which is preposterous. We can't take responsibility for the actions of a madman. Do you know how many homes Queller Healthcare runs? Just in the Bay Area?"

"Fifteen," Andrew answered, but only Jane heard him.

Barlow said, "The kidnappers are calling themselves the Army of the Changing World. You've never heard of them?"

Both Jane and Andrew shook their heads.

Across the room, Danberry closed the fallboard on the piano. Jane felt her heart lurch. The ivory would yellow without sunlight.

Jasper picked up on her distress. He asked her, "Shouldn't that be up?"

She shook her head. Nick would tell her to let the keys yellow. To skip practice. To stop pushing herself so hard. Martin could not punish her from the grave.

"Major Queller?" Barlow was waiting. "Have you heard of the Army of the—"

"Of course not." Jasper edged close to losing his cool, but brought himself back quickly. "I don't have to tell you how damaging those lies are to the company. We were meant to go public this week. We've got some very powerful investors who are getting very antsy about this mess. The charges the kidnappers made are ludicrous. We don't torture sick people, for Chrissakes. This isn't Soviet Russia."

Danberry tried, "Major Queller—"

"My father was a good man," Jasper insisted. "He made some controversial statements, I'll admit, but he always had the good of the family, the good of the country, in his mind. He was a patriot. His mission in life was to serve others, and that's what got him killed."

"No one here is disagreeing with that."

"Look." Jasper moderated his tone. "Laura Juneau obviously had a screw loose. We may never know why she—"

"The why is pretty clear." Andrew spoke quietly, but they

were all listening. "Robert Juneau was kicked out of half a dozen Queller group homes. He should've been hospitalized, but there was no hospital to go to. You can say the system failed him, but we're the system, Jasper. Queller is the system. Ergo—"

"Ergo, shut the hell up, Andy." He glared at Andrew, fire in his eyes. "The company could be ruined by this idiotic bullshit. The investors could pull out completely. Do you understand that?"

"I need some air." Jane stood up. Andrew and Barlow did the same. She felt dizzy. Her stomach flipped. She had to look down at the floor as she walked away. Her boots might as well have been crossing a spinning wheel. She wanted to go to the bathroom and throw up or cry or just sit there, alone, and try to figure out what was happening.

*Where had Nick gone?*

Was he mad at Jane? Had she made a mistake? Had she been silent when Nick wanted her to defend him? Would he be angry? Would he shut her out again?

Jane couldn't be shut out again. She couldn't take it. Not now. *Not when she was carrying his child.*

Instead of going into the bathroom or stopping in the kitchen to leave a desperate message on Nick's answering machine, she walked to the back of the house and went outside.

She stood on the patio with her eyes closed and tried to breathe. The fresh air made her feel like the band around her chest was loosening. She looked up at the cloudy sky. She could see a tiny sliver of sun behind the Golden Gate Bridge. Morning fog still laced the Marin Headlands. There was a chill in the air, but Jane didn't want to go back inside for her sweater.

She saw signs on the wrought iron table that her mother had been here: Annette's lipstick-stained teacup, a full ashtray, the newspaper held down by a cut glass paperweight.

Jane's eyes scanned the front page of the *Chronicle*, though she knew the ransom letter by heart. Nick had bragged about its cleverness, even as Jane worried that it made them sound like evil super villains in a cartoon—

*This is a direct communication from the Army of the Changing World. We have kidnapped Dr. Alexandra Maplecroft, a tool of the fascist regime, a pawn in the dangerous game played by Martin Queller and his so-called healthcare company. We demand an apology for the part that Martin Queller played in the genocide of the Juneau family and other families across the greater California area. Queller Healthcare must be stopped. They have systematically exploited, tortured and beaten patients in their institutions. More lives will be lost if—*

"Nice digs."

Jane startled.

"Sorry." Agent Danberry was standing in the doorway. He had an unlit cigarette in his mouth. He stared at the view with open admiration. "My apartment, I can see the alley I share with my neighbor. If I open the window, I get to smell the puke from the junkies sleeping it off."

Jane didn't know what to say. Her heart was hammering so hard that she was sure he could see it moving beneath her blouse.

"They closed it a few years ago," he said. "The bridge. Wind gusts." He took the cigarette out of his mouth. "That piano in there—probably could pay off my car, right?"

The Bösendorfer could likely buy him fifty new cars, but he wasn't here to talk about pianos.

"What're the extra keys for?" He waited.

And waited.

Jane wiped her eyes. She couldn't just stand here crying. She had to say something—anything—about the bridge, the fog, the view, but her mind was so filled with panic that even the most innocuous observation could not make its way to her mouth.

Danberry nodded, as if this was expected. He lit his cigarette. He stared past the trees at the bridge. The distant bray of foghorns floated up from the rocks.

Jane looked up at the bridge, too. She thought of the first time she'd stood with Nick in the backyard to watch the fog roll in. It wasn't until that moment that Jane had realized that she'd taken the view for granted. Only Nick had understood how lucky they were.

Danberry said, "I saw you play once."

Jane knew what he was doing—trying to steer her to something familiar, to make her comfortable.

"My wife dragged me to a club on Vallejo. Keystone Korner. This was a long time ago. They've moved across the Bay, I heard." He pulled out a chair for Jane. She had no choice but to sit. He said, "I know this is hard for you."

Jane wiped her eyes with her fingers. The skin felt burned by her tears.

He took a seat without being asked. "What were you doing in Germany?"

Jane knew the answer to the question, at least the one she was supposed to give.

"Miss Queller?"

She forced out the word, "Working." Her voice was barely more than a whisper. She had to pull herself together. They had practiced this. It was just like a performance. All the notes were in her head. She just had to coax them out with her fingers.

She rubbed her throat to relax the muscles. She said, "It was meant to be temporary. I was filling in for a friend in Berlin as a session pianist."

"West Berlin, I hope."

He smiled, so Jane smiled.

He told her, "I know what you're thinking: we know what you did over there. We know where you lived. We know where you worked, where you ate lunch, that you went to the East sometimes. We also know your flight to Oslo was out of East Berlin, which isn't unusual over there, right? The fares are cheaper." He looked back at the house. "Not that you need to save money, but who can pass up a bargain?"

Jane felt the panic start to return. Did he really know everything, or was this a trick?

He asked, "How was East Germany?"

She tried to see past his question. Did they think she was a communist? A spy?

He said, "I hear everybody watches you. Like, what you're doing, who you're talking to, what you're saying." He tapped his cigarette into the overfull ashtray. "Kind of like me right now, huh?"

He smiled again, so Jane smiled again.

Danberry asked, "They let them listen to music over there?"

Jane chewed her lip. She heard Nick's voice in her head: *If they try to make you comfortable, let them think they're making you comfortable.*

Danberry said, "A little Springsteen, maybe some Michael Jackson?"

She pushed out the well-rehearsed words, "Popular music is frowned upon, but it's not completely *verboten.*"

"Music is freedom, right?"

Jane shook her head. There was no script for this.

"It's like—" He held out his hands, fingers splayed. "It moves people. Inspires them. Makes them wanna dance or grab a gal and have a good time. It's got power."

Jane felt herself nodding, because that was exactly how she'd felt watching the impromptu concerts the students had put on in Treptow Park. She'd wanted desperately to tell Nick about them, but she had to be careful about Germany because she didn't want him to feel left out.

Danberry asked, "You political?"

She shook her head. She had to play the game.

*They'll know you've never voted.*

She told the agent, "I've never even voted."

"You do a lot of volunteering, though. Soup kitchens. Homeless shelters. Even that AIDS ward they set up over at UCSF. Not afraid you'll catch it?"

Jane watched him smoke his cigarette.

He said, "Rock Hudson shocked the hell out of me. Never would've thought he was one of them." He stared up at the Golden Gate, asking, "Was your dad playing matchmaker?"

*Don't answer the question if you don't understand it.*

Danberry explained, "You went away to Germany for three months. Your boyfriend stayed here catting around with your brother." He glanced at her, then looked back at the bridge. "Ellis-Anne MacMillan said the break-up with Andrew was very unexpected. But they usually are."

*Don't let them surprise you into reacting.*

He asked, "So, the old man flies Mr. Harp to Norway for what? To get you two kids back together?"

*Just give them the facts. Don't over-explain.*

She told him, "Nick and I were never apart. I was in Berlin for a job. He had to stay here for work." Jane knew she should stop talking, but she could not. "Father gave him the job at Queller. He probably wanted Nick in Oslo for himself. The panel with Maplecroft was a big deal. Nick's very charming, very easy to be around. People have always liked him. They're drawn to him. Father was no exception. He wanted to help Nick up the ladder."

"Guys like that always fall up."

Jane chewed the tip of her tongue. She had to look away so that he did not catch the anger in her eyes. She had never been able to abide anyone running down Nick. He'd suffered so much as a child. People like Danberry would never understand that.

"He's got charisma, right?" Danberry put out the cigarette on the bottom of his shoe and tossed the butt into the ashtray. "The pretty face. The quick wit. The cool clothes. But it's more than that, right? He's got that thing some guys have. Makes you want to listen to them. Follow them."

The wind picked up, rustling the edges of the *Chronicle*. Jane folded the paper closed. She saw the garish headline: $1,000,000 RANSOM OR PROF DIES!

A ridiculous headline for a ridiculous manifesto. Nick had made them all sound unhinged.

Danberry said, "'Death to the fascist insect that preys on the life of the people.'"

Jane didn't recognize the line from the ransom note. She pretended to skim the paper.

Danberry said, "It's not in there. I was talking about the Patty Hearst kidnapping. That's how the Symbionese Liberation Army signed all of their screeds—'Death to the fascist insect that preys on the life of the people.'" He studied her face. "Your family has another house near the Hearsts, right? Up in Hillsborough?"

"I was a kid when it happened."

His laugh said that he thought she still was a kid. "Carter couldn't free the hostages, but he got Patty Hearst out of lock-up."

"I told you I don't follow politics."

"Not even in college?" He said, "My old man told me everybody's a socialist until they start paying taxes."

She mirrored his smile again.

"Do you know where the word 'symbionese' comes from?"

Jane waited.

"The SLA's leader, Donald DeFreeze—the jackass didn't know the word 'symbiotic,' so he made up the word 'symbionese.'" Danberry leaned back in the chair, crossed his ankle over his knee. "The newspapers called them terrorists, and they committed acts of terror, but all terror cells are basically cults, and all cults usually have one guy at the center who's driving the bus. Your Manson or your Jim Jones or your Reverend Moon."

*They'll seem almost nonchalant the closer they get to the point.*

"DeFreeze was a black fella, an escaped con doing five-to-life for rolling a hooker, and like a lot of cons, he had a lot of charisma, and the kids who followed him—all of them white, middle class, most of them in college—well, they weren't stupid. They were worse. They were true believers. They felt sorry for him because he was this poor black guy in prison and they were spoiled white kids with everything, and they really believed all the shit that came out of his mouth about fascist insects and everybody living together all Kumbaya. Like I said, he had that thing. Charisma."

*Pay attention to the words they repeat because that's the point of the story.*

Danberry said, "He had everybody in his circle convinced he was smarter than he actually was. More clever than he was. Fact is, he was just another con man running another cult so he could bed the pretty girls and play God with all the boys. He knew when people were pulling away. He knew how to bring them back on side." Danberry looked at the bridge. His shoulders were relaxed. "They were like yo-yos he could snap back with a flick of his wrist."

*Make eye contact. Don't look nervous.*

"So, anyway." Danberry clasped his hands together and rested them on his stomach. "What happened was, most of the kids following him ended up shot in the head or burned to death. And I have to tell you, that's not uncommon. These anarchist groups think they're doing the right thing, right up until they end up in prison or flat on their backs in the morgue."

Jane wiped her eyes. She could see everything he was doing, but felt helpless to stop him.

*What would Nick do? How would he throw it back in Danberry's face?*

"Miss Queller," Danberry said, then, "Jinx." He leaned forward, his knees almost touching her leg.

*They'll get in your space to try to intimidate you.*

He said, "Look, I'm on your side here. But your boyfriend—"

"Have you ever seen someone shot in the head?" The stunned look on his face told Jane she'd found the right mark. Like Nick, she let herself draw power from his mistake. "You were so cavalier when you said those kids ended up getting shot in the head. I'm just wondering if you know what that looks like."

"I didn't—" He reeled back. "What I meant—"

"There's a hole, a black hole no larger than the size of a dime, right here"—she pointed to her own temple where Martin

Queller was shot—"and on the opposite side, where the bullet exits, you see this bloody pulp, and you realize that everything that makes up that person, everything that makes them so who they are, is splattered onto the floor. Something a janitor will mop up and toss down the drain. Gone. Forever."

"I—" His mouth opened and closed. "I'm sorry, Miss Queller. I didn't—"

Jane stood. She went back into the house and slammed the door behind her. She used her hand to wipe her nose as she walked down the hallway. She couldn't keep up this façade much longer. She had to get out of here. To find Nick. To tell him what was going on.

Her purse was on the sideboard. Jane rummaged for her keys, and then she realized that Nick had taken them.

*Where had he gone?*

"Jinx?" Jasper was still in the parlor. He was sitting on the couch beside Andrew. They both had drinks in their hands. Even Agent Barlow, standing by the fireplace, had a glass of whisky.

"What is it?" Jasper stood up when she entered the room.

"Are you okay?" Andrew was standing, too. They both looked alarmed, almost angry. Neither one of them had ever been able to abide seeing her upset.

"I'm all right," she patted her hands in the air to calm them. "Please, could I just have someone's keys?"

"Take mine." Jasper gave Andrew his keys. "Andy, you drive her. She's in no condition."

Jane tried, "I'm not—"

"Where do you want to go?" Andrew was already heading to the closet for their jackets.

Jasper had his hand in his pocket. "Do you need some money?"

"No." Jane didn't have the strength to fight both of her brothers. "I need to find—" She was aware that Barlow was listening. "Air. I need some air."

Barlow asked, "Not enough of it in the backyard?"

Jane turned away from him. She did not wait for Andrew. She grabbed her purse off the table. She walked out the front door, down the front steps. Jasper's Porsche was parked beside the garage.

"I've got it." Andrew had jogged to catch up with her. He reached down to open the door.

"Andy—" Jane grabbed his arm. Her knees felt weak. She could barely stand.

"It's okay," he said, trying to help her into the car. "Just play it cool."

"No," she said. "You don't understand. They know."

# 10

They were too afraid to speak openly in the car. Jasper was not a part of this, but only they knew that. The FBI or CIA or NSA or whoever could have planted bugs in any of the crevices inside the Porsche. Even the car phone could be tapped.

Before Oslo, before every branch of law enforcement had swept down on the Presidio Heights house, before Agent Danberry had cornered Jane in the backyard, it had felt ridiculously paranoid when Nick had told them to assume that every familiar place was monitored, that someone was always going to be listening. To speak openly, they were supposed to find a park or a random café. They had to sneak down alleys and walk through buildings and say the passwords and know the interrogation techniques and practice self-defense and drill themselves over and over again so that they had their stories right.

*The stories had been too right.*

Jane could see that now. As she replayed all the conversations with all the agents over the last five days, she could see how their interrogators had registered certain phrases, certain gestures, in their notepads, to compare later.

*I pretended to recognize the woman whom I thought was Dr. Maplecroft.*

*Only one of us had darker intentions.*

*I wanted to speak to an American after being in Germany for so long.*

"Pull over," Jane told Andrew, fear twisting her stomach into knots. She pushed open the door before the car fully stopped. Her boots skipped across the pavement. They were inside the city proper. There was no grass, just concrete. Jane had no choice but to vomit on the sidewalk.

*I met Laura Juneau at the KLM lounge at Schiphol.*

*I could tell she was an American by the way she was dressed.*

Jane retched so hard that she was on her knees. Her stomach clenched out dark bile. She hadn't been able to eat more than toast and eggs since the murder. The tea that Nick had given her this morning tasted like bark as it burned its way up her throat.

*Nick. She had to find Nick so he could explain how they were all going to be fine.*

"Jinx." Andrew's hand was on her shoulder. He was kneeling beside her.

Jane sat back on her heels. She wiped her mouth. There was a tremble in her fingers that she could not get rid of. It was as if the bones were vibrating beneath her skin.

*Theyknowtheyknowtheyknow . . .*

Andrew asked, "Are you okay?"

Her laugh had an edge of uncontrollability.

"Jane—"

"None of us is okay." Saying the words inserted some sanity into this madness. "It's all closing in on us. They talked to Ellis-Ann."

"I kept her out of this. She doesn't know anything."

"*They* know everything." How could he not see this? "My God, Andy. They think we're in a cult."

He laughed. "Like the People's Temple? The Manson Family?"

Jane wasn't laughing. "What are we going to do?"

"Stick to the plan," he said, his voice low. "That's what it's there for. When in doubt, just let the plan lead the way."

"The plan," Jane repeated, but not with his reverence.

The stupid fucking plan. So carefully plotted, so relentlessly discussed and strategized.

*So wrong.*

"Come on," Andrew said. "We'll find a café and—"

"No." Jane had to find Nick. He could solve this for them. Or maybe he already had. Just the thought of Nick taking control immediately soothed some of her jagged nerves. Maybe what had happened with Danberry and Barlow was part of a larger, secret plan. Nick did that sometimes—made them all think they were about to walk into the path of an oncoming train, only to reveal at the last minute that he was the cunning conductor braking at the last possible moment to keep them out of harm's way. He tested them like this all of the time. Even in Berlin, Nick had asked Jane to do things, to put herself in danger, just to make sure she would obey.

He had so much trouble trusting people. Everyone in his family had turned their backs on him. He had been forced to live on the streets. He had managed to pull himself up entirely on his own. Time and again, he had trusted people who had hurt him. It was no wonder that Jane had to repeatedly prove herself.

*They were like yo-yos he could snap back with a flick of his wrist.*

"Jane," Andrew said.

She felt Danberry's words echoing in her head. Was she like a yo-yo? Was Nick a con man? A cult leader? How different was he from Jim Jones? The People's Temple had started out doing wonderful things. Feeding the homeless. Taking care of the elderly. Working to eradicate racism. And then a decade later, over nine hundred people, many of them children, were killed by cyanide-laced Kool-Aid.

*Why?*

"Jane, come on," Andrew said. "The pigs don't *know* anything. Not for certain."

Jane shook her head, trying to banish the dark thoughts. Nick had said that the police would try to separate them, that their psyches would be poked and prodded in the hope that they would eventually turn on each other.

*If nobody speaks, then no one will know.*

Did Nick really believe the crazy-sounding things that came out of his mouth, or was this how he pulled Jane back in? She had spent six years of her life chasing after him, pleasing him, loving him, fighting with him, breaking up with him. She always went back. No matter what, she always found her way back.

*Snap.*

"Come on. Let's get out of here."

Jane let Andrew help her up. "Take me to Nick's apartment."

"He won't be there."

"We'll wait for him." Jane got back into the car. She searched her purse for some tissue. Her mouth felt like it was rotting from the inside. Maybe it was. Maybe everything was rotting, even the child they had made.

She anticipated Nick's wry reaction—*problem solved.*

"It's going to be okay," Andrew turned the key. The Porsche fishtailed as he pulled away from the curb. "We just need to drive a bit. Maybe we'll swing by Nick's?"

Jane was confused by his avuncular tone, but then she realized that Andrew was talking for the bug that might be in the car.

She told him, "Danberry compared Nick to Donald DeFreeze."

"Field Marshal Cinque?" Andrew gave her a careful look. He instantly got the portent of Danberry's observation. "Does that make you Patricia Hearst?"

She said it again, "They think we're in a cult."

"Do Hare Krishnas drive Porsches?" Andrew didn't realize that she wanted a real answer. He was still speaking for the benefit of a phantom listener. "Come on, Jinx. This is crazy. The pigs don't like Nick, which is understandable. He's being an asshole for no reason. Once they figure out he's playing them, they'll move on to investigating the real bad guys."

Jane wondered if Andrew had accidentally hit on the truth. Why did Nick have to constantly play games? They were supposed to be taking this seriously—and since Oslo, everything had become deadly serious. What they were about to do in San Francisco, Chicago, and New York would bring the full weight of the federal government down on them. Nick couldn't keep flying so close to the sun. They would all end up plummeting into prison cells.

"It's nothing," Andrew said. "We're not a cult, Jinx. Nick has been my best friend for seven years. He's been your boyfriend for six. Those agents are focused on him because they have to focus on someone. There always has to be a boogeyman with those people. Even David Berkowitz blamed his neighbor's dog."

Jane felt no relief from his cavalier words. "What if they don't move on?"

"They'll have to. Our father was murdered in front of our eyes."

Jane winced.

"The FBI won't fail us. Jasper won't let that happen. They'll catch whoever did this."

She shook her head. Tears streamed down her cheeks.

*That was exactly what she was worried about.*

The car banked around a steep curve.

Jane put her hand to her throat. The sickness threatened to return. She looked out the window and watched the houses blur by. She thought about Nick because that was the only thing that kept her from breaking down. Jane had to stop questioning him, even if only in her mind. The one thing Nick could not abide was disloyalty. That was the reason for his tests while she was in Berlin—sending Jane to a biker bar near the Bornholmer checkpoint, airmailing her a dime-bag of cocaine to sell to a university student, sending her into the police station to report a stolen bike that had never existed.

Nick had told her at the time that he was helping Jane practice, honing her ability to adapt to dangerous situations. That she could've been raped in the bar, arrested for the coke or charged with making a false police report had never occurred to him.

Or maybe it had.

Jane took a deep breath as Andrew steered into another curve. She held onto the strap. She watched him weave in and out of traffic with barely a glance over his shoulder.

*Evasive maneuvers.*

They had driven repeatedly to San Luis Obispo and back, three or four cars at a time, working on their driving skills. Nick, predictably, had been the best of all of them, but Andrew was a close second. They were both naturally competitive. They both shared a dangerous disregard for life that allowed them to speed and swerve with moral impunity.

Andrew coughed into the crook of his elbow so he wouldn't have to take his hands off the wheel. They were going deeper into the city. His eyes were trained on the road. In the sunlight, she could see the faint line of a scar along his neck where he'd tried to hang himself. This was three years ago, after he'd taken too many pills but before he'd shot up enough heroin to stop his heart. Jasper had found him hanging in the basement. The rope was thin, a clothesline, really, with a metal wire that had gouged out a slice of Andrew's skin.

Jane was overwhelmed with a mixture of grief and regret every time she saw the scar. The truth was that, at the time of the attempt, she had hated her brother. Not because Andrew was older or because he teased her about her knobby knees and social awkwardness, but because, for most of his life, Andrew had been a drug addict, and there was nothing he would not do in service of his addiction. Robbing Annette. Fighting with Jasper. Stealing from Martin. Relentlessly dismissing Jane.

*Cocaine. Benzodiazepine. Heroin. Speed.*

She was twelve years old when it became clear that Andrew was an addict, and like most twelve-year-olds, she only saw his misery through her own lens of deprivation. As she got older, Jane had been forced to accept that the shape of her life would always bend around her brother. To understand that the entire family would forever be held hostage to what Martin called Andrew's weakness. The arrests, the treatment facilities, the court appearances, the favors called in, the money handed under the table, the political donations—continually sucked away all of her parents' attention. Jane had never had a normal life, but Andrew took away any hope of a peaceful, sometimes ordinary existence.

By the time she'd turned sixteen, Jane had lost track of the family meetings about Andrew's problem, the screaming and blame-laying and accusations and beatings and haranguing and hope—that was the worst part of it all—the hope. Maybe this time he'll quit. Maybe this birthday or Thanksgiving or Christmas he'll show up sober.

And maybe, just maybe, this concert or performance that was so important to Jane; the first one where she had been allowed to choose her own music, the special one to which she had devoted thousands of hours of practice, would not be overshadowed by another overdose, another suicide attempt, another hospitalization, another family meeting where Martin railed and Jasper glowered and Jane sobbed while Andrew pleaded for more chances and Annette drank herself into a blameless stupor.

Then, suddenly, Nick had gotten Andrew clean.

The arrest on the cocaine possession two years ago had been an eye-opener for both of them, but not in the expected, relentlessly hoped for, way. They had been arrested by an Alameda County sheriff's deputy, otherwise Martin would have as usual made the charge go away. The Alameda deputy had dealt with too many spoiled rich kids before. He was determined to see the case through the court system. He'd threatened to go to the newspapers if some kind of justice was not meted out.

Which was how Andrew and Nick had ended up living at the Queller Bayside Home, the last group home that Robert Juneau had been kicked out of.

That was where Laura had found Nick. Nick had introduced her to Andrew. Then Nick had formulated a plan, and that plan had finally given Andrew a cause that urgently demanded his sobriety.

The Porsche screeched to a halt. They were outside Nick's

apartment complex, a squat, low building with a wobbly metal railing around the upper-floor balcony. He didn't live in the best area, but it wasn't the worst the city had to offer, either. The place was clean. The homeless people were kept at bay. Still, Jane hated that Nick couldn't live at the Presidio Heights house with the rest of them.

Except that now he could.

*Right?*

"I'll go check," Andrew said. "You stay here."

Jane opened the car door before Andrew could stop her. A sense of urgency overwhelmed her. All of the doubts she'd had for the last half hour would be wrapped up in Nick's arms and explained away. The sooner she was with him, the better she would feel.

"Jinx," Andrew called, trailing behind her. "Jinx, wait up."

She started to run, tripping over the sidewalk, heading up the rusty metal stairs. Her boots were stiff and hurt her feet but Jane did not care. She could feel that Nick was inside his apartment. That he was waiting. That he might be wondering what had taken them so long, that maybe they no longer cared about him, had lost their faith in him.

She *had* lost faith. She *had* doubted him.

She wasn't a fool. She was a monster.

Jane ran harder. Every step felt like it was taking her farther away. Andrew jogged behind her, calling her name, telling her to slow down, to stop, but Jane could not.

She had let Agent Danberry get into her head. Nick was not a con man or a cultist. He was a survivor. His first memory was of watching his mother screw a police officer, still in uniform, who paid her in heroin. He'd never known his father. A series of pimps had beaten and abused him. He'd attended dozens of schools by the time he hitchhiked across the country to find his grandmother. She'd hated him on sight, woke him up in the middle of the night kicking and screaming at him. He'd been forced into the streets, then lived in a homeless shelter, while he finished school. That Nick had managed to get into Stanford despite all of these hardships proved that he was smarter, more clever, than anybody had ever given him credit for.

Especially Agent Danberry with his missing tooth and cheap suit.

"Jinx," Andrew called from the other end of the balcony. He was walking slowly because he couldn't run anymore. She could hear his coughing from thirty feet away.

Jane reached into her purse for the key—not the one she kept on the chain, but the one for emergencies that she kept in the zippered pocket. Her hands were shaking so hard that she dropped the key. She bent down to get it. Sweat covered her palms.

"Jinx." Andrew was leaning over, hands on his knees, wheezing.

Jane opened the door.

She felt her world tilt off center.

Nick wasn't there.

Worse, his stuff wasn't there. The apartment was almost empty. All of his cherished things—the leather couch he'd spent hours thinking about, the tasteful glass side tables, the hanging lamp, the plush brown carpet—all of it was gone. There was just a large, overstuffed chair facing the back wall. The beautiful brass and glass kitchen table set was gone. The big television. The stereo with its giant speakers. His record collection. The walls were bare; all of his cherished art was gone, even the pieces that Andrew had drawn for him.

She almost fell to her knees. Her hand went to her chest as she felt her heart tear in two.

Had Nick abandoned them?

*Abandoned her?*

She put her hand to her mouth so that she wouldn't start screaming. She walked on shaky legs into the middle of the room. None of his magazines, his books, his shoes left by the balcony door. Each missing item was like an arrow piercing her heart. Jane was so terrified that she almost felt numb. All of the worst thoughts spun through her head—

He had left her. He knew that she was doubting him. That

she had stopped believing in him, if just for a moment. He had disappeared. He had overdosed. He had found someone else.

*He had tried to kill himself.*

Jane's knees buckled as she tried to walk down the hall. Nick had threatened to kill himself more than once and the thought of losing him was so wrenching to Jane that each time she had cried out like a child, begging him to please stay with her.

*I can't live without you. I need you. You are the breath in my body. Please never leave me.*

"Jane?" Andrew had made it to the door. "Jane, where are you?"

Nick's bedroom door was closed. She had to brace herself against the wall as she made her way down the hallway. Past the bathroom—toothbrush, toothpaste, no cologne, no shaving set, no brush and comb.

More arrows slicing open her heart.

Jane stopped outside the bedroom. Her hand could barely grip the doorknob. There was not enough air to fill her lungs. Her heart had stopped its steady beat.

She pushed open the door.

A strangled sound came from her throat.

No bed with its puffy duvet. No side tables with matching lamps. No antique chest of drawers Nick had lovingly refinished. Only a sleeping bag was rolled out on the bare floor.

The closet door was open.

Jane started crying again, almost sobbing from relief, when she saw that his clothes were still hanging on the rack. Nick loved his clothes. He would never leave without them.

"Jinx?" Andrew was beside her, holding her up.

"I thought—" Her knees finally sunk to the floor. She felt sick again. "I thought he—"

"Come back through here." Andrew lifted her to standing and practically carried her out of the room.

Jane leaned into him as they walked up the hallway, her feet dragging across the bare floor. He took her into the living room. He flipped the light switch. Jane squinted from the glare. Even the light fixtures were missing. Bare bulbs hung from the sockets. Except for the massive chair that looked like it belonged on the street, everything that Nick had ever cared for was gone.

His clothes were still in the closet. He would not leave his clothes.

*Would he?*

"Is—" she couldn't say the words. "Andrew, where—"

Andrew put his finger to his lips, indicating that there might be someone listening.

Jane shook her head. She couldn't play this game anymore. She needed words, assurances.

"It's all right." Andrew gave her that careful look again, like she was missing something important.

Jane looked around the room, desperate for some kind of understanding. What could she be missing in this bare space?

*The bare space.*

Nick had gotten rid of his things. He had either sold them or given them away. Was he cleverly foiling the police so they didn't have anywhere to plant their listening devices?

Jane couldn't stand any more. She sat on the floor, tears of relief flooding from her eyes. That had to be the answer. Nick hadn't left them. He was fucking with the pigs. The almost-empty apartment was just another one of Nick's games.

"Jinx?" Andrew was clearly concerned.

"I'm all right." She wiped her tears. She felt foolish for making such a scene. "Please don't tell Nick I was so upset. Please."

Andrew opened his mouth to respond, but a cough came out instead. Jane winced at the wet, congested sound. He coughed again, then again, and finally walked into the kitchen where he found a glass drying by the sink.

Jane wiped her nose with the back of her hand. She looked around the room again, noticing a small cardboard box beside the hideous chair. Her heart fluttered at the sight of the framed photo resting on the top.

Nick had given away almost everything but this—

Jane and Nick last Christmas at the Hillsborough house.

Smiling for the camera, but not for each other, despite the proprietary arm Nick had draped over her shoulders. Jane had been out on tour for the previous three weeks. She had come back to find Nick antsy and distracted. He had kept insisting there was nothing wrong. Jane had kept begging him to speak. It had gone on like that for hours, sunset to sunrise, until finally, Nick had told Jane about meeting Laura Juneau.

He had been smoking a cigarette outside the front gates of the Queller Bayside Home. This was after the cocaine bust in Alameda County. Both he and Andrew were serving their court-mandated sentence. That Nick had met Laura was pure happenstance. For months, she'd been looking for a way into Queller. She had approached countless patients and staff in search of someone, anyone, who could help find proof that her husband had been screwed over by the system.

In Nick, Laura had found a truly sympathetic listener. For most of his life, he had been told by those in authority that he didn't matter, that he wasn't smart enough or from the right family or that he did not belong. Pulling in Andrew must have been even easier. Her brother had spent most of his life focused on his own wants and needs. Directing that attention toward another person's tragedy was his way out of the darkness.

*I felt so selfish when I heard her story*, Andrew had told Jane. *I thought I was suffering, but I had no idea what true suffering really is.*

Jane wasn't sure at what point Nick had brought in other people. That's what he did best—collected stragglers, outsiders, people like him who felt that their voices were not being heard. By that Christmas night at the Hillsborough house when Nick had finally told Jane about the plan, there were dozens of people in other cities who were ready to change the world.

Was it Laura who'd first come up with the idea? Not just Oslo, but San Francisco, Chicago, and New York?

Queller Healthcare was one company in one state doing bad things to good people, but going public would infuse the company with enough cash to take their program of neglect nationwide.

The competition was clearly working from the same business plan. Nick had told Jane stories about treatment facilities in Georgia and Alabama that were kicking patients out into the streets. An institution in Maryland had been caught dropping mentally incapacitated patients at bus stops in the harshest cold of winter. Illinois had a waitlist that effectively denied coverage for years.

As Nick had explained, Martin would be the first target, but meaningful change required meaningful acts of resistance. They had to show the rest of the country, the rest of the world, what was happening to these poor, abandoned people. They had to take a page from ACT UP, the Weather Underground, the United Freedom Front, and shake these corrupt institutions to their very foundations.

Which was fantastical.

*Wasn't it?*

The truth was that Nick was always either outraged or excited about something. He wrote to politicians demanding action. Mailed angry letters to the editors of the *San Francisco Gate*. Volunteered alongside Jane at homeless shelters and AIDS clinics. He was constantly drawing ideas for incredible inventions, or scribbling notes about new business ventures. Jane always encouraged him because Nick following through on these ideas was another matter entirely. Either he thought the people who could help him were too stupid or too intransigent, or he would grow bored and move on to another thing.

She had assumed that Laura Juneau was one of the things Nick would move on from. When she'd realized that this time was different, that Andrew was involved, too, that they were both deadly serious about their fantastical plans, Jane couldn't back out. She was too afraid that Nick would go on without her. That she would be left behind. A niggling voice inside of Jane always reminded her that she needed Nick far more than he needed her.

"Jinx." Andrew was waiting for her attention. He was holding the Christmas photograph in his hands. He opened the back of the frame. A tiny key was taped to the cardboard.

Jane caught herself before she could ask what he was doing. She glanced nervously around the room. Nick had told them cameras could be hidden in lamps, tucked inside potted plants or secreted behind air-conditioning vents.

She realized now that Nick had removed all the vents. Nothing was left but the open mouths of the ducts that had been cut into the walls.

*It's only paranoia if you're wrong.*

Andrew handed Jane the key. She slipped it into her back pocket. He returned the photo to its place on the cardboard box.

As quietly as possible, he pushed the heavy, overstuffed chair over onto its side.

"What—" the word slipped out before she could catch it. Jane stared her curiosity into her brother.

*What the hell is going on?*

Andrew's only response was to yet again put his finger to his lips.

A groan escaped from his mouth as he got down on his knees. He yanked away the material along the bottom of the chair. Jane strangled back the questions that wanted to come. Instead, she watched her brother take apart the chair. He bent back a section of the metal springs. He reached deep into the foam and pulled out a rectangular metal box that was about four inches thick and as tall and wide as a sheet of legal paper.

Jane felt her muscles tense as she thought about all the things that could be inside the box: weapons, explosives, more photographs, all sorts of things that Jane did not want to see because Nick didn't hide something unless he did not want it to be found.

Andrew put the box on the floor. He sat back on his heels. He was trying to catch his breath, though all he'd done was tip over a chair. The harsh lights did his complexion no favors. He looked even sicker now. The dark circles under his eyes were rimmed with tiny dots of broken blood vessels. The wheeze in his breath had not abated.

"Andy?"

He tucked the box under his arm. "Let's go."

"What if Nick—"

"Now."

He shoved the chair back onto its legs. He waited for Jane to walk ahead of him, then he waited for her to lock the door.

Jane kept her mouth closed as she crossed the balcony. She could hear their heavy footsteps against the concrete, the sharp click of her boots, the hard clap of Andrew's loafers. His wheezing was more pronounced. Jane tried to keep the pace slow. They were on the first landing to the stairs when he put out his hand to stop her.

Jane looked up at her brother. The wind rustled his hair. Sunlight cut a fine line across his forehead. She wondered how he was managing to stay upright. His face had taken on the pallor of a dead person.

She felt safe to ask, "What are we doing, Andrew? I don't understand why we had to leave. Shouldn't we wait for Nick?"

He asked, "Back at the house, did you hear Jasper telling those feds what a good man Father was?"

Jane couldn't joke about Jasper right now. She was terrified that he'd somehow get pulled into this thing that none of them could control. "Andrew, please, will you tell me what's going on?"

"Jasper defended Father because he's just like him."

Jane wanted to roll her eyes. She couldn't believe he was doing this now. "Don't be so cruel. Jasper loves you. He always has."

"It's you he loves. And that's fine. It's good that he looks after you."

"I'm not a child who needs a minder." Jane couldn't keep the peevishness out of her tone. They had fought about Jasper since they were little. Andrew always saw the worst in him. Jane saw him as her savior. "Do you know how many times Jasper took me to dinner when Father was in one of his moods, or helped me pick out something to wear when Mother was too drunk, or tried to talk to me about music or listened to me cry about boys or—"

"I get it. He's a saint. You're his perfect baby sister." Andrew sat down on the stairs. "Sit."

Jane begrudgingly sat on the step below him. There were so many things she could say about Jasper that would only hurt Andrew, like the way that, every time Andrew overdosed or disappeared or ended up in the hospital, it was Jasper who made sure that Jane was okay.

Andrew said, "Give me the key."

She retrieved it from her pocket and handed it over. Jane studied his face as he worked the key in the lock. He was still breathing hard, sweating profusely despite the cool breeze.

"Here." Andrew finally opened the lid on the metal box.

Jane saw that it was filled with file folders. She recognized the Queller Healthcare logo printed along the bottoms.

"Look at these." Andrew handed her a stack of files. "You know Father got Nick a job at corporate."

Jane chewed her tongue so she didn't snap that of course she knew that her boyfriend was working for her father's company. She scanned the forms inside the folders, trying to understand why they were important enough for Nick to hide. She easily recognized the patient packets with billing codes and intake forms. Martin routinely brought them home in his briefcase, then Jasper started doing the same when he joined the business.

Andrew said, "Nick's been snooping around."

This, too, was not news. Nick was their man on the inside, as he liked to say. Jane flipped through the forms. Patient names, social security numbers, addresses, billing codes, correspondences with the state, with medical professionals, with accounting. Queller Bayside Home. Queller Hilltop House. Queller Youth Facility.

She told Andrew, "We've seen these before. They're part of the plan. Nick is sending them to the newspapers."

Andrew flipped through the folders until he found what he was looking for. "Read this one."

Jane opened the file. She immediately recognized the name on the admitting form.

ROBERT DAVID JUNEAU.

She shrugged. They knew that Robert Juneau had been at Bayside. Everyone knew. It was the place where all of this had started.

He said, "Look at the admitting dates."

She read aloud: "April 1–22, 1984; May 6–28, 1984; June 21–July 14, 1984." She looked back up at Andrew, confused, because they knew all of this, too. Queller had been gaming the system. Patients who stayed at the facilities for longer than twenty-three days were considered long-term patients, which meant that the state paid a lower daily rate for their care. Martin's way around the lowered rate was to kick out patients before they could hit the twenty-three-day mark, then re-admit them a few days later.

Jane said, "This is going to be released after Chicago and New York. Nick has the envelopes ready to go to the newspapers and the FBI field offices."

Andrew laughed. "Can you really see Nick sitting around stuffing almost one hundred envelopes? Licking stamps and writing out addresses?" He pointed to the file in Jane's hands. "Look at the next page."

She was too stressed and exhausted to play these games, but she turned the form over anyway. She saw more dates and summed them up for Andrew. "Twenty-two days in August, again in September, then in . . . Oh."

Jane stared at the numbers. The revulsion she had felt for her father became magnified.

Robert Juneau had murdered his children, then killed himself, on September 9, 1984. According to the information in his file, he'd continued to be admitted and re-admitted to various facilities for the next six months.

*Queller facilities.*

Her father had not just exploited Robert Juneau's injuries for profit. He had kept the profit rolling in even after the man had committed mass murder and suicide.

Jane had to swallow before she could ask, "Did Laura know that Father did this? I mean, did she know before Oslo?" She looked up at Andrew. "Laura saw these?"

He nodded.

Her hands were shaking when she looked back down. "I feel like a fool," she said. "I was guilty—feeling guilty—this morning. Yesterday. I kept remembering these stupid moments when Father wasn't a monster, but he was—"

"He was a monster," Andrew said. "He exploited the misery of thousands of people, and when the company went public, he would've exploited hundreds of thousands of more, all for his own financial gain. We had to stop him."

Nothing that Nick had said over the last five days had made Jane feel more at peace with what they had done.

She paged to the back of Robert Juneau's file. Queller had made hundreds of thousands of dollars off of Robert Juneau's death. She found paid invoices and billing codes and proof that the government had continued to pay for the treatment of a patient who'd never needed a clean bed or medication or meals.

Andrew said, "Turn to—"

Jane was already looking for the Intervening Report. A senior executive had to sign off on all multiple re-admissions so that an advisory board could convene to discuss the best course of action to get the patient the help that he needed. At least, that was what was supposed to happen because Queller Healthcare was allegedly in the business of helping people.

Jane scanned down to the senior executive's name. Her heart fell into her stomach. She knew the signature as well as she knew her own. It had appeared on school forms and blank checks that she took to the mall to buy clothes or when she got her hair cut or needed gas money.

Jasper Queller.

Her eyes filled with tears. She held up the form to the light. "It must be forged or—"

"You know it's not. That's his signature, Jinx. Probably signed with his special fucking Montblanc that Father got him when he left the Air Force."

Jane felt her head start to shake. She could see where this was going. "Please, Andrew. He's our brother."

"You need to accept the facts. I know you think that Jasper's your guardian angel, but he's been part of it the whole time. Everything Father was doing, he was doing, too."

Jane's head kept shaking, even though she had the proof right in front of her. Jasper had known that Robert Juneau was dead. He'd talked to Jane about the newspaper stories. He'd been just as horrified as Jane that Queller had so spectacularly failed a patient.

And then he had helped the company make money off of it.

Jane grabbed the other files, checked the signatures, because she was certain this had been some kind of mistake. The more she looked, the more desperate she felt.

Jasper's signature was on every single one.

She worked to swallow down her devastation. "Are all of these patients dead?"

"Most of them. Some moved out of state. Their patient credentials are still being used to charge for treatment." Andrew explained, "Jasper and Father were running up the numbers. The investors were getting antsy that the public offering wasn't going to be as much."

*The investors.* Martin had taken them on a few years ago so he could buy out the competition. Jasper was obsessed with the group, as if they were some sort of all-seeing monolith who could destroy them on a whim.

Andrew said, "Jasper has to be stopped. If the company goes public, he'll be sitting on millions of dollars in blood money. We can't let that happen."

Jane felt a quiver of panic. This was exactly how it had started with Martin. One bad revelation had followed another bad revelation and then suddenly Laura Juneau was shooting him in the head.

Andrew said, "I know you want to defend him, but this is indefensible."

"We can't—" Jane had to stop. This was too much. All of this was too much. "I won't hurt him, Andy. Not like Father. I don't care what you say."

"Jasper's not worth the bullet. But he has to pay for this."

"Who are we to play—" She stopped herself again, because they had played God in Oslo and none of them had blinked until the second it was over. "What are you going to do?"

"Release it to the newspapers."

Jane grabbed his arm. "Andy, please. I'm begging you. I know Jasper hasn't been the perfect brother to you, but he loves you. He loves both of us."

"Father would've said the same thing."

His words were like a slap. "You know that's different."

Andrew's jaw was set. "There's a finite amount of money in the system to take care of these people, Jinx. Jasper stole those resources to keep the investors happy. How many more Robert Juneaus are out there because of what our brother did?"

She knew he was right, but this was Jasper. "We can't—"

"It's no use arguing, Jinx. Nick's already put it into play. That's why he told me to come here first."

"First?" she repeated, alarmed. "First before what?"

Instead of answering, Andrew rubbed his face with his hands, the only sign that any of this was bothering him.

"Please." She could not stop saying the word. Her tears were on an endless flow.

*Think of what destroying Jasper will do to me,* she wanted to say. *I can't hurt anyone else. I can't turn off that switch that makes me feel responsible.*

Andrew said, "Jinx, you've got to know that this decision is not up to us."

She understood what he was telling her. Nick wanted revenge—

not just for the bad things that Jasper had done, but for snubbing him at the dinner table, looking down his nose at Nick, asking pointed questions about his background, making it clear that he was not *one of us*.

Andrew reached into the metal box again. Jane cringed when he pulled out a bundle of Polaroid photos. Andrew took off the rubber band and snapped it around his wrist.

She whispered, "Don't."

He ignored her, carefully studying each photo, a catalog of the beating that Jane had endured. "I'll never forgive Father for doing this to you." He showed her the close-up of her pummeled stomach.

The first time, not the last time, that Jane had been pregnant.

"Where was Jasper when this happened, Jane?" Andrew's anger had sparked. He could not be talked down. "I own my part. I was stoned. I didn't give a shit about myself, let alone anybody else. But Jasper?"

Jane looked into the parking lot. Her tears kept falling.

"Jasper was home when this happened, wasn't he? Locked in his room? Ignoring the screaming?"

They had all ignored the screaming when it was happening to someone else.

"Jesus." Andrew studied the next photo, the one that showed the deep gash in her leg. "Every time over the last few months, if I felt my nerve slipping, Nick would take these out to remind us both of what Father did to you." He showed Jane the close-up of her swollen eye. "How many times did Father hit you? How many black eyes did we ignore at the breakfast table? How many times did Mother laugh or Jasper kid you about being so un-coordinated?"

She tried to make light of it, saying her family nickname, "Clumsy Jinx."

Andrew said, "I will never let anyone hurt you again. Ever."

Jane was so tired of crying, but she seemed incapable of stopping herself. She had cried for Laura Juneau's broken family.

She had cried for Nick. She had cried, inexplicably, for Martin, and now she cried from shame.

Andrew sniffed loudly. He put the rubber band back around the Polaroids and dropped them into the box. "I'm not going to ask you if you knew about the gun."

Jane smoothed together her lips. She kept her gaze steady on the parking lot. "I'm not going to ask you, either."

He took in a wheezy, labored breath. "So, Nick—"

"Please don't say it." Jane's hand was pressed flat to her stomach again. She longed for Laura Juneau's serenity, her righteousness of cause.

Andrew said, "Laura had a choice. She could've left when she found the gun in the bag."

The same words from Nick had not brought Jane any comfort. She knew that Laura would never have backed out. The woman was determined, totally at peace with her choice. Maybe even glad of it. There was something to be said for being the master of your own fate. Or, as Nick had said, taking out a bastard with you.

Jane said, "She seemed nice."

Andrew made himself busy closing the lid on the box, checking the lock.

She repeated, "She just seemed really, really nice."

He cleared his throat several times. "She was a wonderful person."

His tone spoke to his anguish. Nick had put Andrew in charge of handling Laura. He was her sole point of contact for the group. It was Andrew who'd walked Laura through the details, given her the money, relayed information on flights, where to meet the forger in Toronto, how to present herself, what secret words would open this door or close the other.

He asked Jane, "Why did you talk to her? In Oslo?"

Jane shook her head. She could not answer the question. Nick had warned them that anonymity was their only protection if things went sideways. Jane, ever-eager to follow his orders, had been hiding in the bar when Laura Juneau walked in. There was less than an hour before the panel. It was too early to drink and Jane knew she shouldn't be drinking anyway. The piano had always worked to soothe her nerves, but for some inexplicable reason, she'd been drawn to Laura sitting alone at the bar.

"We should go," Andrew said.

Jane didn't argue. She just followed him silently down the steps and to the car.

She held the metal box in her lap as he started the engine and headed deeper into the city.

Jane struggled to keep her thoughts away from Jasper. Neither could she ask Andrew where they were going. It wasn't just the possibility of hidden listening devices that was keeping her brother silent. Her gut told her that there was something else going on. Jane's time in Berlin had somehow managed to remove her from the circle. She had noticed it in Oslo and it was especially obvious now that they were all back home. Nick and Andrew had been going for long walks, lurking in corners, their voices quickly dying down when Jane appeared.

At first she had thought they were managing her guilt, but now she wondered if there were other things that they didn't want her to know about.

Were there more hidden boxes?

Who else was Nick planning to hurt?

The car crested a hill. Jane closed her eyes against the sudden, bright sunlight. She let her mind wander back to Laura Juneau. Jane wanted to figure out what had motivated her to approach the woman in the bar. It was exactly the wrong thing to do. Nick had repeatedly warned Jane that she needed to stay far away from Laura, that interacting with her would only make the pigs look at Jane more carefully.

He'd been right.

She had known he was right when she was doing it. Maybe Jane had been rebelling against Nick. Or maybe she had been drawn to Laura's clarity of purpose. Andrew's coded letters had been filled with reverence for the woman. He'd told Jane that, out of all of them, Laura was the one who never seemed to waver.

*Why?*

"Look for a space," Andrew said.

They had already reached the Mission District. Jane was familiar with the area. As a student, she used to sneak down here to listen to punk bands at the old fire station. Around the corner were a homeless shelter and a soup kitchen where she often volunteered. The area had been a focal point for fringe activities as far back as when the Franciscan Friars built the first Mission in the late 1700s. Bear fighting and duels and horse races had given way to impoverished students and homeless people and drug addicts. There was a violent energy emanating from the abandoned warehouses and dilapidated immigrant housing. Anarchist graffiti was everywhere. Trash littered the street. Prostitutes stood on corners. It was the middle of the morning, but everything had the dark, dingy tint of sundown.

She said, "You can't park Jasper's Porsche here. Someone will steal it."

"They've never touched it before."

*Before*, Jane thought. *You mean all of those times the brother you claim to hate drove down here in the middle of the night to rescue you?*

Andrew tucked into a space between a motorcycle and a burned-out jalopy. He started to get out of the car, but Jane put her hand over his. His skin felt rough. There was a patch of dry skin on his wrist just under his watch. She started to comment on it, but she did not want words to intrude on this moment.

They had not been alone together since before they'd left the house. Since Laura Juneau had fired that last bullet into her skull. Since the *politi* had rushed both Jane and Nick from the auditorium.

The policemen had mistaken Nick for Andrew, and by the time they had figured out why Jane was screaming for her brother, Andrew was banging his fists on the door.

He'd looked almost deranged. Blood had stained the front of

his shirt, dripped from his hands, soaked his trousers. Martin's blood. While everyone was running away from the stage, Andrew had run toward it. He had pushed aside the security. He had fallen to his knees. The next day, Jane would see a photograph of this moment in a newspaper: Andrew holding in his lap what was left of their father's head, his eyes raised to the ceiling, his mouth open as he screamed.

"It's funny," Andrew said now. "I didn't remember that I loved him until I saw her pointing the gun at his head."

Jane nodded, because she had felt it, too—a wrenching of her heart, a sweaty, cold second-guessing.

When Jane was a girl, she used to sit on Martin's knee while he read to her. He had placed Jane in front of her first piano. He had sought out Pechenikov to hone her studies. He had attended recitals and concerts and performances. He had kept a notebook in the breast pocket of his suit jacket in which he recorded her mistakes. He had punched her in the back when she slumped at the keyboard. He had switched her legs with a metal ruler when she didn't practice enough. He had kept her awake so many nights, screaming at her, telling her she was worthless, squandering her talent, doing everything wrong.

Andrew said, "I had all of these things I wanted to say to him."

Jane yet again found herself helpless to stop her tears.

"I wanted him to be proud of me. Not now, I knew it couldn't be now, but one day." Andrew turned to face her. He had always been lean, but now, in his grief, his cheeks were so hollow she could see the shape of the bones underneath. "Do you think that would've ever happened? That Father would've been proud of me, eventually?"

Jane knew the truth, but she answered, "Yes."

He looked back into the street. He told her, "There's Paula."

Jane felt the fine hairs on her arms and neck stand on end.

Paula Evans, dressed in her usual combat boots, dirty shift and fingerless gloves, fit in perfectly with the scenery. Her curly hair was frizzed wild. Her lips were bright red. For reasons unknown, she'd blackened under her eyes with a charcoal pencil. She saw the Porsche and flipped them off with both hands. Instead of heading toward the car, she stomped toward the warehouse.

Jane told Andrew, "She scares me. There's something wrong with her."

"Nick trusts her. She would do anything he asked."

"That's what scares me." Jane shuddered as she watched Paula disappear into the warehouse. If Nick was playing Russian roulette with their futures, Paula was the single bullet in the gun.

Jane got out of the car. The air had a greasy stench that reminded her of East Berlin. She left the metal box on the seat so she could slide on her jacket. She found her leather gloves and her scarf in her purse.

Andrew tucked the box under his arm as he locked the car. He told Jane, "Stay close."

They walked into the warehouse, but only to get through to the back. Jane hadn't been here for three months, but she knew the route by heart. They all did, because Nick had made them study diagrams, run up and down alleys, dart into backyards and even slide behind sewer grates.

Which had felt unhinged until now.

Paranoia seized Jane as she made her way down the familiar path. An alley took them through to the next street over. They blended in here, despite their expensive clothes. Thrift stores and dilapidated apartments were filled with students from nearby San Francisco State. Wadded-up newspapers had been shoved into broken windows. Trash cans overflowed with debris. Jane could smell the sickly-sweet odor of a thousand joints being lit to welcome the new morning.

The safe house was on 17th and Valencia, a block from Mission. At some point, it had been a single-family Victorian, but now it was chopped up into five one-bedroom apartments that appeared to be inhabited by a drug dealer, a group of strippers and a young couple with AIDS who had lost everything but each other. As with a lot of structures in this area, the house had been condemned. As with a lot of structures in the area, the inhabitants did not care.

They both climbed the wobbly front steps to the front door. For the hundredth time, Andrew glanced over his shoulder before going in. The front hall was narrow enough that he had to turn his shoulders sideways to walk through to the open kitchen door. The backyard contained an old shed-like structure that had been converted into living space. An orange extension cord that draped from the house to the shed served as electrical service. There was no plumbing. The top floor balanced precariously on what was originally meant to be a storage area. Music throbbed against the closed windows. Pink Floyd's screechy "Bring the Boys Back Home."

Andrew looked up at the second floor, then looked back over his shoulder yet again. He knocked twice on the door. He paused. He knocked one last time and the door flew open.

"Idiots!" Paula grabbed Andrew by his shirt and yanked him inside. "What the fuck were you thinking? We all said dye packs. Who put that fucking gun in the bag?"

Andrew straightened his shirt. The metal box had fallen to the floor. He tried, "Paula, we—"

The air went cold.

Paula said, "What did you call me?"

Andrew didn't respond for a moment. In the silence, all Jane could hear was the record playing upstairs. She dropped her purse on the floor in case she had to help her brother. Paula's fists were clenched. Nick had told them only to use their code names, and as with everything else that came out of his mouth, Paula had taken his order as gospel.

"Sorry," Andrew said. "I meant Penny. As in, Penny, we can talk about this later?"

Paula did not back down. "Are you in charge now?"

"Penny," Jane said. "Stop this."

Paula reeled on her. "Don't you—"

Quarter cleared his throat.

Jane startled at the noise. She hadn't seen him when they'd walked in. He was sitting at the table. A red apple was in his hand. He lifted his chin toward Jane, then Andrew, by way of solidarity. He told Paula, "What's done is done."

"Are you fucking kidding me?" Paula's hands went to her hips. "This is murder, you fucking idiots. Do you know that? We're all part of a conspiracy to commit murder."

"In Norway," Quarter said. "Even if they manage to extradite us, we'll get seven years, tops."

Paula snorted in disgust. "You think the United States government is going to let us stand trial in a foreign country? It was you, wasn't it?" Paula was pointing her finger at Jane. "You put the gun in the bag, you dumb bitch."

Jane refused to be bullied by this festering asshole. "Are you pissed at me because Nick didn't tell you about the gun or because Nick is fucking me instead of you?"

Quarter chuckled.

Andrew sighed as he leaned down to pick up the metal box. Then he froze.

They all froze.

Someone was outside. Jane heard feet stamping. She held her breath as she waited for the secret knock—twice, then a pause, then another knock.

*Nick?*

Jane felt her heart leap at the possibility, but still, she was racked with anxiety until she opened the door and saw the smile on his face.

"Hello, gang." Nick gave Jane a kiss on the cheek. His mouth was at her ear. He whispered, "Switzerland."

Jane felt a rush of love for him.

*Switzerland.*

Their dreamed-about little flat in Basel, surrounded by students in a country that had no formal extradition treaty with the United States. Nick had talked about Switzerland that same Christmas night that he had revealed the plan. Jane had been shocked that he'd been able to focus so acutely not just on the mayhem they would cause, but on how they would extricate themselves from the fallout.

*My darling*, he had whispered in her ear. *Don't you know I've thought of everything?*

"Now." Nick clapped together his hands. He addressed the group. "All right, troops? How are we doing?"

Quarter pointed to Paula. "This one was freaking out."

"I was not," Paula insisted. "Nick, what happened in Norway was—"

"Exceptional!" He grabbed her by the arms, his excitement flowing through the room like a ray of light. "It was tremendous! Absolutely the single most important thing that has happened to an American in this century!"

Paula blinked, and Jane could see her mind instantly shift to Nick's way of thinking.

Nick clearly noted the change, too. He said, "Oh, Penny, if only you had been there to witness the act. The room was shocked. Laura pulled the revolver right as Martin was waxing poetic about the costs of floor cleaner. Then"—he made a gun of his fingers and thumb—"Pow. A gunshot heard around the world. Because of us." He winked at Jane, then expanded his arms to include the group. "My God, troops. What we've done, what we are about to do, is nothing short of heroic."

"He's right." As usual, Andrew rushed in to back him up. "Laura had a choice. We all had a choice. She decided to do what she did. We decided to do what we're doing. Right?"

"Right," Paula said, eager to be the first to agree. "We all knew what we were getting into."

Nick looked at Jane, waited for her to nod.

Quarter grunted, but his loyalty was never in question. He asked Nick, "What's going on with the pigs?"

Jane tried, "Agent Danberry—"

"It's not just the pigs," Nick interrupted. "It's every federal agency in the country. And Interpol." He seemed delighted by the last part. "It's what we wanted, gang. The eyes of the world are upon us. What we're doing now—in New York, Chicago, Stanford, what's already happened in Oslo—we're going to change the world."

"That's right," Paula said, a congregant calling back to the preacher.

"Do you know how rare it is to make change?" Nick's eyes were still glowing with purpose. It was infectious. They were all leaning toward him, a physical manifestation of hanging on his every word.

Nick asked, "Do each of you know how truly, genuinely rare it is that simple people like us are able to make a difference in the lives of—well, it'll be the lives of millions, won't it? Millions of people who are sick, others who have no idea that their tax dollars are being used to line the coffers of soulless corporations while real people, everyday people who need help, are left behind."

He looked around the room and made eye contact with every single one of them. This was what Nick fed off, knowing that he was inspiring all of them to reach toward greatness.

He said, "Penny, your work in Chicago is going to shock the world. Schoolchildren will be taught about your integral part in this. They will know that you stood for something. And Quarter, your logistical help—it's unfathomable that we'd be here without you. Your Stanford plans are the linchpin of this entire operation. And Andrew, our dear Dime. My God, how you handled Laura, how you put together all the pieces. Jane—"

Paula snorted again.

"Jane." Nick rested his hands on Jane's shoulders. He pressed his lips to her forehead and she felt awash with love. "You, my darling. You give me strength. You make it possible for me to lead our glorious troops toward greatness."

Paula said, "We're gonna get caught." She no longer seemed furious about the prospect. "You guys know that, right?"

"So what?" Quarter had taken out his knife. He was peeling the apple. "Are you afraid now? All your big-talk bullshit and now—"

"I'm not afraid," Paula said. "I'm in this. I said I was in this, so I'm in it. You can always count on me, Nick."

"Good girl." Nick rubbed Jane's back. She almost curled into him like a kitten. It was that easy for him. All he had to do was put his hand in the right place, say the right word, and she was firmly back at his side.

*Was Jane a yo-yo?*

Or was she a true believer, because what Nick was saying was right? They had to wake people up. They could not sit idly by while so many people were suffering. Inaction was unconscionable.

Nick said, "All right, troops. I know the gun in Oslo was a surprise, but can't you see how fantastic things are for us now? Laura did us a tremendous favor by pulling that trigger and sacrificing her life. Her words resonate far more now than if she'd been shouting them from behind prison bars. She is a martyr—a celebrated martyr. And what we do next, the steps we take, will make people realize that they can't just run along like sheep anymore. Things will have to change. People will have to change. Governments will have to change. Corporations will have to change. Only we can make that happen. We're the ones who have to wake up everyone else."

They were all beaming at him, his willing acolytes. Even Andrew was glowing under Nick's praise. Maybe their blind devotion was what allowed Jane's anxiety to keep seeping back in.

Things had changed while she was away in Berlin. The energy in the room was more kinetic.

Almost fatalistic.

Had Paula cleaned out her apartment, too?

Had Quarter gotten rid of all of his most prized possessions?

Andrew had broken things off with Ellis-Ann. He was visibly unwell, yet he kept refusing to go to the doctor.

*Was their blind devotion another form of sickness?*

All of them but Jane had been in one psychiatric facility or another. Nick had purloined their files at Queller, or in the instances of the other members of the cells, found someone who would give them access. He knew about their hopes and fears and breakdowns and suicide attempts and eating disorders and criminal histories and, most importantly, Nick knew how to exploit this information for effect.

*Yo-yos unraveling or rolling back up at Nick's whim.*

"Let's do this." Quarter reached into his pocket. He slapped a quarter on the table beside the peeled apple. He said, "The Stanford Team is ready."

*Manic depression. Schizoid tendencies. Violent recidivism.*

Paula fell into a chair as she placed a penny on the table. "Chicago's been ready for a month."

*Anti-social behavior. Kleptomania. Anorexia nervosa. Akiltism.*

Nick flipped a nickel into the air. He caught it in his hand and dropped it onto the table. "New York is raring to go."

*Sociopathy. Impulse control disorder. Cocaine addiction.*

Andrew looked at Jane again before reaching into his pocket. He placed a dime with the other change and sat down. "Oslo is complete."

*Anxiety disorder. Depression. Suicidal ideation. Drug-induced psychosis.*

They all turned to Jane. She reached into her jacket pocket, but Nick stopped her.

"Take this upstairs, would you, darling?" He handed Jane the apple that Quarter had peeled.

"I can do it," Paula offered.

"Can you be quiet?" Nick was not telling her to shut up. He was asking a question.

Paula sat back down.

Jane took the apple. The fruit made a wet spot on her leather glove. She felt around on the secret panel until she found the button to push. One of Nick's clever ideas. They wanted to make it as hard as possible for anyone to find the stairs. Jane pulled back the panel, then used the hook to close it firmly behind her.

There was a sharp click as the release mechanism went back in place.

She climbed the stairs slowly, trying to make out what they were saying. The Pink Floyd song blaring from a tinny speaker was doing too good a job. Only Paula's raised voice could be heard over the soaring instrumental of "Comfortably Numb."

"Fuckers," she kept saying, obviously trying to impress Nick with her rabid devotion. "We'll show those stupid mother-fuckers."

Jane could feel an almost animalistic excitement rising through the floorboards as she reached the top of the stairs. There was incense burning inside the locked room. She could smell lavender. Paula had likely brought one of her voodoo talismans to keep the spirits at peace.

Laura Juneau had kept lavender in her house. This was one of the many stray details that Andrew had managed to relay in his coded letters. Like that Laura enjoyed pottery. That, like Andrew, she was a fairly good painter. That she had just come from the garden outside her house and was on her knees in the living room looking for a vase in the cupboard when Robert Juneau had used his key to unlock the front door.

A single shot to the head of a five-year-old.

Two bullets into a sixteen-year-old's chest.

Two more bullets into the body of a fourteen-year-old girl.

One of those bullets lodged into Laura Juneau's spine.

The last bullet, the final bullet, had entered Robert Juneau's skull from beneath his chin.

*Thorazine. Valium. Xanax. Round-the-clock care. Doctors. Nurses. Accountants. Janitors. Mop & Glo.*

"Do you know how much it costs to commit a man full-time?" Martin had demanded of Jane. They were sitting at the breakfast table. The newspaper was spread in front of them, garish head-lines capturing the horror of a mass murder: MAN MURDERS FAMILY THEN SELF. Jane was asking her father how this had happened—why Robert Juneau had been kicked out of so many Queller Homes.

"Almost one hundred thousand dollars a year." Martin was stirring his coffee with an antique Liberty & Company silver spoon that had been gifted to a distant Queller. He asked Jane, "Do you know how many trips to Europe that represents? Cars for your brothers? How many road trips and tours and lessons with your precious Pechenikov?"

*Why did you give up performing?*

*Because I could no longer play with blood on my hands.*

Jane found the key on a hook and pushed it into the deadbolt lock. On the other side of the door, the record had reached the part where David Gilmour took over the chorus—

*There is no pain, you are receding . . .*

Jane walked into the room. The smell of lavender enveloped her. A glass vase held fresh cut flowers. Incense burned on a metal tray. Jane realized these were not meant to ward off bad spirits, but to cover the odor of shit and piss in the bucket by the window.

*When I was a child, I had a fever . . .*

There were only two windows in the small space, one facing the Victorian in the front, the other facing the house that was on the street behind them. Jane opened both, hoping the cross-breeze would alleviate some of the odor.

She stood in the middle of the room holding the peeled apple. She let the song play through to the guitar solo. She followed the notes in her head. Visualized her fingers on the strings. She had played guitar for a while, then the violin, cello, mandolin and, just for the sheer joy of it, a steel-stringed fiddle.

Then Martin had told her that she had to choose between being good at many things or perfect at one.

Jane lifted the needle from the record.

She heard them downstairs. First, Andrew's coughing with its worrisome rattle. Nick's pithy little asides. Quarter told them all to keep their voices down, but then Paula started another *fucking pigs will pay* diatribe that drowned them all out.

"Come now," Nick spoke in a teasing tone. "We're so close. Do you know how important we're going to be when this is all over?"

*When this is all over . . .*

Jane put her hand to her stomach as she walked across the room.

*Would this ever be over?*

Could they go on after this? Could they bring a child into this world that they were trying to create? Was there really a flat waiting for them in Switzerland?

Jane reminded herself again: Nick had sold his furniture. Stripped away the fixtures in his apartment. He was sleeping on the floor. Was that a man who thought there was a future?

*Was that a man who could be a father to their child?*

Jane kneeled beside the bed.

She lowered her voice a few octaves, warning, "Don't say a word."

She pulled down the gag from the woman's mouth.

Alexandra Maplecroft started screaming.

August 23, 2018

# 11

Andy hefted a heavy box of old sneakers out of the back of the Reliant. Fat drops of rain smacked the cardboard. Steam came off the asphalt. The sky had opened after days of punishing heat, so now in addition to the punishing heat she had to deal with getting wet. She sprinted back and forth between the hatch and the open storage unit, head cowed every time a bolt of lightning slipped between the afternoon clouds.

She had taken a page from her mother and rented two different storage units in two different facilities in two different states to hide the gazillion dollars of cash inside the Reliant. Actually, Andy had done Laura one better. Instead of just piling the money on the floor of the unit like she was Skyler in *Breaking Bad*, she had cleaned out the back room of a Salvation Army store in Little Rock, then hidden the stacks of cash underneath old clothes, camping gear and a bunch of broken toys.

That way, anyone watching would think Andy was doing what most Americans did and paying to store a bunch of crap they didn't want instead of donating it to people who could actually use it.

Andy ran back to the Reliant and grabbed another box. Rain splashed inside her brand-new sneakers. Her new socks took on the consistency of quicksand. Andy had stopped at another Walmart after leaving the first storage facility on the Arkansas

271

side of Texarkana. She was finally wearing clothes that were not from the 1980s. She'd bought a messenger bag and a $350 laptop. She had sunglasses, underwear that didn't sag around her ass, and, weirdly, a sense of purpose.

*I want you to live your life*, Laura had said back at the diner. *As much as I want to make it easier for you, I know that it'll never take unless you do it all on your own.* Andy was certainly on her own now. But what had changed? She couldn't quite articulate even to herself why she felt so different. She just knew that she was sick of floating between disaster points like an amoeba inside a petri dish. Was it the realization that her mother was a spectacular liar? Was it the feeling of shame for being such a gullible believer? Was it the fact that a hired gun had followed Andy all the way to Alabama, and instead of listening to her gut and taking off, she had tried to hook up with him?

Her face burned with shame as she slid another box out of the back of the Reliant.

Andy had stayed in Muscle Shoals long enough to watch Mike Knepper's truck drive past the motel twice in the space of two hours. She had waited through the third hour and into the fourth to make certain that he wasn't coming back, then she'd packed up the Reliant and hit the road again.

She had been shaky from the outset, loaded with caffeine from McDonald's coffee, still terrified to pull over to go to the restroom because, at that point, she still had the cash hidden inside of the car. The drive to Little Rock, Arkansas, had taken five hours, but every single one of them had weighed on her soul.

Why had Laura lied to her? Who was she so afraid of? Why had she told Andy to go to Idaho?

More importantly, why was Andy still blindly following her mother's orders?

Andy's inability to answer any of these questions had not been helped by lack of sleep. She had stopped in Little Rock because it was a town she had heard of, then she had stopped at the first hotel with an underground parking deck because she figured she should hide the Reliant in case Mike was somehow following her.

Andy had backed the station wagon into a space so that any would-be thieves would have trouble accessing the hatch. Then she had gotten back into the car and pulled forward so that she could take the sleeping bag and the beach tote out of the trunk. Then she had backed into the space again, then she had checked into the hotel, where she had slept for almost eighteen hours straight.

The last time she had slept that long, Gordon had taken her to the doctor because he was afraid she had narcolepsy. Andy thought of the Arkansas sleep as therapeutic. She was not gripping a steering wheel. She was not screaming or sobbing into the empty car. She was not checking Laura's cell phone every five minutes. She was not fretting about all the money that tethered her to the Reliant. She was not worrying that Mike had followed her because she had actually crawled under the car and checked for any GPS tracking devices.

*Mike.*

With his stupid *K* in his last name and his stupid grasshopper on his truck and his stupid kissing her in the parking lot like some kind of psychopath because he was clearly there to follow Andy, or torture her, or do something horrible, and instead he had seduced her.

Worse, she had let him.

Andy grabbed the last box from the back of the car and approximated a walk of shame into the unit. She dropped the box onto the floor. She sat down on a wooden stool with a wobbly third leg. She rubbed her face. Her cheeks were on fire.

*Idiot,* she silently admonished herself. *He saw right through you.*

The painful truth was, there was not much of a story to tell about Andy's sex life. She would always trot out the affair with her college professor as a way to sound sophisticated, but she left out the part where they'd had sex only three and a half times. And that the guy was a pothead. And mostly impotent.

And that they usually ended up sitting on his couch while he got high and Andy watched *Golden Girls* reruns.

Still, he was better than her high school boyfriend. They had met in drama club, which should have been a giant freaking clue. But they were best friends. And they had both decided that their first times should be with each other.

Afterward, Andy had been underwhelmed, but lied to make him feel better. He had been just as underwhelmed, but failed to extend her the same courtesy.

*You get too wet*, he had told her, shuddering dramatically, and even though he admitted he was probably gay in the next sentence, Andy had carried that debilitating criticism with her for the ensuing decade and a half.

*Too wet*. She mulled the phrase in her mind as she stared at the wall of rain outside the storage unit. There were so many things she would say to that jackass now if he would just accept her friend request on Facebook.

Which brought her to her New York boyfriend. Andy had thought that he was so gentle and kind and considerate and then Andy had been in the bathroom at a friend's apartment when she'd overheard him talking to his buddies.

*She's like the ballerina in a jewelry box*, he had confided. *The second you bend her over, the music stops.*

Andy shook her head like a dog. She ran back to the car, got the light blue Samsonite suitcase, and dragged it into the unit. With the door closed, she changed into dry clothes. There was nothing she could do about her sneakers but at least she had socks that weren't peeling at her already sore feet. By the time she rolled the door up, the rain had tapered off, which was the first good luck she'd had in days.

Andy used one of her Walmart padlocks on the latch. Instead of a key, she had chosen a combination lock that used letters rather than numbers. The Texarkana code was FUCKR because she was feeling particularly hostile when she programmed it. For the Hook 'Em & Store outside of Austin, Texas, she'd gone with the more obvious KUNDE, as in—

*I could talk to Paula Kunde.*

*I hear she's in Seattle.*

*Austin. But good try.*

Andy had decided back in Little Rock that she was not going to amoeba her way to Idaho like Laura had told her to. If she could not get answers from her mother, then maybe she could get them from Professor Paula Kunde.

She reached up to close the hatch on the wagon. The sleeping bag and beach tote were still loaded up with cash, but she figured she might as well keep them in the car. She should probably put the little cooler and the box of Slim Jims in the storage unit, but Andy was antsy to get back on the road.

The Reliant's engine made a whirly Chitty-Chitty-Bang-Bang sound when she pulled away. Instead of heading toward the interstate, she took the next right into McDonald's. She used the drive-thru to order a large coffee and get the Wi-Fi password.

Andy chose a parking space close to the building. She dumped the coffee out the window because she was pretty sure her heart would explode if she drank any more caffeine. She got her new laptop out of the messenger bag and logged onto the network.

She stared at the flashing cursor on the search bar.

As usual, she had a moment of indecision about whether or not to create a fake Gmail account and send something to Gordon. Andy had composed all kinds of drafts in her mind, pretending to be a Habitat for Humanity coordinator or a fellow Phi Beta Sigma, contriving some kind of coded message that let her father know that she was okay.

*Just asking if you saw that great Subway coupon offering two-for-one?*

*Saw a story about Knob Creek bourbon I thought you might enjoy!*

As usual, Andy decided against it. There wasn't a hell of a lot she trusted about her mother right now, but even the slightest chance of putting Gordon in harm's way was too much of a risk.

She typed in the web address for the *Belle Isle Review*.

The photo of Laura and Gordon at the Christmas party was still on the front page.

Andy studied her mother's face, wondering how the familiar woman smiling at the camera could be the same woman who'd deceived her only daughter for so many years. Then she zoomed in closer, because Andy had never given the bump in her mother's nose a second thought. Had it been broken at some point and healed crookedly?

The Polaroids from her mother's storage unit told Andy that the explanation was possible.

*Would she ever know the truth?*

Andy scrolled down the page. The article about the body that had washed up under the Yamacraw Bridge had not changed, either. Still no identity on the man in the hoodie. No report of his stolen vehicle. Which meant that Laura had not only kept a battalion of police officers out of her house, she had somehow managed to drag an almost two hundred pound man to her Honda, then dump him in the river twenty miles away.

With one arm strapped to her chest and barely a set of legs to walk on.

Her mother was a criminal.

That was the only explanation that made sense. Andy had been thinking of Laura as passive and reactionary when all of the evidence pointed to her being logical and devious. The almost one million bucks in cash had not come from helping stroke patients work on their diction. The fake IDs were scary enough, but Andy had walked that back a step and realized that Laura not only had a fake ID, she had a contact—a forger—who could make documents for her. Every time Laura had crossed into Canada to renew the license or the car tag, she had broken federal law. Andy doubted the IRS knew about the cash, which broke all kinds of other federal laws. Laura wasn't afraid of the police. She knew that she could refuse an interrogation. She had a preternatural coolness around law enforcement. That didn't come from Gordon, which meant that Laura had learned it on her own.

Which meant that Laura Oliver was not a *good guy*.

Andy closed the laptop and returned it to the messenger bag. There wasn't enough memory on the machine to start listing all the things that her mother needed to explain. At this point, how Laura had disposed of Hoodie's dead body wasn't even in the top three.

Rain tapped at the windshield. Dark clouds had rolled in. Andy backed out of the space and followed the signs toward UT-AUSTIN. The sprawling campus took up forty acres of prime real estate. There was a medical school and hospital, a law school, all kinds of liberal arts programs and, despite not having its own football team, countless Texas Longhorns flags and bumper stickers.

According to the class schedule on the school's website, Dr. Kunde had taught a morning class called Feminist Perspectives on Domestic Violence and Sexual Assault followed by an hour set aside for student advisory. Andy checked the time on the radio. Even assuming Paula's sessions had run long or she'd stopped for lunch, or maybe met a colleague for another meeting, she was probably home by now.

Andy had tried to do more research on the woman's background, but there wasn't a hell of a lot about Paula Kunde on the internet. The UT-Austin site listed tons of academic papers and conferences, but nothing about her personal life. ProfRatings. com gave her only one half of a star, but when Andy dug into the student reviews, she saw they were mostly whining about bad grades that Dr. Kunde refused to change or offering long, adverb-riddled diatribes about how Dr. Kunde was a harsh bitch, which was basically the hallmark of her generation's contribution to higher education.

The only easy part of the investigoogling was finding the professor's home address. Austin's tax records were online. All Andy had to do was enter Paula Kunde's name and not only was she able to see that the property taxes had been paid consistently for the last ten years, she was able to click onto Google Street View and see for herself the low-slung one-story house in a section of the city called Travis Heights.

Andy checked her map again as she turned down Paula's street. She had studied the street on her laptop, like she was some kind of burglar casing the joint, but the images had been taken in the dead of winter when all the shrubs and trees lay dormant—nothing like the lush, overflowing gardens she passed now. The neighborhood had a trendy feel, with hybrids in the driveways and artistic yard ornaments. Despite the rain, people were out jogging. The houses were painted in their own color schemes, regardless of what their neighbors chose. Old trees. Wide streets. Solar panels and one very strange-looking miniature windmill in front of a dilapidated bungalow.

She was so intent on looking at the houses that she drove past Paula's on the first go. She went down to South Congress and turned back around. This time, she looked at the street numbers on the mailboxes.

Paula Kunde lived in a craftsman-style house, but with a kind of funkiness to it that wasn't out of touch with the rest of the neighborhood. An older model white Prius was parked in front of the closed garage door. Andy saw dormers stuck into the garage roof. She wondered if Paula Kunde had a daughter in her apartment that she couldn't get rid of, too. That would be a good opening line, or at least a second or a third, because the onus was going to be on Andy to talk her way into the house.

*This could be it.*

All the questions she'd had about Laura might be answered by the time Andy got back into the Reliant.

The thought made her knees rubbery when she stepped out of the car. Talking had never been her forte. Amoebas didn't have mouths. She threw her new messenger bag over her shoulder. She checked the contents to give her brain something else to concentrate on as she walked toward the house. There was some cash in there, the laptop, Laura's make-up bag with the burner phone, hand lotion, eye drops, lip gloss—just enough to make her feel like a human woman again.

Andy searched the windows of the house. All of the lights were off inside, at least from what she could see. Maybe Paula wasn't home. Andy had only guessed by the online schedule. The Prius could belong to a tenant. Or Mike could've changed out his truck.

The thought sent a shiver down her spine as she navigated the path to the front door. Leggy petunias draped over wooden planters. Dead patches in the otherwise neatly trimmed yard showed where the Texas sun had burned the ground. Andy glanced behind her as she climbed the porch stairs. She felt furtive, but wasn't sure whether or not the feeling was justified.

*I'm not going to hurt you. I'm just going to scare the shit out of you.*

Maybe that's why Mike had kissed Andy. He knew that threats had not worked against Laura, so he'd figured he would do something awful to Andy and use that for leverage.

"Who the fuck are you?"

Andy had been so caught up in her own thoughts that she hadn't noticed the front door had opened.

Paula Kunde gripped an aluminum baseball bat between her hands. She was wearing dark sunglasses. A scarf was tied around her neck. "Hello?" She waited, the bat still reared back like she was ready to swing it. "What do you want, girl? Speak up."

Andy had practiced this in the car, but the sight of the baseball bat had erased her mind. All she could get out was a stuttered, "I-I-I—"

"Jesus Christ." Paula finally lowered the bat and leaned it inside the doorframe. She looked like her faculty photo, but older and much angrier. "Are you one of my students? Is this about a grade?" Her voice was scratchy as a cactus. "Trigger warning, dumbass, I'm not going to change your grade, so you can dry your snowflake tears all the way back to community college."

"I—" Andy tried again. "I'm not—"

"What the hell is wrong with you?" Paula tugged at the scarf around her neck. It was silk, too hot for the weather, and didn't match her shorts and sleeveless shirt. She looked down her long nose at Andy. "Unless you're going to talk, get your ass—"

"No!" Andy panicked when she started to shut the door. "I need to talk to you."

"About what?"

Andy stared at her. She felt her mouth trying to form words. The scarf. The glasses. The scratchy voice. The bat by the door. "About you getting suffocated. With a bag. A plastic bag."

Paula's lips pressed into a thin line.

"Your neck." Andy touched her own neck. "You're wearing the scarf to hide the scratch marks and your eyes probably have—"

Paula took off her sunglasses. "What about them?"

Andy tried not to gawk. One of the woman's eyes was milky white. The other was streaked with red as if she had been crying, or strangled, or both.

Paula asked, "Why are you here? What do you want?"

"To talk—my mother. I mean, do you know her? My mother?"

"Who's your mother?"

*Good question.*

Paula watched a car drive past her house. "Are you going to say something or stand there like a little fish with your mouth gaping open?"

Andy felt her resolve start to evaporate. She had to think of something. She couldn't give up now. Suddenly, she remembered a game they used to play in drama, an improv exercise called *Yes, And* . . . You had to accept the other person's statement and build on it in order to keep the conversation going.

She said, "Yes, and I'm confused because I've recently found out some things about my mother that I don't understand."

"I'm not going to be part of your *bildungsroman*. Now cheese it or I'll call the police."

"Yes." Andy almost screamed. "I mean, yes, call the police. And then they'll come."

"That's kind of the point of calling the police."

"Yes," Andy repeated. She could see where the game really required two people. "And they'll ask lots of questions. Questions you don't want to answer. Like about why your eye has petechiae."

Paula looked over Andy's shoulder again. "Is that your car in my driveway, the one that looks like a box of maxi pads?"

"Yes, and it's a Reliant."

"Take off your shoes if you're going to come inside. And stop that 'Yes, And' bullshit, Jazz Hands. This isn't drama club."

Paula left her at the door.

Andy felt weirdly terrified and excited that she had managed to get this far.

*This was it. She was going to find out about her mother.*

She dropped the messenger bag on the floor. She rested her hand on the hall table. A glass bowl of change clicked against the marble top. She slipped off her sneakers and left them in front of the aluminum baseball bat. Her wet socks went inside the shoes. She was so nervous that she was sweating. She pulled at the front of her shirt as she stepped down into Paula's sunken living room.

The woman had a stark sense of design. There was nothing craftsman inside the house except some paneling on the walls. Everything had been painted white. The furniture was white. The rugs were white. The doors were white. The tiles were white.

Andy followed the sound of a chopping knife down the back hall. She tried the swinging door, pushing it just enough to poke her head in. She found herself looking in the kitchen, surrounded by still more white: countertops, cabinets, tiles, even light fixtures. The only color came from Paula Kunde and the muted television on the wall.

"Come in already." Paula waved her in with a long chef's knife. "I need to get my vegetables in before the water boils off."

Andy pushed open the door all the way. She walked into the room. She smelled broth cooking. Steam rose off a large pot on the stove.

Paula sliced broccoli into florets. "Do you know who did it?"

"Did . . ." Andy realized she meant Hoodie. She shook her head, which was only partially lying. Hoodie had been sent by somebody. Somebody who was clearly known to Laura. Somebody who might be known to Paula Kunde.

"He had weird eyes, like . . ." Paula's voice trailed off. "That's all I could tell the pigs. They wanted to set me up with a sketch artist, but what's the point?"

"I could—" Andy's ego cut her off. She had been about to offer to draw Hoodie, but she hadn't drawn anything, even a doodle, since her first year in New York.

Paula snorted. "Good Lord, child. If I had a dollar bill every time you left a sentence hanging, I sure as shit wouldn't be living in Texas."

"I was just—" Andy tried to think of a lie, but then she wondered if Hoodie had really come here first. Maybe Andy had misunderstood the exchange in Laura's office. Maybe Mike had been sent to Austin and Hoodie had been sent to Belle Isle.

She told Paula, "If you've got some paper, maybe I could do a sketch for you?"

"Over there." She used her elbow to indicate a small desk area at the end of the counter.

Andy opened the drawer. She was expecting to find the usual junk—spare keys, a flashlight, stray coins, too many pens—but there were only two items, a sharpened pencil and a pad of paper.

"So, art's your thing?" Paula asked. "You get that from someone in your family?"

"I—" Andy didn't have to see the look on Paula's face to know that she'd done it again.

Instead, she flipped open the notebook, which was filled with blank pages. Andy didn't give herself time to freak out about what she was about to do, to question her talents or to talk herself out of having the hubris to believe she still had any skills left in her hands. Instead, she knocked the sharp point off the pencil and sketched out what she remembered of Hoodie's face.

"Yep." Paula was nodding before she'd finished. "That looks like the bastard. Especially the eyes. You can tell a lot about somebody from their eyes."

Andy found herself looking into Paula's blank left eye.

Paula asked, "How do you know what he looks like?"

Andy didn't answer the question. She turned to a fresh page. She drew another man, this one with a square jaw and an Alabama baseball cap. "What about this guy? Have you ever seen him around here?"

Paula studied the image. "Nope. Was he with the other guy?"

"Maybe. I'm not sure." She felt her head shaking. "I don't know. About anything, actually."

"I'm getting that."

Andy had to buy herself some time to think. She returned the pad and pencil to the drawer. This whole conversation was going sideways. Andy wasn't so stupid that she didn't know she was being played. She'd come here for answers, not more questions.

Paula said, "You look like her."

Andy felt a bolt of lightning shoot from head to toe.

*You-look-like-her-you-look-like-her-you-look-like-your-mother.*

Slowly, Andy turned around.

"The eyes, mostly." Paula used the point of a large chef's knife to indicate her eyes. "The shape of your face, like a heart."

Andy felt frozen in place. She kept playing back Paula's words in her head because her heart was pounding so loudly that she could barely hear.

*The eyes . . . The shape of your face . . .*

Paula said, "She was never as timid as you. Must get that from your father?"

Andy didn't know because she didn't know anything except that she had to lean against the counter and lock her knees so she didn't fall down.

Paula resumed chopping. "What do you know about her?"

"That . . ." Andy was having trouble speaking again. Her stomach had filled with bees. "That she's been my mother for thirty-one years."

Paula nodded. "That's some interesting math."

"Why?"

"Why indeed."

The sound of the knife *thwapping* the chopping board resonated inside of Andy's head. She had to stop reacting. She needed to ask her questions. She'd made a whole list of them in her head on the seven-hour drive and now—

"Could you—"

"Dollar bill, kid. Could I what?"

Andy felt dizzy. Her body was experiencing the odd numbness of days before. Her arms and legs wanted to float up toward the ceiling, her brain had disconnected from her mouth. She couldn't fall back into old patterns. Not now. Not when she was so close.

"Can—" Andy tried a third time, "How do you know her? My mother?"

"I'm not a snitch."

*Snitch?*

Paula had looked up from her chopping. Her expression was unreadable. "I'm not trying to be a bitch. Though, admittedly, being a bitch is kind of my thing." She diced together a bundle of celery and carrots. The pieces were all identical in size. The knife moved so fast that it looked still. "I learned how to cook in the prison kitchen. We had to be fast."

*Prison?*

"I always wanted to learn." Paula scooped the vegetables into her hands and walked over to the stove. She dropped everything into a stew pot as she told Andy, "It took over a decade for me to earn the privilege. They only let the older gals handle the knives."

*Over a decade?*

Paula asked, "I gather you didn't see that when you googled me."

Andy realized her tongue was stuck to the roof of her mouth. She was too astonished to process all of these revelations.

*Snitch. Prison. Over a decade.*

Andy had been telling herself for days that Laura was a criminal. Hearing the theory confirmed was like a punch to her gut.

"I pay to keep that out of the top searches. It's not cheap, but—" She shrugged, her eyes on Andy again. "You *did* google me, right? Found my address through the property tax records.

Saw my course schedule, read my shitty student reviews?" She was smiling. She seemed to like the effect she was having. "Then, you looked at my CV, and you asked yourself, UC-Berkeley, Stanford, West Connecticut State. Which one of those doesn't belong? Right?"

Andy could only nod.

Paula started chopping up a potato. "There's a women's federal corrections facility near West Conn. Danbury—you probably know it from that TV show. They used to let you do a higher ed program. Not so much anymore. Martha Stewart was a guest, but that was after my two dimes."

*Two dimes?*

Paula glanced up at Andy again. "People at the school know. It's not a secret. But I don't like to talk about it, either. My revolutionary days are over. Hell, at my age, pretty much most of my life is over."

Andy looked down at her hands. The fingers felt like cat whiskers. What awful thing did a person have to do to be sentenced to a federal prison for twenty years? Should Laura have been in prison for the same amount of time, only she had stolen a bunch of money, run away, created a new life, while Paula Kunde was counting the days until she was old enough to work in the prison kitchen?

"I should—" Andy's throat was so tight she could barely draw air. She needed to think about this, but she couldn't do that in this stuffy kitchen under this woman's watchful eye. "Leave, I mean. I should—"

"Calm down, Bambi. I didn't meet your mother in prison, if that's what you're freaking out about." She started on another potato. "Of course, who knows what you're thinking, because you're not really asking me any questions."

Andy swallowed the cotton in her throat. She tried to remember her questions. "How—how do you know her?"

"What's her name again?"

Andy didn't understand the rules of this cruel game. "Laura Oliver. Mitchell, I mean. She got married, and now—"

285

"I know how marriage works." Paula sliced open a bell pepper. She used the sharp tip of the blade to pick out the seeds. "Ever hear of QuellCorp?"

Andy shook her head, but she answered, "The pharmaceutical company?"

"What's your life like?"

"My li—"

"Nice schools? Fancy car? Great job? Cute boyfriend who's gonna do a YouTube video when he proposes to you?"

Andy finally picked up on the hard edge to the woman's tone. She wasn't being matter-of-fact anymore. The smile on her face was a sneer.

"Uh—" Andy started to edge toward the door. "I really should—"

"Is she a good mother?"

"Yes." The answer came easy when Andy didn't think about it.

"Chaperoned school dances, joined the PTA, took pictures of you at the prom?"

Andy nodded to all of this, because it was true.

"I saw her murdering that kid on the news." Paula turned her back on Andy as she washed her hands at the sink. "Though they're saying she's cleared now. She was trying to save him. Please don't move."

Andy stood perfectly still. "I wasn't—"

"I'm not saying 'Please don't move' to you, kid. 'Please' is a patriarchal construct designed to make women apologize for their vaginas." She wiped her hands on a kitchen towel. "I was talking about what your mother said before she murdered that boy. It's all over the news."

Andy looked at the muted television on the wall. The diner video was showing again. Laura was holding up her hands in that strange way, four fingers raised on her left, one on her right, to show Jonah Helsinger how many bullets he had left. The closed captioning scrolled, but Andy was incapable of processing the information.

"The experts have weighed in," Paula said. "They claim to know what your mother said to Helsinger—*Please don't move*, as in *Please don't move or the inside of your throat will splat onto the floor*."

Andy put her hand to her own neck. Her pulse tapped furiously against her fingers. She should be relieved that her mother was in the clear, but every bone in her body was telling her to leave this house. No one knew she was here. Paula could gut her like a pig and no one would be the wiser.

"It's funny, isn't it?" Paula leaned her elbows on the counter. She pinned Andy with her one good eye. "Your sweet little ol' mother kills a kid in cold blood, but walks because she thought to say *Please don't move* instead of *Hasta la vista*. Lucky Laura Oliver." Paula seemed to roll the phrase around on her tongue. "Did you see the look on her face when she did it? Gal didn't look bothered to me. Looked like she knew exactly what she was doing, right? And that she was a-okay with it. Just like always."

Andy was frozen again, but not from fear. She wanted to hear what Paula had to say.

"Cool as a cucumber. Never cries over spilled milk. Trouble rolls off her like water off a duck's back. That's what we used to say about her. I mean, those of us who said anything. You know Laura Oliver, but you don't *know* her. There's only the surface. Still waters don't run deep. Have you noticed?"

Andy wanted to shake her head, but she was paralyzed.

"I hate to say it kid, but your mother is full of the worst type of bullshit. That dumb bitch has always been an actress playing the role of her life. Haven't you noticed?"

Andy finally managed to shake her head, but she was thinking— *Mom Mode. Healing Dr. Oliver Mode. Gordon's Wife Mode.*

"Stay here." Paula left the room.

Andy could not have followed if she'd wanted to. She felt like her bare feet were glued to the tiled floor. Nothing this scary stranger had said about Laura was new information, but Paula had framed it in such a way that Andy was beginning to understand that the different facets of her mother weren't pieces of a whole; they were camouflage.

*You have no idea who I am. You never have and you never will.*

"Are you still there?" Paula called from the other side of the house.

Andy rubbed her face. She had to forget what Paula had said for now and get the hell out of here. The woman was still dangerous. She was clearly working some kind of angle. Andy should never have come here.

She opened the desk drawer. She ripped the drawings of Hoodie and Mike out of the pad, shoved them into her back pocket, then pushed open the kitchen door.

She was met by Paula Kunde pointing a shotgun at her chest.

"Jesus Christ!" Andy fell back against the swinging door.

"Hold up your hands, you dimwit."

Andy's hands went up.

"Are you wired?"

"What?"

"Bugged. Mic'd." Paula patted the front of Andy's shirt first, then her pockets, down her legs and back up. "Did she send you here to trap me?"

"What?"

"Come on." Paula pressed the muzzle into Andy's sternum. "Speak, you little monkey. Who sent you?"

"N-n-body."

"Nobody." Paula snorted. "Tell your mother your stupid deer in the headlights act almost got me. But if I ever see you again, I'll pull the trigger on this thing until it's empty. And then I'll reload and come after her."

Andy almost lost control of her bladder. Every part of her body was shaking. She kept her hands up, her eyes on Paula, and walked backward down the hallway. She stumbled on the stair down into the sunken living room.

Paula rested the shotgun on her shoulder. She glared at Andy for another few seconds, then walked back into the kitchen.

Andy choked back bile as she turned to run. She sprinted past the couch, up the single stair to the foyer, and stumbled again on the tile floor. Pain shot into her knee, but she caught herself on the side table. Change spilled out of the glass bowl and tapped against the floor. Every nerve in her body was trapped inside the teeth of a bear trap. She could barely wedge her foot into her shoe. Then she realized the fucking socks were wadded up inside. She checked over her shoulder as she jammed the socks into her messenger bag and shoved her feet into the sneakers. Her hand was so sweaty she almost couldn't turn the knob to open the front door.

*Fuck.*

Mike was standing on the front porch.

He grinned at Andy the same way he'd grinned at her when they were outside the bar in Muscle Shoals.

He said, "What a strange coinci—"

Andy grabbed the baseball bat.

"Whoa-whoa-whoa!" Mike's hands shot into the air as she cocked the bat over her shoulder. "Come on, beautiful. Let's talk this—"

"You shut the fuck up, you fucking psycho." Andy gripped the bat so tight that her fingers were cramping. "How did you find me?"

"Well, that's a funny story."

Andy jerked the bat higher.

"Wait!" he said, his voice raking up. "Hit me here"—he pointed down at his side—"you can fracture a rib, easy. I'll probably drop like a flaming sack of shit. Or punch it into the center of my chest. There's no such thing as the solar plexus but—"

Andy swung the bat, but not hard, because she wasn't trying to hit him.

Mike easily caught the end of the bat with his hand. He had to step back to do it. His legs were about a shoulder-width apart. Or a foot's width, which Andy soon found out when she kicked him in the nuts as hard as she could.

He dropped to the ground like a flaming sack of shit.

"Fuh—" He coughed, then coughed again. He was squeezing his hands between his legs, rolling on the front porch. Foam came out of his mouth, the same as Hoodie, but this time was different because he wasn't going to die, he was just going to suffer.

"Well done."

Andy jumped.

Paula Kunde was standing behind her. The shotgun was still resting against her shoulder. She said, "That's the guy from the second drawing, right?"

Andy's fear of Paula was overridden by her rage at Mike. She was sick of people treating her like a crash-test dummy. She patted his pockets. She found his wallet, his stupid rabbit's foot keychain. He put up absolutely no resistance. He was too busy clutching his balls.

"Wait," Paula said. "Your mother didn't send you here, did she?"

Andy shoved the wallet and keys into her messenger bag. She stepped over Mike's writhing body.

"I said wait!"

Andy stopped. She turned around and gave Paula the most hateful look she could muster.

"You'll need this." Paula dug around to the bottom of the change bowl and found a folded dollar bill. She handed it to Andy. "Clara Bellamy. Illinois."

"What?"

Paula slammed the door so hard that the house shook.

*Who the hell was Clara Bellamy?*

*Why was Andy listening to a fucking lunatic?*

She crammed the dollar bill into her pocket as she walked down the steps. Mike was still huffing like a broken muffler. Andy did not want to feel guilty for hurting him, but she felt guilty. She felt guilty as she got into the Reliant. She felt guilty as she pulled away from the house. She felt guilty as she turned onto the next street. She felt guilty right up until she saw Mike's white truck parked around the corner.

*Motherfucker.*

He had changed the magnetic sign on the side of the door.

LAWN CARE BY GEORGE

Andy jerked the Reliant to a stop in front of the truck. She popped the hatch. She found the box of Slim Jims and ripped it open. Nothing but Slim Jims. She opened the little cooler, something she hadn't done since she'd found it back at Laura's storage unit.

*Idiot.*

There was a tracker taped to the underside of the cooler lid. Small, jet black, about the size of an old iPod. The red light was blinking, sending back the coordinates of her location to a satellite somewhere in space. Mike must've put it there while Andy was passed out in the Muscle Shoals motel.

She chucked the cooler lid across the street like a Frisbee. She reached into the hatch and pulled out the sleeping bag and beach tote. She threw both into the front of Mike's truck. Then she grabbed two weedeaters and a set of trimmers from the back and dropped them onto the sidewalk. The magnetic signs easily peeled off the doors. She slapped them onto the hood of the Reliant. Andy thought about leaving him the key, but fuck that. All the money was sitting in storage units. He could drive around in the Maxi-Pad box for a while.

She got into Mike's truck. Her messenger bag went onto the seat beside her. The steering wheel had a weird fake leather wrap. A pair of dice hung from the rearview mirror. Andy jammed the key into the ignition. The engine roared to life. Dave Matthews warbled through the speakers.

Andy pulled away from the curb. Her brain summoned up a map as she drove toward the university. She figured she had about one thousand miles ahead of her, which was around twenty hours of driving, or two full days if she broke it up the right way. Dallas first, then straight up to Oklahoma, then Missouri, then Illinois, where she hoped like hell she could find a person or thing named Clara Bellamy.

July 31, 1986

# 12

Alexandra Maplecroft's screams were like a siren pitching higher and higher. The sirens from a police car. From the FBI. From the prison van.

Jane knew that she should do something to stop the wailing, but she could only stand there listening to the woman's desperate pleas for help.

"Jane!" Andrew called from downstairs.

The sound of her brother's voice broke Jane from her trance. She struggled to put the gag back in place. Maplecroft started thrashing in the bed, pulling at the restraints around her wrist and ankles. Her head jerked back and forth. The blindfold slipped up. One eye spun desperately around before she found Jane. Suddenly, one of the woman's hands was loose, then a foot. Jane leaned over to hold her down, but she wasn't fast enough.

Maplecroft punched Jane so hard in the face that she fell back onto the floor, literal stars dancing in front of her eyes.

"Jane!" Andrew screamed. She could hear footsteps pounding up the stairs.

Maplecroft heard it too. She struggled so hard against the ropes that the metal bed frame tipped over onto the floor. She worked furiously to untie her other hand while her leg jerked back and forth to work away the bindings.

Jane tried to stand. Her legs felt wonky. Her feet would not find purchase. Blood was streaming down her face, gagging her throat. She somehow found the strength to push herself up. All she could think to do was throw her body on top of Maplecroft's and pray that she could hold her down long enough for help to arrive.

Seconds later, it did.

"Jane!" The door flew open. Andrew reached her first. He pulled Jane up, wrapped his arm around her.

Maplecroft was standing, too. She was in the middle of the floor, fists up like a boxer, one ankle still tied to the bed. Her clothes were torn, her eyes wild, her hair matted to her skull with filth and sweat. She screamed unintelligibly as she moved back and forth between her feet.

Paula snorted a laugh. She was blocking the door. "Give it up, bitch."

"Let me go!" Maplecroft screamed. "I won't tell anyone. I won't—"

"Stop her," Nick said.

Jane didn't know what he meant until she saw Quarter raise his knife.

"No—" she yelled, but it happened too fast.

Quarter slashed down. The blade flashed in the sunlight.

Jane stood helpless, watching the knife arc down.

But then it stopped.

Maplecroft had caught the knife in her hand.

The blade pierced the center of her palm.

The effect hit them all like a stun grenade. No one could speak. They were too shocked.

Except for Maplecroft.

She had known exactly what she was going to do. While they all stood transfixed, she wrenched her arm across her body, preparing to backhand the blade in Jane's direction.

Nick's fist snaked out, punching Maplecroft square in the face.

Blood shot out of her nose. The woman spun in a half-circle, wildly slicing the air with the blade that pierced her hand.

Nick punched her again.

Jane heard the sharp *snap* of her nose breaking.

Maplecroft stumbled. The bed frame dragged back with her foot.

"Nick—" Jane tried.

He punched her a third time.

Maplecroft's head jerked back on her neck. She started to fall, but her pinned leg pulled her sideways. Her temple bounced against the metal edge of the bed frame with a sickening *pop* before she hit the floor. A pool of blood flowered from beneath her, rolled across the wood, seeped into the cracks between the boards.

Her eyes were wide. Her lips gaped apart. Her body was still.

They all stared at her. No one could speak until—

"Jesus," Andrew whispered.

Paula asked, "Is she dead?"

Quarter knelt down to check, but he leapt back when Alexandra Maplecroft's eyes blinked.

Jane screamed once before she could cover her mouth with both hands.

"Christ," Paula whispered.

Urine puddled from between the woman's legs. They could almost hear the sound of her soul leaving her body.

"Nick," Jane breathed. "What have you done? What have you done?"

"She—" Nick looked scared. He never looked scared. He told Jane, "I didn't mean—"

"You killed her!" Jane screamed. "You punched her, and she fell, and she—"

"It was me," Quarter said. "I'm the one who put the knife in her."

"Because Nick told you to!"

"I didn't—" Nick tried. "I said to stop her, not to—"

"What have you done?" Jane felt her head shaking furiously side to side. "What have we done? What have we done?" She couldn't ask the question enough. This had crossed the line of insanity. They were all psychotic. Every single one of them. "How could you?" she asked Nick. "How could you—"

"He was protecting you, dumb bitch," Paula said, unable or unwilling to keep the derision out of her voice. "This is your fault."

"Penny," Andrew said.

Nick tried, "Jinx, you have to believe—"

"You punched—you killed—" Jane's throat felt strangled. They had all watched it happen. She didn't have to give them a replay. Maplecroft had been spinning out of control after the first hit. Nick could've grabbed her arm, but he had punched her two more times and now her blood was sliding along the cracks in the floor.

Paula told Jane, "You're the one who let her get untied. So much for our ransom demand. That's our leverage pissing on her own grave."

Jane walked to the open back window. She tried to pull air into her lungs. She couldn't witness this, couldn't be here. Nick had crossed the line. Paula was making excuses for him. Andrew was keeping his mouth shut. Quarter had been willing to murder for him. They had all completely lost their senses.

Nick said, "Darling—"

Jane braced her hands on the windowsill. She looked at the back of the house across the alley because she couldn't bear to look at Nick. A pair of pink sheers wistfully furled in the late morning breeze. She wanted to be back home in her bed. She wanted to take back Oslo, to rewind the last two years of her life and leave Nick before he had pulled them all into the abyss.

"Jane," Andrew said. He was using his patient voice.

She turned around, but not to look at her brother. Her eyes automatically found the woman lying on the floor. "Don't," she begged Andrew. "Please don't tell me to calm—"

Maplecroft blinked again.

Jane didn't scream like the first time, because the more this kept happening, the more it felt normal. That's how Nick had gotten them. The drills and the rehearsals and the constant state of paranoia had all hypnotized them into believing that what they were doing was not just reasonable, but necessary.

Paula broke the silence this time. "We have to finish it."

Jane could only stare at her.

Paula said, "Put the pillow over her head, or just use your hands to cover her mouth and pinch her nose closed. Unless you want to try to stab her in the heart? Drown her in that bucket of piss?"

Jane felt bile stream up her throat. She turned, but not quickly enough. Vomit spewed onto the floor. She pressed her hands against the wall. She opened her mouth and tried not to wail.

*How could she bring a child into this terrible, violent world?*

"Christ," Paula said. "You can watch your own daddy being shot, but a gal bumps her head—"

"Penny," Andrew cautioned.

"Jinx," Nick tried to put his hand on Jane's back, but she shrugged him off. "I didn't mean to do it. I just—I wasn't thinking. She hurt you. She was still trying to hurt you."

"It's moot." Quarter was pressing two fingers to the woman's neck. "She doesn't have a pulse."

"Well, fuck," Paula mumbled. "What a surprise."

"It doesn't matter," Andrew said. "What's done is done." He, too, was looking at Jane. "It's all right. I mean, no, of course it's not all right, but it was an accident, and we have to get past it because there are more important things at play here."

"He's right," Quarter said. "We still have Stanford, Chicago, New York."

Paula said, "You know I'm still in. I'm not like little Miss Princess here. You should've stuck to your volunteer work with the other rich ladies. I knew you'd wimp out the second things got messy."

Jane finally allowed herself to look at Nick. His chest was heaving. His fists were still clenched. The skin along the back of his knuckles was torn where he'd punched Alexandra Maplecroft in the face.

*Who was this man?*

"I can't—" Jane started, but she could not say the words.

"You can't what?" Nick wiped the back of his hand on his pants. Blood smeared across like dirty fingerprints. There was more blood on the sleeve of his shirt. Jane looked down at her trousers. Red slashes crossed her legs. Speckles dotted her blouse.

"I can't—" she tried again.

"Can't what?" Nick asked. "Jinx, talk to me. What can't you do?"

*Do this, be a part of this, hurt more people, live with the secrets, live with the guilt, give life to your child because I will never, ever be able to explain to her that you are her father.*

"Jinxie?" Nick had recovered from his shock. He was giving her his half grin. He wrapped his hands around her arms. He pressed his lips to her forehead.

She wanted to resist. She told herself to resist. But her body moved toward his and then he was holding her and she was letting herself take comfort from the warmth of his embrace.

*The yo-yo flipping back on itself.*

Andrew said, "Let's go downstairs and—"

Suddenly, Quarter made a gulping sound.

His entire body jerked, his arms flying into the air. Blood burst from his chest.

A millisecond later, Jane heard the loud crack of a rifle firing, the sound of glass breaking in the windowpane.

She was already lying flat on the floor when she realized what was happening.

Someone was shooting at them.

Jane could see the crazy red dots from rifle scopes slipping along the walls as if they were in an action movie. The police had found them. They had tracked Jasper's car or someone in the neighborhood had reported them or they had followed Andrew and Jane and none of that mattered now because Quarter was dead. Maplecroft was dead. They were all going to die in this horrible room with the bucket of shit and piss and Jane's vomit on the floor.

Another bullet broke out the rest of the glass. Then another zinged around the room. Then another. Then they were suddenly completely swallowed by the sharp percussion of gunfire.

"Move!" Nick yelled, upending the mattress to block the front window. "Let's go, troops! Let's go!"

They had trained for this. It had seemed preposterous at the time, but Nick had made them drill for this exact scenario.

Andrew ran in a crouch toward the open door at the top of the stairs. Paula crawled on her hands and knees toward the back window. Jane started to follow, but a bullet pinged past her head. She flattened back to the floor. The vase of flowers shattered. Holes pierced the flimsy walls, lines of sunlight creating a disco effect.

"Over here!" Paula was already at the window.

Jane started to crawl again, but she stopped, screaming as Quarter's body bucked into the air. They were shooting him. She heard the sickening suck of bullets punching into his dead flesh. Maplecroft's head cracked open. Blood splattered everywhere. Bone. Brain. Tissue.

Another explosion downstairs; the front door blowing open.

"FBI! FBI!" The agents screamed over each other like a crescendo building. Jane heard their boots stomping through the lower floor, fists banging on the walls, looking for the stairs.

"Don't wait for me!" Andrew had already closed the door. Jane watched him heft up the heavy post that fit into the brackets on either side of the jamb.

"Jane, hurry!" Nick shouted. He was helping Paula guide the extension ladder out the back window. It was too heavy for just one person to manage. They knew this from the training exercise. Two people on the ladder. One person barring the door. Mattress against the window.

*Duck and run, move fast, don't stop for anything.*

Paula was first out the window. The rickety ladder clanged as she crawled on hands and knees to the house on the other side of the alley. The distance between the two windows was fifteen feet. Below was a pile of rotting garbage filled with needles and broken glass. No one would willingly go into the pit. Not unless the ladder broke and they plummeted twenty feet down.

"Go-go-go!" Nick yelled. The pounding downstairs was getting louder. The agents were still looking for the stairs. Wood started to splinter as they used the butts of their shotguns on the walls.

"Fuck!" a man yelled. "Get the fucking sledgehammer!"

Jane went on the ladder next. Her hands were wet with sweat. The cold metal rungs dug into her knees. There was a vibration in the ladder from a sledgehammer pounding into the walls below.

"Hurry!" Paula kept looking down at the pile of garbage. Jane chanced a peek and saw that there were three FBI agents in blue jackets swarming around the pile, trying to find a way in.

A gunshot rang out—not from the agents, but from Nick. He was leaning out the window, giving Andrew cover as he made his way across the ladder. The going was slower for her brother. The metal box was clutched under his arm. He could only use one hand. Jane couldn't even remember him bringing the box up the stairs.

"Fuckers!" Paula screeched as she shook her fist at the agents on the ground. She was drawing a sick sort of excitement from the carnage. "Fascist fucking pig cunts!"

Andrew slipped on the ladder. Jane gasped. She heard him curse. He'd almost dropped the box.

"Please," she whispered, begged, pleaded.

*Forget the box. Forget the plan. Just get us out of this. Make us sane again.*

"Nickel!" Paula yelled. "Throw it to me!"

She meant the gun. Nick tossed it across the fifteen-foot span. Paula caught it with both hands just as Andrew was coming off the ladder.

Jane had her arms around him before his feet hit the floor.

"Fuckers!" Paula started shooting at the FBI agents. Her eyes were closed. Her mouth was open. She was yelling like a madwoman because of course she was mad. They were all deranged, and if they died here today that was exactly what they deserved.

"Take my hand!" Andrew reached out to Nick, yanking him across the last few feet. They both fell back onto the floor.

Jane stood at the window. She looked across at the shed. The stairs had been found. The snipers had stopped firing. There was an agent, an older man cut from Danberry and Barlow's same cloth, standing directly across from her.

He raised his gun and pointed it at Jane's chest.

"Idiot!" Paula pulled Jane down into a crouch just as the gun fired. She reached up with both hands to push the ladder off the edge of the windowsill.

They heard the metal bang against the house, then clatter into the debris.

"This way." Andrew took the lead, crouching as he ran across the room. They were down the stairs, on the main floor, when they heard cars pull up in the street outside, which was fine, because leaving by the front door had never been the plan.

Andrew felt along the wall with his fingers. He found another secret button, accessed another secret panel, and revealed the steps to the basement.

This was why Nick had chosen the two-story shed after months of searching. He'd told the group that they needed a safe place to keep Alexandra Maplecroft, but they also needed a safe route of escape. There were very few basements in the Mission District, at least as far as the city knew. The water table was too high, the sand too swampy. The shallow basement under the Victorian was one of the city's many remnants from the original Armory. Soldiers had hidden in the dungeons when the Mission was under siege. Nick knew about the passages from his homeless days. There was a tunnel connecting the house to a warehouse one street over.

Nick clicked the panel closed behind them. Jane felt a chill as the temperature dropped. At the bottom of the stairs, Andrew was trying to push away the bookcase that covered the tunnel entrance.

Nick had to help him. The bookcase slid across the concrete. Jane saw scrapes across the floor and prayed like hell the FBI would not see them until it was too late.

Paula slapped a flashlight into Jane's hand and pushed her into the tunnel. Nick helped Andrew tug on the rope that pulled the bookcase back into its spot. Quarter was supposed to pull the rope. He was the carpenter of the group, the one who had turned all of Nick's sketches into actual working designs.

And now he was dead.

Jane switched on the flashlight before the bookcase sent them into complete darkness. Her job was to lead them through the tunnel. Nick had made her run through dozens of times, sometimes with a working flashlight, sometimes without. Jane had not been down here in three months, but she still remembered all the irregular rocks that could snag against a shoe or cause a bone-breaking fall.

Like the one Alexandra Maplecroft had experienced.

"Stop dawdling," Paula hissed, shoving Jane hard in the back. "Move."

Jane tripped over a stone she knew was there. None of the practice runs mattered. Adrenaline could not be faked. The deeper they went underground, the more claustrophobic she felt. The dome of light was too narrow. The darkness was overpowering. She felt a scream bubbling into her throat. Water from Mission Creek seeped in from every crevice, splashed up under their shoes. The tunnel was forty-eight feet long. Jane put her hand on the wall to steady herself. Her heart was pushing into her throat. She felt the need to vomit again but dared not stop. Now that she was out of Nick's embrace, away from his calming influence, the same question kept darting around inside of her head—

*What the hell were they doing?*

"Move it." Paula pushed Jane again. "Hurry."

Jane picked up the pace. She reached out in front of her, because she knew that they had to be close. Finally, the flashlight picked out the wooden back of the second bookcase. Jane didn't ask for help. She made an opening that was wide enough for them to squeeze through.

They all blinked in the sudden light. There were windows high in the basement walls. Jane could see feet shuffling past. She ran up the stairs, some sort of internal autopilot clicking on. She took a right because she had trained to take a right. Thirty yards later, she took a left because she had trained to take a left. She pushed open a door, climbed through a break in the wall, and found the van parked in a cavernous bay that smelled of black pepper from the building's previous life as a spice storage facility.

Paula ran ahead of Jane, because the first person to reach the van was the person who got to drive. Jane was second, so she pulled back the side door. Nick was already heading toward the bay door. There was a combination lock.

8-4-19.

They all knew the combination.

Andrew threw the metal box into the van. He tried to get in, but he started to fall backward. Jane grabbed at his arm, desperate to get him inside. Nick rolled up the bay door. He sprinted back to the van. Jane closed the sliding door behind him.

Paula was already driving out of the warehouse. She had tied up her hair and stuck a brown hat on her head. A matching brown jacket covered the top of her shift dress. The sunlight razored through the windshield. Jane squeezed her eyes shut. Tears slid down the side of her face. She was on her back, lying between Nick and Andrew. They were on a futon mattress, but every bump and pothole in the road reverberated into her bones. She craned her neck, trying to see out the window. They were on Mission within seconds, then turning deeper into the city, when they heard the sirens whizzing past.

"Keep cool," Nick whispered. He was holding Jane's hand. Jane was holding Andrew's. She could not remember when this had happened, but she was so grateful to be safely between them, to be alive, that she could not stop weeping.

They all lay there on their backs, clinging to each other, until Paula told them they had reached the 101.

"Chicago is thirty hours away." Paula had to shout to be heard over the road noise that echoed like a dentist's drill inside the van. "We'll stop in Idaho Falls to let them know we're on the way to the safe house."

*Safe house.*

A farm just outside of Chicago with a red barn and cows and horses and what did it matter because they were never going to be safe again?

Paula said, "We'll change drivers in Sacramento after we drop Nick at the airport. We'll follow the speed limit. We'll obey all traffic laws. We'll make sure to not draw attention to ourselves." She was mimicking Nick's instructions. They were all mimicking Nick's instructions because he claimed to always know what he was doing, even when everything was out of control.

*This was madness. It was absolute madness.*

"Je-sus Christ, that was close." Nick sat up, stretching his arms into the air. He gave Jane one of his rakish grins. He had that internal switch, too—the one that Laura Juneau had when she murdered Martin, then herself. Jane could see it so clearly now. For Nick, everything that had happened in the shed was behind him.

Jane could not look at him. She studied Andrew, still lying beside her. His face was ashen. Streaks of blood crisscrossed his cheeks. Jane could not begin to know the source. When she thought of the shed, she could only see death and carnage and bullets ricocheting around like mosquitos.

Andrew coughed into the crook of his arm. Jane reached out to touch his face. His skin had the texture of cotton candy.

Nick said, "Glad you practiced now, aren't you, troops?" Like Andrew, his face was splattered with blood. His hair had fallen into his left eye. He had that familiar look of exhilaration, as if everything was perfect. "Imagine going over that ladder for the first time without having your training to—"

Jane sat up. She should have gone to Nick, but she leaned

her back against the hump over the tire. Could she call Jasper? Could she find a telephone, beg him for help, and wait for her big brother to swoop in and save them all? How would she tell him that she had been responsible for helping to kill their father? How could she look him in the eye and say that everything they had done until this point was not the result of some form of collective derangement?

*A cult.*

"Jinx?" Nick asked.

She shook her head, but not at Nick. Even Jasper could not save her now. And how would she reward him if he tried, by being part of a plot to send him to prison for healthcare fraud?

Nick crawled on his knees to the locked box that Quarter had bolted to the floor. He dialed in the combination on the lock—

6-12-32.

They all knew the combination.

Jane watched him push up the lid. He removed a blanket, a Thermos filled with water. All part of the escape plan. There were Slim Jims, a small cooler, various emergency supplies and, secreted beneath a false bottom, $250,000 in cash.

Nick poured some water into the cup of the Thermos. He found the handkerchief in his back pocket and cleaned his face, then leaned over and wiped at Andrew's cheeks until they turned ruddy.

Jane watched her lover clean blood from her brother's face.

*Maplecroft's? Quarter's?*

She said, "We don't even know his real name."

They both looked at her.

"Quarter," she said. "We don't know his name, where he lives, who his parents are, and he's dead. We watched him die, and we don't even know who to tell."

Nick said, "His name was Leonard Brandt. No children. Never married. He lived alone at 1239 Van Duff Street. He worked as a carpenter over in Marin. Of course I know who he is, Jinx. I know everyone who is involved in this because I am responsible for their lives. Because I will do whatever it takes to try to protect all of you."

Jane couldn't tell whether or not he was lying. His features were blurred by the tears streaming from her eyes.

Nick put the cup back on the Thermos, telling him, "You don't look so good, old pal."

Andrew tried to muffle a cough. "I don't feel so good."

Nick grabbed Andrew's shoulders. Andrew grabbed Nick's arms. They could've been in a football scrimmage.

"Listen," Nick said. "We've had a hard time, but we're back on track. You'll rest at the safe house, you and Jane. I'll be back from New York as soon as I can, and we'll watch the world fall down together. Yes?"

Andrew nodded. "Yes."

*Jesus.*

Nick patted Andrew's cheek. He slid across the van toward Jane, because it was her turn for the rousing pep talk that pulled her back on side.

"Darling." His arm looped around her waist. His lips brushed her ear. "It's okay, my love. Everything is going to be okay."

Jane's tears came faster. "We could've died. All of us could've—"

"Poor lamb." Nick pressed his lips to the top of her head. "Can't you believe me when I tell you that we're all going to be okay?"

Jane's mouth opened. She tried to pull breath into her shaking lungs. She wanted so desperately to believe him. She told herself the only things that mattered right now in this moment: Nick was safe. Andrew was safe. The baby was safe. The ladder had saved them. The tunnel had saved them. The van had saved them.

*Nick had saved them.*

He'd made Jane keep up her training while she was in Berlin. So far away from everything, Jane had thought it was silly to go through the movements every morning, her hands whipping past each other, fists boxing out, as if she expected to go to war. The thing that had driven her most back in San Francisco was the pleasure of kicking Paula's ass every time they sparred. With Paula gone, and in truth with Nick gone, Jane had found herself slipping—away from her resolve, away from the plan, away from Nick.

*What have you been up to, my darling?* he would ask across the scratchy, international telephone line.

*Nothing*, she would lie. *I miss you too much to do more than sulk and mark the days off the calendar.*

Jane did miss him, but only a certain part of him. The part that was charming. That was loving. That was pleased with her. That didn't willfully, almost hedonistically, push everything to the breaking point.

What Jane had not realized until she was safely tucked away in Berlin was that for as long as she had been conscious of being alive, she had always had a ball of fear that slept inside of her stomach. For years, she had told herself that being neurotic was the bane of a solo artist's success, but in truth, the thing that kept her walking carefully, self-censoring her words, conforming her emotions, was the heavy presence of the two men in her life. Sometimes Martin would wake her fear. Sometimes Nick. With their words. With their threats. With their hands. And sometimes, occasionally, with their fists.

In Berlin, for the first time in her memory, Jane had experienced what it was to live a life without fear.

She went to clubs. She danced with lanky, stoned German guys with tattoos on their hands. She attended concerts and art openings and underground political meetings. She sat in cafés arguing about Camus and smoking Gauloises and discussing the tragedy of the human condition. At a distance, Jane would sometimes catch a glimpse of what her life was supposed to be like. She was a world-class performer. She had worked for two decades to get to this place, this exalted position, and yet—

She had never been a child. She had never been a teenager. She had never been a young woman in her twenties. She had never really been single. She had belonged to her father, then Pechenikov and then Nick.

In Berlin, she had belonged to no one.

"Hey." Nick snapped his fingers in front of her face. "Come back to us, my darling."

Jane realized that they'd all been having a conversation without her.

Nick said, "We were talking about when to release Jasper's files. After Chicago? After New York?"

Jane shook her head. "We can't," she told Nick. "Please. Enough people have been hurt."

"Jane," Andrew said. "We're not doing this on a whim. People have been hurt, have died, over this. We can't back out because we've lost our nerve. Not when they took a bullet for us."

"Literally," Nick said, as if Jane needed to be reminded. "Two people. Two bullets. Laura and Quarter really believed in what we're doing. How can we let them down now?"

"I can't," she told them both. There was nothing more to add. She just couldn't anymore.

"You're exhausted, my love." Nick tightened his arm around Jane's waist, but he didn't tell her what she wanted to hear: that they were going to stop now, that Jasper's files would be destroyed, that they would find their way to Switzerland and try to atone for the damage they had done.

He said, "We should take turns sleeping." Then he raised his voice so that Paula could hear. "I'll fly to New York from Chicago. It's too hot for me to go out of Sacramento. Paula, you'll stay with your team and make sure they're set for Chicago. We'll coordinate times when we get to the safe house."

Jane waited for Paula to chime in, but she was uncharacteristically silent.

"Jinx?" Andrew asked. "Are you okay?"

She nodded, but he could tell that she was lying. "I'm okay," she repeated, unable to keep her voice from wavering.

Nick told Andrew, "Go sit with Penny. Keep her awake. Jane and I will sleep, then we'll take the next shift."

Jane wanted to tell him no, that Andrew should go first, but she hadn't the energy and besides, Andrew was already struggling to his knees.

She watched her brother crawl to the front of the van. He sat beside Paula. Jane heard a groan come out of his mouth as he reached toward the radio. The news station was at a low murmur. They should've listened to it, but Andrew turned the knob until he found an oldies station.

Jane turned to Nick. "He needs a doctor."

"We've got bigger problems than that."

Jane knew instantly the problem he was talking about—not that things had gone sideways, but that Nick knew she was doubting him.

He said, "I told you what happened to Maplecroft was an accident." His voice was so low that only Jane could hear him. "I went crazy when I saw what she'd done to your beautiful face."

Jane touched her nose. The pain was instantaneous. So much had happened since that awful moment that she had forgotten about Maplecroft punching her.

Nick said, "I know I should've just grabbed her, or—something else. I don't know what happened to me, darling. I just felt so angry. But I wasn't out of control. Not completely. I promised you that I would never let that happen again."

*Again.*

Jane tried not to think about the baby growing inside of her.

"Darling," Nick said. "Tell me it's okay. We're okay. Tell me, please."

Jane reluctantly nodded. She lacked the energy to argue otherwise.

"My love."

He kissed her on the mouth with a surprising passion. She found herself unable to summon any desire as their tongues touched. Still, she wrapped her arms around him because she desperately needed to feel normal. They hadn't made love in Oslo, even after three months of separation. They'd both been too anxious, then the shooting had happened and they were terrified of saying or doing the wrong thing, then they were back in San Francisco and he had left her alone until this morning. Jane hadn't wanted him then, either, but she remembered keenly craving the *after*. To be held in his arms. To press her ear to his chest and listen to the steady, content beat of his heart. To tell him about the baby. To see the happiness in his expression.

*He hadn't been happy the first time.*

"Come on, love." Nick gave her a chaste kiss on the forehead. "Let's get some sleep."

Jane let him pull her down to the futon mattress. His mouth went to her ear again, but only to brush his lips against her skin. He wrapped his body around hers. Legs intertwined, arms holding her close. He made a pillow for her head out of the crook of his elbow. Instead of feeling the usual sense of peace, Jane felt like she was trapped in place by an octopus.

She stared up at the ceiling of the van. She had no thoughts in her mind. She was too exhausted. Her body felt numb, but in a different way from before. She wasn't being shot at or fretting about Danberry's interrogation or mourning Martin or worrying that they would all get caught. She was looking at her future and realizing that she was never going to get out of this. Even if every facet of Nick's plan worked, even if they managed to escape to Switzerland, Jane was always going to be living inside of a cartwheel.

Nick's breathing started to slow. She could feel his body relax. Jane thought to slide out from his grasp, but she hadn't the strength. Her eyelids began to flutter. She could almost taste every beat of her heart. She let herself give in to it, falling asleep for what she thought was just a moment, but they both woke up when Paula stopped at a gas station just inside the Nevada state line.

They were the only customers. The attendant inside barely glanced up from the television when they all climbed out of the van.

"Snacks?" Paula asked. No one answered, so she loped off

to the store with her hands stuck into the pockets of the brown jacket.

Andrew worked the gas pump. He closed his eyes and leaned against the van as the tank started to fill.

Nick didn't speak to anyone. He didn't clap together his hands and try to rally the troops. He walked a few yards away from them. His hands were in his back pockets. He stared out at the road. Jane watched him look up at the sky, then out at the vast, brown landscape.

Everyone was subdued. Jane couldn't tell if it was from shellshock or debilitating fatigue. There was an almost tangible feel among them that they had reached a point of no return. The giddy high they had foolishly experienced when they'd talked about being on the lam from the law, as if they were gangsters in a James Cagney movie, had been eviscerated by reality.

Nick was the only one who could reliably pull them out of free fall. Jane had seen it happen so many times before. Nick could walk into a room and instantly make everything better. She had witnessed it this morning at the shed. Andrew and Jane were quarreling with Paula, who was about to kill them all, then Nick had somehow turned them all into a single, working group again. Everyone looked to him for his strength, his surety of purpose.

*His charisma.*

Nick turned away from the road. His eyes skipped over Jane as he walked toward the bathrooms on the side of the building. His shoulders were slumped. His feet dragged across the asphalt. Her heart broke at the sight of him. Jane had only seen him like this a handful of times before, so stuck in a fugue of depression that he could barely lift his head.

It was her fault.

She had doubted him, the one betrayal that Nick could not abide. He was a man, not an all-seeing god. Yes, what had happened in the shed was terrible, but they were still alive. Nick had made that happen. He had designed drills and made sketches to map out their escape. He had insisted they practice until their arms and legs felt weak. To keep them safe. To keep them on track. To keep their spirits up and their minds focused and their hearts motivated. No one else had the ability to do all of those things.

And no one, especially Jane, had stopped to think what a toll these responsibilities were taking on him.

She followed Nick's path to the men's bathroom. She didn't think about what she would find when she pushed open the door, but she felt sick with her own complicity when she saw Nick.

His hands were braced on the sink. His head was bent. When he looked up at Jane, tears were streaming from his eyes.

"I'll be out in a minute." He turned away, grabbing a handful of paper towels. "Maybe you could help Penny with—"

Jane wrapped her arms around him. She pressed her face to his back.

He laughed, but only at himself. "I seem to be falling apart."

Jane squeezed him as tight as she dared.

His chest heaved as he took a shuddered breath. His arms covered hers. He shifted his weight into her and Jane held him up because that was what she did best.

"I love you," she told him, kissing the back of his neck.

He misread her intentions. "Afraid I'm not up for any hijinks, my Jinx, but it means the world to me that you're offering."

She loved him even more for trying to sound like his old, confident self. She made him turn around. She put her hands on his shoulders the same way he always did with everyone else. She put her mouth to his ear the same way he only did with her. She said the three words that mattered most to him, not *I love you*, but—

"I'm with you."

Nick blinked, then he laughed, embarrassed by his obvious swell of emotion. "Really?"

"Really." Jane kissed him on the lips, and inexplicably,

everything felt right. His arms around her. His heart beating against hers. Even standing in the filthy men's room felt right.

"My love," she said. Over and over again. "My only love."

Andrew was fast asleep in the passenger's seat when they got back to the van. Paula was too wired to do anything but keep driving. Nick helped Jane into the back. He did the same thing as before, wrapping his arms and legs around her as they lay on the futon. This time, Jane curled into him. Instead of closing her eyes to sleep, she started talking—mundane nonsense at first, like the feeling of joy the first time she had nailed a performance, or the excitement of a standing ovation. She wasn't bragging. She was giving Nick context because nothing compared to the absolute elation Jane had experienced the first time Nick had kissed her, the first time they had made love, the first time she'd realized that he belonged to her.

Because Nick did belong to her, just as surely as Jane belonged to him.

She told him how her heart had floated up like a hot-air balloon when she'd first seen him roughhousing with Andrew in the front hall. How her spirits had soared when Nick had walked into the kitchen, kissed her, then backed away like a thief. Then she told Nick how much she had ached for him in Berlin. How she had missed the taste of his mouth. How nothing she did could chase away the longing she'd had for his touch.

Then they were in Wyoming, then Nebraska, then Utah, then finally Illinois.

Over the twenty-eight remaining hours it took to drive to the outskirts of Chicago, Jane spent almost every waking moment telling Nick how much she loved him.

*She was a yo-yo. She was Patricia Hearst. She had drunk the Kool-Aid. She was taking orders from her neighbor's dog.*

Jane did not care if she was in a cult or if Nick was Donald DeFreeze. Actually, she no longer cared about the plan. Her part was over, anyway. The other cell members were on the frontlines now. Of course, she still felt outraged by the atrocities committed by her father and older brother. She mourned Laura and Robert Juneau's loss. She felt bad for what had happened to Quarter and Alexandra Maplecroft in the shed. But Jane did not really have to believe in what they were doing or why.

All she had to do was believe in Nick.

"Turn left up here," Paula said. She was kneeling behind the driver's seat. She put her hand on Jane's shoulder, which was alarming because Paula never touched except to hurt. "Look for a driveway on the right. It's kind of hidden in the trees."

Jane saw the driveway a few yards later. She put on the turn signal even though the van was the only vehicle for miles.

Paula punched Jane's arm. "Dumb bitch."

Jane listened to her disappear into the back of the van. Paula's mood had lifted because Nick's mood had lifted. The same had happened with Andrew. The effect was magical. The moment they had seen Nick's easy grin, any feelings of worry or doubt had vanished.

Jane had made that happen.

"Jinx?" Andrew stirred in the passenger's seat as the tires bumped onto the gravel driveway.

"We're here." Jane let out a slow sigh of relief as they cleared the stand of trees. The farm was just as she had pictured it from Andrew's coded letters. Cows grazed in the pasture. A huge, red barn loomed over a quaint, one-story house that was painted a matching color. Daisies were planted in the yard. There was a small patch of grass and a white picket fence. This was the sort of happy place you could raise a child.

Jane rested her hand on her stomach.

"Okay?" Andrew asked.

She looked at her brother. The sleep had done him no good. Improbably, he looked worse than before. "Should I be worried?"

"Absolutely not." His smile was unconvincing. He told her, "We'll be able to rest here. To be safe."

"I know," Jane said, but she would not feel safe until Nick returned from New York.

The front tire hit a rut in the gravel drive. Jane winced as tree limbs lashed the side of the van. She almost said a prayer of thanks when she finally parked beside two cars in front of the barn.

"Hello, Chicago!" Nick called as he slid open the side door. He jumped to the ground. He stretched his arms and arched his back, his face looking up at the sky. "My God, it's good to be out of that tin box."

"No shit." Paula groaned as she tried to stretch. She was only a few years older than Nick, but rage had curled her body in on itself.

Jane sighed again as her feet touched solid ground. The air was sharp, the temperature considerably lower than what they had left in California. She rubbed her arms to warm them as she looked out at the horizon. The sun hung heavy over the treetops. She guessed it was around four o'clock in the afternoon. She didn't know what day it was, where they were exactly, or what was going to happen next, but she was so relieved to be out of the van that she could've cried.

"Stay here." Paula stomped toward the house. Her boots kicked up a cloud of dust. She had taken off her fingerless gloves, wiped the black charcoal from under her eyes. The back of her hair corkscrewed into a cowlick. The hem of her shift was filthy. Like the rest of them, she had slashes of blood on her clothes.

Jane looked past her to the farmhouse. She wasn't going to think about the blood anymore. She was either with Nick or she wasn't.

All or none; the Queller way.

The front door opened. A small woman stood with a shawl wrapped around her narrow shoulders. Beside her, a tall man with long hair and an elaborate, handlebar mustache held a shotgun in his hands. He saw Paula, but did not lower the gun until she placed a penny in the palm of the woman's open hand.

This was Nick's idea. Penny, nickel, quarter, dime—each representing a cell, each cell using the coins as a way of indicating to each other that it was safe to talk. Nick delighted in the play on their name, the Army of the Changing World. He'd made them all dress in black, even down to their underwear, and stand in a line like soldiers as he placed a coin in each of their hands to designate their code names.

*The jackass didn't know the word "symbiotic," so he made up the word "symbionese."*

Jane gritted her teeth as she banished Danberry's words from her mind.

She had made her choice.

"I don't know about you, troops, but I'm starving." Nick looped his arm around Andrew's shoulders. "Andy, what about you? Is it feed a cold and starve a fever, or the other way around?"

"I think it's give them both whisky and sleep in a real bed." Andrew trudged toward the house, Nick beside him. They were both noticeably exhausted, but Nick's energy was carrying them through, just as it always did.

Jane did not follow them toward the house. She wanted to stretch her legs and look at the farm. The thought of a moment alone in the silence appealed to her. She had grown up in the city. The Hillsborough house was too close to the airport to be called the country. While other girls Jane's age learned horseback riding and attended Girl Scout retreats, she was sitting in front of her piano for five and six hours at a time, trying to sharpen the fine motor movements of her fingers.

Her hand, as always, found its way to her stomach.

*Would her daughter play the piano?*

Jane wondered how she was so certain that the child was a girl. She wanted to name her something wonderful, not plain Jane or silly Jinx or the cartoony Janey that Nick sometimes called her. She wanted to give the girl all of her strengths and none of her weaknesses. To make sure that she did not pass on that sleeping ball of fear to her precious child.

She stopped at the wooden fence. Two white horses were grazing in the field. She smiled as they nuzzled each other.

Andrew and Jane would be here for at least a week, maybe more. When Nick got back from New York, they would lie low for another week before crossing into Canada. Switzerland was their dream, but what would it feel like to raise her baby on a farm like this one? To walk her to the end of the driveway and wait for the school bus? Hide Easter eggs in bales of hay? Take the horses out into the field and lay a picnic—Jane, her baby, and Nick.

*Next time*, Nick told her the last time. *We'll keep it next time.*

"Hello." The thin woman with the shawl called to Jane. She was making her way past the barn. "I'm sorry to bother you. They're asking for you. Tucker can move the van into the barn. Spinner and Wyman are already inside."

Jane gave a solemn nod. The lieutenants in each cell had all been assigned code names from past Secretaries of the United States Treasury. When Nick had first told Jane the idea, she had struggled not to laugh. Now, she could see that the cloak and dagger had been for a reason. The identities of the Stanford cell had died with Quarter.

"Oh," the woman had stopped in her tracks, her mouth rounded in surprise.

Jane was just as shocked to see the familiar face. They had never met before, but she knew Clara Bellamy from magazines and newspapers and posters outside the State Theater at Lincoln Center. She was a *prima ballerina*, one of Balanchine's last shining stars, until a debilitating knee injury had forced her into retirement.

"Well now." Clara resumed walking toward Jane with a grin on her face. "You must be Dollar Bill."

Another necessary part of spycraft. She told Clara, "We decided calling me 'DB' is easier than Dollar Bill. Penny thinks it stands for 'Dumb Bitch.'"

"That's Penny for you." Clara had easily picked up on Paula's prickliness. "Nice to meet you, DB. They call me Selden."

Jane shook the woman's hand. Then she laughed to let her know she recognized that the two of them meeting on a secluded farm outside of Chicago was wild.

"It's a funny old world, isn't it?" Clara looped her arm through

Jane's as they slowly headed toward the farmhouse. There was a slight limp to her walk. "I saw you at Carnegie three years ago. Brought me to tears. Mozart's Concerto Number 24 in C Minor, I believe."

Jane felt her lips curve into a smile. She loved it when people really loved music.

Clara said, "That green dress was amazing."

"I thought the shoes were going to kill me."

She smiled in commiseration. "I remember it was right after Horowitz's Japan concert. To see a man who's so accomplished fail so spectacularly—you must've been on pins and needles when you walked onto that stage."

"I wasn't." Jane was surprised by her own honesty, but someone like Clara Bellamy would understand. "Every note I played came with this sense of déjà vu, as if I had already played it perfectly."

"A fait accompli." Clara nodded her understanding. "I lived for those moments. They never happened often enough. Makes you understand drug addicts, doesn't it?" She had stopped walking. "That was your last classical performance, wasn't it? Why did you give it up?"

Jane was too ashamed to answer. Clara Bellamy had stopped dancing because she had no choice. She wouldn't understand choosing to walk away.

Clara offered, "Pechenikov put it around that you lacked ambition. They always say that about women, but that can't be the truth. I saw your face when you performed. You weren't just playing the music. You *were* the music."

Jane looked past Clara's shoulder to the house. She had wanted to keep her spirits up for Nick, but the reminder of her lost performing life brought back her tears. She had loved playing classical, then she had loved the energy of jazz, then she'd had to find a way to love being alone inside a studio with no feedback from anyone but the chain-smoking man on the other side of the soundproofed glass.

"Jane?"

She shook her head, dismissing her grief as a foolish luxury. As usual, she told a version of the truth that the listener could relate to. "I used to think my father was proud of me when I played. Then one day, I realized that everything I did, every award and gig and newspaper or magazine story reflected well on him. That's what he got out of it. Not admiration for me, but admiration for himself."

Clara nodded her understanding. "I had a mother like that. But you won't give it up for long." Without warning, she pressed her palm to Jane's round belly. "You'll want to play for her."

Jane felt a narrowing in her throat. "How did—"

"Your face." She stroked Jane's cheek. "It's so much fuller than in your photos. And you have this bump in your belly, of course. You're carrying high, which is why I assumed it was a girl. Nick must be—"

"You can't tell him." Jane's hand flew to her mouth as if she could claw back the desperation in her tone. "He doesn't know yet. I need to find the right time."

Clara seemed surprised, but she nodded. "I get it. What you guys are going through, it's not easy. You want some space around it before you tell him."

Jane forced a change in subject. "How did you get involved with the group?"

"Edwin—" Clara laughed, then corrected herself. "Tucker, I mean. He met Paula while they were both at Stanford. He was in law school. She was in poly-sci. Had a bit of a fling, I expect. But he's mine now."

Jane tried to hide her surprise. She couldn't see Paula as a student, let alone having a fling. "He's handling any legal issues that come up?"

"That's right. Nick is lucky to have him. Tucker dealt with some nasty contract problems for me when my knee blew out. We kind of hit it off. I've always been a sucker for a man with interesting facial hair. Anyway, Paula introduced Tucker to Nick, I mean, Nickel. Tucker introduced Nickel to me, and, well, you know how it is when you meet Nick. You believe every word that comes out of his mouth. It's a good thing he didn't try to sell me a used car."

Jane laughed because Clara laughed.

Clara said, "I'm not a true believer. I mean, yeah, I get what you're doing and of course it's important, but I'm a big chicken when it comes to putting myself on the line. I'd rather write some checks and provide safe harbor."

"Don't dismiss what you're doing. Your contributions are still important." Jane felt like she was channeling Nick, but they all had to do their part. "More important, actually, because you keep us safe."

"Lord, you do sound like him."

"Do I?" Jane knew that she did. This was the cost of giving herself to Nick. She was starting to become him.

"I want lots of babies," Clara said. "I couldn't when I was dancing, but now"—she indicated the farm—"I bought this so I can raise my kids here. To let them grow up happy, and safe. Edwin's learning to take care of the cows. I'm learning to cook. That's why I'm helping Nick. I want to help make a better place for my children. Our children."

Jane studied the woman's face for a tell-tale grin.

"I really believe that, Jane. I'm not just blowing smoke up your ass. It's exciting to be a part of it, even on the periphery. And I'm not taking a big risk, but there's still a risk. One or all of you could end up in an interrogation room. Imagine the kind of press you could get for pointing the finger at me." She gave a startled laugh. "Do you know, I'm sort of jealous, because I think you're more famous than I am, so I'm already hating you for hogging all of the press."

Jane didn't laugh because she had been in the spotlight long enough to know that the woman was not really joking.

"Edwin thinks we'll be okay. I set great store by his opinion."

"Do you—" Jane stopped herself, because she had been about to say the exact wrong thing.

*Do you know that Quarter got shot? That Maplecroft was killed? What if the buildings aren't really empty? What if we kill a security guard or a policeman? What if what we're doing is wrong?*

"Do I what?" Clara asked.

"Cough medicine," Jane said, the first thing that came to mind. "Do you have any? My brother—"

"Poor Andy. He's really gone downhill, hasn't it?" Clara frowned in sympathy. "It's come as quite a shock. But we've both seen it happen so many times before, haven't we? You can't be in the arts without knowing dozens of extraordinary men who are infected."

*Infected?*

"Jinx?" Nick was standing at the open front door. "Are you coming in? You need to see this. Both of you."

Clara hastened her step.

Jane could barely find the strength to lift her legs.

Her mouth had gone dry. Her heart was jerking inside of her chest. She struggled to maintain the forward momentum. Up the front walk. The stairs to the porch. To the front door. Into the house.

*Infected?*

Inside, Jane had to lean against the wall, to lock her knees so that she did not collapse. The numbness was back. Her muscles were liquid.

*We've both seen it happen so many times before.*

Jane had known so many young, vigorous men who had coughed like Andrew was coughing. Who had looked sick the same way that Andrew looked sick. Same pale skin tone. Same heavy droop to his eyelids. A jazz saxophonist, a first chair cellist, a tenor, an opera singer, a dancer, another dancer, and another—

*All dead.*

"Come, darling." Nick waved Jane into the room.

They were all gathered around the television. Paula was on the couch beside the man who was probably Tucker. The two others, Spinner and Wyman, a woman and man respectively, sat in folding chairs. Clara sat on the floor because dancers always sat on the floor.

"Andrew's asleep." Nick was on his knees, adjusting the volume on the set. "It's amazing, Jinx. Apparently, they've been doing special reports for the last two days."

Jane saw his mouth move, but it was as if the sound was traveling through water.

Nick sat back on his heels, elated by their notoriety.

Jane watched because everyone else was watching.

Dan Rather was reporting on the events in San Francisco. The camera cut to a reporter standing outside the Victorian house that fronted the shed.

The man said, "According to sources from the FBI, listening devices helped them ascertain that Alexandra Maplecroft had already been murdered by the conspirators. The likely culprit is their leader, Nicholas Harp. Andrew Queller was joined by a second woman who helped them escape through an adjacent building."

Jane flinched when she saw first Nick's face, then Andrew's, flash up. Paula was represented by a shadowy outline with a question mark in the center. Jane closed her eyes. She summoned the photo of Andrew that she had just seen. One year ago, at least. His cheeks were ruddy. A jaunty scarf was tied around his neck. A birthday party, or some kind of celebration? He looked happy, vibrant, alive.

She opened her eyes.

The television reporter said, "The question now is whether Jinx Queller is another hostage or a willing accomplice. Back to you in New York, Dan."

Dan Rather stacked together his papers on the top of his news desk. "William Argenis Johnson, another conspirator, was shot by snipers while trying to escape. A married father of two who worked as a graduate student at Stanford Uni—"

Nick turned off the volume. He did not look at Jane.

"William Johnson." She whispered the words aloud because she did not understand.

*His name was Leonard Brandt. No children. Never married. He lived alone at 1239 Van Duff Street. He worked as a carpenter over in Marin.*

"A fucking question mark?" Paula demanded. "That's all I rate is a fucking question mark?" She stood up, started to pace. "Meanwhile, poor Jinx Queller gets off scot fucking free. How about I write them a fucking letter and tell them you're fucking willing and able and ready? Would that make you happy, Dumb Bitch?"

"Penny," Nick said. "We don't have time for this. Troops, listen to me. We have to move everything up. This is bigger than even I had hoped for. Where are we with Chicago?"

"The bombs are ready," Spinner said, as if she was telling them that she'd just put dinner on the table. "All we have to do is plant them in the underground parking garage, then be within fifty feet of the building when we press the button on the remote."

"Fantastic!" Nick clapped together his hands. He was bouncing on the toes of his feet, amping them all back up again. "It should be the same with the explosives in New York. I'll rest here a few hours, then start driving. Even without my photo on the news, the FBI will heighten security at the airports. I'm not sure my ID will hold up to that kind of scrutiny."

Wyman said, "The forger in Toronto—"

"Is expensive. We blew our wad on Maplecroft's credentials because none of this would've mattered without Laura getting into that conference." Nick rubbed his hands together. Jane could almost see his brain working. This was the part he had always loved, not the planning, but holding them all rapt. "Nebecker and Huston are waiting for me at the safe house in Brooklyn. We'll drive the van into the city after rush hour, plant the devices, then go back the following morning and set them off."

Paula asked, "When do you want my team to set up?"

"Tomorrow morning." Nick watched their faces as realization set in. "Don't set up, *do it*. Plant the explosives first thing in the morning before anyone shows up for work, get as far away as you can, then blow the motherfucker down."

"Fuck yeah!" Paula raised her fist into the air. The others joined in.

"We're doing this, troops!" Nick shouted to be heard over the din. "We're going to make them stand up and take notice! We have to tear down the system before we can make it better."

"Damn right!" Wyman shouted.

"Hell yeah!" Paula was still pacing. She was like an animal ready to break out of her cage. "We're gonna show those mother-fucking pigs!"

Jane looked around the room. They were all wound up the same way, clapping their hands, stomping their feet, whooping as if they were watching a football game.

Tucker said, "Hey! Listen! Just listen!" He'd stood up, hands raised for attention. This was Edwin, Clara's lover. With his handlebar mustache and wavy hair, he looked more like Friedrich Nietzsche than a lawyer, but Nick trusted him, so they all trusted him.

He said, "Remember, you have a legal right to refuse to answer any and all questions from law enforcement. Ask the pigs, 'Am I under arrest?' If they say no, then walk away. If they say yes, shut your mouth—not just to the pigs, but to everybody, especially on the phone. Make sure you have my number memorized. You have a legal right to call your lawyer. Clara and I will be in the city standing by in case I need to go to the jail."

"Good man, Tuck, but it's not going to come to that. And fuck taking a rest. I'm leaving now!"

There was another round of whooping and cheering.

Nick was grinning like a fool. He told Clara, "Go wake up Dime. I'll need someone to help swap out the driving. It's only twelve hours, but I think—"

"No," Jane said. But she hadn't said it. She had shouted it.

The ensuing silence felt like a needle scratching off a record. Jane had ruined the game. No one was smiling anymore.

"Christ," Paula said. "Are you going to start whining again?"

Jane ignored her.

Nick was all that mattered. He looked confused, probably because he'd never heard Jane say *no* before.

"No," she repeated. "Andrew can't. You can't ask him to do

anything more. He did his part. Oslo was our part, and it's over and—" She was crying again, but this was different from the last week of crying. She wasn't grieving over something that had already happened. She was grieving over something that was going to happen very soon.

Jane saw it so clearly now—every sign she had missed in the months, the days, before. Andrew's sudden chills. The exhaustion. The weakness. The sores in his mouth that he'd mentioned in passing. The stomach aches. The weird rash on his wrist.

*Infection.*

"Jinx?" Nick was waiting. They were all waiting.

Jane walked down the hallway. She'd never been in the house before, so she had to open and close several doors before she finally found the bedroom where Andrew was sleeping.

Her brother was lying face-down in bed, fully clothed. He hadn't bothered to undress or get under the covers or even take off his shoes. Jane put her hand to his back. She waited for the up and down of his breathing before she allowed herself to take in her own breath.

She gently slid off his shoes. Carefully rolled him onto his back.

Andrew groaned, but didn't wake. His breath was raspy through his chapped lips. His skin was the color of paper. She could see the blue and red of his veins and arteries as easily as if she had been looking at a diagram. She unbuttoned his shirt partway down and saw the deep purple lesions on his skin. Kaposi's sarcoma. There were probably more lesions in his lungs, his throat, maybe even his brain.

Jane sat down on the bed.

She had lasted no more than six months volunteering at UCSF's AIDS ward. Watching so many men walk through the doors knowing that they would never walk out had proven to be too overwhelming. Jane had thought that the rattle in their chests as they gasped for their last breaths would be the worst sound that she would ever hear.

Until now, when she heard the same sounds coming from her brother.

Jane carefully buttoned his shirt back up.

There was a blue afghan on the back of a rocking chair. She draped it over her brother. She kissed his forehead. He felt so cold. His hands. His feet. She tucked the afghan around his body. She stroked the side of his pale face.

Jane had been seventeen years old when she'd found the old cigar box in the glove box of Andrew's car. She'd thought she'd caught him stealing Martin's cigars, but then she had opened the lid and gasped out loud. A plastic cigarette lighter. A bent silver teaspoon from one of her mother's precious sets. Stained cotton balls. The bottom of a Coke can. A handful of filthy Q-tips. A tube of skin cream squeezed in the middle. A length of rubber tubing for a tourniquet. Insulin syringes with black dots of blood staining the tips of the sharp needles. Tiny rocks of debris that she recognized from her years backstage as tar heroin.

Andrew had given it up eighteen months ago. After meeting Laura. After Nick had developed a plan.

But it was too late.

"Jinx?" Nick was standing in the doorway. He nodded for her to come into the hall.

Jane walked past Nick and went into the bathroom. She wrapped her arms around her waist, shivering. The room was large and cold. A cast iron tub was underneath the leaky window. The toilet was the old-fashioned type with the tank mounted high above the bowl.

Just like the one in Oslo.

"All right." Nick closed the door behind him. "What's got you so worked up, Ms. Queller?"

Jane looked at her reflection in the mirror. She saw her face, but it wasn't her face. The bridge of her nose was almost black. Dried blood caked the nostrils. What was she feeling? She couldn't tell anymore.

*Uncomfortably numb.*

"Jinx?"

She turned away from the mirror. She looked at Nick. His face, but not his face. Their connection, but not really a connection.

He had lied about knowing Quarter's name. He had lied about their future. He had lied every time that he had pretended that her brother was not dying.

And now, he had the audacity to look at his watch. "What is it, Jinx? We haven't much time."

"Time?" she had to repeat the word to truly understand the cruelty. "You're worried about time?"

"Jane—"

"You robbed me." Her throat felt so tight that she could barely speak. "You stole from me."

"Love, what are you—"

"I could've been here with my brother, but you sent me away. Thousands of miles away." Jane clenched her hands. She knew what she was feeling now: rage. "You're a liar. Everything that comes out of your mouth is a lie."

"Andy was—"

She slapped him hard across the face. "He's sick!" She screamed the words so loud that her throat ached. "My brother has AIDS, and you sent me to fucking Germany."

Nick touched his fingers to his cheek. He looked down at his open hand.

He'd been slapped before. Over the years, he'd told Jane about the abuse he'd suffered as a child. The prostitute mother. The absent father. The violent grandmother. The year of homelessness. The disgusting things people had wanted him to do. The self-loathing and hate and the fear that it would happen no matter how hard he tried to run away.

Jane understood the emotions all too well. From the age of eight, she had known what it was like to desperately want to run away. From Martin's hand clamping over her mouth in the middle of the night. From all the times he grabbed the back of her head and pressed her face into the pillow.

Which Nick had known about.

Which is why his stories were so effective. Jane saw it happen over and over again with every person he met. He mirrored your darkest fear with stories of his own.

That's how Nick got you: he inserted himself into the common ground.

Now, he simply asked, "What do you want me to say, Jinx? Yes, Andy has AIDS. Yes, I knew about it when you left for Berlin."

"Is Ellis-Anne . . ." Jane's voice trailed off. Andrew's girlfriend of two years. So sweet and devoted. She had called every day since Oslo. "Is she positive, too?"

"She's fine. She took the ELISA test last month." Nick's tone was filled with authority and reason, the same as it had been when he'd lied about Quarter's real name.

He told Jane, "Listen, you're right about all of this. And it's horrible. I know Andrew is close to the end. I know that having him out here is likely causing him to spiral down faster. And I've been so worried about him, but I have the whole group depending on me, expecting me to lead them and—I can't let myself think about it. I have to look ahead, otherwise I'd just curl into a useless ball of grief. I can't do that, and neither can you, because I need you, darling. Everyone thinks I'm so strong, but I'm only strong when you're standing beside me."

Jane could not believe he was giving her one of his rallying speeches. "You know how they die, Nick. You've heard the stories. Ben Mitchell—do you remember him?" Jane's voice lowered as if she was saying a sacrament. "I took care of him on the ward, but then his parents finally said it was okay for him to come home to die. They took him to the hospital and none of the nurses would touch him because they were afraid of getting infected. Do you remember me telling you about it? They wouldn't even give him morphine. Do you remember?"

Nick's face was impassive. "I remember."

"He suffocated on the fluid inside his lungs. It took almost eight agonizing minutes for him to die, and Ben was awake for every single second of it." She waited, but Nick said nothing. "He was terrified. He kept trying to scream, clawing at his neck, begging people to help. No one would help him. His own mother had to leave the room. Do you remember that story, Nick? Do you?"

He only said, "I remember."

"Is that what you want for Andrew?" She waited, but again, he said nothing. "He's coughing the same way Ben did. The same way Charlie Bray did. The same thing happened to him. Charlie went home to Florida and—"

"You don't have to give me a play-by-play, Jinx. I told you: I remember the stories. Yes, how they died was horrible. All of it was horrible. But we don't have a choice."

She wanted to shake him. "Of course we have a choice."

"It was Andy's idea to send you to Berlin."

Jane knew he was telling the truth, just as she knew that Nick was a surgeon when it came to transplanting his ideas onto other people's tongues.

Nick said, "He thought if you knew he was sick, that you would . . . I don't know, Jinx. Do something stupid. Make us stop. Make everything stop. He believes in this thing that we're doing. He wants us to finish it. That's why I'm taking him to Brooklyn. You can come too. Take care of him. Keep him alive long enough to—"

"Stop." She couldn't listen to his bullshit. "I am not going to let my brother suffocate to death in the back of that filthy van."

"It's not about his life anymore," Nick insisted. "It's about his legacy. This is how Andy wants to go out. On his own terms, like a man. That's what he's always wanted. The overdoses, the hanging, the pills and needles, showing up in places he shouldn't be, hanging out with the wrong people. You know what hell his life has been. He got clean for this thing that we're doing—that we're all doing. This is what gave him the strength to stop using, Jane. Don't take that away from him."

She gripped her fists in frustration. "He's doing it for you, Nick. All it would take is one word from you and he'd go to the hospital where he can die in peace."

"You know him better than me?"

"I know *you* better. Andy wants to please you. They all want to please you. But this is different. It's cruel. He'll suffocate like—"

"Yes, Jane, I get it. He'll suffocate on the fluids in his lungs. He'll have eight minutes of agonizing terror, and that's—well, agonizing—but you need to listen to me very carefully, darling, because this part is very important," Nick said. "You have to choose between him or me."

*What?*

"If Andy can't make the trip with me, then you need to go with me in his place."

*What?*

"I can't trust you anymore." Nick's shoulder went up in a shrug. "I know how your mind works. The minute I leave, you'll take Andy to the hospital. You'll stay with him because that's what you do, Jinx. You stay with people. You've always been loyal, sitting with homeless men down at the shelter, helping serve soup at the mission, wiping spittle from the mouths of dying men at the infection ward. I won't say you're a good little dog, because that's cruel. But your loyalty to Andrew will land us all in prison, because the moment you walk into the hospital, the police will arrest you, and they'll know we're in Chicago, and I can't let that happen."

She felt her mouth gape open.

"I'll only give you this one chance. You have to choose right here, right now: him or me."

Jane felt the room shift. This couldn't be happening.

He looked at her coldly, as if she was a specimen under glass. "You must have known it would come to this, Jane. You're naïve, but you're not stupid." Nick waited a moment. "Choose."

She had to rest her hand on the sink so that she wouldn't slide to the floor. "He's your best friend." Her voice was no more than a whisper. "He's my brother."

"I need your decision."

Jane heard a high-pitched sound in her ears, as if her skull had been struck by a tuning fork. She didn't know what was happening. Panic made her words brim with fear. "Are you leaving me? Breaking up with me?"

"I said me or him. It's your choice, not mine."

"Nick, I can't—" She didn't know how to finish the sentence. Was this a test? Was he doing what he always did, gauging her loyalty? "I love you."

"Then choose me."

"I—you know you're everything to me. I've given up—" She held out her arms, indicating the world, because there was nothing left that she had not abandoned for him. Her father. Jasper. Her life. Her music. "Please, don't make me choose. He's dying."

Nick stared at her, icy cold.

Jane felt a wail come out of her mouth. She knew how Nick looked when he was finished with a person. Six years of her life, her heart, her love, was evaporating in front of her eyes. How could he so easily throw it all away? "Nicky, please—"

"Andrew's impending death should make your choice easy. A few more hours with a dying man or the rest of your life with me." He waited. "Choose."

"Nick—" Another sob cut her off. She felt like she was dying. He couldn't leave her. Not now. "It's not just a few more hours. It's hours of terror, or—" Jane couldn't think about what Andrew would go through if he was abandoned. "You can't mean this. I know you're just testing me. I love you. Of course I love you. I told you I'm with you."

Nick reached for the door.

"Please!" Jane grabbed him by the front of his shirt. He turned away his head when she tried to kiss him. Jane pressed her face to his chest. She was crying so hard that she could barely speak. "Please, Nicky. Please don't make me choose. You know that I can't live without you. I'm nothing without you. Please!"

"Then you'll go with me?"

She looked up at him. She had cried so hard for so long that her eyelids felt like barbed wire.

"I need you to say it, Jane. I need to hear your choice."

"I c-can't—" she stuttered out the word. "Nick, I can't—"

"You can't choose?"

"No." The realization almost stopped her heart. "I can't leave him."

Nick's face gave nothing away.

"I—" Jane could barely swallow. Her mouth had gone dry. She was terrified, but she knew that what she was doing was right. "I will not let my brother die alone."

"All right." Nick reached for the door again, but then something changed his mind.

For just a moment, she thought that he was going to tell her it was okay.

But he didn't.

His hands shot out. He shoved Jane across the room. Her head whipped back, broke the glass out of the window.

She was dumbstruck. She felt the back of her head, expecting to find blood. "Why did—"

Nick punched her in the stomach.

Jane collapsed to her knees. Bile erupted from her mouth. She tasted blood. Her stomach spasmed so hard that she doubled over, her forehead touching the floor.

Nick grabbed her hair, jerked her head back up. He was kneeling in front of her. "What did you think would happen after we did this, Janey, that we would run off to a little flat in Switzerland and raise our baby?"

*The baby—*

"Look at me." His fingers wrapped around her neck. He shook her like a doll. "Were you stupid enough to think I'd let you keep it? That I'd turn into some fat old man who reads the Sunday paper while you do the dishes and we talk about Junior's class project?"

Jane couldn't breathe. Her fingernails dug into his wrists. He was choking her.

"Don't you understand that I know everything about you, Jinx? We've never been whole people. We only make sense when we're together." He tightened his grip with both hands. "Nothing can come between us. Not a whining baby. Not your dying brother. Nothing. Do you hear me?"

She clawed at him, desperate for air. He banged her head against the wall.

"I'll kill you before I let you leave me." He looked her in the eye, and Jane knew that this time, Nick was telling the truth. "You belong to me, Jinx Queller. If you ever try to leave me, I will scorch the earth to get you back. Do you understand?" He shook her again. "Do you?"

His hands were too tight. Jane felt a darkness edging around her vision. Her lungs shuddered. Her tongue would not stay inside of her mouth.

"Look at me." Nick's face was glowing with sweat. His eyes were on fire. He was smiling his usual self-satisfied grin. "How does it feel to suffocate, darling? Is it everything you imagined?"

Her eyelids started to flutter. For the first time in days, Jane's vision was clear. There were no more tears left.

Nick had taken them away, just like he had taken everything else.

August 26, 2018

# 13

Andy sat at a booth in the back of a McDonald's outside of Big Rock, Illinois. She had been so happy to be out of Mike's truck after two and a half monotonous days of driving that she'd treated herself to a milkshake. Worrying about her cholesterol and lack of exercise was a problem for Future Andy.

Present Andy had enough problems already. She was no longer an amoeba, but there were some obsessive tendencies that she had to accept were baked into her DNA. She had spent the first day of the trip freaking out over all of the mistakes she had made and was probably still making: that she had never checked the cooler in the Reliant for a GPS tracker, that she had left the unregistered revolver in the glove box for Mike to find, that she had possibly broken his testicles and actually stolen his wallet and was committing a felony by taking a stolen vehicle across multiple state lines.

This was the really important one: had Mike heard Paula tell Andy to look for Clara Bellamy in Illinois, or had he been too concerned that his nuts were imploding?

*Future Andy would find out eventually.*

She chewed the straw on her milkshake. She watched the screensaver bounce around the laptop screen. She would have to save her neurosis about Mike for when she was trying to fall asleep and needed something to torment herself over. For now, she had to figure out what the hell had landed Paula Kunde in prison for twenty years and why she so clearly held a grudge against Laura.

Andy had so far been stymied in her computer searches. Three nights spent in three different motels with the laptop propped open on her belly had resulted in nothing more than an angry red rectangle of skin on her stomach.

The easiest route to finding shit on people was always Facebook. The night Andy had left Austin, she'd created a fake account in the name of Stefan Salvatore and used the Texas Longhorns' logo as her profile photo. Unsurprisingly, Paula Kunde was not on the social media site. ProfRatings.com let Andy use her Facebook credentials to log in as a user. She went onto Paula's review page with its cumulative half-star rating. She sent dozens of private messages to Paula's most vocal critics, the texts all saying the same thing:

*DUDE!!! Kunde in FEDERAL PEN 20 yrs?!?!?! MUST HAVE DEETS!!! Bitch won't change my grade!!!*

Andy hadn't heard back much more than *Fuck that fucking bitch I hope you kill her*, but she knew that eventually, someone would get bored and do the kind of deep dive that took knowing the number off your parents' credit card.

A toddler screamed on the other side of the McDonald's.

Andy watched his mother carry him toward the bathroom. She wondered if she had ever been to this McDonald's with her mother. Laura hadn't just pulled Chicago, Illinois, out of her ass for Jerry Randall's birth and death place.

*Right?*

Andy slurped the last of the milkshake. Now was not the time to dive into the silly string of her mother's lies. She studied the scrap of paper at her elbow. The second that Andy was safe enough outside of Austin, she had pulled over to the side of the road and scribbled down everything she could remember about her conversation with Paula Kunde.

—Twenty years in Danbury?

—QuellCorp?

—Knew Hoodie, but not Mike?

—31 years—interesting math?

—Laura full of the worst type of bullshit?

—Shotgun? What made her change her mind—Clara Bellamy???

Andy had started with the easiest searches first. The Danbury Federal Penitentiary's records were accessible through the BOP. gov inmate locator, but Paula Kunde was not listed on the site. Nor was she listed on the UC-Berkeley, Stanford or West Connecticut University alumni pages. The obvious explanation was that Paula had at some point gotten married and, patriarchal constructs aside, changed her last name.

*I know how marriage works.*

Andy had already checked marriage and divorce records in Austin, then in surrounding counties, then done the same in Western Connecticut and Berkeley County and Palo Alto, then Andy had decided that she was wasting her time because Paula could've flown to Vegas and gotten hitched and actually, why did Andy believe that a shotgun-wielding lunatic had told her the truth about being in prison in the first place?

*Snitch* and *two dimes* were basically in every prison show ever. All it took was saying them with attitude, which Paula Kunde had plenty of.

Regardless, the BOP search was a dead end.

Andy tapped her fingers on the table as she studied the list. She tried to think back to the conversation inside of Paula's kitchen. There had been a definite before and after. Before, meaning when Paula was talking to her, and after, meaning when she'd gone to fetch her shotgun and told Andy to get the hell out.

Andy couldn't think of what she'd said wrong. They had been talking about Laura, and how she was full of bullshit—the worst type of bullshit—

And then Paula had told Andy to wait and then threatened to shoot her.

Andy could only shake her head, because it still didn't make sense.

Even more puzzling was the after-after, because Paula hadn't given up Clara Bellamy's name until after Andy had kicked the shit out of Mike. Andy could take it at face value and assume that Paula had been impressed by the violence, but something told her she was on the wrong track. Paula was fucking smart. You didn't go to Stanford if you were an idiot. She had played Andy like a fiddle from the moment she'd opened the front door. She was very likely playing Andy even now, but trying to figure out a maniac's end game was far beyond Andy's deductive skills.

She looked back at her notes, focusing on the item that still niggled most at her brain:

—31 years—interesting math?

Had Paula gone to prison thirty-one years ago while a pregnant Laura ran off with nearly one million bucks and a fake ID to live her fabulous life on the beach for thirty-one years until suddenly the diner video appeared on the national news, pointing the bad guys to her location?

Hoodie had strangled both Laura and Paula, so obviously both women had information that someone else wanted.

The mysterious *they* who could track Andy's emails and phone calls?

Andy returned to the laptop and tried QuellCorp.com again, because all she could do now was go back and see if she'd missed anything the last twenty times she had looked at the website.

The splash page offered a Ken Burns–effect photo slowly zooming onto a young, multicultural group of lab-coated scientists staring intently at a beaker full of glowing liquid. Violins played in the background like Leonardo da Vinci had just discovered the cure for herpes.

Andy muted the sound.

She was familiar with the pharmaceutical company the same way everybody was familiar with Band-Aids. QuellCorp made everything from baby wipes to erectile dysfunction pills. The only information Andy could find under HISTORY was that a guy named Douglas Paul Queller had founded the company in the 1920s, then his descendants had sold out in the 1980s, then by the early 2000s QuellCorp had basically swallowed the world, because that's what evil corporations did.

*They* could certainly be an evil corporation. That was the plot of almost every sci-fi movie Andy had seen, from *Avatar* to all of the *Terminator*s.

She closed the QuellCorp page and pulled up the wiki for Clara Bellamy.

If it was strange that Laura knew Paula Kunde, it was downright shocking that Paula Kunde knew a woman like Clara Bellamy. She had been a *prima ballerina*, which according to another wiki page was an honor only bestowed on a handful of women. Clara had danced for George Balanchine, a choreographer whose name even Andy recognized. Clara had toured the world. Danced on the most celebrated stages. Been at the top of her field. Then a horrific knee injury had forced her to retire.

Because Andy had had nothing better to do after driving all day, she had seen almost every video of Clara Bellamy that YouTube had to offer. There were countless performances and interviews with all kinds of famous people, but Andy's favorite was from what she believed was the first Tchaikovsky Festival ever staged by the New York City Ballet.

Since Andy was a theater nerd, the foremost thing she'd noticed about the video was that the set was spectacular, with weird translucent tubes in the background that made everything look like it was encased in ice. She had assumed that it would be boring to watch tiny women spinning on their toes to old-people music, but there was something almost hummingbird-like about Clara Bellamy that made her impossible to look away from. For a woman Andy had never heard of, Clara had been extraordinarily famous. *Newsweek* and *Time* had both featured her on the cover. She was constantly showing up in the *New York Times Magazine* or highlighted in the *New Yorker*'s "Goings On About Town" section.

That was where Andy's searches had hit a wall. Or, to be more exact, a pay wall. She was only allowed a certain number of articles on a lot of the websites, so she had to be careful about what she clicked on. It wasn't like she could just pull out a credit card and buy more access.

As far as she could tell, Clara had disappeared from public life around 1983. The last photo in the *Times* showed the woman with her head down, tissue held to her nose, as she left George Balanchine's funeral.

As with Paula, Andy assumed that Clara Bellamy had been married at some point and changed her name, though why anybody would work so hard to create a famous name, then change it, was hard to fathom. Clara had no Facebook page, but there was a closed appreciation group and a public thinspo one that was grossly obsessed with her weight.

Andy had not been able to locate any marriage or divorce documents for Clara Bellamy in New York, or Chicago's Cook County or the surrounding areas, but she had found an interesting article in the *Chicago Sun Times* about a lawsuit that had taken place after Clara's knee injury.

The *prima ballerina* had sued a company called EliteDream BodyWear for payment on an endorsement contract. The lawyer who'd represented her was not named in the article, but the accompanying photo showed Clara leaving the courthouse with a lanky, mustachioed man who looked to Andy like the perfect embodiment of a hippie lawyer, or a hipster Millennial trying to look like one. More importantly, when the photographer had clicked the button to take the photo, Hippie Lawyer was looking directly at the camera.

Andy had taken several photography classes at SCAD. She knew how unusual it was to have a candid where someone wasn't blinking or moving their lips in a weird way. Hippie Lawyer had defied the odds. Both of his eyes were open. His lips were slightly parted. His ridiculously curled handlebar mustache was on center. His silky, long hair rested square on his shoulders. The image was so clear that Andy could even see the tips of his ears sticking out from his hair like tiny pistachios.

Andy had to assume that Hippie Lawyer had not changed that much over the years. A guy who in his thirties took his facial hair grooming cues from Wyatt Earp did not suddenly wake up in his sixties and realize his mistake.

She entered a new search: *Chicago+Lawyer+Mustache+Hair*.

Within seconds, she was looking at a group called the Funkadelic Fiduciaries, a self-described "hair band." They played every Wednesday night at a bar called the EZ Inn. Each one had some weird facial hair going on, whether it was devilish Van Dykes or Elvis sideburns, and there were enough man-buns to start an emo colony. Andy zoomed in on each face in the eight-member group and spotted the familiar curl of a handlebar mustache on the drummer.

Andy looked down at his name.

Edwin Van Wees.

She rubbed her eyes. She was tired from driving all day and staring at computer screens all night. It couldn't be that easy.

She found the old photo from the newspaper to do a comparison. The drummer was a little plumper, a lot less hairy and not as handsome, but she knew that she had the right guy.

Andy looked out the window, taking a moment to acknowledge her good luck. Was finding Edwin, who might know how to find Clara Bellamy, really that easy?

She opened another browser window.

As with Clara, Edwin Van Wees did not have his own Facebook page, but she was able to find a homemade-looking website that listed him as partially retired but still available for speaking gigs and drum solos. She clicked on the *about* tab. Edwin was a Stanford-trained, former ACLU lawyer with a long, successful career of defending artists and anarchists and rabble-rousers and revolutionaries who had happily posted photos of themselves grinning beside the lawyer who'd kept them out of prison. Even some of the ones who'd ended up going to jail still had glowing things to say about him. It made perfect sense that a guy like Edwin would know a crazy bitch like Paula Kunde.

*My revolutionary days are over.*

Andy believed with all of her heart that Edwin Van Wees still knew how to get in touch with Clara Bellamy. It was the familiar way she was touching his arm in the courthouse photo. It was also the nasty look Edwin was giving the man behind the lens. Maybe Andy was reading too much into it, but if the professor from Andy's Emotions of Light in Black and White Photography class had tasked her with finding a photo of a fragile woman holding onto her strong protector, this was the picture Andy would've chosen.

The toddler started screaming again.

His mother snatched him up and took him to the bathroom again.

Andy closed the laptop and shoved it into her messenger bag. She tossed her trash and got back into Mike's truck. Stone Temple Pilots' "Interstate Love Song" was still playing. Andy reached down to turn it off, but she couldn't. She hated that she loved Mike's music. All of his mix-CDs were awesome, from Dashboard Confessional to Blink 182 and a surprising amount of J-Lo.

Andy checked the time on the McDonald's sign as she pulled onto the road. Two twelve in the afternoon. Not the worst time to drop by unannounced. On his website, Edwin Van Wees had listed his office address at a farm about an hour and a half drive from Chicago. She assumed that meant he worked from home, which made it highly likely that he would be there when Andy pulled up. She had mapped out the directions on Google Earth, zooming in and out of the lush farmlands, locating Edwin's big red barn and matching house with its bright metal roof.

From the McDonald's, it took her ten minutes to find the farm. She almost missed the driveway because it was hidden in a thick stand of trees. Andy stopped the truck just shy of the turn. The road was deserted. The floorboard vibrated as the engine idled.

She didn't feel the same nervousness she'd felt when she walked toward Paula's house. Andy understood now that there was no guarantee that finding a person meant that the person was going to tell you the truth. Or even that the person was not going to shove a shotgun in your chest. Maybe Edwin Van Wees would do the same thing. It kind of made sense that Paula Kunde would send Andy to someone who would not be happy to see her. The drive from Austin had given Paula plenty of time to call ahead and warn Clara Bellamy that Laura Oliver's kid might be looking for her. If Edwin Van Wees was still close to Clara, then Clara could've called Edwin and—

Andy rubbed her face with her hands. She could spend the rest of the day doing this stupid dance or she could go find out for herself. She turned the wheel and drove down the driveway. The trees didn't clear for what felt like half a mile, but soon she saw the top of the red barn, then a large pasture with cows, then the small farmhouse with a wide porch and sunflowers planted in the front yard.

Andy parked in front of the barn. There were no other cars in sight, which was a bad sign. The front door to the house didn't open. There was no fluttering of curtains or furtive faces in the windows. Still, she wasn't too much of an imbecile to leave without knocking on the door.

Andy started to climb out of the truck, but then she remembered the burner phone that Laura was supposed to call her on when the coast was clear. In truth, she had lost hope around Tulsa that it would ever ring. The *Belle Isle Review* had provided the salient facts: Hoodie's body remained unidentified. After analyzing the video from the diner, the police had reached the same conclusion as Mike. Laura had tried to stop Jonah Helsinger from killing himself. She would not be charged with his murder. The kid's family was still making noises, but police royalty or not, public sentiment had turned away from them, and the local prosecutor was a political weathervane of the vilest kind. In short, whatever lurking danger was keeping Andy away from home was either unrelated or simply another part of Laura's colossal web of lies.

Andy unzipped the make-up bag and checked the phone to make sure the battery was full before slipping it into her back pocket. She saw Laura's Canada license and health card. Andy studied the photo of her mother, trying to ignore the pang of longing that she did not want to feel. Instead, she looked at her own reflection in the mirror. Maybe it was Andy's crappy diet or lack of sleep or the fact that she had started wearing her hair down, but as each day passed, she had started to look more and more like her mother. The last three hotel clerks had barely glanced up when Andy had used the license to check in.

She shoved it back into her messenger bag beside a black leather wallet.

Mike's wallet.

For the last two and a half days, Andy had been studiously avoiding opening the wallet and staring at Mike's handsome face, especially when she was lying in bed at night and trying not to think about him because he was a psychopath and she was pathetic.

She looked up at the farmhouse, then checked the driveway, then opened the wallet.

"Oh for fucksakes," she muttered.

He had four different driver's licenses, each of them pretty damn good forgeries: Michael Knepper from Alabama; Michael Davey from Arkansas; Michael George from Texas; Michael Falcone from Georgia. There was a thick flap of leather dividing the wallet. Andy picked it open.

*Holy shit.*

He had a fake United States marshal badge. Andy had seen the real thing before, a gold star inside of a circle. It was a good replica, as convincing as all of the fake IDs. Whoever his forger was had done a damn good job.

There was a tap at the window.

"Fuck!" Andy dropped the wallet as her hands flew up.

Then her mouth dropped open, because the person who had knocked on the window looked a hell of a lot like Clara Bellamy.

"You," the woman said, a bright smile to her lips. "What are you doing sitting out here in this dirty truck?"

Andy wondered if her eyes were playing tricks, or if she had looked at so many YouTube videos that she was seeing Clara Bellamy everywhere. The woman was older, her face lined, her long hair a peppered gray, but undoubtedly Andy was looking at the real-life person.

Clara said, "Come on, silly. It's chilly out here. Let's go inside."

*Why was she talking to Andy like she knew her?*

Clara pulled open the door. She held out her hand to help Andy down.

"My goodness," Clara said. "You look tired. Has Andrea been keeping you up again? Did you leave her at the hotel?"

Andy opened her mouth, but there was no way to answer. She looked into Clara's eyes, wondering who the woman saw staring back at her.

"What is it?" Clara asked. "Do you need Edwin?"

"Uh—" Andy struggled to answer. "Is he—is Edwin here?" She looked at the area in front of the barn. "His car isn't here."

Andy waited.

"I just put Andrea down for a nap," she said, as if she hadn't two seconds ago asked if Andrea was at the hotel.

Did she mean Andrea as in Andy, or someone else?

Clara said, "Should we have some tea?" She didn't wait for an answer. She looped her arm through Andy's and led her back toward the farmhouse. "I have no idea why, but I was thinking about Andrew this morning. What happened to him." She put her hand to the base of her throat. She had started to cry. "Jane, I'm so very sorry."

"Uh—" Andy had no idea what she was talking about, but she felt a strange desire to cry, too.

*Andrew? Andrea?*

Clara said, "Let's not talk about depressing things today. You've got enough of that going on in your life right now." She pushed open the front door with her foot. "Now, tell me how you've been. Are you all right? Still having trouble sleeping?"

"Uh," Andy said, because apparently that's all she was capable of coming up with. "I've been . . ." She tried to think of something to say that would keep this woman talking. "What about you? What have you been up to?"

"Oh, so much. I've been clipping magazine photos with ideas

for the nursery and working on some scrapbooks from my glory years. The worst kind of self-aggrandizement, but you know, it's such a strange thing—I've forgotten most of my performances. Have you?"

"Uh . . ." Andy still didn't know what the hell the woman was talking about.

Clara laughed. "I bet you remember every single one. You were always so sharp that way." She pushed open a swinging door with her foot. "Have a seat. I'll make us some tea."

Andy realized she was in another kitchen with another stranger who might or might not know everything about her mother.

"I think I have some cookies." Clara started opening cupboards.

Andy took in the kitchen. The space was small, cut off from the rest of the house, and probably not much changed since it was built. The metal cabinets were painted bright teal. The countertops were made from butcher's blocks. The appliances looked like they belonged on the set of *The Partridge Family*.

There was a large whiteboard on the wall by the fridge. Someone had written:

*Clara: it's Sunday. Edwin will be in town from 1–4pm. Lunch is in the fridge. Do not use the stove.*

Clara turned on the stove. The starter clicked several times before the gas caught. "Chamomile?"

"Uh—sure." Andy sat down at the table. She tried to think of some questions to ask Clara, like what year it was or who was the current president, but none of that was necessary because you don't put notes on a board like that unless a person has memory problems.

Andy felt an almost overwhelming sadness that was quickly chased by a healthy dose of guilt, because if Clara had early-onset Alzheimer's, then what had happened to her last week was gone, but what had happened to her thirty-one years ago was probably close to the surface.

Andy asked, "What colors were you thinking of for the nursery?"

"No pinks," Clara insisted. "Maybe some greens and yellows?"

"That sounds pretty." Andy tried to keep her talking. "Like the sunflowers outside."

"Yes, exactly." She seemed pleased. "Edwin says we'll try as soon as this is over, but I don't know. It seems like we should start now. I'm not getting any younger." She put her hand to her stomach as she laughed. There was something so beautiful about the sound that Andy felt it pull at her heart.

Clara Bellamy exuded kindness. To try to trick her felt dirty.

Clara asked, "How are you feeling, though? Are you still exhausted?"

"I'm better." Andy watched Clara pour cold water into two cups. She hadn't heated the kettle. The flame flickered high on the stove. Andy stood up to turn it off, asking, "Do you remember how we met? I was trying to recall the details the other day."

"Oh, so horrible." Her fingers went to her throat. "Poor Andrew."

*Andrew again.*

Andy sat back down at the table. She wasn't equipped for this kind of subterfuge. A smarter person would know how to get information out of this clearly troubled woman. Paula Kunde would likely have her singing like a bird.

Which gave Andy an idea.

She tried, "I saw Paula a few days ago."

Clara rolled her eyes. "I hope you didn't call her that."

"What else would I call her?" Andy tried. "Bitch?"

Clara laughed as she sat down at the table. She had put tea bags in the cold water. "I wouldn't say that to her face. Penny would probably just as soon see us all dead right now."

*Penny?*

Andy mulled the word around in her head. And then she remembered the dollar bill that Paula Kunde had shoved into her hand. Andy was wearing the same jeans from that day. She dug into her pocket and found the bill wadded into a tight ball. She smoothed it out on the table. She slid it toward Clara.

"Ah." Clara's lips turned up mischievously. "Dumb Bitch, reporting for duty."

*Another spectacular success.*

Andy had to stop being subtle. She asked, "Do you remember Paula's last name?"

Clara's eyebrow went up. "Is this some sort of test? Do you think I can't remember?"

Andy tried to decipher Clara's suddenly sharp tone. Was she irritated? Had Andy ruined her chances?

Clara laughed, breaking the tension. "Of course I remember. What's gotten into you, Jane? You're acting so strange."

*Jane?*

Clara said the name again. "Jane?"

Andy played with the string on her tea bag. The water had turned orange. "I've forgotten, is the problem. She's using a different name now."

"Penny?"

*Penny?*

"I just—" Andy couldn't keep playing these games. "Just tell me, Clara. What's her last name?"

Clara reeled back at the demand. Tears seeped from her eyes.

Andy felt like an asshole. "I'm sorry. I shouldn't have snapped at you."

Clara stood up. She walked to the refrigerator and opened it. Instead of getting something out, she just stood there.

"Clara, I'm so—"

"It's Evans. Paula Louise Evans."

Andy's elation was considerably tempered by her shame.

"I'm not completely bonkers." Clara's back was stiff. "I remember the important things. I always have."

"I know that. I'm so sorry."

Clara kept her own counsel as she stared into the open fridge.

Andy wanted to slide onto the floor and grovel for forgiveness. She also wanted to run outside and get her laptop, but she needed internet access to look up Paula Louise Evans. She hesitated, but only slightly, before asking Clara, "Do you know the—" She stopped herself, because Clara probably had no idea what Wi-Fi was, let alone knew the password.

Andy asked, "Is there an office in the house?"

"Of course." Clara closed the fridge and turned around, the warm smile back in place. "Do you need to make a phone call?"

"Yes," Andy said, because agreeing was the quickest way forward. "Do you mind?"

"Is it long-distance?"

"No."

"That's good. Edwin's been grousing at me about the phone bill lately." Clara's smile started to falter. She had lost her way in the conversation again.

Andy said, "When I finish my phone call in the office, we could talk some more about Andrew."

"Of course." Clara's smile brightened. "It's this way, but I'm not sure where Edwin is. He's been working so hard lately. And obviously the news has made him very upset."

Andy didn't ask what news because she couldn't bear to risk setting the woman off again.

She followed Clara back through the house. Even with the bad knee, the dancer's walk was breathtakingly graceful. Her feet barely touched the floor. Andy couldn't fully appreciate watching her move because so many questions flooded her mind: Who was Jane? Who was Andrew? Why did Clara cry every time she said the man's name?

And why did Andy feel the desire to protect this fragile woman she had never met before?

"Here." Clara was at the end of the hall. She opened the door to what had likely been a bedroom at some point, but was now a tidy office with a wall of locked filing cabinets, a roll-top desk and a MacBook Pro on the arm of a leather couch.

Clara smiled at Andy. "What did you need?"

Andy hesitated again. She should go back to the McDonald's and use their Wi-Fi. There was no reason to do this here. Except that she still wanted to know answers. What if Paula Louise Evans wasn't online? And then Andy would have to drive back, and Edwin Van Wees would probably be home by then, and he would probably not want Clara talking to Andy.

Clara asked, "Can I help you with something?"

"The computer?"

"That's easy. They're not as scary as you think." Clara sat on the floor. She opened the MacBook. The password prompt came up. Andy expected her to struggle with the code, but Clara pressed her finger to the Touch ID and the desktop was unlocked.

She told Andy, "You'll have to sit here, otherwise the light from the window blacks out the screen."

She meant the giant window behind the couch. Andy could see Mike's truck parked in front of the red barn. She could still leave. Edwin would be home in less than an hour. Now would be the time to go.

Clara said, "Come, Jane. I can show you how to use it. It's not terribly complicated."

Andy sat down on the floor beside Clara.

Clara put the open laptop on the seat of the couch so they could both see it. She said, "I've been looking at videos of myself. Does that make me terribly vain?"

Andy looked at this stranger sitting so close beside her, who kept talking to her like they had been friends for a long time, and said, "I watched your videos, too. Almost all of them. You were—are—such a beautiful dancer, Clara. I never thought I liked ballet before, but watching you made me understand that it's lovely."

Clara touched her fingers to Andy's leg. "Oh, darling, you're so sweet. You know I feel the same about you."

Andy did not know what to say. She reached up to the laptop. She found the browser. Her fingers fumbled on the keyboard. She was sweaty and shaky for no reason. She squeezed her hands into fists in an attempt to get them back under control. She rested her fingers on the keyboard. She slowly typed.

PAULA LOUISE EVANS.

Andy's pinky finger rested on the ENTER key but did not press it. This was the moment. She would find out something—

at least one thing—about the horrible woman who had known her mother thirty-one years ago.

Andy tapped ENTER.

*Motherfucker.*

Paula Louise Evans had her own Wikipedia page.

Andy clicked on the link.

The warning at the top of the page indicated the information was not without controversy. Which made sense, because Paula struck Andy as a woman who loved controversy.

She felt a nervous energy take hold as she skimmed the contents, scrolling through an extensive bio that listed everything from the hospital where Paula had been born to her inmate number at Danberry Federal Penitentiary for Women.

*Raised in Corte Madera, California . . . Berkeley . . . Stanford . . . murder.*

Andy's stomach dropped.

Paula Evans had murdered a woman.

Andy looked up at the ceiling for a moment. She thought about Paula pointing the shotgun at her chest.

Clara said, "There's so much information about her. Is it horrible that I'm a bit jealous?"

Andy scrolled down to the next section:

INVOLVEMENT WITH THE ARMY OF THE CHANGING WORLD.

There was a blurry photo of Paula. The date underneath read "July 1986."

*Thirty-two years ago.*

Andy could remember doing the math back in Carrollton at the library computer. She had been looking for events that had taken place around the time she would've been conceived.

Bombings and plane hijackings and shoot-outs at banks.

Andy studied the photo of Paula Evans.

She was wearing a weird dress that looked like a cotton slip. Thick, black lines of make-up were smeared beneath her eyes. Fingerless gloves were on her hands. Combat boots were on her feet. She was wearing a beret. A cigarette dangled from her mouth. She had a revolver in one hand and a hunting knife in the other. It would've been funny except for the fact that Paula had murdered someone.

And been involved in a conspiracy to bring down the world, apparently.

"Jane?" Clara had pulled a blue afghan around her shoulders. "Should we have some tea?"

"In a moment," Andy said, doing a search for the word *JANE* on Paula's Wikipedia page.

Nothing.

*ANDREW.*

Nothing.

She clicked on the link that took her to the wiki page for THE ARMY OF THE CHANGING WORLD.

*Starting with the assassination of Martin Queller in Oslo . . .*

"QuellCorp," Andy said.

Clara made a hissing sound. "Aren't they awful?"

Andy skipped down the page. She saw a photo of their leader, a guy who looked like Zac Efron with Charles Manson's eyes. The Army's crimes were bullet-pointed past the Martin Queller assassination. They had kidnapped and murdered a Berkeley professor. Been involved in a shoot-out, a nationwide manhunt. Their crazy-ass leader had written a manifesto, a ransom note that had appeared on the front page of the *San Francisco Chronicle*.

Andy clicked on the note.

She read the first part about the fascist regime and then her eyes started to glaze over.

It was like something Calvin and Hobbes would concoct during a meeting of G.R.O.S.S. to get back at Susie Derkins.

Andy returned to the Army page and found a section called MEMBERS. Most of the names were in blue hyperlinks amid the sea of black text. Dozens of people. How had Andy never seen a Dateline or Lifetime movie about this insane cult?

William Johnson. Dead.

Franklin Powell. Dead.

Metta Larsen. Dead.

Andrew Queller—

Andy's heart flipped, but Andrew's name was in black, which meant he didn't have a page. Then again, you didn't have to be Scooby-Doo to link him back to QuellCorp and its assassinated namesake.

She scrolled back up to Martin Queller and clicked his name. Apparently, there were a lot more famous Quellers out there that Andy didn't know about. His wife, Annette Queller, née Logan, had a family line that would take hours to explore. Their eldest son, Jasper Queller, was hyperlinked, but Andy already knew the asshole billionaire who kept trying and failing to run for president.

The cursor drifted over the next name: Daughter, Jane "Jinx" Queller.

"Jane?" Clara asked, because she had Alzheimer's and her mind was trapped in a time over thirty years ago when she knew a woman named Jane who looked just like Andy.

Just as Andy looked like the Daniela B. Cooper photo in the fake Canada driver's license.

*Her mother.*

Andy started to cry. Not just cry, but sob. A wail came out of her mouth. Tears and snot rolled down her face. She leaned over, her forehead on the seat of the couch.

"Oh, sweetheart." Clara was on her knees, her arms wrapped around Andy's shoulders.

Andy shook with grief. Was Laura's real name Jane Queller? Why did this one lie matter so much more than the others?

"Here, let me." Clara slid the laptop over and started to type. "It's okay, my darling. I cry when I watch mine sometimes, too, but look at this one. It's perfect."

Clara slid the laptop back to the center.

Andy tried to wipe her eyes. Clara put a tissue in her hand. Andy blew her nose, tried to stanch her tears. She looked at the laptop.

Clara had pulled up a YouTube video.

!!!RARE!!! JINX QUELLER 1983 CARNEGIE HALL!!!
*What?*

"That green dress!" Clara's eyes glowed with excitement. She clicked the icon for full screen. "A fait accompli."

Andy did not know what to do but watch the video as it autoplayed. The recording was fuzzy and weirdly colored, like everything else from the eighties. An orchestra was already on stage. A massive, black grand piano was front and center.

"Oh!" Clara unmuted the sound.

Andy heard soft murmurs from the crowd.

Clara said, "This was my favorite part. I always peeked out to feel their mood."

For some reason, Andy held her breath.

The audience had gone silent.

A very thin woman in a dark green evening gown walked out of the wings.

"So elegant," Clara murmured, but Andy barely registered the comment.

The woman crossing the stage was young-looking, maybe eighteen, and obviously uncomfortable walking in such dressy shoes. Her hair was bleached almost white, permed within an inch of its life. The camera swept to the audience. They were giving her a standing ovation before she even turned to look at them.

The camera zoomed in on the woman's face.

Andy felt her stomach clench.

*Laura.*

In the video, her mother performed a slight bow. She looked so cool as she stared into the faces of thousands of people. Andy had seen that look before on other performers' faces. Absolute certainty. She had always loved watching an actor's transformation from the wings, had been in awe that they could walk out in front of all of those judgmental strangers and so believably pretend to be someone else.

Like her mother had pretended for all of Andy's life.

*The worst type of bullshit.*

The cheering started to die down as Jinx Queller sat down in front of the piano.

She nodded to the conductor.

The conductor raised his hands.

The audience abruptly silenced.

Clara turned up the volume as loud as it would go.

Violins strummed. The low vibration tickled her eardrums. Then the tempo bounced, then calmed, then bounced again.

Andy didn't know music, especially classical. Laura never listened to it at home. The Red Hot Chili Peppers. Heart. Nirvana. Those were the groups that Laura played on the radio when she was driving around town or doing chores or working on patient reports. She knew the words to "Mr. Brightside" before anyone else did. She had downloaded "Lemonade" the night it dropped. Her eclectic taste made her the cool mom, the mom that everyone could talk to because she wouldn't judge you.

Because she had played Carnegie Hall and she knew what the fuck she was talking about.

In the video, Jinx Queller was still waiting at the piano, hands resting in her lap, eyes straight ahead. Other instruments had joined the violins. Andy didn't know which ones because her mother had never taught her about music. She had discouraged Andy from joining the band, winced every time Andy picked up the cymbals.

Flutes. Andy could see the guys in front pursing their lips.

Bows moved. Oboe. Cello. Horns.

Jinx Queller still patiently awaited her turn at the grand piano.

Andy pressed her palm to her stomach as if to calm it. She was sick with tension for the woman in the video.

Her mother.

*This stranger.*

What was Jinx Queller thinking while she waited? Was she wondering how her life would turn out? Did she know that she would one day have a daughter? Did she know that she had only four years left before Andy came along and somehow took her away from this amazing life?

At 2:22, her mother finally raised her hands.

There was an appreciable tension before her fingers lightly touched the keys.

Soft at first, just a few notes, a slow, lazy progression.

The violins came back in, then her hands moved faster, floating up and down the keyboard, bringing out the most beautiful sound that Andy had ever heard.

*Flowing. Lush. Rich. Exuberant.*

There weren't enough adjectives in the world to describe what Jinx Queller coaxed from the piano.

*Swelling*—that's what Andy felt. A swelling in her heart.

*Pride. Joy. Confusion. Euphoria.*

Andy's emotions matched the look on her mother's face as the music went from solemn to dramatic to thrilling, then back again. Every note seemed to be reflected in Jane's expression, her eyebrows lifting, her eyes closing, her lips curled up in pleasure. She was absolutely enraptured. Confidence radiated off the grainy video like rays from the sun. There was a smile on her mother's lips, but it was a secret smile that Andy had never seen before. Jinx Queller, still so impossibly young, had the look of a woman who was exactly where she was meant to be.

Not in Belle Isle. Not at a parent–teacher conference or on the couch in her office working with a patient, but on stage, holding the world in the palm of her hand.

Andy wiped her eyes. She could not stop crying. She did not understand how her mother had not cried every day for the rest of her life.

*How could anyone walk away from something so magical?*

Andy sat completely transfixed for the entire length of the video. She could not take her eyes off the screen. Sometimes her mother's hands flicked up and down the length of the piano, other times they seemed to be on top of each other, the fingers moving independently across the white and black keys in a way that reminded Andy of Laura kneading dough in the kitchen.

The smile never left her face right up until the ebullient last notes.

Then it was over.

Her hands floated to her lap.

The audience went crazy. They were on their feet. The clapping turned into a solid wall of sound, more like the constant shush of a summer rain.

Jinx Queller stayed seated, hands in her lap, looking down at the keys. Her breath was heavy from physical exertion. Her shoulders had rolled in. She started nodding. She seemed to be taking a moment with the piano, with herself, to absorb the sensation of absolute perfection.

She nodded once more. She stood up. She shook the conductor's hand. She waved to the orchestra. They were already standing, saluting her with their bows, furiously clapping their hands.

She turned to the audience and the cheering swelled. She bowed stage left, then right, then center. She smiled—a different smile, not so confident, not so joyful—and walked off the stage.

That was it.

Andy closed the laptop before the next video could play.

She looked up at the window behind the couch. The sun was bright against the blue sky. Tears dripped down into the collar of her shirt. She tried to think of a word to describe how she was feeling—

*Astonished? Bewildered? Overcome? Dumbfounded?*

Laura had been the one thing that Andy had wanted to be close to all of her life.

*A star.*

She studied her own hands. She had normal fingers—not too long or thin. When Laura was sick and unable to take care of herself, Andy had washed her mother's hands, put lotion on them, rubbed them, held them. But what did they really look like? They had to be graceful, enchanted, imbued with an other-worldly sort of grace. Andy should have felt sparks when she massaged them, or spellbound, or—*something*.

Yet they were the same normal hands that had waved for Andy to hurry up or she'd be late for school. Dug soil in the garden when it was time to plant spring flowers. Wrapped around the back of Gordon's neck when they danced. Pointed at Andy in fury when she did something wrong.

*Why?*

Andy blinked, trying to clear the tears from her eyes. Clara had disappeared. Maybe she hadn't been able to handle Andy's grief, or the perceived pain that Jane Queller experienced when she watched her younger self playing. The two women had clearly discussed the performance before.

*That green dress!*

Andy reached into her back pocket for the burner phone.

She dialed her mother's number.

She listened to the phone ring.

She closed her eyes against the sunlight, imagining Laura in the kitchen. Walking over to her phone where it was charging on the counter. Seeing the unfamiliar number on the screen. Trying to decide whether or not to answer it. Was it a robocall? A new client?

"Hello?" Laura said.

The sound of her voice cracked Andy open. She had longed for nearly a week to have her mother call, to hear the words that it was safe to come back home, but now that she was on the phone, Andy was incapable of doing anything but crying.

"Hello?" Laura repeated. Then, because she had gotten similar calls before, "Andrea?"

Andy lost what little shit she had managed to keep together. She leaned over her knees, head in her hand, trying not to wail again.

"Andrea, why are you calling me?" Laura's tone was clipped. "What's wrong? What happened?"

Andy opened her mouth, but only to breathe.

"Andrea, please," Laura said. "I need you to acknowledge that you can hear me." She waited. "Andy—"

"Who are you?"

Laura did not make a sound. Seconds passed, then what felt like a full minute.

Andy looked at the screen, wondering if they had been disconnected. She pressed the phone back to her ear. She finally heard the gentle slap of waves from the beach. Laura had walked outside. She was on the back porch.

"You lied to me," Andy said.

Nothing.

"My birthday. Where I was born. Where we lived. That fake picture of my fake grandparents. Do you even know who my father is?"

Laura still said nothing.

"You used to be somebody, Mom. I saw it online. You were on stage at-at-at Carnegie Hall. People were worshipping you. It must've taken years to get that good. All of your life. You were somebody, and you walked away from it."

"You're wrong," Laura finally said. There was no emotion in her tone, just a cold flatness. "I'm nobody, and that's exactly who I want to be."

Andy pressed her fingers into her eyes. She couldn't take any more of these fucking riddles. Her head was going to explode.

Laura asked, "Where are you?"

"I'm nowhere."

Andy wanted to close the phone, to give Laura the biggest silent *fuck you* she could, but the moment was too desperate for hollow gestures.

She asked Laura, "Are you even my real mother?"

"Of course I am. I was in labor for sixteen hours. The doctors thought they were going to lose both of us. But they didn't. We didn't. We survived."

Andy heard a car pulling into the driveway.

*Fuck.*

"An-Andrea," Laura struggled to get out her name. "Where are you? I need to know you're safe."

Andy knelt on the couch and looked out the window. Edwin Van Wees with his stupid handlebar mustache. He saw Mike's truck and practically fell out of his car as he scrambled toward the front door.

"Clara!" he yelled. "Clara, where—"

Clara answered, but Andy couldn't make out the words.

Laura must have heard something. She asked, "Where are you?"

Andy listened to heavy boots pounding down the hallway.

"Andrea," Laura said, her tone clipped. "This is deadly serious. You need to tell me—"

"Who the fuck are you?" Edwin demanded.

Andy turned around.

"Shit," Edwin muttered. "Andrea."

"Is that—" Laura said, but Andy pressed the phone to her chest.

She asked the man, "How do you know me?"

"Come away from the window." Edwin motioned Andy out of the office. "You can't be here. You need to go. Now."

Andy didn't move. "Tell me how you know me."

Edwin saw the phone in her hand. "Who are you talking to?"

When Andy didn't answer, he wrenched the phone out of her hand and put it to his ear.

He said, "Who is—fuck." Edwin turned his back to Andy, telling Laura, "No, I have no idea what Clara told her. You know she's been unwell." He started nodding, listening. "I didn't tell her—no. Clara doesn't know about that. It's privileged information. I would never—" He stopped again. "Laura, you need to calm down. No one knows where it is except for me."

*They knew each other. They were arguing the way old friends argued. Edwin had known Andy by sight. Clara had thought she was Jane, who was really Laura . . .*

Andy's teeth had started to chatter. She could hear them clicking inside of her head. She rubbed her arms with her hands. She felt cold, almost frozen.

"Laura, I—" Edwin leaned down his head and looked out the window. "Listen, you just need to trust me. You know I would never—" He turned around and looked at Andy. She watched his anger soften into something else. He smiled at her the same way Gordon smiled at her when she fucked up but he still wanted her to know that he loved her.

*Why was a man she had never met looking at her like her father?*

Edwin said, "I will, Laura. I promise I'll—"

There was a loud *crack*.

Then another.

Then another.

Andy was on the floor, the same as the last time she had heard a sudden burst of gunfire.

Everything was exactly the same.

Glass broke. Papers started to fly. The air filled with debris.

Edwin took the brunt of the bullets, his arms jerking up, his skull almost vaporizing, bone and chunks of his hair splattering against the couch, the walls, the ceiling.

Andy was flat on her belly, hands covering her head, when she heard the nauseating *thunk* of his body hitting the floor.

She looked at his face. Nothing but a dark hole with white shards of skull stared back. His mustache was still curled up at the ends, held in place with a thick wax.

Andy tasted blood in her mouth. Her heart felt like it was beating inside of her eardrums. She thought that she had lost her hearing, but there was nothing to hear.

The shooter had stopped.

Andy scanned the room for the burner phone. She saw it fifteen feet away in the hall. She had no idea if it was still working, but she heard her mother's voice as clear as if she was in the room—

*I need you to run, darling. He can't reload fast enough to hurt you.*

Andy tried to stand. She could barely get to her knees before throwing up from the pain. The McDonald's milkshake was pink with blood. Every time she heaved, it felt like fire was ripping down her left side.

*Footsteps. Outside. Getting closer.*

Andy forced herself up onto her hands and knees. She crawled toward the door, her palms digging into broken glass, her knees sliding across the floor. She made it as far as the hallway before the searing pain made her stop. She fell over onto her hip. She pushed herself up to sitting. Pressed her back to the wall. Her skull was filled with a high-pitched whining noise. Shards of glass porcupined from her bare arms.

Andy listened.

She heard a strange sound from the other side of the house. *Click-click-click-click.*

The cylinder spinning in the revolver?

She looked at the burner phone. The screen had been shattered. There was nowhere to go. Nothing to do but wait.

Andy reached down to her side. Her shirt was soaked with blood. Her fingers found a tiny hole in the material.

Then the tip of her finger found another hole in her skin.

She had been shot.

August 2, 1986

# 14

Jane felt the ivory keys of the Steinway Concert Grand soften beneath the tips of her fingers. The stage lights warmed the right side of her body. She allowed herself a furtive glance at the audience, picked out a few of their faces under the lights.

*Rhapsodic.*

Carnegie had sold out within one day of the tickets going on sale. Over two thousand seats. Jane was the youngest woman ever to take center stage. The hall's acoustics were remarkable. The reverb poured like honey into her ears, bending and elongating each note. The Steinway gave Jane more than she had dared hope for; the key action was loose enough to bring a nuanced delicacy that bathed the room in an almost ethereal wave of sound. She felt like a wizard pulling off the most wondrous trick. Every keystroke was perfect. The orchestra was perfect. The audience was perfect. She lowered her gaze past the lights, taking in the front row.

Jasper, Annette, Andrew, Martin—

*Nick.*

He was clapping his hands. Grinning with pride.

Jane missed a note, then another, then she was playing along to the staccato of Nick's hands like she had not done since Martin first sat her down on the bench and told her to play. The noise sharpened as Nick's clapping amplified through the hall. Jane had to cover her ears. The music stopped. Nick's mouth twisted into a sneer. He kept clapping and clapping. Blood began to seep from his hands, down his arms, into his lap. He clapped harder. Louder. Blood splattered onto his white shirt, onto Andrew, her father, the stage.

Jane opened her eyes.

The room was dark. Confusion and fear mixed to bring her heart into her throat. Slowly, Jane's senses came back to her. She was lying in bed. She pulled away the afghan covering her body. She recognized the blue color.

The farmhouse.

She sat up so fast that she was almost knocked back by a wave of dizziness. She fumbled for the switch on the lamp.

A syringe and vial were on the table.

*Morphine.*

The syringe was still capped, but the bottle was almost empty. Panicked, Jane checked her arms, legs, feet for needle marks. Nothing, but what was she afraid of? That Nick had drugged her? That he had somehow infected her with Andrew's tainted blood?

Her hand went to her neck. Nick had strangled her. She could still remember those last moments in the bathroom as she desperately gasped for air. Her throat pulsed beneath her fingers. The skin was tender. Jane moved her hand lower. The round swell of her belly filled her palm. Slowly, she inched down farther and checked between her legs for the tell-tale spots of blood. When she pulled back her hand, it was clean. Relief nearly took her breath away.

Nick had not beaten another child out of her body.

This time, at least for this moment, they were safe.

Jane found her socks on the floor, tugged on her boots. She walked over to the large window across from the bed and drew back the curtains. Darkness. Her eyes picked out the silhouette of the van parked in front of the barn, but the other two cars were gone.

She listened to the house.

There were low voices, at least two people talking, on the far side of the house. Chopping sounds. Pots and pans clattering.

Jane leaned over to buckle her boots. She had a moment where she remembered doing the same thing days ago. Before they walked downstairs to speak with agents Barlow and Danberry. Before they had left in Jasper's Porsche without realizing that they would never go back. Before Nick had made Jane choose between him or her brother.

*These anarchist groups think they're doing the right thing, right up until they end up in prison or flat on their backs in the morgue.*

The door opened.

Jane didn't know who she expected to see. Certainly not Paula, who barked, "Wait in the living room."

"Where's Andrew?"

"He went for a run. Where the fuck do you think?" Paula stalked off, her footsteps like two hammers hitting the floor.

Jane knew she should look for Andrew, but she had to compose herself before she spoke with her brother. The last hours or days of his life should not be filled with recriminations.

She went across the hall to the bathroom. She used the toilet, praying that she did not feel the sharp pain, see the spots of blood.

Jane looked down at the bowl.

*Nothing.*

The tub drew her attention. She had not fully bathed in almost four days. Her skin felt waxen, but the thought of getting undressed and finding soap and locating towels was too much. She flushed the toilet. Her eyes avoided the mirror as she washed her hands, then her face, with warm water. She looked for a rag and wiped under her arms and between her legs. She felt another wave of relief when she saw there was still no blood.

*Were you stupid enough to think I'd let you keep it?*

Jane walked into the living room. She looked for a telephone, but there wasn't one. Calling Jasper was likely pointless, anyway. All of the family phone lines would be tapped. Even if Jasper was inclined to help, his hands would be tied. Jane was completely on her own now.

She had made her choice.

From the sound of it, someone had rolled the TV into the kitchen. She blinked, and time shifted back. Nick was on his knees in front of the set, adjusting the volume, insisting they all watch their crimes being cataloged for the nation. The group had arrayed themselves around him like blades on a fan. Clara on the floor taking in the frenetic energy. Edwin solemn and watchful. Paula beaming at Nick like he was the second coming of Christ. Jane standing there, dazed from the news that Clara had given her.

Even then, Jane had stayed in the room rather than finding Andrew because she still did not want to let Nick down. None of them did. That was the biggest fear they all had—not that they would get caught, or die, or be thrown into prison for the rest of their lives, but that they would disappoint Nick.

She knew that now there would be a reckoning for her defiance. Nick had left her here with Paula for a reason.

Jane rested her hand on the swinging door to the kitchen and listened.

She heard a knife blade striking a cutting board. The murmur of a television program. Her own breathing.

She pushed open the door. The kitchen was small and cramped, the table wedged against the end of the laminate countertop. Still, it had its charms. The metal cabinets were painted a cheery yellow. The appliances were all new.

Andrew was sitting at the table.

Jane felt her heart stir at the sight of him. He was here. He was still alive, though the smile he gave her was weak.

He motioned for Jane to turn down the television. She twisted the knob. Her eyes stayed on his.

*Did he know what Nick had done to Jane in the bathroom?*

Paula said, "I told you to wait in there." She threw seasoning into a pot on the stove. "Hey, Dumb Bitch, I said—"

Jane gave her the finger as she sat down with her back to Paula.

Andrew chuckled. The metal box was open in front of him. Folders were spread out on the table. The tiny key was by his elbow. A large envelope was addressed to the *Los Angeles Times*. He was doing his part for Nick. Even at death's door, still the loyal trooper.

Jane worked to keep the sorrow out of her expression. Impossibly, he looked even more pale. His eyes could have been lined in red crayon. His lips were starting to turn blue. Every breath was like a saw grinding back and forth across a piece of wet wood. He should be resting comfortably in a hospital, not struggling to stay upright in a hard wooden chair.

She said, "You're dying."

"But you're not," he said. "Nick took the ELISA test last month. He's clean. You know he's terrified of needles. And the other way—he's never been into that."

Jane felt a cold sweat break out. The thought had not even crossed her mind, but now that it was there, she felt sickened by the realization that, even if Nick had been infected, he probably would've never told her. They would've kept making love and Jane would've kept growing their child and she would've not found out the truth until it came from a doctor's mouth.

Or a medical examiner's.

"You'll be okay," Andrew said. "I promise."

Now was not the time to call her brother a liar. "What about Ellis-Anne?"

"She's clean," Andrew said. "I told her to get tested as soon as . . ." He let his voice trail off. "She wanted to stay with me. Can you believe that? I couldn't let her do it. It wasn't fair. And we had all this going on, so . . ." His voice trailed off again in a long sigh. "Barlow, the FBI agent. He told me they talked to her. I know she must've been afraid. I regret—well, I regret a lot of things."

Jane did not want him to dwell on regrets. She reached for his hands. They felt heavy, weighted somehow by what was to come. His shirt collar was open. She could see the purplish lesions on his chest.

He couldn't stay here in this too-warm house with less than half a thimbleful of morphine. She wouldn't allow it.

"What is it?" he asked.

"I love you."

Andrew was never one to return the sentiment, but he squeezed her hands, smiled again, so that she knew he felt the same.

Paula mumbled, "Christ."

Jane turned to glare at her. She had started cutting up a tomato. The knife was dull. The skin tore like paper.

Paula asked, "You two into incest now?"

Jane turned back around.

Andrew told her, "I'm going to rest for a while. Okay?"

She nodded. They would stand a better chance of leaving if Andrew was not involved in the negotiation.

"Get a scarf," Paula said. "Keep your neck warm. It helps the cough."

Andrew raised a skeptical eyebrow at Jane as he tried to stand. He shrugged off her offer of help. "I'm not that far gone."

She watched him lurch toward the swinging door. His shirt was soaked with sweat. The back of his hair was damp. Jane turned away from the door only when it stopped swinging.

She took Andrew's seat parallel to Paula because she did not want her back to the woman. She looked down at the files on the table. These were the two things that Nick had valued most: Jasper's signature attesting to his part in the fraud. The Polaroids with their red rubber band.

Paula said, "I know what you're thinking, and you're not going anywhere."

Jane had thought that she was incapable of feeling any more emotions, but she had never abhorred Paula so much as she did in this moment. "I just want to take him to the hospital."

"And let the pigs know where we are?" Paula huffed out a laugh. "You might as well take off your fancy boots, 'cause you ain't goin' anywhere."

Jane turned away from her, clasped her hands together on the table.

"Hey, Dumb Bitch." Paula lifted up her shirt and showed Jane the handgun tucked into the waist of her jeans. "Don't get any ideas. I'd love to shoot six new holes into that asshole you call a face."

Jane looked at the clock on the wall. Ten in the evening. The Chicago team would already be in the city. Nick was on his way to New York. She had to find a way out of here.

She asked, "Where are Clara and Edwin?"

"Selden and Tucker are in position."

Edwin's apartment in the city. He was supposed to wait for phone calls in case anyone was arrested.

Jane said, "Northwestern can't be far from here. They're a teaching hospital. They'll know how to take care of—"

"Northwestern is straight down I-88, about forty-five minutes away, but it might as well be on the moon because you're not fucking going anywhere and neither is he." Paula rested her hand on her hip. "Look, bitch, they can't do anything for him. You did your rich girl slumming at the AIDS ward. You know how this story ends. The prince doesn't ride again. Your brother is going to die. As in tonight. He's not going to see the sunrise."

Hearing her fears confirmed brought a lump into Jane's throat. "The doctors can make him comfortable."

"Nick left a vial of morphine for that."

"It's almost empty."

"That's all we could find on short notice, and we're lucky we could get that. It'll probably be enough, and if it's not—" She shrugged her shoulder. "Nothing we can do about it."

Jane thought again of Ben Mitchell, one of the first young men she'd met on the AIDS ward. He'd been desperate to go back to Wyoming to see his parents before he died. They had finally relented, and the last eight minutes of Ben's life had been spent in terror as he suffocated on his own fluids because the rural hospital staff were too frightened to stick a tube down his throat to help him breathe.

Jane knew the panic that came from not being able to breathe. Nick had strangled her before. Once during sex. Once the last time she was pregnant. Once a few hours ago, when he was threatening to kill her. No matter how many times it happened, there was no way to prepare for that terrifying sensation of not being able to pull air into your lungs. The way her heart felt like it was filling with blood. The searing pain from her muscles cramping. The burning in her lungs. The numbness in her hands and feet as the body gave up on everything but staying alive.

Jane could not let her brother experience that terror. Not for one minute, certainly not for eight.

She told Paula, "The doctors can knock him out so that he's unconscious for the worst of it."

"Maybe he wants to be conscious," she said. "Maybe he wants to feel it."

"You sound like Nick."

"I'll take that as a compliment."

"Don't," Jane said. "It's meant to make you think about what you're doing, because it's wrong. All of this is wrong."

"The concept of *right* and *wrong* are patriarchal constructs to control the populace."

Jane turned her head to look at the woman. "You can't be serious."

"You're too fucking blind to see it. At least now you are." Paula had picked up a knife. She chopped brutally at a bundle of carrots. "I heard you with him in the van. All that lovey-dovey bullshit, telling Nick how wonderful he is, how much you love him, how you believe in what we're doing, and then you get here and suddenly you're abandoning him."

"Did you hear him in the bathroom, strangling me into unconsciousness?"

"I could happily hear that every day for the rest of my life."

A piece of carrot landed on the floor beside Jane.

If Jane stood up, if she took one small step, she could close the distance between them. She could grab the knife from Paula's hand, wrench the gun from her waist.

*And then what?*

Could Jane kill her? There was a difference between despising someone and murdering them.

Paula said, "It happened before Berlin, right?" She motioned down at her own stomach with the knife. "I thought you were getting fat, but—" She blew out air between her lips. "No such luck."

Jane looked down at her stomach. She had been so nervous about telling people about the baby, but everyone seemed to have figured it out on their own.

Paula said, "You don't deserve to carry his child."

Jane watched the knife move up and down. Paula wasn't paying attention to Jane.

*Stand up, take one step, grab the knife—*

"If it was up to me, I'd cut it out of you." Paula pointed the blade at Jane. "Want me to?"

Jane tried to pretend that the threat had not sent an arrow into her heart. She had to think about her child. This wasn't just about Andrew. If she attacked Paula and failed, then she could lose her baby before she even had the chance to hold it.

"That's what I thought." Paula turned back to the carrots with a grin on her face.

Jane tucked her chin to her chest. She had never been good at confrontation. Her way was to remain silent and hope that the explosion would pass. That was what she had always done with her father. That's what she did with Nick.

She looked at the bundle of Polaroids on the table. The photo on top showed the deep gash in her leg. Jane touched her leg in that same spot now, feeling the ridge of the pink scar.

*Bite mark.*

She remembered clearly when the pictures had been taken. Jane and Nick were staying in Palm Springs while Jane's cuts and bruises healed. Nick had gone out for lunch and returned with the camera and instant film.

*I'm sorry, my darling, I know you're hurting, but I've just had the best idea.*

Back home, Andrew had been wavering about the plan. There

were good reasons. Andrew didn't want Laura Juneau to go to prison for attacking Martin with the red dye packs. He was especially conflicted about hurting Martin's pride. Despite the beatings and the disappointments and even the awful things that Nick had uncovered while working at Queller Healthcare, Andrew still had a sliver of love for their father.

Then, when they returned from Palm Springs, Nick had shown him the Polaroids.

*Look at what your father did to your sister. We have to make him pay for this. Martin Queller has to pay for all of his sins.*

Nick had assumed that Jane would play along, and why wouldn't she? Why wouldn't she keep from her brother the fact that it was Nick who had beaten her face, who had ripped open her skin with his teeth, who had pummeled her stomach until blood had poured from between her legs and their baby was gone?

*Why wouldn't she?*

Jane dropped the Polaroids into the metal box. She wiped her sweaty hands on her legs. She thought about sitting with Agent Danberry in the backyard. In less than a week, the cops had seen right through Nick.

*He had everybody in his circle convinced he was smarter than he actually was. More clever than he was.*

Paula said, "I used to be so jealous of you. Did you know that?"

Jane stacked the files and put them back in the box. "No shit."

"Yeah, well." Paula had moved on to chopping a potato. She was using a meat cleaver. "The first time I met you, I thought, 'What's that snooty bitch doing here? Why does she want to change shit when all the shit in the world benefits her?'"

Jane didn't have an answer anymore. She had hated her father. That's where it had started. Martin had raped her when she was a child, beaten her throughout her teenage years, terrorized her into her twenties, and Nick had given Jane a way to make it stop. Not for herself, but for other people. For Robert Juneau.

For Andrew. For all the other patients who had been hurt. Jane was not strong enough to pull away from Martin for her own sake, so Nick had contrived a plan to wrench Martin away from Jane.

She put her hand to her mouth. She wanted to laugh, because she had just now realized that Nick had done the same with Andrew, using the Polaroids to weaponize his anger on behalf of Jane.

*They were like yo-yos he could snap back with a flick of his wrist.*

Paula said, "Andy has everything, too, but he's so conflicted about it, you know? He struggles with it." She used her teeth to tear the plastic wrap around a bundle of celery. "You never seemed to struggle, but I guess that's the point with gals like you, right? All the right schools and the right clothes and the right hair. They Pygmalion your skinny white asses from birth so you don't ever seem to struggle with anything. You know what forks to use, and who painted what Mona Lisa and blah-dee-duh-blah. But underneath, you're just—" She clenched her hands into tight fists. "So fucking angry."

Jane had never thought of herself as angry, but she understood now that it had lived just beneath the fear all along. "Rage is a luxury."

"Rage is a fucking narcotic." Paula laughed as she attacked the celery with her knife. "That's why Nick is so good for me. He helped me turn my rage into power."

Jane felt her eyebrows go up. "You're babysitting his girlfriend while he's out planting bombs."

"Shut your fucking mouth." Paula threw the knife on the counter. "You think you're so fucking clever? You think you're better than me?" When Jane didn't answer, she demanded, "Look at me, Dumb Bitch. Say that to my face. Say you're better than me. I fucking dare you."

Jane turned sideways in the chair so that she was facing Paula. "Did Nick ever fuck you?"

Paula's jaw dropped. She was evidently thrown by the question.

Jane wasn't sure where it had come from, but now, she pressed on. "It's all right if he did. I'm pretty sure he fucked Clara." Jane laughed, because she could see it so clearly now. "He's always been drawn to fragile, famous women. And fragile, famous women are always drawn to guys like Nick."

"That's bullshit."

Jane found herself puzzled that the thought of Nick and Clara together elicited not even a flicker of jealousy. Why was Jane so okay with it? Why was all of her envy directed at Clara, who had somehow managed to get what she wanted out of Nick without losing herself completely?

Jane told Paula, "I bet he didn't fuck you." She could tell from Paula's pained expression that this was true. "It's not that he wouldn't fuck you if he needed to, but you're so brazenly desperate for any show of kindness. Not giving it to you was much more effective than giving it to you. Right? And it provides your drama with a villain—me—because I'm the only thing keeping him from being with you."

Paula's lower lip started to tremble. "Shut up."

"One of the FBI agents called it days ago. He said that Nick was just another con man running another cult so he could bed the pretty girls and play God with all the boys."

"I said shut your goddamn mouth." The bluster had gone out of her tone. She pressed her palms to the edge of the counter. Tears dripped down her cheeks. She kept shaking her head. "You don't know. You don't know anything about us."

Jane closed the lid on the metal box. There was a tiny handle on the side, too small for Andrew's hand, but Jane's fingers easily slid through the loop.

She stood up from the table.

Paula reached for the knife as she started to turn.

Jane took a step forward. She swung the box at Paula's head.

*Pop.*

Like a toy gun going off.

Paula's mouth dropped open.

The knife slipped from her hand.

She crumpled to the floor.

Jane leaned over Paula and found the steady pulse in her neck. She pressed open her eyelids. There was a milky white in her left eye, but the pupil in her right eye dilated in the harsh overhead light.

Jane pushed through the swinging door, the box tucked under her arm. She walked through the living room and down the hall. Andrew was sleeping in the bedroom. The morphine bottle was empty. She shook him, saying, "Andy. Andy, wake up."

He turned toward her voice, a glassy look in his eyes. "What is it?"

"Didn't you hear the phone?" Jane could only think of one lie that would move him. "Nick called. We have to get out of here."

"Where's—" He struggled to sit up. "Where's Paula?"

"She took off. There was another car parked on the road." Jane struggled to get him up. "I've got the box. We have to go, Andrew. Now. Nick said we had to get out."

He tried to stand. Jane had to lift him to his feet. He was so thin that holding him up was almost effortless.

He asked, "Where are we going?"

"We have to hurry." Jane almost dropped the metal box as she guided him down the hall, out the front door. The walk to the van seemed to take hours. She should've gagged Paula. Tied her up. How long before she woke up and started screaming? Would Andrew leave if he thought they were betraying Nick and the plan?

Jane couldn't risk it.

"Come on," she begged her brother. "Keep moving. You can sleep in the van, all right?"

"Yeah," was all he could manage between raspy breaths.

Jane had to drag him the last few yards. She leaned him against the van, her knee keeping his knees from bending, so that she could open the door. She was buckling him into the seat when she remembered—

The keys.

"Stay here."

Jane ran back to the house. She pushed through the door into the kitchen. Paula was on her hands and knees, head shaking like a dog.

Without thinking, Jane kicked her in the face.

Paula *oofed* out a sound, then collapsed flat to the floor.

Jane patted Paula's pockets until she found the keys. She was halfway to the van when she remembered the gun in Paula's waistband. She could go back and get it, but what was the point? It was better to leave than risk giving Paula another chance to stop them.

"Jay—" Andrew watched her climb behind the wheel. "How did . . . how did they find . . ."

"Selden," she told him. "Clara. She backed out. She changed her mind. Nick said we have to hurry." Jane threw the van into reverse. She pressed the gas pedal to the floor as she drove back up the driveway. She checked the rearview mirror. All she saw was dust. Her heart kept pounding into her throat as she drove down the winding roads outside the farm. It wasn't until they'd finally reached the interstate that Jane felt her breathing return to normal. She looked over at Andrew. His head was lolling to the side. She counted his arduous breaths, the painful in and out as he strained for air.

For the first time in almost two years, Jane felt at peace. An eerie calmness had taken over. This was the right thing to do. After giving herself over to Nick's insanity for so long, she was finally lucid again.

Jane had been to Northwestern Hospital once before. She was in the middle of a tour and suffering from an earache. Pechenikov had driven her to the emergency room. He had fussed around her, telling the nurses that Jane was the most important patient that they would ever care for. Jane had rolled her eyes at the praise but been secretly pleased to be handled with such care. She had loved Pechenikov so much, not just because he was a teacher, but because he was a decent and loving man.

Which was likely why Nick had made Jane leave him.

*Why did you give it up?*

*Because my boyfriend was jealous of a seventy-year-old homosexual.*

An ambulance whizzed by on Jane's right. She followed it up the exit. She saw the Northwestern Memorial Hospital sign glowing in the distance.

"Jane?" The ambulance siren had woken Andrew. "What are you doing?"

"Nick told me to take you to the hospital." She pushed up the turn signal, waited for the light.

"Jane—" Andrew started coughing. He covered his mouth with both hands.

"I'm just doing what Nick told me to do," she lied. Her voice was shaking. She had to keep strong. They were so close. "He made me promise, Andrew. Do you want me to break my promise to Nick?"

"You don't—" he had to stop to catch his breath. "I know what you're—that Nick didn't—"

Jane looked at her brother. He reached out, his fingers gently touching her neck.

She glanced into the mirror, saw the bruises from Nick's hands strangling her. Andrew knew what had happened in the bathroom, that Jane had chosen to stay with him.

She realized now that Nick must have given Andrew the same ultimatum. Andrew had not driven to New York with Nick. He had stayed at the farmhouse with Jane.

She told her brother, "We're quite a pair, aren't we?"

He closed his eyes. "We can't," he said. "Our faces—on the news—the police."

"It doesn't matter." Jane mumbled a curse at the red light, then another at herself. The van was the only vehicle in sight. It was the middle of the night and she was obeying traffic laws.

She pressed the gas and blew through the light.

"Jane—" Andrew broke off for another coughing fit. "Y-you can't do this. They'll catch you."

Jane took another right, followed another blue sign with a white H on it.

"Please." He rubbed his face with his hands, something he used to do when he was a boy and things got too frustrating for him to handle.

Jane coasted through another red light. She was on autopilot now. Everything inside of her was numb again. She was a machine as much as the van, a mode of conveyance that would take her brother to the hospital so he could die peacefully in his sleep.

Andrew tried, "Please. Listen to—" Another coughing fit took hold. There was no rattle, just a straining noise, as if he was trying to suck air through a reed.

She said, "Try to save your breath."

"Jane," he repeated, his voice no more than a whisper. "If you leave me, you have to leave me. You can't let them catch you. You have to—" His words broke off into more coughing. He looked down at his hand. There was blood.

Jane swallowed back her grief. She was taking him to the hospital. They would put a tube down his throat to help him breathe. They would give him drugs to help him sleep. This was likely the last conversation they would ever have.

She told him, "I'm sorry, Andy. I love you."

His eyes were watering. Tears slid down his face. "I know that you love me. Even when you hated me, I know that you loved me."

"I never hated you."

"I forgive you, but—" He coughed. "Forgive me, too. Okay?"

Jane pushed the van to go faster. "There's nothing to forgive you for."

"I knew, Janey. I knew who he was. What he was. It's my—" he wheezed. "Fault. My fault. I'm so . . ."

Jane looked at him, but his eyes were closed. His head tilted back and forth with the motion of the van.

"Andrew?"

"I knew," he mumbled. "I knew."

She banked a hard left. Her heart shook at the sight of the NORTHWESTERN sign outside of the emergency room.

"Andy?" Jane panicked. She couldn't hear him breathing anymore. She held onto his hand. His flesh was like ice. "We're almost there, my darling. Just hang on."

His eyelids fluttered open. "Trade—" He choked a cough. "Trade him."

"Andy, don't try to speak." The hospital sign was getting closer. "We're almost there. Just hang on, my darling. Hang on for just a moment more."

"Trade all . . ." Andrew's eyelids fluttered again. His chin dropped to his chest. Only the whistling sound of air being sucked through his teeth told her that he was still alive.

The hospital.

Jane almost lost control of the wheel when the tires bumped over a curb. The van fishtailed. She somehow managed to screech to a halt in front of the entrance to the ER. Two orderlies were smoking on a nearby bench.

"Help!" Jane jumped out of the van. "Help my brother. Please!"

The men were already off the bench. One ran back into the hospital. The other opened the van door.

"He has—" Jane's voice caught. "He's infected with—"

"I gotcha." The man wrapped his arms around Andrew's shoulders as he helped him out of the van. "Come on, buddy. We're gonna take good care of you."

Jane's tears, long dried, started to flow again.

"You're all right," the man told Andrew. He sounded so kind that she wanted to fall to the ground and kiss his feet. He asked Andrew, "Can you walk? Let's go to this bench and—"

"Where—" Andrew was looking for Jane.

"I'm right here, my darling." She put her hand to his face. She pressed her lips to his forehead. His hand reached out. He was touching the round swell of her stomach.

"Trade . . ." he whispered, ". . . all of them."

The other orderly ran back through the door with a gurney.

The two men lifted Andrew off his feet. He was so light that they barely had to strain to get him onto the gurney. Andrew turned his head, looking for Jane.

He said, "I love you."

The men started to roll the gurney inside. Andrew kept his eyes on Jane for as long as he could.

The doors closed.

She watched through the glass as Andrew was rolled into the back of the emergency room. The double doors swung open. Nurses and doctors swarmed around him. The doors closed again, and he was gone.

*They'll catch you.*

Jane breathed in the cool night air. No one rushed out of the hospital with a gun, telling her to get down on the ground. None of the nurses were on the phone behind the desk.

She was safe. Andrew was being taken care of. She could leave now. No one knew where she was. No one could find her unless she wanted to be found.

Jane walked back to the van. She closed the passenger's side door. She climbed back behind the wheel. The engine was still running. She tried to remember everything Andrew had said. Moments before, she had been talking to her brother, and now Jane knew that she would never hear Andrew's voice ever again.

She put the car in gear.

Jane drove aimlessly, passing the marked parking spaces for the emergency room. Passing the parking deck for the hospital, for the university, for the shopping center at the end of the street.

*Canada. The forger.*

Jane could create a new life for herself and her child. The two hundred and fifty thousand dollars in cash was probably still in the back of the van. The small cooler. The Thermos of water. The box of Slim Jims. The blanket. The futon. Toronto was just over eight hours away. Skirt around the top of Indiana, through Michigan, then into Canada. That had been the plan after Nick's triumphant return from New York. They would stay in the farmhouse for a few weeks during the fallout from the bombings, then drive into Canada, buy more documents from the forger on East Kelly Street, and fly to Switzerland.

Nick had thought of everything.

A horn beeped behind Jane. She startled at the noise. She'd stopped in the middle of the road. Jane looked in the rearview mirror. The man behind her was waving his fist. She waved back an apology, pressing the gas pedal.

The angry driver passed her for no reason other than to prove that he could. Jane drove another few yards, but then she slowed the van and followed a sign toward a long-term parking garage. The temperature inside the van cooled as she spiraled down the ramp. She located a spot between two sedans on the lowest basement level. She backed into the space. She checked to make sure she wasn't being watched. No cameras on the walls. No two-way mirrors.

Nick's precious metal box was on the floor between the seats. Jane tucked it under her arm just as her brother always had. She crouched as she made her way into the back of the van. The padlock hung from the box that was bolted to the floor.

6-12-32.

They all knew the combination.

The cash was still there. The Thermos. The cooler. The box of Slim Jims.

Jane added Nick's box to the stash. She peeled off three hundred dollars, then closed the lid. She spun the lock. She got out of the van. She walked around to the back.

The steel bumper was hollow inside. Jane balanced the key on the rim. Then she walked back up the winding ramp. There was no after-hours parking attendant, just a stack of envelopes and a mail drop. Jane wrote down the space number for the van, then put the three hundred dollars in the envelope, enough for the van to park for one month.

Outside, she followed the cold breeze to Lake Michigan. Her thin blouse whipped in the wind. Jane could remember the first time she'd flown into Milwaukee to play at the Performing Arts Center. She had thought the plane had overshot its mark and ended up at the Atlantic because, even from twenty thousand feet, she could not see the edge of the massive lake. Pechenikov had told her that you could take the entire island of Great Britain and put it in the lake without the edges touching the sides.

Jane was shaken by a deep and unwelcome sadness. Part of her had thought—had hoped—that one day, she would be able to go back. To performing. To Pechenikov. Not anymore. Her touring days were over. She would probably never fly in an airplane again. She would never tour again. Perform again.

She laughed at a sudden revelation.

The last notes she had played on the piano were the jumpy, glib opening bars to A-ha's "Take On Me."

The hospital's waiting room was packed. Jane became aware of how she must look. Her hair had not been washed in days. She had blood on her clothes. Her nose felt broken. Black bruises had come up around her neck. Probably the familiar pinprick dots of broken blood vessels riddled the whites of her eyes. She could see the questions in the nurses' eyes.

*Battered woman? Junkie? Call girl?*

Sister was the only title left to her. She found Andrew behind a curtain in the back of the emergency room. They had finally intubated him. Jane was glad that he could breathe, but she understood that she would never, ever hear his voice again. He would never tease her or make a joke about her weight or meet the baby that was growing inside of her.

The only thing that Jane could do for her brother now was hold his hand and listen to the monitor announce the ever-slowing beats of his heart. She held onto him while they wheeled him to the elevator, when they took him to his room in the ICU. She refused to leave his side even after the nurses told her that visitors were not allowed to stay more than twenty minutes at a time.

There were no windows in Andrew's room. The only glass was the window and sliding door that looked onto the nurses' station. Jane had never had track of the time, so she didn't know

how long it took for someone—a doctor, an orderly, a nurse—
to recognize their faces. The tone of their voices changed. Then
a lone policeman appeared outside the closed glass door. He
didn't come inside. No one came into Andrew's small room but
the ICU nurse, whose previously chatty demeanor was gone.
Jane waited for an hour, then another hour, then she lost count.
There were no agents from the CIA, NSA, Secret Service, FBI,
Interpol. There was no one to stop Jane when she put her head
beside Andrew's on the bed.

She put her lips to his ear. How many times had Nick done
the same thing to her, put his mouth close, confided in Jane in
such a way that made her believe they were the only two people
who mattered in the world?

"I'm pregnant," she told her brother, the first time she had
said the words aloud to anyone. "And I'm happy. I'm so happy,
Andy, that I'm going to have a baby."

Andrew's eyes moved beneath his eyelids, but the nurse had
told Jane not to read too much into it. He was in a coma. He
would not wake up again. There was no way for Jane to know
whether or not her brother knew she was there. But Jane knew
she was there, and that was all that mattered.

*I will never let anyone hurt you ever again.*

"Jinx?"

Her older brother was standing in the doorway. Jane should
have guessed that Jasper would eventually find his way here.
Her big brother always swooped in to save her. She wanted to
stand up and hug him, but she didn't have the strength to do
more than slump into the chair. Jasper looked equally incapacitated as he closed the sliding glass door. The cop gave him a
nod before walking across the hall to the nurses' station. It was
the Air Force uniform, wrinkled but still impressive. Jasper
obviously hadn't changed since she'd last seen him in the parlor
of the Presidio Heights house.

He turned around, his mouth a clenched straight line. Jane
felt sick with guilt. Jasper's skin was ashen. His hair was
cowlicked in the back. His tie was askew. He must have come

straight from the airport after the four-hour flight from San Francisco.

Four hours in the air. Thirty hours in the van. Twelve hours to New York.

Nick had to be in Brooklyn by now.

Jasper asked, "Are you all right?"

Jane would have wept if she'd had any tears left. She held onto Andrew's hand and reached out to Jasper with the other. "I'm glad you're here."

He held her fingers for a moment before letting them go. He walked back a few steps. He leaned against the wall. She expected him to ask about her part in Martin's murder, but instead, he told Jane, "A bomb went off at the Chicago Mercantile Exchange."

The information sounded strange coming out of his mouth. They had planned it for so long, and now it had actually happened.

Jasper said, "At least one person's dead. Another was critically injured. The cops think they were trying to set the detonator when the bomb went off."

*Spinner and Wyman.*

He said, "That's the only reason the police aren't swarming all over you right now. Every guy with a badge or a uniform is over there trying to pick through the pieces in case there are more casualties."

Jane held tight to Andrew's hand. His face was slack, his skin the same color as the sheets. She said, "Jasper, Andy is—"

"I know about Andrew." Jasper's tone was flat, indecipherable. He had not once looked at Andrew since he'd walked into the room. "We have to talk. You and I."

Jane knew he was going to ask her about Martin. She looked at Andrew because she did not want to see the hope, then disappointment, then disgust, in Jasper's face.

He said, "Nick is a fraud. His name isn't even Nick."

Jane's head swiveled around.

"That FBI agent—Danberry—he told me that Nick's real name

is Clayton Morrow. They identified him through the fingerprints in your bedroom."

Jane was without words.

"The real Nicholas Harp died of an overdose six years ago, his first day at Stanford. I've seen the death certificate. It was heroin."

*The real Nicholas Harp?*

"The real Nick's drug dealer, Clayton Morrow, assumed his identity. Do you understand what I'm saying, Jinx? Nick isn't really Nick. His real name is Clayton Morrow. He stole a dead man's identity. Maybe he even gave Harp the fatal overdose. Who knows what he's capable of?"

*Stole a dead man's identity?*

"Clayton Morrow grew up in Maryland. His father's a pilot with Eastern. His mother is the president of the PTA. He's got four younger brothers and a sister. The state police believe he murdered his girlfriend. Her neck was broken. She was beaten so badly they had to use dental films to identify her body."

*Her neck was broken.*

"Jinx, I need you to tell me you understand what I'm saying." Jasper had slid down the wall, rested his elbows on his knees, so he could be at her level. "The man you know as Nick lied to us. He lied to us all."

"But—" Jane struggled to make sense of what he'd said. "Agent Barlow told us all in the parlor that Nick's mother had sent him to California to live with his grandmother. That's the same story Nick told us."

"The real Nick's mother sent him out west." Jasper worked to keep the frustration out of his voice. "He knocked up a girl back home. They didn't want his life to be over. They sent him out here to live with his grandmother. That part was true, about the move, but the rest was just bullshit to make us feel sorry for him."

Jane had no more questions because none of this felt real. The prostitute mother. The abusive grandmother. The year of homelessness. The triumphant acceptance to Stanford.

Jasper said, "Don't you see that Clayton Morrow used just

KARIN SLAUGHTER

enough of the real Nick's story to make the lies he told us believable?" He waited, but Jane still had no words. "Do you hear what I'm saying, Jinx? Nick, or Clayton Morrow, or whoever he is, was a fraud. He lied to all of us. He was nothing but a drug dealer and a con man."

*. . . just another con man running another cult so he could bed the pretty girls and play God with all the boys.*

Jane felt a noise force its way out of her throat. Not grief, but laughter. She heard the sound bounce around the tiny room, so incongruous with the machines and pumps. She put her hand to her mouth. Tears streamed down her cheeks. Her stomach muscles cramped, she laughed so hard.

"Christ." Jasper stood back up. He was looking at her as if she had lost her mind. "Jinx, this is serious. You're going to go to prison if you don't make a deal."

Jane wiped her eyes. She looked at Andrew, so close to death that his flesh was nearly translucent. This was what he'd been trying to tell Jane in the van. The real Nick had been his assigned roommate at Stanford. She could easily see Nick persuading Andrew to play along, just as she could see Andrew doing whatever it took to befriend the dead man's drug dealer.

She wiped her eyes again. She held tight to Andrew's hand. None of it mattered. She forgave him everything, just as he had forgiven her.

"What is wrong with you?" Jasper asked. "You're laughing about the asshole who murdered our father."

Now he was finally getting to the point. She said, "Laura Juneau murdered our father."

"You think anybody in that fucking cult makes a move without his orders?" Jasper hissed out the words between clenched teeth. "This is serious, Jinx. Get yourself together. If you want to have anything like a normal life, you're going to have to turn your back on the troops."

*Troops?*

"They've already captured that idiot woman from San Francisco. She stole a car and shot at a police officer." He loosened his tie as he paced the tiny room. "You have to talk before she does. They'll give a deal to the first person who squeals. If we're going to save your life, we have to act fast."

Jane watched her brother's nervous pacing. Sweat was pouring off of him. He looked agitated, which for anyone else would be a typical response. But Jasper's greatest gift was his ability to always keep his cool. Jane could count on one hand the number of times Jasper had really lost it.

For the first time in hours, she let go of Andrew's hand. She stood to tuck the blanket around him. She pressed her lips to his cool forehead. She wished for a moment that she could see into his mind, because he had clearly known so much more than her.

She told Jasper, "You called them troops."

Jasper stopped pacing. "What?"

"You were in the Air Force for fifteen years. You're still in the Reserves. You wouldn't dishonor that word by using it to describe the members of a cult." In her mind, Jane could see Nick clapping together his hands, preparing to deliver one of his rallying speeches. "That's what Nick calls us. His *troops*."

Jasper might have called her bluff, but he couldn't stop himself from nervously glancing at the cop across the hallway.

Jane said, "You knew about it. Oslo, at least."

He shook his head, but it made sense that Nick had found a way to pull him into their folly. Jasper had left the Air Force to run the company. Martin kept promising to step aside, but then the deadline would come and he would find another excuse to stay.

She said, "Tell me the truth, Jasper. I need to hear you say it."

"Stop talking." His voice was barely more than a whisper. He closed the space between them, his face inches from hers. "I'm trying to help you out of this."

"Did you give money?" Jane asked, because a lot of people had given money to the cause. Of all of them, only Jasper would personally benefit from Martin's public humiliation.

He said, "Why would I give that asshole money?"

Jasper's haughtiness gave him away. She had watched him use it as a weapon her entire life, but he had never, ever directed it toward Jane.

She told him, "Taking the company public would've been a lot more lucrative if Father was forced to resign. All of his essays and speeches about the Queller Correction made him too controversial."

Jasper's jaw worked. She could tell from his face that she was right.

"Nick was bribing you," Jane guessed. The stupid metal box with Nick's trophies. How smug he must have been when he told Jasper he'd stolen the forms right under his nose. "Tell me the truth, Jasper."

His eyes went back to the cop. The man was still across the hall talking to a nurse.

Jane said, "I'm on your side, whether you believe me or not. I never wanted you to get hurt. I only found out about the papers before everything went to hell."

Jasper cleared his throat. "What papers?"

She wanted to roll her eyes. There was no point to this game. "Nick stole the intervening reports with your signature on them. You verified billing for patients who were dead, like Robert Juneau, or ones who had already left the program. That's fraud. Nick had you dead to rights, and I know he used it to—"

Jasper's expression was almost comical in its astonishment. His eyebrows shot up. The whites of his eyes were completely visible. His mouth opened in a perfect circle.

"You didn't know?" Even as she asked the question, Jane knew the answer. Nick had double-crossed her brother. He hadn't been content to take his money. Jasper had to pay for snubbing Nick at the dinner table, looking down his nose, asking pointed questions about Nick's background, making it clear that he was not *one of us*.

"Christ." Jasper pressed his hands to the wall. His face had gone completely white. "I think I'm gonna be sick."

"I'm sorry, Jasper, but it's all right."

"I'll go to prison. I'll—"

"You won't go anywhere." Jane rubbed his back, tried to assuage his fears. "Jasper, I have the—"

"Please." He grabbed her arms, suddenly desperate. "You have to support me. Whatever Nick says, you have to—"

"Jasper I have—"

"Shut up, Jinx. Listen to me. We can say—we can—It was Andrew, all right?" He finally looked at their brother, dying only a few feet away. "We'll tell them it was all Andrew."

Jane concentrated on the pain from his fingers gouging into her skin.

"He forged my signature on the reports," Jasper decided. "He's done it before. He forged Father's signature on school forms, checks, credit card slips. There's a long history we can document. I know Father kept everything in his safe. I'm sure they—"

"No," Jane said, firmly enough to be heard. "I'm not going to let you do that to Andrew."

"He's dying, Jinx. What does it matter?"

"His legacy matters. His reputation."

"Are you fucking nuts?" Jasper shook her so hard her teeth clicked together. "Andrew's legacy is just like the rest of them— he was a faggot, and he's dying a faggot's death."

Jane tried to pull away, but Jasper held her in his grip.

"Do you know how many times I rescued him from yet another fag in the Tenderloin? How much cash I gave him so he could pay off whatever twink was threatening to go to Father?"

"Ellis-Anne—"

"Doesn't have AIDS because Andy could never get it up to screw her." Jasper finally let her go. He put his hand to his forehead. "Christ, Jinx, you never wondered why Nick would stick his tongue down your throat or grab your ass whenever Andrew was around? He was taunting him. We all saw it, even Mother."

Jane saw it now—more signs that she had missed. She laced her fingers through Andrew's again. She looked at his ravaged face. She had never noticed before, but his forehead had premature lines from his constant worrying.

*Why had he never told Jane?*

She wouldn't have stopped loving him. Maybe she would have loved him more, because suddenly, his lifetime of self-hatred and torture made sense.

She told Jasper, "It doesn't matter. I won't dishonor his death."

"Andy's the one who dishonored his death," Jasper said. "Don't you see he's getting exactly what he deserves? With any luck, all of them will."

Jane felt ice shoot through her veins. "How can you say that? He's still our brother."

"Think for a minute." Jasper had collected himself. He was back to trying to control everything. "Andy can finally be useful to both of us. You can tell the cops that he and Nick kidnapped you. Look at you—your nose is probably broken. Somebody tried to strangle the life out of you. Andy let it happen. He helped murder our father. He didn't care that people were going to die. He didn't try to stop it."

"We can't—"

"What's happening to him now is a Correction." Jasper invoked Martin Queller's theory as if it was suddenly gospel. "We have to accept that our brother is an abomination. He defied the natural order. He fell in love with Nick. He brought him into our house. You should've let Andy rot in the street. I should've let him hang in the basement. None of this would have happened without his disgusting perversion."

Jane could barely look at this man she had admired her entire life. She'd contorted herself to defend him. She had fought with Andrew to keep him out of harm's way.

Jasper said, "Save yourself, Jinx. Save me. We can still pull this family's name out of the gutter. In six months, maybe a year, we can take the company public. It won't be easy, but it will work if we stick together. Andrew's nothing more than a pus we have to drain from the Queller line."

Jane sank down onto Andrew's bed, her hand resting on his leg. She silently repeated Jasper's words, because in the future, if she ever wavered about never talking to her brother again, she wanted to remember in detail everything he had said.

She told him, "I have the paperwork, Jasper. All of it. I'll testify in front of any judge that it's your signature. I'll tell them that you knew about Oslo, and I'll tell them that you wanted to frame Andrew for everything."

Jasper stared at her. "How can you choose him over me?"

Jane was sick of men thinking they could give her ultimatums. "I've been standing here listening to you try to justify your crimes and talk about Andrew as if he's an aberration, but it's you I'm most ashamed of."

He huffed a disgusted laugh. "You're judging *me*?"

"You went along with Oslo because you wanted power and money and the private jets and another Porsche and the only way you could take control was to get Father out of the way. That makes you worse than all of us combined. At least we did it because it was something that we believed in. You did it for greed."

Jasper walked toward the door. Jane thought he was going to leave, but instead he closed the curtain across the glass. The cop lifted his chin to make sure everything was okay. Jasper waved him off again.

He turned around. He smoothed down his tie. He told Jane, "You don't understand how this works."

"Tell me."

"Everything you said is true. Father's academic bullshit was jeopardizing our valuation on the Stock Exchange. We were going to lose millions. Our investors wanted him to go, but he was refusing."

"So you thought the dye packs would do the trick."

"There's no trick to this, Jinx. These are very, very wealthy men we're dealing with. They will be very pissed off if they lose their money because of a spoiled little bitch who can't keep her mouth shut."

"I'm going to prison, Jasper." Hearing the words out loud didn't scare her as much as she thought they would. "I'm going to tell the FBI everything we did. I don't care about the collateral damage. The only way to atone for our atrocities is to stand up and tell the truth."

"Are you really so stupid that you think they can't kill us in prison?"

"They?"

"The investors." He looked at her as if she was a stubborn child to be dealt with. "I know too much. It's not just the fraud. You have no idea what kind of crooked shit Father was doing to inflate the numbers. I won't make it to lock-up, Jinx. They can't risk me making a deal to save my ass. They'll kill me, and then they'll kill you."

"They're wealthy men, not thugs."

"*We* are wealthy, Jinx. Look at what Father did to Robert Juneau. Look at what all three of us did to him." He lowered his voice. "Do you really think we're the only family in the world that is capable of conspiring to murder our enemies in cold blood?"

He was hovering over her.

Jane stood up to make him back away.

He said, "You will be signing your death warrant if you say one word against them." He jabbed his finger into her chest. "They'll chase you down and put a bullet in your head."

Jane's hand fluttered to her stomach.

*Trade him.*

"I'm not fucking around," Jasper said.

"Do you think I am? It's not just me I have to think about."

Jasper glanced down at her stomach. He had figured it out, too. "That's why you need to carefully consider what you're doing. They don't have daycare in prison."

*Trade all of them.*

He said, "These men, they've got long fucking memories. If you go against them—"

"What time is it?"

"What?"

She turned his hand so she could see his watch: 3:09 a.m. "Is this Chicago time?"

"You know I always change it when I land."

She dropped his hand. "You need to go home, Jasper. I never want to see you again."

He looked stunned.

"Live your corrupt life. Fuck over whoever you want. Keep your dangerous men happy, but remember I have those papers, and I can blow up your life, and their lives, anytime I please."

"Don't do this."

"What I do is no longer your business. I don't need you to save me. I'm saving myself."

He laughed, then he saw she was serious. "I hope you're right, Jinx, because if any of your shit blows back on me, I will not hesitate to tell them how to find you. You made your choice."

"You're damn right I did," Jane told him. "And if anybody comes looking for me, I'll use those papers to make sure you go down right beside me."

Jane pulled back the privacy curtain. She slid open the glass door.

The cop had already turned around. His hand was on his gun.

She told him, "Tell the FBI they've got less than three hours to offer me a deal or there's going to be a massive explosion in New York City."

August 26, 2018

# 15

Andy felt the tip of her finger slip through the hole in her skin. *She had been shot.*

She leaned her head back against the wall. She sucked in air through her teeth and tried not to pass out.

Edwin Van Wees was on the floor of his office. Broken glass was scattered around his body. Pieces of paper. Blood. The MacBook that Andy had used to find out about her mother.

*Laura.*

Andy reached out, her fingers brushing the edge of the burner phone. The screen was cracked. She closed her eyes, concentrated on listening. Was that her mother's voice? Was she still on the phone?

A woman's scream came from the other side of the house.

Andy's heart stopped.

The second scream was louder, abruptly cut off by a loud *smack*.

Andy clamped her jaw shut so she would not scream, too.

*Clara.*

Andy couldn't stay frozen this time. She had to do something. Her legs shook as she tried to push herself up against the wall. The pain almost ripped her open. She had to hunch over to stop the cramping. Blood dribbled from the bullet hole in her side. Andy's legs shook as she tried to move forward. This was her fault. All of it. Laura had warned her to be careful and still, Andy had led them here.

*They.*

To kill Edwin. To kill Clara.

Andy's shoulder slid along the wall as she tried to find Clara, to give herself up, to stop this awful mess she had made. Her feet got caught up on the rug. Pain sliced into her side. Her head bumped against the photographs that lined the hallway. She had to stop to catch her breath. Her eyes kept going in and out of focus. She stared at the pictures on the wall. Different frames, different poses, some color, some black and white. Clara and Edwin with two women around Andy's age. A few snapshots of the women when they were younger, in high school, in kindergarten, and then—

Toddler Andy in the snow.

Andy felt numb as she stared at the image of her younger self.

Was it Edwin's hand she had been holding? The adjacent photo showed baby Andy sitting in Clara and Edwin's lap. Laura had cut Andy out of their lives and superimposed her onto the stock photo of the fake Randall grandparents.

"Nice, right?"

Andy turned her head. She had been expecting to find Mike, but it was a woman's voice. A woman she knew all too well.

Paula Kunde stood at the end of the hallway.

She pointed a familiar-looking revolver at Andy. "Thanks for leaving this for me in your car. Did you rub off the serial number, or was that Mommy?"

Andy didn't answer. She couldn't catch her breath.

"You're hyperventilating," Paula said. "Pick up the phone."

Andy turned her head. The burner phone was on the floor behind her. In the stillness, she could hear her mother wailing.

"Jesus." Paula stomped down the hall, scooped up the phone and held it to her ear. "Shut up, Dumb Bitch."

Laura didn't shut up. Her tinny voice was vibrating with rage.

Paula turned on the speakerphone.

"... *touch a fucking hair on her*—"

"She's dying." Paula smiled at Laura's abrupt silence. She held the phone under Andy's chin. "Tell her, sweetheart."

Andy clutched her hand to her side. She could feel the blood seeping out of her.

"Andrea?" Laura said. "Please, talk to—"

"Mom . . ."

"Oh, my darling," Laura cried. "Are you okay?"

Andy broke down, a strangled cry coming from deep inside her body. "Mom—"

"What happened? Please—oh, God, please tell me you're okay!"

"I—" Andy didn't know if she could get the words out. "I was shot. She shot me in the—"

"That's enough." Paula raised the gun and Andy went silent. She told Laura, "You know what I want, Dumb Bitch."

"Edwin—"

"Is dead." Paula raised her eyebrows at Andy, as if this was a game.

"You stupid fucking idiot," Laura hissed. "He's the only one who knows—"

"Shut up with your bullshit," Paula said. "You know where it is. How much time do you need?"

"I can—" Laura stopped. "Two days."

"Sure, no problem." Paula grinned at Andy. "Maybe your kid will go into shock before she bleeds out."

"You fucking cunt."

Andy was rattled by the hateful words. She had never heard her mother like this.

Laura said, "I will slice open your fucking throat if you hurt my daughter. Do you understand me?"

"You dumb bitch," Paula said. "I'm hurting her right now."

Andy saw a flash.

Everything went black.

*   *   *

Andy was aware that something was wrong even before she opened her eyes. There was not a moment where it all came back to her, because she had never for a moment forgotten what had happened.

She had been shot. She was inside the trunk of a car. Her hands and feet were bound by some configuration of handcuffs. A towel was duct-taped around her waist to stanch the bleeding. The gag in her mouth had a rubber ball that made it hard for her to breathe because her nose was filled with blood from being pistol-whipped into unconsciousness.

As with everything else, Andy could recall the blows from the revolver. She hadn't really blacked out. She had felt more as if she'd been caught between the edge of sleep and wakefulness. When Andy was in art school, she had craved that stasis because it was where she found her best ideas. Her mind seemingly blank but still working through the various shades of black and white she would elicit from her pencil.

*Did she have a concussion?*

She should've been panicked, but the panic had gurgled back down like water circling a drain. An hour ago? Two hours? Now, her only overriding feeling was intense discomfort. Her lip was split. Her cheek felt bruised. Her eye was swollen. Her hands were numb. Her wrists had fallen asleep. If she lay the right way, if she kept her spine bent, if her breathing remained shallow, the burning in her side was manageable.

The guilt was another matter.

In her head, Andy kept playing back what happened inside the farmhouse, trying to identify the point at which everything had gone wrong. Edwin had told her to leave. Could Andy have left before the front of his shirt was ripped open by the bullets riddling his back?

She squeezed her eyes shut.

*Click-click-click-click.*

The revolver's cylinder spinning.

Andy tried to analyze Clara's two different screams, the startled quality of the first one, the *smack* that had cut off the second one. Not a hand slapping or a fist punching. Paula had struck Andy with the revolver. Had Clara suffered a similar fate? Had she awoken dazed in her own kitchen, walked down the hallway and found Edwin lying dead?

Or had she never opened her eyes again?

Andy cried out as the car hit a bump in the road.

Paula slowed for a turn. Andy felt the change in speed, the pull of gravity. The glow of the brake lights filled the darkness. Andy saw the stub of the emergency trunk release that Paula had cut off so that Andy could not escape.

They were in a rental car with Texas plates. Andy had seen as much when she'd been shoved into the trunk. Paula couldn't fly with the gun. She must have driven from Austin, the same as Andy, but Andy had been checking sporadically for Mike. Which meant that Paula had known exactly where Andy would eventually end up. She had played right into the bitch's hands.

Andy tasted bile in her throat.

*Why hadn't she listened to her mother?*

The car slowed again, but this time came to a full stop.

Paula had stopped once before. Twenty minutes ago? Thirty? Andy wasn't sure. She had tried to keep count, but her eyes kept closing and she'd end up having to jerk herself awake and start all over again.

*Was she dying?*

Her brain felt weirdly indifferent to everything that was happening. She was terrified, but her heart was not pounding, her hands were not sweating. She was hurting, but she wasn't hyperventilating or crying or begging for it to stop.

*Was she in shock?*

Andy heard the clicking of a turn signal.

The car wheels bumped onto a gravel road.

She tried not to remember all the horror movies that started with a car driving down a gravel road to a deserted campsite or an abandoned shack.

"*No.*" She said the word aloud into the darkness of the trunk. She would not let her panic ramp up again, because it would only make her blind to any opportunities of escape. Andy was being held hostage. Laura had something that Paula wanted. Paula would not kill Andy until she got that thing.

*Right?*

The brakes whined as the car stopped again. This time, the engine turned off. The driver side door opened, then closed.

Andy waited for the trunk to open. She had gone through all kinds of scenarios in her head of what she was going to do when she saw Paula again, primary among them to raise her feet and kick the bitch in the face. The problem was, you needed stomach muscles to raise your feet, and Andy could barely breathe without feeling like a blow torch was blazing open her side.

She let her head rest on the floor of the trunk. She listened for sounds. All she could hear was the engine block cooling.

*Click-click-click-click.*

Like the cylinder spinning in the gun, but slower.

Andy started counting to give herself something to do. Being stuck in the Reliant, then Mike's truck, for so many hours had made her the type of person who said things out loud just to break the monotony.

"One," she mumbled. "Two . . . three . . ."

She was at nine hundred and eight-five when the trunk finally opened.

Andy blinked. It was dark outside, no moon in the sky. The only light came from the stairwell across from the open trunk. She had no idea where they were, except for another shitty motel in another shitty town.

"Look at me." Paula jammed the revolver underneath Andy's chin. "Don't fuck with me or I'll shoot you again. All right?"

Andy nodded.

Paula tucked the gun into the waist of her jeans. She worked the keys into the handcuffs. Andy groaned with relief when her arms and legs were finally released. She clawed at the ball gag. The pink leather straps snapped in the back. It looked like something from a *50 Shades of Grey* catalog.

Paula had the revolver out again. She glanced around the parking lot. "Get out and keep your mouth shut."

Andy tried to move, but the wound and her long confinement made it impossible.

"Christ." Paula jerked Andy up by her arm.

Andy could only roll, falling against the bumper and stumbling to the ground. There was so much pain in her body that she could not locate one source. Blood dribbled from her mouth. She had bitten her own tongue. Her feet were beset by pins and needles as the circulation returned.

"Stand up." Paula grabbed Andy's arm and pulled her to her feet.

Andy howled, bending over at the waist to stop the spasms.

"Stop whining," Paula said. "Put this on."

Andy recognized the white polo button-down from the blue Samsonite suitcase. Part of Laura's go-bag from the Carrollton storage unit.

"Hurry." Paula looked around the parking lot again as she helped Andy into the shirt. "If you're thinking about screaming, don't. I can't shoot you, but I can shoot anybody who tries to help you."

Andy started on the buttons. "What did you do to Clara?"

"Your second mommy?" She chuckled at Andy's expression. "She raised you for almost two years, her and Edwin. Did you know that?"

Andy was desperate not to give her a reaction. She kept her head down, watched her fingers work the buttons.

*Had Edwin looked at her like her father because he was her father?*

Paula said, "They wanted to keep you, but Jane took you for herself because that's the kind of selfish bitch she is." Paula was watching Andy carefully. "Seems like you're not surprised to hear that your mother's real name is Jane."

"Why did you kill Edwin?"

"Jesus, kid." She grabbed some handcuffs from the trunk. "Did you go through your entire life with a fish hook in your mouth?"

Andy mumbled, "Evidently."

Paula slammed the trunk shut. She picked up two plastic bags in one hand. The gun went into the waist of her jeans, but she kept her hand on the grip. "Move."

"Is Edwin—" Andy tried to think of a clever way of tricking her into admitting the truth, but her brain was incapable of any acrobatics. "Is he my father?"

"If he was your father, I would've already shot you in the chest and shit in the hole." She waved for Andy to get moving. "Up the stairs."

Andy found walking relatively easy, but climbing the stairs almost cut her in two. She kept her hand on her side, but there was no way to stop the feeling of a knife twisting her flesh. Each time she lifted her foot, she wanted to scream. Screaming would probably bring people out of their rooms, then Paula would shoot them, then Andy would have more than Edwin Van Wees and Clara Bellamy's deaths on her conscience.

"Left," Paula said.

Andy walked down a long, dark hallway. Shadows danced in front of her eyes. The nausea had returned. The dull pain had become sharp again. She had to put her hand to the wall so she would not trip or fall over. Why was she going along with everything like a lemming? Why didn't she scream in the parking lot? People didn't run out to help anymore. They would call the police, and then the police would—

"Here." Paula waved the keycard to open the door.

Andy entered the room ahead of her. The lights were already on. Two queen-sized beds, a television, a desk, small bistro table with two matching chairs. The bathroom was by the door. The curtains were closed on the window that probably looked out onto the parking lot.

Paula dropped the plastic grocery bags onto the table. Bottles of water. Fruit. Potato chips.

Andy sniffed. Blood rolled down her throat. She felt like the entire left side of her face was filled with hot water.

"All right." Paula's hand rested on the butt of the gun. "Go ahead and holler if you want. This entire wing is empty, and anyway, this ain't the kind of hotel where people worry if they hear a gal begging for help."

Andy stared all of her hate into the woman.

Paula grinned, feeding off the rage. "If you need to piss, do it now. I won't offer again."

Andy tried to close the bathroom door, but Paula stopped her. She watched Andy labor to sit on the toilet without using her stomach muscles. A yelp slipped from Andy's lips as her ass hit the seat. She had to lean over her knees to keep the pain at bay. Normally, Andy's bladder was shy, but after so long in the car, she had no problem going.

Standing was another matter. Her knees started to straighten and then she was back on the toilet, groaning.

"Fucksakes." Paula yanked up Andy by the armpit. She zipped and buttoned Andy's jeans like she was three, then shoved her into the room. "Go sit down at the table."

Andy kept her back bent as she navigated her way into the rickety chair. The side of her body lit up like a bolt of lightning.

Paula shoved the chair underneath the table. "You need to do what I say when I say it."

"Fuck you." The words slipped out before Andy could stop them.

"Fuck you, too." Paula grabbed Andy's left arm. She clamped a handcuff on her wrist, then jerked her hand under the table and attached the cuff to the metal base.

Andy pulled at the restraint. The table rattled. She pressed her forehead to the top.

*Why hadn't she gone to Idaho?*

Paula said, "If your mother caught the first flight out, she won't be here for at least another two hours." She found an ibuprofen bottle in one of the bags. She used her teeth to rip off the safety seal. "How bad does it hurt?"

"Like I've been shot, you fucking psycho."

"Fair enough." Instead of being mad, Paula seemed delighted by Andy's anger. She put four gelcaps on the table. She opened one of the bottles of water. "Barbecue or regular?"

Andy stared at her.

Paula held up two bags of potato chips. "You have to eat something or you'll get a tummy ache from the pills."

Andy didn't know what to say but, "Barbecue."

Paula opened the bag with help from her teeth. She unwrapped two sandwiches. "Mustard and mayo?"

Andy nodded, watching the madwoman who'd shot and kidnapped her use a plastic knife to spread mayonnaise and mustard onto the bread of her turkey sandwich.

*Why was this happening?*

"Eat at least half." Paula slid over the sandwich and started adding mustard to her own. "I mean it, kid. Half. Then you can take the pills."

Andy picked it up, but she had an idiotic flash of the sandwich squirting out of the hole in her side. And then she remembered, "You're not supposed to eat before surgery."

Paula stared at her.

"The bullet. I mean, if—when—my mom gets here, and—"

"They won't operate. Easier to let the bullet stay inside. It's infection you should be worried about. That shit'll kill you." Paula turned on the television. She channeled around until she found Animal Planet, then muted the sound.

*Pitbulls and Parolees.*

"This is a good episode." Paula swiveled back around. She squirted mayonnaise onto her sandwich. "I wish they'd had this program at Danbury."

Andy watched her use the plastic knife to evenly spread the mayo across the bread.

This should've felt strange, but it didn't feel strange. Why would it? Andy had started the week by watching her mother kill a kid, then Andy had murdered a gun for hire, then she was on the run and kicking a thug in the balls and getting one, maybe two more people killed, so why wouldn't it feel natural to be handcuffed to a table, watching parolees try to reform abused animals with a psycho ex-con college professor?

Paula pressed the sandwich back together. She tugged at the

scarf around her neck, the same scarf she had been wearing two and a half days ago in Austin.

Andy said, "I thought you'd been suffocated."

Paula took a large bite. She spoke with her mouth full. "I'm getting a cold. You gotta keep your neck warm to stop the coughing."

Andy didn't bother to correct the asinine health advice. A cold explained Paula's raspy voice, but Andy said, "Your eye—"

"Your fucking mother." Food dropped from Paula's mouth, but she kept talking. "She whacked me in the head. They didn't do shit for me in jail. The left one went white, I got an infection in the right one. Still sensitive to light, so that's why I wear the sunglasses. Thanks to your mom, that's been my look for thirty-two years."

*Interesting math.*

Paula said, "What else you wanna know?"

Andy felt like she had nothing left to lose. She asked, "You sent the guy to Mom's house, right? To torture her?"

"Samuel Godfrey Beckett." Paula snorted, then coughed when the sandwich went down the wrong way. "Worth the money just for his stupid name. I thought for sure Jane would give it up. She's never been good at confrontation. Then again, she killed that kid in the diner. I about shit myself when I recognized her face on the news. *Fucking Laura Oliver.* Living on a goddamn beach while the rest of us rotted in jail."

Andy pressed her tongue to the roof of her mouth. The gun was still tucked into Paula's jeans, but her hands were occupied with eating. Could Andy push the table into Paula's gut, reach over with her free hand and grab the gun?

"What else, kid?"

Andy mentally walked herself through the motions. None of them worked out. Her handcuffed wrist was stretched too far under the table. She would end up impaling herself if she reached for the gun with her free hand.

"Come on." Paula bit off another chunk of sandwich. "Ask me all the questions you can't ask your mother."

Andy looked away. At the ugly floral bedspread. At the door almost twenty feet away. Paula was offering her everything, but after searching for so long, Andy didn't just want answers. She wanted an explanation, and that was something she could only get from her mother.

Paula looked for a napkin in the bag. "You turning shy on me?"

Andy did not want to, but she asked, "How will I know you're telling the truth?"

"I'm more honest than that whore you call a mother."

Andy chewed at the tip of her already sore tongue to keep from lashing out. "Who did you kill?"

"Some bitch who tried to stab me in prison. They couldn't prosecute me for Norway. Maplecroft wasn't my fault. Quarter was the one who snatched her. The other stuff wasn't on me." She stopped to chew. "I pleaded guilty to fleeing the scene of a crime. That got me six years, the bitch I shivved was self-defense, but they took me up to two dimes. Ask another question."

"How did you get your job at the university?"

"They were looking for a diversity hire and I lucked up with my sad sack reformed felon story. Ask another."

"Is Clara okay?"

"Ha, good try. How about this: why do I hate your dumb bitch of a mother?"

Andy waited, but Paula was waiting, too.

Andy made her tone as bored and disinterested as she could, asking, "Why do you hate my mother?"

"She turned on us. All of us except Edwin and Clara, but that was only because she wanted to control them." Paula waited for a reaction that Andy could not give her. "Jane was put into witness protection in exchange for her testimony. She got a sweetheart deal because the clock was literally ticking. We had another bomb ready to go, but her big fucking mouth stopped it all."

Andy searched Paula's expression for guile, but she saw none. *Witness protection.*

Andy tried to wrap her brain around the information, to figure out how it made her feel. Laura had lied to her, but Andy had become accustomed to the fact that her mother lied. Maybe what she was feeling was a slight sense of relief. All of this time, Andy had assumed that Laura was a criminal. And she was a criminal, but she had actually done something good by turning them all in.

*Right?*

Paula said, "The pigs still put her in prison for two years. They can do that, you know. Even with witness protection. And Jane did some heinous shit. We all did, but we did it for the cause. Jane did it because she was a spoiled bitch who got bored spending her daddy's money."

"QuellCorp," Andy said.

"Billions," Paula said. "All from the suffering and exploitation of the sick."

"So you're holding me ransom for money?"

"Hell no. I don't want her fucking blood money. This has nothing to do with QuellCorp. The family divested years ago. None of them have anything to do with it. Except raking in the dough from their stock options."

Andy wondered if that's where the cash came from in the Reliant. You had to pay taxes on stock gains, but if Laura was in witness protection, then everything would be above-board.

*Right?*

Paula said, "Jane never told you any of this?"

Andy didn't bother to confirm what the woman already knew.

"Did she tell you who your father is?"

Andy kept her mouth shut. She knew who her father was.

"Don't you want to know?"

Gordon was her father. He had raised her, taken care of her, put up with her maddening silences and indecision.

Paula gave a heavy, disappointed sigh. "Nicholas Harp. She never told you?"

Andy felt her curiosity rise, but not for the obvious reason. She recognized the name from the Wikipedia page. Harp had died of an overdose years before Andy was born.

She told Paula, "You're lying."

"No, I'm not. Nick is the leader of the Army of the Changing World. Everybody should know his name, but especially you."

"Wiki said that Clayton Morrow—"

"Nicholas Harp. That's your father's chosen name. Half of that bullshit on Wikipedia is lies. The other half is speculation." Paula leaned across the table, excited. "The Army of the Changing World stood for something. We really were going to change the world. Then your mother lost her nerve and it all turned into a shitshow."

Andy shook her head, because all they had done was kill people and terrorize the country. "That professor was murdered in San Francisco. Most of the people in your group are dead. Martin Queller was assassinated."

"You mean, your grandfather?"

Andy felt jarred. She had not had time to make the connection. *Martin Queller was her grandfather.*

He had been married to Annette Queller, her grandmother.

Which meant that Jasper Queller, the asshole billionaire, was her uncle.

*Was Laura a billionaire, too?*

"Finally putting it together, huh?" Paula tossed a stray piece of deli meat into her mouth. "Your father has been in prison for three decades because of Jane. She kept you away from him. You could've had a relationship, gotten to know who he is, but she denied you that honor."

Andy knew exactly who Clayton Morrow was, and she wanted nothing to do with him. He was not her father any more than Jerry Randall was. She had to believe that, because the alternative would have her curled into a ball on the floor.

"Come on." Paula wiped her mouth with the back of her hand. "Give me some more questions."

Andy thought through the last few days, the list of unknowns she had jotted down after meeting Paula. "What changed your mind back in Austin? One minute you were telling me to leave, the next minute you were telling me to look for Clara Bellamy."

Paula nodded, as if she approved of the question. "The pig whose nuts you marshmallowed. I figured you wouldn't have done that if you were working with your mother."

"What?"

"The pig. The US marshal."

Andy felt a flush work its way up her neck.

"You fucked up his shit. That bitch was lying on my front porch for an hour."

Andy leaned her head onto the table so that Paula couldn't see her face.

*Mike.*

The Marshal Service was in charge of administering the witness protection program. They could make all the driver's licenses they wanted because making new documents was part of their job—fake birth certificates and fake tax returns and even fake obituaries for a made-up guy named Jerry Randall.

Andy felt her bowels swirl.

Mike was Laura's handler. That's why he was at the hospital when she came out. Was that why he was following Andy? Was he trying to help her because she had unwittingly been in the program, too?

Had she taken out the only person who might be able to save them from this monster?

"Hey." Paula rapped her knuckles on the table. "More questions. Spit 'em out. We got nothing better to do."

Andy shook her head. She tried to put together Mike's involvement since the beginning. His truck in the Hazeltons' driveway with his rabbit's foot keychain. The magnetic signs he changed out with each new city.

*The GPS tracker on the cooler.*

Mike must have planted it while Andy was passed out in the Muscle Shoals motel. Then he'd gone across the street for a congratulatory beer and improvised when Andy walked through the door.

She had assumed that he was friends with the bartender, but guys like Mike made friends wherever they went.

"Hey," Paula repeated. "Focus on me, kid. If you're not going to keep me entertained, then I'm gonna truss you back up and watch my shows."

Andy had to shake her head to clear it. She lifted her chin up, rested it against her free hand. She didn't know what else to do but return to her list. "Why did you send me to find Clara?"

"Bitch refused to talk to me back when she had her marbles, and Edwin threatened to rat me to my P.O. I was hoping seeing you would trigger her memories. Then I could snatch you up and you could give me the information and happy ending for everybody. Except Edwin got in the way. But you know what? Fuck him for working Jane's deal to keep her out of prison for thirty years." Paula crammed a handful of chips into her mouth. "Your mother was part of a conspiracy to kill your grandfather. She watched Alexandra Maplecroft die. She was there when Quarter was shot in the heart. She helped drive the van to the farm. She was with us one hundred percent every step of the way."

"Until she wasn't," Andy said, because that was the part that she wanted to hold onto.

"Yeah, well, we took down the Chicago Mercantile before it was all over." She caught Andy's blank look. "That's where commodities are exchanged. Derivatives. You've heard of those? And Nick was on his way into Manhattan when they caught him trying to blow up the Stock Exchange. It would've been glorious."

Andy had watched along with everyone else planes hitting buildings and trucks mowing down pedestrians and all of the horrors in between. She knew that attacks like that were not glorious, just as she knew that no matter what these crazy groups tried to take down, it always got rebuilt—taller, stronger, better.

She asked Paula, "So why am I here? What do you want from my mom?"

"Took you long enough to get to that question," Paula said. "Jane has some papers your uncle Jasper signed."

*Uncle Jasper.*

Andy couldn't get used to having a family, though she wasn't sure the Quellers were a family that she wanted.

Paula said, "Nick's been up for parole six times in the last twelve years." She wadded up the potato chip bag and threw it toward the trash can. "Every single fucking time, Jasper Fucking Queller climbs up on his podium wearing his stupid Air Force insignia and American flag pin and starts whining about how Nick killed his father and infected his brother and made him lose his sister and wah-wah-wah."

"Infected his brother?"

"Nick had nothing to do with that. Your uncle was a fag. He died of AIDS."

Andy physically reeled from the invective.

Paula snorted. "Your generation and its fucking political correctness."

"Your generation and its fucking homophobia."

Paula snorted again. "Christ, if I'd known all it took to make your balls drop was to shoot you, I would've done you the favor back in Austin."

Andy closed her eyes for a second. She hated this brutal back and forth. "What's in the papers? Why are they so important?"

"Fraud." Paula raised her eyebrows, waiting for Andy to react. "Queller Healthcare was kicking patients out on the street, but still billing the state for their care."

Andy waited for more, but apparently, that was it. She asked, "And . . . ?"

"What do you mean, *and* . . . ?"

"I could go online right now and find dozens of videos showing poor people being kicked out of hospitals." Andy shrugged. "The hospitals just apologize and pay a fine. Sometimes they don't even do that. Nobody loses their job, except maybe the security guard who was following orders."

Paula was clearly thrown by her nonchalance. "It's still a crime."

"Okay."

"Do you ever watch the news or read a paper? Jasper Queller wants to be president."

Andy wasn't so sure that a fraud conviction would stop him. Paula was still fighting by 1980s rules, before spin doctors and crisis management teams had become part of the vernacular. All Jasper would have to do was go on an apology tour, cry a little, and he'd be more popular than before it all started.

Paula crossed her arms. She had a smug look on her face. "Trust me, Jasper will crumble at the first whiff of scandal. All he cares about is the Queller family reputation. We'll work him like a marionette."

Andy had to be missing something. She tried to work it out. "You saw my mom on TV. You hired a guy to torture her for the location of these documents, and now you're holding me ransom for them because you're going to blackmail Jasper into being silent so Clayton—Nick—will be paroled?"

"It's not rocket science, kid."

It wasn't even model rocket science.

*How had her mother fallen in with these idiots?*

Paula said, "I've got everything ready for Nick when he gets out. We'll get some art for the walls, find the right furniture. Nick has such a great eye. I wouldn't presume to choose those things without him."

Andy remembered the institutional blandness inside of Paula's house. Twenty years in prison, at least a decade on the outside, and she was still waiting for Clayton Morrow to tell her what to do.

She asked, "Did Nick put you up to this?" She remembered something Paula had said. "That's why you haven't killed me, right? Because I'm his daughter."

She grinned. "I guess you're not as stupid as you look."

Andy heard a cell phone vibrating.

Paula searched the bags and found the broken burner phone. She winked at Andy before answering. "What is it, Dumb Bitch?" Her eyebrows went up. "Porter Motel. I know you're familiar. Room 310."

Andy watched her close the phone. "She's on her way?"

"She's here. Guess she used some of those Queller billions to charter a flight." Paula stood up. She adjusted the gun in her waistband. "We're in Valparaiso, Indiana. I figured you'd want to see where you were born."

Andy had already chewed her tongue raw. She started on her cheek.

"Dumb Bitch was too good to be thrown into the general prison population. Edwin wrangled her a stay in the Porter County jail. She was in solitary the whole time, but so fucking what? Beats worrying some bitch is gonna shiv you in the back because you said her ass was big."

Andy's brain couldn't handle all the information at once. She said, "What about—"

Paula took off her scarf and shoved it deep into Andy's mouth.

"Sorry, kid, but I can't be distracted by your bullshit." She got on her knees and released the handcuff from the base of the table. "Put your right arm underneath."

Andy stretched both arms toward the base, and Paula ratcheted down the cuffs.

"Uhn," Andy tried. The scarf was shoved too far down her throat. She tried to work it out with her tongue.

"If your mom does what she's supposed to do, you'll be fine." Paula took a spool of clothesline out of the bag. She bound Andy's ankles to the chair leg. "Just in case you get any ideas."

Andy started to cough. The more she struggled to push out the scarf, the deeper it went.

"You know your dead uncle tried to hang himself with this stuff once?" She reached into the plastic bag again. She found a pair of scissors. She used her teeth to break them out of the packaging. "No, I guess you don't know. Left a scar on his neck, here—" She used the tip of the scissors to point to her neck, just below a smattering of dark moles.

Andy hoped she had skin cancer.

"Jasper saved him that time." Paula cut the end of the clothesline. "Andy was always needing saving. Weird that your mom calls you by his name."

Laura didn't like to call Andy by her dead brother's name. She winced every time she used anything other than Andrea.

Paula checked the handcuffs again, then the knots, to make sure they were secure. "All right. I'm gonna pee." She stuck the scissors into her back pocket. "Don't do anything stupid."

Andy waited until the bathroom door shut, then she looked for something stupid to do. The burner phone was still on the table. Her hands were out of the question, but maybe she could use her head. She tried to inch the chair forward but the burning was so intense that vomit spilled up her throat.

The scarf pushed it back down.

*Fuck.*

Andy let her eyes scan the room from floor to ceiling. Ice bucket and plastic cups on the desk under the TV. Water bottles. Trash can. Andy wrapped her fingers around the base of the table. She tested the weight as much as she could. Too heavy. And also, she had a bullet inside her body. Even if she managed to bite back the pain and lift the table, she would fall flat on her face because her ankles were tied to the chair.

The toilet flushed. The sink faucet ran. Paula came out with a towel in her hands. She tossed it onto the desk. Instead of addressing Andy, she sat down on the edge of the bed and watched television.

Andy let her forehead rest on the table. She closed her eyes. She felt a groan vibrate inside of her throat. It was too much. All of it was just too damn much.

Mike was a US marshal.

Her mother was in the witness protection program.

Her birth father was a murderous cult leader.

Edwin Van Wees was dead.

Clara Bellamy—

Andy could still clearly hear the *smack* that had cut off Clara's scream.

The *click-click-click-click* of the revolver's cylinder.

The ballerina and the lawyer had taken care of Andy for the

first two years of her life, and she had not remembered one detail about them.

There was a sound in the hallway.

Andy's heart jumped. She raised her head.

Two knocks rattled the door, then there was a pause, then another knock.

Paula snorted. "Your mom thinks she's being sneaky getting here sooner than she said." She turned off the TV. She pressed her finger to her lips as if Andy was capable of anything but silence.

The revolver was in Paula's hand by the time she opened the door.

*Mom.*

Andy started to cry. She couldn't help it. The relief was so overwhelming that she felt like her heart was going to explode.

Their eyes met.

Laura shook her head once, but Andy didn't know why.

*Don't do anything?*

*This is the end?*

Paula jammed the gun in Laura's face. "Move it. Hurry."

Laura leaned heavily on an aluminum cane as she walked into the room. Her coat was wrapped around her shoulders. Her face was drawn. She looked frail, like a woman twice her age. She asked Andy, "Are you okay?"

Andy nodded, alarmed by her mother's fragile appearance. She'd had almost a week to recover from her injuries. Was she sick again? Did she get an infection from the wound in her leg, the knife cut in her hand?

"Where are they?" Paula pressed the muzzle of the gun to the back of Laura's head. "The files. Where are they?"

Laura kept her gaze locked with Andy's. It was like a laser beam between them. Andy could remember the same look passing between them when the nurses were wheeling Laura into surgery, off to radiation therapy, into the chemo ward.

This was her mother. This woman, this stranger, had always been Andy's mother.

"Come on," Paula said. "Where—"

Laura shrugged her right shoulder, letting the coat slip to the floor. Her left arm was in a sling instead of strapped to her waist. A packet of file folders was tucked inside. The splint from the hospital was gone. She was wearing an Ace bandage that ballooned around her hand. Her swollen fingers curled from the opening like a cat's tongue.

Paula snatched away the files and opened them on the desk under the TV. The gun stayed trained on Laura while she thumbed through the pages. Paula's head swiveled back and forth like she was afraid Laura would pounce. "Is this all of them?"

"It's enough." Laura still would not look away from Andy.
*What was she trying to say?*

"Spread your legs." Paula roughly patted down Laura with her hands, clapping up and down her body. "Take off the sling."

Laura didn't move.

"Now," Paula said, an edge to her voice that Andy had never heard before.

Was Paula afraid? Was the fearless bitch really scared of Laura?

"Take it off," Paula repeated. Her body was tense. She was shifting her weight back and forth between her feet. "Now, Dumb Bitch."

Laura sighed as she rested the cane against the bed. She reached up to her neck. She found the Velcro closure and carefully pulled away the sling. She held her wrapped hand away from her body. "I'm not wearing a wire."

Paula lifted Laura's shirt, ran her finger around the waistband.

Laura's eyes found Andy. She shook her head again, just once.
*Why?*

Paula said, "Sit on the bed."

"You have what you asked for." Laura's voice was calm, almost cold. "Let us go and no one else will get hurt."

Paula jammed the gun into Laura's face. "You're the only one who's going to get hurt."

Laura nodded at Andy, as if this was exactly what she had expected. She finally looked at Paula. "I'll stay. Let her go."

*No!* The word got caught in Andy's throat. She worked furiously to spit out the scarf. *No!*

"Sit down." Paula shoved her mother back onto the bed. There was no way for Laura to catch herself with one arm. She fell on her side. Andy watched her mother's expression contort in pain.

Anger seized Andy like a fever. She started groaning, snorting, making every noise she could manage.

Paula kicked away the aluminum cane. "Your daughter's going to watch you die."

Laura said nothing.

"Take this." Paula tossed the spool of clothesline at Laura.

She caught it with one hand. Her eyes went to Andy. Then she looked back at Paula.

*What?* Andy wanted to scream. *What am I supposed to do?*

Laura held up the spool. "Is this supposed to make me feel sad?"

"It's supposed to tie you up like a pig so I can gut you."

*Gut you?*

Andy started pulling at the handcuffs. She pressed her chest into the edge of the table. The pain was almost unbearable, but she had to do something.

"Penny, stop this." Laura slid toward the edge of the bed. "Nick wouldn't want—"

"What the fuck do you know about what Nick wants?" Paula gripped the gun with both hands. She was shaking with fury. "You fucking cold bitch."

"I was his lover for six years. I gave birth to his child." Laura's feet went flat to the ground. "Do you think he'd want his daughter to witness her mother's brutal murder?"

"I should just shoot you," Paula said. "Do you see my eye? Do you see what you did to me?"

"I'm actually quite proud of that."

Paula swung the gun into Laura's face.

*Smack.*

Andy felt her stomach clench as Laura struggled to stay upright.

Paula raised the gun again.

Andy squeezed her eyes closed, but she heard the horrible crunching sound of metal hitting bone. She was back at the farmhouse. Edwin was dead. Clara had screamed her first scream, then—

*Click-click-click-click.*

The cylinder spinning in the revolver.

Andy's eyes opened.

"Fucking bitch." Paula struck Laura across the face again. The skin had opened. Her mouth was bleeding.

*Mom!* Andy's yell came out like a grunt. *Mom!*

"It's gonna get worse," Paula told Andy. "Pace yourself."

*Mom!* Andy yelled. She looked at Laura, then looked at the gun, then looked back at Laura.

*Think about it!*

Why was Paula threatening to gut her? Why hadn't she shot Clara at the farmhouse? Why wasn't she shooting Laura and Andy right now?

The clicking back at the farmhouse was the sound of Paula checking to see if all of the cartridges in the revolver were spent.

*She didn't have any bullets left in the gun.*

*Mom!* Andy shook the chair so hard that fresh blood oozed out of her side. The table bumped into her chest. She twisted her wrists, trying to hold up her hands so that Laura could see them.

*Look!* Andy groaned, straining her vocal cords, begging her mother for attention.

Laura took another blow from the gun. Her head rolled to the side. She was dazed from the beating.

*Mom!* Andy shook the table harder. Her wrists were raw. She waved her hands, furiously trying to get Laura's attention.

"Come on, kid," Paula said. "All you're gonna do is knock yourself over."

Andy grunted, shaking her hands in the air so hard that the cuffs cut into her skin.

*Look!*

With painful slowness, Laura's eyes finally focused on Andy's hands.

Four fingers raised on the left. One finger raised on the right.

The same number of fingers Laura had shown Jonah Helsinger at the diner.

*It's why you haven't pulled the trigger yet. There's only one bullet left.*

While Laura watched, Andy raised the thumb of her left hand.

Six fingers.

Six bullets.

The gun was empty.

Laura sat up on the bed.

Paula was thrown by her sudden recovery from the beating, which was exactly what Laura needed.

She grabbed the gun with her right hand. Her left hand corkscrewed through the air, punching Paula square in the throat.

Everything stopped.

Neither woman moved.

Laura's fist was pressed to the front of Paula's neck.

Paula's hand was wrapped around Laura's arm.

A clock was ticking somewhere in the room.

Andy heard a gurgling sound.

Laura wrested away her injured hand.

A ribbon of red sagged into the collar of Paula's shirt. Her throat had been sliced open, the skin gaping in a crescent-shaped wound.

Blood dripped from the razorblade Laura held between her fingers.

*I will slice open your fucking throat if you hurt my daughter.*

That was why Laura wasn't wearing the splint. She needed her fingers free so that she could hold onto the blade and punch it into Paula's neck.

Paula coughed a spray of blood. She was shaking—not from fear this time, but from white hot fury.

Laura leaned in. She whispered something into Paula's ear.

Rage flickered like a candle in her eyes. Paula coughed again. Her lips trembled. Her fingers. Her eyelids.

Andy pressed her forehead down to the table.

She found herself feeling detached from the carnage. She wasn't shocked by sudden violence anymore. She finally understood the serenity on her mother's face when she had killed Jonah Helsinger.

She had seen it all before.

# ONE MONTH LATER

*I felt a cleaving in my Mind—*
*As if my Brain had split—*
*I tried to match it—Seam by Seam—*
*But could not make them fit.*

*The thought behind, I strove to join*
*Unto the thought before—*
*But Sequence ravelled out of Sound*
*Like Balls—upon a Floor.*

                                        *—Emily Dickinson*

# EPILOGUE

Laura Oliver sat on a wooden bench outside the Federal Corrections Institute in Maryland. The complex resembled a large high school. The adjacent satellite facility was more akin to a boys' summer camp. Minimum security, mostly white-collar criminals who'd skimmed from hedge funds or forgotten to pay decades of taxes. There were tennis and basketball courts and two running tracks. The perimeter fence felt cursory. The guard towers were sparse. Many of the inmates were allowed to leave during the day to work at the nearby factories.

Given the seriousness of his crimes, Nick didn't belong here, but he had always been good at inserting himself into places he did not belong. He'd been convicted of manslaughter for killing Alexandra Maplecroft, and conspiracy to use a weapon of mass destruction for the New York piece of the plan. The jury had decided not only to spare Nick's life, but to give him the possibility of parole. Which was likely how he had wrangled his transfer to Club Fed. The worst thing that inmates had to worry about inside the blue-roofed pods spoking out from the main building was boredom.

Laura knew all about the boredom of incarceration, but not of the rarefied kind that Nick was experiencing. Per her plea deal, her two-year sentence had been spent in solitary confinement. At first, Laura had thought she would go mad. She had

wailed and cried and even fashioned a keyboard on the frame
of the bed, playing notes that only she could hear. Then, as her
pregnancy had progressed, Laura had been overcome with
exhaustion. When she wasn't sleeping, she was reading. When
she wasn't reading, she was waiting for mealtimes or staring up
at the ceiling having conversations with Andrew that she
would've never had with him in person.

*I can be strong. I can change this. I can get away.*

She was mourning the loss of her brothers; Andrew to
death, Jasper to his own greed. She was mourning the loss
of Nick, because she had loved him for six years and felt the
absence of that love as she would the loss of a limb. Then
Andrea was born, and she was mourning the loss of her infant
daughter.

Laura had been allowed to hold Andy only once before Edwin
and Clara had taken her away. Of all the things that Laura had
lost in her life, missing the first eighteen months of Andy's life
was the one wound that would never heal.

Laura found a tissue in her pocket. She wiped her eyes. She
turned her head, and there was Andy walking toward the bench.
Her beautiful daughter was holding her shoulders straight, head
high. Being on the road had changed Andy in ways that Laura
could not quite get used to. She had worried for so long that
her daughter had inherited all of her weakness, but now Laura
saw that she'd passed on her resilience, too.

"You were right." Andy sat down on the bench beside her.
"Those toilets were disgusting."

Laura wrapped her arm around Andy's shoulders. She kissed
the side of her head even as Andy pulled away.

"Mom."

Laura relished the normalcy of her annoyed tone. Andy had
been bristling about the over-protectiveness since she'd been
released from the hospital. She had no idea how much Laura
was holding back. Given the choice, she would have gladly
pulled her grown daughter into her lap and read her a story.

Now that Andy knew the truth—at least the part of the truth

that Laura was willing to share—she was constantly asking Laura for stories.

Andy said, "I talked to Clara's daughters yesterday. They've found a place for her that specializes in people with Alzheimer's. A nice place, not, like, a nursing home but more like a community. They say she hasn't been asking about Edwin as much."

Laura rubbed Andy's shoulder, swallowing back her jealousy. "That's good. I'm glad."

Andy said, "I'm nervous. Are you nervous?"

Laura shook her head, but she wasn't sure. "It's nice to be out of the splint." She flexed her hand. "My daughter is safe and healthy. My ex-husband is speaking to me again. I think, in the scheme of things, I've got more to be happy about than not."

"Wow, that's some class-A misdirection."

Laura gave a surprised laugh, startled that the things Andy used to say inside of her head were finally coming out of her mouth. "Maybe I'm a little nervous. He was my first love."

"He beat the shit out of you. That's not love."

The Polaroids.

Andy had been the first person to whom Laura had told the truth about who'd beaten her. "You're right, sweetheart. It wasn't love. Not at the end."

Andy smoothed together her lips. She seemed to vacillate between wanting to know everything about her birth father and not wanting to know anything at all. "What was it like? The last time you saw him?"

Laura didn't have to think very hard to summon her memories of being on the witness stand. "I was terrified. He acted as his own lawyer, so he had a right to question me in open court." Nick had always thought he was so much smarter than everyone else. "It went on for six days. The judge kept asking me to speak up because I could hardly do more than whisper. I felt so powerless. And then I looked at the jury, and I realized that they weren't buying his act. That's the thing with con men—it takes time. They study you and figure out what's missing inside of you, then they make you feel like they're the only one who can fill the hole."

Andy asked, "What was missing inside of you?"

Laura pursed her lips. She had decided to spare Andy the details of Martin's sexual abuse. On good days, she was even able to persuade herself that she was holding back for Andy's sake rather than her own. "I had just turned seventeen when Andrew brought Nick home. I'd spent most of my life alone in front of a piano. I only got a few hours at school and then I was with a tutor and then . . ." Her voice trailed off. "I was so desperate to be noticed." She shrugged. "It sounds ludicrous, looking back on it now, but that's all it took for me to get hooked. He noticed me."

"Is that where you went when you disappeared on weekends?" Andy had moved away from Nick again. "Like when you went to the Tubman Museum and brought me back the snowglobe?"

"I was meeting with my WitSec handler. Witness security."

"I know what WitSec means." Andy rolled her eyes. She considered herself an expert on the criminal justice system since she'd been on the lam.

Laura smiled as she stroked back her hair. "I was on parole for fifteen years. My original handler was much more laid-back about the whole thing than Mike, but I still had to check in."

"I guess you don't like Mike?"

"He doesn't trust me because I'm a criminal and I don't trust him because he's a cop."

Andy kicked at the ground with the toe of her shoe. She was clearly still trying to reconcile Laura's sordid past with the woman she had always known as her mother. Or maybe she was trying to make peace with her own crimes.

"You can't tell Mike what happened," Laura reminded her. "We're damn lucky he hasn't figured it out."

Andy nodded, but still said nothing. She no longer seemed to feel guilty about killing the man they had all started calling Hoodie, but like Laura, she struggled to forgive herself for her part in jeopardizing Gordon's safety.

The night Andy had fled the house, Laura had sat on the floor of her office, Hoodie's dead body a few feet away, and waited for the police to bust down the door and arrest her.

Instead, she'd heard men screaming on her front lawn.

Laura had opened the door to find Mike lying flat on the ground. Half a dozen cops were pointing their guns at his prone body. He'd been knocked out, likely by Hoodie. Which served him right for lurking around her front yard. If Laura had wanted the US Marshals Service involved in the Jonah Helsinger affair, she would've called Mike herself.

Then again, she shouldn't be too hard on him, considering Mike was the only reason that Laura had not been arrested that night.

Andy's text had been fairly nondescript:

*419 Seaborne Ave armed man imminent danger pls hurry*

If Laura was adept at anything, it was subterfuge. She'd told the cops she'd panicked when she saw a man outside her window, that she'd had no idea it was Mike, that she had no idea who'd hit him, and she had no idea why they wanted to come into the house but she knew she had the legal right to refuse them entry.

The only reason they had believed her was because Mike was too dazed to call bullshit. The ambulance had taken him to the hospital. Laura had waited until sun-up to call Gordon. They had waited until sundown to take the body from the house and put it in the river.

This was the transgression Andy could not get past. Killing Hoodie had been self-defense. Gordon's involvement in covering up her crime was more complicated.

Laura tried to assuage her guilt. "Darling, your father has no regrets. He's told you that over and over again. What he did was wrong, but it was for the right reason."

"He could get into trouble."

"He won't if we all keep our mouths shut. You have to remember that Mike wasn't following you around to keep you safe. He was trying to see what you were up to because he thought that I was breaking the law." Laura held onto Andy's hand. "We'll be fine if we all stick together. Trust me on this. I know how to get away with a crime."

Andy glanced up at her, then looked away. Her silences had meaning now. They were no longer a symptom of her indecision. They were usually followed by a difficult question.

Laura held her breath and waited.

This was the moment when Andy would finally ask about Paula. Why Laura had killed her instead of grabbing the empty gun. What she'd whispered in Paula's ear as she was dying. Why she had told Andy to tell the police that she was unconscious when Paula had died.

Andy said, "There was only one suitcase in the storage unit."

Laura let out the breath. Her brain took a moment to dial back the anxiety and find the correct response. "Do you think that's the only storage unit?"

Andy raised her eyebrows. "Is the money from your family?"

"It's from the safe houses, the vans. I wouldn't take Queller money."

"Paula said the same thing."

Laura held her breath again.

Andy said, "Isn't it all blood money?"

"Yes." Laura had told herself that the stash money was different; she had justified keeping it because she was terrified Jasper would come after her. The make-up bag hidden inside the couch. The storage units. The fake IDs she had bought off the same forger in Toronto who had worked on Alexandra Maplecroft's credentials. All of her machinations had been done in case Jasper figured out where she was.

And all of her fears had been misplaced, because Andy was right.

Jasper clearly did not give a shit about the fraudulent paperwork. The statute of limitations on the fraud had run out years ago, and his public apology tour had actually raised his numbers in the early presidential polls.

Andy kept stubbing the toe of her shoe into the ground. "Why did you give it up?"

Laura almost laughed, because she had not been asked the question in such a long time that her first thought was, *Give up what?*

She said, "The short answer is Nick, but it's more complicated than that."

"We've got time for the long answer."

Laura didn't think there were that many hours left in her lifetime, but she tried, "When you play classical, you're playing the exact notes as written. You have to practice incessantly because you'll lose your dynamics—that's basically how you express the notes. Even a few days away, you can feel the dexterity leaving your fingers. Keeping it takes a lot of time. Time away from other things."

"Like Nick."

"Like Nick," Laura confirmed. "He never came out and told me to quit, but he kept making comments about the other things we could be doing together. So, when I gave up the classical part of my career, I thought I was making the decision for myself, but really, he was the one who put it into my head."

"And then you played jazz?"

Laura felt herself smiling. She had adored jazz. Even now she couldn't listen to it because the loss was too painful. "Jazz isn't about the notes, it's about the melodic expression. Less practice, more emotion. With classical, there's a wall between you and the audience. With jazz, it's a shared journey. Afterward, you don't want to leave the stage. And from a technical perspective, it's a completely different touch."

"Touch?"

"The way you press the keys; the velocity, the depth; it's hard to put into words, but it's really your essence as a performer. I loved being part of something so vibrant. If I had known what it was like to play jazz, I never would've gone the classical route. And Nick saw that, even before I did."

"So he talked you into giving that up, too?"

"It was my choice," Laura said, because that was the truth. Everything had been her choice. "Then I was in the studio, and

I found a way to love that, and Nick started making noises again and—" She shrugged. "He narrows your life. That's what men like Nick do. They pull you away from everything you love so that they are the only thing you focus on." Laura felt the need to add, "If you let them."

Andy's attention had strayed. Mike Falcone was getting out of his car. He was wearing a suit and tie. A grin split his handsome face as he approached them. Laura tried to ignore the way Andy perked up. Mike was charming and self-deprecating and everything about him set Laura's teeth on edge.

*Charisma.*

When he got close enough, Andy said, "What a coincidence."

He pointed to his ear. "Sorry, can't hear you. One of my testicles is still lodged in my ear canal."

Andy laughed, and Laura felt her stomach tense.

He said, "Beautiful day to visit a whackjob."

"You're selling yourself short," Andy teased. There was an easy grin on her face that Laura had never seen. "How are your three older sisters?"

"That part was true."

"And that thing about your dad?"

"Also true," he said. "You wanna explain how you ended up at Paula Kunde's house? She's at the top of your mom's no-fly list."

Laura felt Andy stiffen beside her. Her own nerves were rattled every time she thought about Andy eavesdropping on her conversation with Hoodie. Laura would never forgive herself for inadvertently sending her daughter into the lions' den.

Still, Andy held her own, just shrugging at Mike's question.

He tried, "What about those bricks of cash in your back pockets? Put quite a damper on the mood."

Andy smiled, shrugging again.

Laura waited, but there was nothing more except the weight of sexual tension.

Mike asked Laura, "Nervous?"

"Why would I be?"

He shrugged. "Just an average day where you meet a guy you sent to prison for the rest of his life."

"He sent himself to prison. You people are the jackasses who keep letting him go in front of the parole board."

"It takes a village." Mike pointed to the pink scar on his temple where he'd been hit in the head. "You ever figure out who knocked me out in your front yard?"

"How do you know it wasn't me?"

Laura smiled because he smiled.

He gave a slight bow of surrender, indicating the prison. "After you, ladies."

They walked ahead of Mike toward the visitors' entrance. Laura looked up at the tall building with bars over reinforced glass in the windows. Nick was inside. He was waiting for her. Laura felt a sudden shakiness after days of certainty. Could she do this?

*Did she have a choice?*

Her shoulders tensed as they were buzzed through the front doors. The guard who met them was massive, taller than Mike, his belly jutting past his black leather belt. His shoes squeaked as he led them through security. They stored their purses and phones in metal lockers, then he led them down a long corridor.

Laura fought a shudder. The walls felt like they were closing in. Every time a door or gate slammed shut, her stomach clenched. She had only been confined for two years, but the thought of being trapped alone in a cell again brought on a cold sweat.

*Or was she thinking about Nick?*

Andy slipped her hand into Laura's as they reached the end of the corridor. They followed the guard into a small, airless room. Monitors showed feeds from all of the cameras. Six guards sat with headphones on, eavesdropping on inmate conversations inside the visitors' room.

"Marshal?" There was a man standing with his back to the wall. Unlike the others, he was wearing a suit and tie. He shook Mike's hand. "Marshal Rosenfeld."

"Marshal Falcone," Mike said. "This is my witness. Her daughter."

Rosenfeld nodded to each of them as he pulled a small plastic case out of his pocket. "These go in your ears. They'll transmit back to the station over there where we will record everything that's said between you and the inmate."

Laura frowned at the plastic earbuds in the case. "They look like hearing aids."

"That's by design." Rosenfeld took the listening devices and placed them in her open hand. "Your words will be picked up through the vibrations in your jawbone. In order for us to pick up Clayton Morrow, he needs to be close. There's a lot of ambient noise in the visitation room. All the inmates know how to work the dead zones. If you want to get him on tape, you need to be no more than three feet away."

"That won't be a problem." Laura was more concerned with vanity. She did not want Nick to think she was an old woman who needed hearing aids.

Rosenfeld said, "If you feel threatened, or like you can't do it, just say the phrase, 'I would like a Coke.' There's a machine in there. He won't notice anything's off. We'll tell the closest guard to step in, but if Morrow somehow has a shiv or a weapon—"

"I'm not worried about that. He would only use his hands."

Andy gave an audible gulp.

"I'll be fine, sweetheart. It's just a conversation." Laura pushed the plastic buds into her ears. They felt like pebbles. She asked Rosenfeld, "What does he need to say, exactly? What's incriminating?"

"Anything that gives ownership to Paula Evans-Kunde's actions. Like, if Morrow says he sent her to the farm, that's enough. He doesn't have to say he sent her to kill anybody, or kidnap your daughter. That's the beauty of conspiracy. All you have to do is get him on tape taking credit for her actions."

The old Nick gladly took credit for everything, but Laura had absolutely no idea whether or not the present-day Nick had learned his lesson. "All I can do is try."

"Good to go." One of the guards raised his thumb into the air. "The sound is coming through perfect."

Rosenfeld gave him a thumbs-up in response. He asked Laura, "Ready?"

Laura felt a lump in her throat. She smiled at Andy. "I'm good."

Mike said, "Gotta say, it makes us all a little bit nervous, having you in the same room with this guy."

Laura knew he was trying to lighten the mood. "We'll try not to blow anything up."

Andy guffawed.

Mike said, "I'll walk you as far as the door. You still okay with Andy hearing all this?"

"Of course." Laura squeezed Andy's hand, though uncertainty nagged at her thoughts. She was worried that Nick would somehow sway Andy to his side. She was worried for her own sanity, because he had pulled her back in hundreds of times, but she had only managed to escape once.

"You're gonna do great, Mom." Andy grinned, and the gesture was so reminiscent of Nick that Laura felt her breath catch. "I'll be here when it's over. Okay?"

All Laura could do was nod.

Mike stepped back so that Laura could follow the guard down yet another long corridor. He kept his distance, but she could hear his heavy footsteps behind her. Laura touched her fingers to the wall to stop herself from wringing her hands together. She felt butterflies in her stomach.

She had taken a month to prepare for this, and now that she was here, she found herself terrifyingly unprepared.

"How's she doing?" Mike said, obviously trying to distract her again. "Andy. How's she doing?"

"She's perfect," Laura said, which was not that much of an exaggeration. "The surgeon got out most of the bullet. There won't be any lasting damage." Mike hadn't been asking about her physical recovery, but Laura wasn't going to talk about personal things with a man who had so openly flirted with her daughter. "She's found an apartment in town. I think she might go back to college."

"She should try the Marshals Service. She was a damn good detective out there on the road."

Laura gave him a sharp look. "I would lock her in the basement before I let my daughter become a pig."

He laughed. "She's ridiculously adorable."

Laura had forgotten the earbuds. He was talking for Andy's benefit. She opened her mouth to cut him down to size, but any pithy comment Laura might have made was drowned out by the buzz of distant conversations.

Her throat tightened. Laura still remembered what a visitation room sounded like.

The guard worked his key in the lock.

"Ma'am." Mike gave her a salute, then walked back toward the monitoring room.

Laura gritted her teeth as the guard opened the door. She walked through. He closed the door, then looked for a key to the next one.

She could not help but start to wring together her hands. This was what she remembered most from her time in jail: a series of locked doors and gates, none of which she could open on her own.

Laura looked up at the ceiling. She gritted her teeth even harder. She was back in the courtroom with Nick. She was on the stand, wringing her hands, trying not to look into his eyes because she knew if she allowed herself that one weakness, she would crumble and it would all be over.

*Trade him.*

The guard opened the door. The conversations grew louder. She heard children laughing. Ping-pong balls hitting paddles. She touched the plastic earbuds, making sure they hadn't fallen out. Why was she so damn nervous? She wiped her hands on her jeans as she stood at the locked gate, the last barrier between her and Nick.

Everything felt wrong.

She wanted to rewind her day to this morning and start all over again. She had refused to dress up for the occasion, but now she found herself picking apart her choice of a simple black sweater and blue jeans. She should've worn heels. She should've dyed the gray out of her hair. She should've paid more attention to her make-up. She should've turned around and left, but then the gate was open and she was going around a corner and she saw him.

Nick was sitting at one of the tables in the back of the room. He lifted his chin by way of greeting.

Laura pretended not to notice, pretended that her heart was not trembling, her bones were not vibrating inside of her body.

She was here for Andrew, because his dying wish had to mean something.

She was here for Andrea, because her life had finally found purpose.

She was here for herself, because she wanted Nick to know that she had finally gotten away.

Laura caught flashes of movement as she walked through the large, open space. Fathers in khaki uniforms lifting babies into the air. Couples talking quietly and holding hands. A few lawyers speaking in hushed tones. Children playing in a roped-off corner. Two ping-pong tables manned by happy-looking teenagers. Cameras mounted every ten feet, microphones jutting from the ceiling, guards standing by the doors, the Coke machine, the emergency exit.

Nick was sitting only a few yards away. Laura looked past him, still unprepared for eye contact. Her heart jumped at the sight of the upright piano on the back wall. The Baldwin Hamilton School Model in walnut satin. The fallboard was missing. The keys were worn. She imagined that it was rarely tuned. She was so taken by the sight of the piano that she almost walked past Nick.

"Jinx?" He had his hands clasped together on the table. Improbably, he looked exactly the same as she remembered. Not in the courtroom, not when Laura was passing out in the bathroom at the farmhouse, but downstairs in the shed. Alexandra Maplecroft was still alive. None of the bombs had gone off yet.

Nick was unbuttoning his navy peacoat as he kissed her on the cheek.

*Switzerland.*

"Should I call you Clayton?" she asked, still unable to look at him.

He indicated the seat across the table. "My darling, you may call me anything you like."

Laura almost gasped, ashamed that the smooth sound of his voice could still touch her. She took the seat. Her eyes measured the space between them, judging that they were well within the three feet required. She clasped her hands together on the table. For only a moment, she allowed herself the pleasure of looking at his face.

Still beautiful.

A little lined, but not much. His energy was the constant, as if a spring was wound tight inside of him.

*Charisma.*

"Is it Laura now?" Nick grinned. He had always basked under close scrutiny. "After our hero from Oslo?"

"It was random," she lied, looking past him, first at the wall, then at the piano. "Witness security doesn't let you set your own terms. You either go along or you don't."

He shook his head, as if the details didn't interest him. "You look the same."

Laura's fingers went nervously to her gray hair.

"Don't be ashamed, my love. It suits you. But then, you always did everything so gracefully."

She finally looked him in the eye.

The flecks of gold in his irises were a pattern as familiar as the stars. His long eyelashes. The flicker of curiosity mixed with awe, as if Laura was the most interesting person he had ever met.

He said, "There's my girl."

Laura struggled against the thrilling shock of his attention, that inexplicable rush of *need*. She could so easily fall into his vortex again. She could be seventeen years old, her heart floating out of her chest like a hot-air balloon.

Laura broke off first, looking behind him at the piano.

She reminded herself that, just down the corridor, Andy was in that small, dark room listening to everything they said. Mike, too. Marshal Rosenfeld. The six guards with their headphones and monitors.

Laura was not a lonely teenaged girl anymore. She was fifty-five years old. She was a mother, a cancer survivor, a business-woman.

That was her life.

Not Nick.

She cleared her throat. "You look the same, too."

"Not much stress around here. Everything gets planned for me. I just have to show up. Still—" He turned his head to the side, looking at her ear. "Age is a cruel punishment for youth."

Laura touched the earbud. The lie came easily enough. "All those years of concerts finally caught up with me."

He carefully studied her expression. "Yes, I've heard about that. Something to do with the nerve cells."

"Hair cells inside the middle ear." She knew he was testing her. "They translate the sounds into electrical signals that activate the nerves. That is, if they're not destroyed by too much loud music."

He seemed to accept the explanation. "Tell me, my love. How have you been?"

"I'm good. And you?"

"Well, I'm in prison. Did you not hear about what happened?"

"I think I saw something in the news."

He leaned over the table.

Laura reeled back as if from a snake.

Nick grinned, the glow in his eyes sparking into flames. "I was just trying to get a look at the damage."

She held up her left hand so that Nick could see the scar where Jonah Helsinger's knife had gone through.

He said, "Pulled a Maplecroft, did you? A bit more successfully than the poor old gal could manage."

"I'd rather not joke about the woman you killed."

His laugh was almost jubilant. "Manslaughter, but yes, I get your point."

Laura gripped her hands under the table, physically forcing herself to take back control. "I assume you saw the diner video."

"Yes. And our daughter. She's so lovely, Jinx. Reminds me of you."

Her heart lurched into a violent pounding. Andy was listening. What would she make of the compliment? Could she still see that Nick was a monster? Or were these verbal volleys somehow normalizing him?

She asked, "Did you hear about Paula?"

"Paula?" He shook his head. "Doesn't ring a bell."

Laura was wringing her hands again. She made herself stop—again.

She said, "Penny."

"Ah, yes. Dear Penny. Such a loyal soldier. She always had it out for you, didn't she? I guess no matter how glowing the personality, there are always detractors."

"She hated me."

"She did." He shrugged. "A bit jealous, I think. But why bring up the old days when we were having so much fun?"

Laura fumbled for words. She couldn't keep doing this. She had come here for a reason and that reason was slipping through her fingers. "I'm a speech pathologist."

"I know."

"I work with patients who—" She had to stop to swallow. "I wanted to help people. After what we did. And when I was in jail, the only book I had was this textbook on speech—"

Nick interrupted her with a loud groan. "You know, it's sad, Jinxie. We used to have so much to talk about, but you've changed. You're so . . ." He seemed to look for the right word. "Suburban."

Laura laughed, because Nick had clearly wanted her to do

the opposite. "I *am* suburban. I wanted my daughter to have a normal life."

She waited for him to correct her about who Andy belonged to, but Nick said, "Sounds fascinating."

"It is, actually."

"Married a black fella, too. How cosmopolitan of you."

*Black fella.*

About a million years ago, Agent Danberry had used the same words to describe Donald DeFreeze.

Nick said, "You got a divorce. What happened, Jinx? Did he cheat on you? Did you cheat on him? You always had a wandering eye."

"I didn't know what I had," she said, keenly aware of her audience in the distant room. "I thought that being in love meant being on pins and needles all of the time. Passion and fury and arguing and making up."

"But it's not?"

She shook her head, because she had learned at least one thing from Gordon. "It's taking out the trash and saving up for vacations. Making sure the school forms are signed. Remembering to bring home milk."

"Is that really how you feel, Jinx Queller? You don't miss the excitement? The thrill? The fucking the shit out of each other?"

Laura tried to keep the blush off her face. "Love doesn't keep you in a constant state of turmoil. It gives you peace."

He pressed his forehead to the table and pretended to snore.

She laughed, though she didn't want to.

Nick opened one eye, smiled up at her. "I've missed that sound."

Laura looked over his shoulder at the piano.

"I heard you had breast cancer."

She shook her head. She wasn't going to talk to him about that.

He said, "I can remember what it felt like to put my mouth on your breasts. The way you used to moan and squirm when

447

I licked between your legs. Do you ever think about that, Jinx? How good we were together?"

Laura stared at him. She wasn't worried about Andy anymore. Nick's fatal flaw had reared its ugly head. He always overplayed his hand.

She asked, "How do you live with it?"

He raised an eyebrow. She had piqued his interest again.

"The guilt?" she asked. "For killing people. For putting it all into motion."

"*People?*" he asked, because the jury had been divided over his part in the Chicago bombing. "You tell me, darling. Jonah Helsinger? Was that his name?" He waited for Laura to nod. "Ripped out his throat, though they blur that part on TV."

She chewed the inside of her cheek.

"How do you live with it? How do you feel about murdering that boy?"

Laura let a tiny part of her brain think about what she had done. It was hard—for so long she had managed to face each day by discarding the day before. "Do you remember the look on Laura Juneau's face? When we were in Oslo?"

Nick nodded, and she marveled at the fact that he was the only person left alive with whom she could talk about one of the most pivotal moments of her life.

Laura said, "She seemed almost at peace when she pulled the trigger. Both times. I remember wondering how she did it. How she had turned off her humanity. But I think what happened was that she turned it on. Does that make sense? She was completely at peace with what she was doing. That's why she looked so serene."

He raised his eyebrow again, and this time she knew that he was waiting for her to get to the point.

"I kept saying I didn't want to see the video from the diner, but then I finally broke down and watched, and the look on my face was the exact same as Laura's. Don't you think?"

"Yes," Nick said. "I noticed that, too."

"I'll do anything I can to protect my daughter. Anything. Poor Penny found that out the hard way."

He raised his eyebrows, waiting.

Laura left the bait on the line, though if she thought about it hard enough, she could feel Paula's hot blood dripping down her hand.

She asked, "Have you seen Jasper on the news?"

Nick chuckled. "His grand apology tour. You know, it's cruel to say, but I'm quite enjoying the fact that he got very, very fat."

Laura kept her expression neutral.

"I suppose there's been some kind of family reunion? A replenishment of the bank accounts from the Queller coffers?"

Laura didn't answer.

"I will tell you, it's been a pleasure seeing Major Jasper in person every fucking time my parole comes up. He's so eloquent when he explains how my actions caused him to lose his entire family."

"He was always good at public speaking."

"Gets that from Martin, I suppose," Nick said. "I was very surprised when Jasper went liberal. He could barely tolerate Andrew's addiction, but when he found out he was a raving queer—" Nick made a slicing motion across his neck. "Oh, dear, is that too close to Penny?"

Laura felt her mouth go dry. Her guard had slipped just enough for him to wound her.

Nick said, "Poor, desperate Andrew. Did you give him a good death? Was it worth your choice, Jinx?"

"We laughed at you," she told Nick, because she knew that was the easiest way to wound him. "Because of the envelopes. Do you remember those? The ones you said were going to be mailed to all the FBI field offices and all the major newspapers?"

Nick's jaw tightened.

"Andrew laughed when I mentioned them. For good reason. You were never good with follow-through, and that's too bad, because if you had kept your word, Jasper would've been in prison a long time ago, and you would've been on parole picking out furniture with Penny."

"Furniture?" Nick said.

"I saw your letters with Penny."

Nick raised an eyebrow.

The warden and the marshals who screened his mail had been clueless because they didn't know the code.

Laura did.

Nick had made them all memorize the code.

She said, "You were still stringing her along. Telling her that you would be together if only you could find a way to get out of here."

He shrugged. "Idle chatter. I didn't think she'd actually do anything. She was always a bit crazy."

Mike had said that a jury would see it the same way. Even writing in code, Nick was still careful.

*It's only paranoia if you're wrong.*

Laura said, "When it all started to happen, I never once thought it was you." She had to be careful about Hoodie because Mike would have questions, but she wanted Nick to know, "You never even crossed my mind."

It was Nick's turn to look at the room over Laura's shoulder.

She told him, "I thought it was Jasper, that he had seen me in the diner video, and he was coming after me." Laura paused, again choosing her words carefully. "When I heard Penny's voice on the phone at the farmhouse, I was shocked."

Nick was always good at ignoring what he didn't like. He leaned his elbows on the table, rested his chin in his hands. "Tell me about the gun, Jinx."

She hesitated, anxiously shifting gears. "What gun?"

"The revolver Laura Juneau found taped to the back of the toilet and used to murder your father." He winked at her. "How did it get to Oslo?"

Laura glanced around the room. At the cameras mounted on the walls, the microphones jutting down from the ceiling, the guards standing sentry. She felt her nerves rattle.

Nick said, "We're just having a conversation, my love. What do you have to worry about? Is someone listening?"

Laura smoothed together her lips. The table next to them had emptied. All she could hear were the constant pops of the ping-pong ball bouncing across the table.

"My darling?" Nick said. "Is our visit over so soon?" He reached out his hands to her. "We're allowed to touch in here."

Laura stared at his hands. Like his face, they were almost suspended in time.

"Jane?"

Without thinking, she was reaching across the table, lacing her fingers through his. The connection was instantaneous, a plug sliding into an outlet. Her heart lifted. She wanted to cry as she felt that familiar magnetic energy flowing through her body.

That Nick could so easily unravel her was devastating.

"Tell me." He leaned across the table. His face was close to hers. The visitation room faded away. She was in the kitchen again reading a magazine. He walked in, wordlessly kissed her, then backed away.

Nick said, "If you keep your voice low, they can't hear."

"Can't hear what?"

"Where did you get the gun, Jane? The one Laura Juneau used to murder your father. That wasn't from me. I didn't know about it until I saw her pull it out of the bag."

Laura shifted her gaze to the piano behind him. She had not played for Andy yet. First her injured hand, then her anxiety, had stopped her.

"Darling," Nick whispered. "Tell me about the revolver."

Laura pulled her attention away from the piano. She looked down at their intertwined fingers. Her hands looked old, the creases more pronounced. She had arthritis in her fingers. The scar from Jonah Helsinger's hunting knife was still red and angry. Nick's skin felt as soft as it had always been. She remembered what his hands had felt like on her body. The gentle way he had stroked her. The intimate, lingering touches at the curve of her back. He had been the first man who had ever made love to her. He had touched Laura in a way that no one had ever touched her before or since.

"Tell me," he said.

She had no choice but to give him what he wanted. Very softly, she said, "I bought the gun in Berlin for eighty marks."

He smiled.

"I—" Laura's throat tightened around the hoarse whisper. She could almost smell the cigarette smoke from the underground bar that Nick had sent her to. The bikers licking their lips. Jeering at her. Touching her. "I took a flight out of East Berlin because the security was lax. I brought the gun to Oslo. I put it in a paper bag. I taped it to the back of the tank for Laura Juneau to find."

Nick smiled. "The old girl didn't hesitate, did she? It was magnificent."

"Did you send Penny to find Jasper's papers?" Nick tried to pull away, but she held onto his hands. "You wanted the paperwork from the metal box. You thought you could leverage your parole. You sent Penny to get it."

Nick's grin told her he was bored with this game. He slipped his hands from hers. He crossed his arms over his chest.

Still, Laura tried, "Did you know what Penny was doing? Did you know she was going to kidnap my daughter? Try to murder me?" She waited, but Nick said nothing. "Penny killed Edwin. She beat Clara so badly that her cheekbone was broken. Are you okay with that, Nick? Is that what you wanted her to do?"

He turned his head. He brushed imaginary lint off his pants.

Laura felt her stomach drop. She knew the look Nick got on his face when he was finished with someone. Her plan hadn't worked. The marshals. The earbuds. Andy waiting down the hall. Everything had gone to hell because she had pushed him too hard.

Was it on purpose?

Had Laura sabotaged everything because Nick's power over her was still too strong?

She stared at the piano, longing, aching, yearning, for a way to make this work.

Nick asked, "Do you still play?"

Laura's heart flipped inside of her chest, but she kept her gaze on the piano.

"You keep staring at it." He turned around to look for himself. "Do you still play?"

"I wasn't allowed." A nerve twitched in her eyelid as she tried not to give herself away. "Someone might recognize my sound, and then—"

"The gig is up—literally." He grinned at the pun. "Did you know, my love, that I've been taking piano lessons?"

"Really?" Laura imbued the word with sarcasm, but underneath, she could barely breathe.

He said, "It was collecting dust in the rec room for years, but then some fool started a petition to move it in here for the children, and of course everyone signed on *for the children.*" He rolled his eyes. "You can't imagine how painful it is, hearing three-year-olds peck out 'Chopsticks.'"

She took a quick breath so she could say, "Play something for me."

"Oh, no, Jinxie. That's not where this is going." He stood up. He motioned for the guard's attention and pointed to the piano. "My friend here wants to play, if that's all right?"

The guard shrugged, but Laura shook her head. "No, I don't. I won't."

"Oh, my darling. You know I hate it when you refuse me."

His tone was joking in that way that wasn't joking. Laura felt the old fear start to stir. Part of her would always be that terrified girl who had passed out in the bathroom.

He said, "I want to hear you play again, Jinx. I made you give it up once. Can't I make you pick it back up again?"

Her hands quivered in her lap. "I haven't played since—since Oslo."

"Please." He could still say the word without it sounding like a request.

"I don't—"

Nick walked around to her side of the table. Laura didn't flinch this time. He wrapped his fingers lightly around her arm and gently pulled. "It's the least you can do for me. I promise I won't ask for anything else."

Laura let him pull her up to standing. She reluctantly walked toward the piano. Her nerves were shot through with adrenaline. She was suddenly terrified.

*Her daughter was listening.*

"Come now, don't be shy." Nick had blocked the guard's view. He pushed her down on the bench so hard that she felt a jarring in her tailbone. "Play for me, Jinx."

Laura's eyes had closed of their own accord. She felt her stomach clench. The ball of fear that had lain dormant for so long began to stir.

"Jane." He dug his fingers into her shoulders. "I said play something for me."

She forced open her eyes. She looked at the keys. Nick was standing close, but not pressing against her. It was his fingers biting into her shoulders that fully awakened her old fear.

"Now," he said.

Laura raised her hands. She gently placed her fingers on the keys but did not press them. The plastic veneer was worn. Strips of wood showed like splinters.

"Something jaunty," Nick told her. "Quickly, before I get bored."

She wasn't going to warm up for him. She didn't know if there was any value in trying. She considered playing something specifically for Andy—one of those awful bubblegum bands that she loved. Her daughter had spent hours watching old Jinx Queller videos on YouTube, listening to bootlegs. Laura didn't have anything classical left in her fingers. Then she remembered that smoky bar in Oslo, her conversation with Laura Juneau, and it came to her that things should end up where they had started.

She took a deep breath.

She walked the bass line with her left hand, playing the notes that were so familiar in her head. She vamped on the E minor, then A, then back to E minor, then down to D, then the triplet punches on the C before hitting the refrain in the major key, G to D, then C, B7 and back to the vamp on E minor.

In her head, she heard the song coming together—Ray Manzerek mastering the schizophrenic bass and piano parts. Robby Krieger's guitar. John Densmore coming in on the drums, finally, Jim Morrison singing—

*Love me two times, baby . . .*

"Fantastic," Nick raised his voice to be heard over the music.

*Love me two times, girl . . .*

Laura let her eyes close again. She fell into the bouncy triplets. The tempo was too fast. She didn't care. There was a swelling in her heart. This had been her first true love, not Nick. Just to play again was a gift. She didn't care that her fingers were old and clumsy, that she lagged the *fermate*. She was back in Oslo. She was tapping out the beat on the bar. Laura Juneau had seen the chameleon inside of Jane Queller, had been the first person to really appreciate the part of her that was constantly adapting.

*If you can't play the music people appreciate, then you play the music that they love.*

"My darling."

Nick's mouth was at Laura's ear.

She tried not to shudder. She had known it would come to this. She had felt him hovering at her ear so often, first during their six years together, then in her dreams, then in her nightmares. She had prayed if she could only get him to the piano, he wouldn't be able to resist.

"Jane." His thumb stroked the side of her neck. He thought the piano was canceling out his voice. "Are you still afraid of being suffocated?"

Laura squeezed her eyes closed. She tapped her foot to keep the beat, heightened the pitch of her fingers. It was simple, really. That was the beauty of the song. It was almost like a ping-pong match, the same notes being volleyed back and forth.

"I remember you saying that about Andrew—that being suffocated felt like a bag was being tied around your head. For twenty seconds, was it?"

He was taking credit for sending Hoodie. Laura hummed with the song, hoping the vibrations in her jawbone would cancel out Mike's recording.

*Yeah, my knees got weak . . .*

"Were you scared?" Nick asked.

She shook her head, hitting the damper pedal to bring out the vibration in the strings.

*Last me all through the week . . .*

Nick said, "This is all your fault, my love. Can't you see that?"

Laura stopped humming. She knew the rhythm of Nick's threats as well as the notes of the song.

"It's your fault I had to send Penny to the farmhouse."

The feel of his mouth on her ear was like sandpaper, but she did not pull away.

"If you had just given me what I wanted, Edwin would be alive, Clara wouldn't have been hurt, Andrea would've been safe. It's all on you, my love, because you wouldn't listen to me."

*Conspiracy.*

Laura kept playing even as she felt the air begin to seep from the balloon in her heart. He'd confessed to sending Paula. They had him on the recording back in the dark little room. Nick's days at Club Fed were over.

But he wasn't finished.

His lips brushed the tip of her ear. "I'm going to give you another choice, my darling. I need our daughter to speak on my behalf. To tell the parole board that she wants her daddy to come home. Can you make her do that?"

He pressed his thumb against her carotid artery, the same as he'd done when he'd strangled her into unconsciousness.

"Or do I have to force you to make another choice? Not Andrew this time, but your precious Andrea. It'd be awful if you lost her after all of this. I don't want to hurt our child, but I will."

*Terroristic threats. Intimidation. Extortion.*

Laura kept playing, because Nick never knew when to quit.

"I told you I would scorch the earth to get you back, my darling. I don't care how many people I have to send, or how many people die. You still belong to me, Jinx Queller. Every part of you belongs to me."

He waited for her reaction, his thumb pressed to her pulse for the tell-tale sign of panic.

She wasn't panicked. She was elated. She was playing music again. Her daughter was listening. Laura could've stopped right now—Nick had given them enough—but she was not going to deny herself the pleasure of finishing what she had started. Up to the A, then back to the E minor, down to the D, then she was hitting the triplets on the C again and she was at the Hollywood Bowl. She was at Carnegie. Tivoli. Musikverein. Hansa Tonstudio. She was holding her baby. She was loving Gordon. She was pushing him away. She was struggling with cancer. She was sending Andrea away. She was watching her daughter finally grow into a vibrant, interesting young woman. And she was holding onto her, because Laura was never going to give up another thing that she loved for this loathsome man.

*One for tomorrow . . . one just for today . . .*

She had hummed the words to the song in her jail cell. Tapped it out on her imaginary bed frame keyboard the same way she had tapped it on the bar top for Laura Juneau. Even now with Nick still playing the devil on her shoulder, Laura allowed herself the joy of playing the song right up until the final, sharp staccato brought her to the abrupt end—

*I'm goin' away.*

Laura's hands floated to her lap. She kept her head bowed.

There was the usual dramatic pause and then—

Clapping. Cheering. Feet stamping the floor.

"Fantastic," Nick shouted. He was basking in the glow of the applause, as if it was meant entirely for him. "That's my girl, ladies and gentlemen."

Laura stood up, shrugging off his hand. She walked past Nick, past the picnic tables and the children's play area, but then she realized that this was truly the last time she would ever see the man who called himself Nicholas Harp again.

She turned around. She looked him in the eye. She told him, "I'm not damaged anymore."

There was a stray clap before the room went silent.

"Darling?" Nick's smile held a sharp warning.

"I'm not hurt," she told him. "I healed myself. My daughter healed me—*my* daughter. My husband healed me. My life without you healed me."

He chuckled. "All right, Jinxie. Run along now. You've got a decision to make."

"No." She said the word with the same determination she had expressed three decades ago in the farmhouse. "I will never choose you. No matter what the other option is. I don't choose you."

His teeth were clenched. She could feel his rage winding up.

She told him, "I'm magnificent."

He chuckled again, but he was not really laughing.

"I am magnificent," she repeated, her fists clenched at her side. "I'm magnificent because I am so uniquely me." Laura pressed her hand to her heart. "I am talented. And I am beautiful. I am amazing. And I found my way, Nick. And it was the right way because it was the path that I set out for myself."

Nick crossed his arms. She was embarrassing him. "We'll talk about this later."

"We'll talk about it in hell."

Laura turned around. She walked around the corner, stood at the locked gate. Her hands shook as she waited for the guard to find his key. The vibrations moved up her arms, into her torso, inside her chest. Her teeth had started to chatter by the time the gate swung open.

Laura walked through. Then there was another door. Another key.

Her teeth were clicking like marbles. She looked through the window. Mike was standing between the two locked doors. He looked worried.

He should be worried.

Laura felt a wave of nausea as she realized what had just happened. Nick had threatened Andy. He had told her to choose. Laura had made her choice. It was all happening again.

*I don't want to hurt our child, but I will.*

The door opened.

She told Mike, "He threatened my daughter. If he comes after us—"

"We'll take care of it."

"No," she told him. "I'll take care of it. Do you understand me?"

"Whoa." Mike held up his hands. "Do me a favor and call me first. Like you could've called me before you went to that hotel room. Or when you were in a shoot-out at the mall. Or—"

"Just keep him away from my family." Laura got a burning sensation in her spine that told her to be careful. Mike was a cop. She had been held blameless for Paula's death, but Laura of all people knew the government could always find a way to fuck you if they wanted.

"He'll be in a SuperMax," Mike said. "He won't be writing letters or getting visitors. He'll get one shower a week, maybe an hour of daylight, if he's lucky."

Laura took out the earbuds. She dropped them into Mike's hand. The burst of adrenaline was tapering off. Her fingers were steady. Her heart wasn't quivering like a cat's whisker anymore. She had done what she'd come here to do. It was over. She never had to see Nick again.

*Not unless she chose to.*

Mike said, "I gotta admit, I thought you had a screw loose when you told me to figure out a way to get that piano moved."

Laura knew she had to stay in his good graces. "The petition was a clever trick."

"Marshal School 101: you can get an inmate to do anything for potato chips." Mike was preening, his chest puffed out. He clearly loved the game. "The way you kept looking at the piano like a kid staring at a bag of candy. You really worked him."

Laura saw Andy through the window in the door. She looked older now, more like a woman than a girl. Her brow was creased. She was worried.

Laura told Mike, "I will do whatever it takes to keep my daughter safe."

"I can name a couple of corpses who found that out the hard way."

She turned to look at him. "Keep that in mind if you ever consider asking her out on a date."

The door opened.

"Mom—" Andy rushed into Laura's arms.

"I'm fine." Laura willed it to be true. "Just a little shaken."

"She was great." Mike winked at Laura, as if they were in this together. "She worked him like Tyson. The boxer, not the chicken."

Andy grinned.

Laura looked away. She could not abide seeing pieces of Nick in her child.

She told Mike, "I need to get out of here."

He waved for the guard. Laura almost tripped over the man's shoes as they exited back through security. She waited for Andy to get her purse out of the locker, her phone and keys.

"I've been thinking about something," Mike said, because he was incapable of being silent. "The old Nickster didn't know you already confessed to transporting the gun to Oslo, right? That's why you got two years in the slammer. The judge sealed that part of your immunity agreement. He didn't want to exacerbate international tensions. If the Germans found out an American smuggled a gun from West to East for the purposes of murder, there would've been hell to pay."

Laura took her purse from Andy. She checked to make sure her wallet was inside.

Mike said, "So, when you told Nick that stuff about the gun, he thought you were implicating yourself. But you weren't."

Laura said, "Thank you, Michael, for narrating back to me

exactly what just happened." She shook his hand. "We've got it from here. I know you have a lot of work to do."

"Sure. I thought I'd scrapbook through some of my feelings, maybe open a pinot." He winked at Laura as he held out his hand to Andy. "Always a pleasure, beautiful."

Laura wasn't going to watch her daughter flirt with a pig. She followed the guard to the last set of doors. Finally, blissfully, she was outside, where there were no more locks and bars.

Laura took a deep breath of fresh air, holding it in her lungs until they felt like they might burst. The bright sunlight brought tears into her eyes. She wanted to be on the beach drinking tea, reading a book and watching her daughter play in the waves.

Andy looped her hand through Laura's arm. "Ready?"

"Will you drive?"

"You hate when I drive. It makes you nervous."

"You can get used to anything." Laura climbed into the car. Her leg was still sore from the shrapnel in the diner. She looked up at the prison. There were no windows on this side of the building, but part of her could not shake the feeling that Nick was watching.

In truth, she'd had that feeling for over thirty years.

Andy backed out of the parking space. She drove through the gate. Laura didn't let herself relax until they were finally on the highway. Andy's driving had improved on her interminable road trip. Laura only gasped every twenty minutes instead of every ten.

Laura said, "That part about loving Gordon, I meant it. He was the best thing that ever happened to me. Other than you. And I didn't know what I had."

Andy nodded, but the little girl who prayed for her parents to get back together was gone.

Laura asked, "Are you all right, sweetheart? Was it okay hearing his voice, or—"

"Mom." Andy checked the mirror before passing a slow-moving truck. She leaned her elbow on the door. She pressed her fingers against the side of her head.

Laura watched the trees blur past. Pieces of her conversation with Nick kept coming into her mind, but she would not let herself dwell on what was said. If there was one thing Laura had learned, it was that she had to keep moving forward. If she ever stopped, Nick would catch up with her.

Andy said, "You talk like him." When Laura didn't answer, she said, "He calls you darling and my love, just like you call me."

"I don't talk like him. He talks like my mother." She stroked back Andy's hair so she could see her face. "Those were the words she used with me. They always made me feel loved. I wasn't going to let Nick keep me from using the same words with you."

"'She always knew where the tops to her Tupperware were,'" Andy quoted, one of the few things Laura could come up with to capture the essence of her mother.

Now, she told Andy, "It's more like she knew which china set was from the Queller side and where the Logan silverware was cast and all the other unimportant things she felt gave her control over her life." Laura said something that she'd only recently realized was the truth: "My mother was as much a victim of my father as the rest of us."

"She was an adult."

"She wasn't raised to be an adult. She was raised to be a rich man's wife."

Andy seemed to mull over the distinction. Laura thought she was finished asking questions, but then she said, "What did you say to Paula when she was dying?"

Laura had dreaded being asked about Paula for so long that she needed a moment to prepare. "Why are you asking now? It's been over a month."

Andy's shoulder went up in a shrug. Instead of going into one of her protracted silences, she said, "I wasn't sure you would tell me the truth."

Laura didn't acknowledge the point, which she proved by saying, "It was a variation of what I told Nick. That I would see her in hell."

"Really?"

"Yes." Laura wasn't sure why her last words to Paula made it on the long list of pieces of herself that she still kept hidden from Andy. Perhaps she did not want to test the boundaries of her daughter's newfound moral ambiguity. Telling a crazy woman with a razorblade lodged in her throat *Nick is never going to fuck you now* seemed jealous and petty.

Which was probably why Laura had said it.

She asked Andy, "Does what I did to Paula bother you?"

Andy shrugged again. "She was a bad person. I mean—I guess you could break it down and say that she was still a human being and maybe there was another way to do it, but it's easy to say that when it's not your own life in danger."

*Your life,* Laura wanted to say, because she had known when she hid the razorblade inside her bandaged hand that she was going to kill Paula Evans for hurting her daughter.

Andy asked, "Back in the prison, when you were walking away, why didn't you tell him about the earbuds? That everything he said in your ear was recorded? Like, a final *fuck you.*"

"I said what I needed to say," Laura told her, though with Nick, she was never sure of herself. It felt so good to say those things to his face. Now that she was away from him, she had doubts.

*The yo-yo snapping back again.*

Andy seemed content to end the conversation there. She turned on the radio. She scanned the stations.

Laura asked, "Did you like the song I played?"

"I guess. It's kind of old."

Laura put her hand to her heart, wounded. "I'll learn something else. Name it."

"How about 'Filthy'?"

"How about something that's actually music?"

Andy rolled her eyes. She punched at the buttons on the tuner, likely searching for a sound that had the depth of cotton candy. "I'm sorry about your brother."

Laura closed her eyes against the sudden tears.

"You did right by him," Andy said. "You stood up for him. That took a lot."

Laura found a tissue and dried her eyes. She still couldn't come to terms with what had happened. "I never left his side. Even when we were negotiating the deal with the FBI."

Andy stopped fiddling with the radio.

Laura said, "Andrew died about ten minutes after the plea agreement was signed. It was very peaceful. I was holding his hand. I got to say goodbye to him."

Andy sniffed back tears. She had always been sensitive to Laura's moods. "He stayed around long enough to make sure you were going to be okay."

She stroked Andy's hair behind her ear again. "That's what I like to think."

Andy wiped her eyes. She left the radio alone as she drove down the near-empty interstate. She was clearly thinking about something, but just as clearly content to keep her thoughts to herself.

Laura rested her head back against the seat. She watched the trees blur by. She tried to enjoy the comfortable silence. Not a night had gone by since Andy had returned home without Laura waking up in a cold sweat. She wasn't suffering post-traumatic stress or worrying about Andy's safety. She had been terrified of seeing Nick again. That the trick with the piano and the earbuds would not work. That he would not walk into the open trap. That she would walk blindly into one of his.

She hated him too much.

That was the problem.

You didn't hate someone unless part of you still loved them. From the beginning, the two extremes had always been laced into their DNA.

For six years, even while she'd loved him, part of Laura had hated Nick in that childish way that you hate something you can't control. He was headstrong, and stupid, and handsome, which gave him cover for a hell of a lot of the mistakes he continually made—the same mistakes, over and over again, because why try new ones when the old ones worked so well in his favor?

He was charming, too. That was the problem. He would charm her. He would make her furious. Then he would charm her back again so that she did not know if Nick was the snake or if she was the snake and Nick was the handler.

*The yo-yo snapping back into the palm of his hand.*

So Nick sailed along on his charm, and his fury, and he hurt people, and he found new things that interested him more, and the old things were left broken in his wake.

Jane had been one of those broken, discarded things. Nick had sent her away to Berlin because he was tired of her. At first, she had enjoyed her freedom, but then she had panicked that he might not want her back. She had begged and pleaded with him and done everything she could think of to get his attention.

Then Oslo had happened.

Then her father was dead and Laura Juneau was dead and then, quite suddenly, Nick's charm had stopped working. A trolley car off the tracks. A train without a conductor. The mistakes could not be forgiven, and eventually, the second same mistake would not be overlooked, and the third same mistake had dire consequences that had ended with Alexandra Maplecroft's life being taken, a death sentence being passed on Andrew, then—almost—resulted in the loss of another life, her life, in the farmhouse bathroom.

Inexplicably, Laura had still loved him. Perhaps loved him even more.

Nick had let her live—that was what she kept telling herself while she went mad inside of her jail cell. He had left Paula at the farmhouse to guard her. He had planned to come back for her. To take her to their much-dreamed-of little flat in Switzerland, a country that had no extradition treaty with the US.

Which had given her a delirious kind of hope.

Andrew was dead and Jasper was gone and Laura had stared

up at the jailhouse ceiling, tears running down her face, her neck still throbbing, her bruises still healing, her belly swelling with his child, and desperately loved him.

Clayton Morrow. Nicholas Harp. In her misery, she did not care.

Why was she so stupid?

How could she still love someone who had tried to destroy her?

When Laura had been with Nick—and she was decidedly with him during his long fall from grace—they had raged against the system that had so irrevocably exploited Andrew, and Robert Juneau, and Paula Evans, and William Johnson, and Clara Bellamy, and all the other members who eventually comprised their little army: The group homes. The emergency departments. The loony bin. The mental hospital. The squalor. The staff who neglected their patients. The orderlies who ratcheted tight the straitjackets. The nurses who looked the other way. The doctors who doled out the pills. The urine on the floor. The feces on the walls. The inmates, the fellow prisoners, taunting, wanting, beating, biting.

The spark of rage, not the injustice, was what had excited Nick the most. The novelty of a new cause. The chance to annihilate. The dangerous game. The threat of violence. The promise of fame. Their names in lights. Their righteous deeds on the tongues of schoolchildren who were taught the lessons of change.

*A penny, a nickel, a dime, a quarter, a dollar bill . . .*

In the end, their deeds became part of the public record, but not in the way Nick had promised. Jane Queller's sworn testimony laid out the plan from concept to demise. The training. The rehearsals. The drills. Jane had forgotten who'd first had the idea, but as with everything else, the plan had spread from Nick to all of them, a raging wildfire that would, in the end, consume every single one of their lives.

What Jane had kept hidden, the one sin that she could never confess to, was that she had ignited that first spark.

Dye packs.

That was what they had all agreed would be in the paper

bag. This was the Oslo plan: That Martin Queller would be stained with the proverbial blood of his victims on the world stage. Paula's cell had infiltrated the manufacturer outside of Chicago. Nick had given the packs to Jane when she had arrived in Oslo.

As soon as he was gone, Jane had thrown them into the trash.

It had all started with a joke—not a joke on Jane's part, but a joke made by Laura Juneau. Andrew had relayed it in one of his coded letters to Berlin:

*Poor Laura told me that she would just as soon find a gun in the bag as a dye pack. She has a recurring fantasy of killing Father with a revolver like the one her husband used to murder their children, then turning the gun on herself.*

No one, not even Andrew, had known that Jane had decided to take the joke seriously. She'd bought the revolver off a German biker in the dive bar, the same dive bar that Nick had sent her to when she'd first arrived in Berlin. The one where Jane was afraid that she would be gang-raped. The one that she had stayed at for exactly one hour because Nick had told her he would know if she left a minute sooner.

For over a week, Jane had left the gun on the counter of her studio apartment, hoping it would be stolen. She had decided not to take it to Oslo, and then she had taken it to Oslo. She had decided to leave it in her hotel room, and then she had taken it from her room. And then she was carrying it in a brown paper bag to the ladies room. And then she was taping it behind the toilet tank like a scene from *The Godfather*. And then she was sitting on the front row, watching her father pontificate on stage, praying to God that Laura Juneau would not follow through on her fantasy.

And also praying that she would.

Nick had always been drawn to new and exciting things. Nothing bored him more than the predictable. Jane had hated her father, but she had been motivated by much more than vengeance. She was desperate to have Nick's attention, to prove that she belonged by his side. She had desperately hoped that the violent shock of helping Laura Juneau commit murder would make Nick love her again.

And it had worked. But then it hadn't.

And Jane was crushed by guilt. But then Nick had talked her out of it.

And Jane persuaded herself that it all would've happened the same way without the gun.

*But then she wondered . . .*

Which was the typical pattern of their six years together. The push and pull. The vortex. The yo-yo. The rollercoaster. She worshipped him. She despised him. He was her weakness. He was her destroyer. Her ultimate all or none. There were so many ways to describe that tiny piece of herself that Nick could always nudge into insanity.

Laura had only ever been able to pull herself back for the sake of other people.

First for Andrew, then for Andrea.

That was the real reason she had gone to the prison today: not to punish Nick, but to push him away. To keep him locked up so that she could be free.

Laura had always believed—vehemently, with great conviction—that the only way to change the world was to destroy it.

# Acknowledgments

Thanks very much to my editor, Kate Elton, and my team at Victoria Sanders and Associates, including but not limited to Victoria Sanders, Diane Dickensheid, Bernadette Baker-Baughman and Jessica Spivey. There are so many folks at HarperCollins International and Morrow who should be thanked: Liate Stehlik, Emily Krump, Heidi Richter-Ginger, Kaitlin Harri, Chantal Restivo-Alessi, Samantha Hagerbaumer and Julianna Wojcik. Also a big hats off to all the fantastic divisions I visited last year and the folks I got to spend time with in Miami. I also want to include Eric Rayman on the team roster—thank you for all you do.

Writing this book took me down many different research paths, some of which did not end up being incorporated into the book, but I have a list of folks who were crucial to helping me capture certain moods and feelings. My good friend and fellow author Sara Blaedel put me in contact with Anne Mette Goddokken and Elisabeth Alminde for some Norwegian background. Another fantastic author and friend, Regula Venske, spoke to me about Germany; I so regret that only one percent of our fascinating conversation in Düsseldorf made it into the narrative. Elise Diffie gave me some help with cultural touchstones. I am very grateful to both Brandon Bush and Martin Kearns for offering insight into the life of a professional pianist.

A very heartfelt thank you goes to Sal Towse and Burt Kendall, my dear friends and resident San Francisco experts.

Sarah Ives and Lisa Palazzolo won the "have your name appear in the next book" contests. Adam Humphrey, I hope you're enjoying all the winning.

To my daddy—thank you so much for taking care of me while I'm in the throes of writing and trying to navigate life. Best for last to DA, my heart, for being nobody, too.

## About the author

## About the book

## Read on

Insights,
Interviews
& More...

# Meet Karin Slaughter

Alison Rosa

KARIN SLAUGHTER is one of the world's most popular and acclaimed storytellers. Published in 120 countries with more than 35 million copies sold across the globe, her eighteen novels include the Grant County and Will Trent books, as well as the Edgar-nominated *Cop Town* and the instant *New York Times* bestselling novels *Pretty Girls*, *The Good Daughter*, and *Pieces of Her*. Slaughter is the founder of the Save the Libraries project—a nonprofit organization established to support libraries and library programming. A native of Georgia, she lives in Atlanta. ❧

# An Interview with Karin Slaughter

*Q: You're exceptionally well-traveled, and your novels are published all around the world. How is this reflected in* Pieces of Her? *What do you think gives this story global appeal?*

**A:** When I first started touring with my Grant County series, I realized that Europe is just a series of small towns, and so a small town like Grant County felt relatable. Then I realized that small towns are universal. Even in New York City, if I'm in the middle of Manhattan and I say to someone who lives there, "Where do you live?" they don't say "New York City," they say "Upper West Side," or "I'm in Chelsea," and that neighborhood is as much a part of their identity as it would be if they were living in Tumbleweed, Oklahoma. It's just the same in Atlanta. Someone from Buckhead, or Midtown, or Virginia-Highland, Decatur— I know exactly who they are. Everybody knows the shorthand for geography. But with Andy in *Pieces of Her*, there are two things to keep in mind about her road trip. One is a physical thing; the farther away she gets from Laura, the stronger she becomes, the more independent she is. So there's the sense that geography is benefitting her in a way. But also I'm writing about states I started touring when I was Andy's exact age, and I know from my own experience how meeting different people, seeing different things, can pull you out of yourself.

*Q: How is writing a standalone different for you than writing the Will Trent series? Does your process differ at all?*

**A:** It's not a different process because every book starts with that first chapter and I just try to think of something awful that's going to open the book. Each type of novel has its easy parts and its hard parts. The hard part for a standalone is that they're all new characters and I'm still getting to know them. When I'm finished writing, I have to go back and check for character. I'll just read the Andy parts, or the Laura parts, and I'll make sure the character you read in the first chapter makes as much sense ▶

as the character I leave you with. So if Andy had some grand epiphany that made her go to medical school, when I previously established that she barely passed high school biology, that's not a genuine arc for her character. What I wanted to concentrate on with her was the process of growing up. As the book evolves she has more self-confidence, more understanding of how the world works. That kind of knowledge will, I hope, lead her into some kind of transformation. But she's not suddenly going to have a Super Girl cape. And it's the same with Laura. I wanted to make sure she made sense all the way through. That's a lot of work, but with a standalone, you have to make sure it all hangs together or the reader will feel cheated. Now, when I'm writing a Will Trent book, I know that character work is pretty much done. But the problem is, I need to find new things to say about Will and Sara for the people who have read every Will Trent book, and then I have to find a way to tell people who have never read a Will Trent book about these characters without boring the pants off the first set of readers. It's quite a tightrope. I think the best thing I ever did was give myself permission to say, "Okay, if *The Kept Woman* is the first book you've read in the series, I don't have to tell you everything about Will and Sara. I'll say a handful of things that are important, but if you want to know about his past, or how he met Sara, or Sara's past, you can go back and read the other books. I don't necessarily have to cover everything in this new book. That would be just like ten pages of, 'I was born . . .'"

**Q: Your novels are so character driven. Where do you draw your inspiration? Do people in your day-to-day life ever see themselves reflected in your books?**

**A:** I don't think anyone ever really sees themselves in my books. Even if I take pieces of them, it's sort of like when you hear your voice on a voicemail and you say, "Where's my sultry voice? Who's this twelve-year-old?" I learned that lesson pretty early on because I did put one of my neighbors, growing up, in my first book. And she was really mean—I say this because she's dead now—she was this old lady who lived on the corner. The houses were on really big lots because we were in a country setting. It was much faster to go home through her yard, and she wouldn't let us—she'd turn the hose on us. There were certain things she did and said, that if you heard them, you'd say, "Oh that's Miss So-and-So." I put those characteristics in the book. This woman was at one of my first signings. She came up and said, "I know who that character is . . ." And I was thinking, "Oh, crap." And she goes, "It's Mrs. So-and-So down the street!" And I was like, "Yes, ma'am, please don't tell her." So, I think there are things that other people see in you that you don't see in yourself. I don't think any person sees another person the exact same way. There are all different kinds of shades. But honestly, in *Pieces of Her*, I wanted to write about how things have changed for women. If you look at Laura's generation of women, which isn't that far off from my generation, there weren't a lot of options for what you could do with your life. You'd get married, have kids, maybe you would have a job. Maybe you might have a career, but it would be nursing or teaching or one of those womanly types of jobs, and your focus would be your children and home. Then you look at where Andy is in her life, and in some ways she's at a stalemate because she has so much choice. She could be a doctor, a lawyer, an astronaut, anything. In a way, Laura as a young woman was paralyzed by her limited choices, and now Andy is paralyzed by having *too many* choices. That was something I wanted to write about. I also think that women in their thirties today are more like women in their twenties when I was growing up. There's sort of this ten-year soft-landing that young women get, (and young men, too) that we didn't get when I was that age. I remember very clearly when I graduated from high school, my dad took me aside and said, "I'm so proud, you can do anything you want. You just can't move back home." For my generation it would have been a stigma to move back home. It would have been a failure. And it's interesting because I travel a lot, and when I'm in France, or Denmark, or whatever, every place I've visited has a phrase for "helicopter parents." In Denmark it's called "curling parents"—like the Olympic sport of curling where you move the broom ahead of the stone, so it has an easier way to go. I think there's a desire for all parents to want their kids' lives to be easier and do what they can. ▶

**An Interview with Karin Slaughter** *(continued)*

**Q: Pieces of Her** *has a relentless sense of momentum. Jane in the past, and Andy in the present day, are in almost constant motion. How did that make the book different to you, and how does it help or complicate plotting?*

**A:** In Andy's forward movement, and Laura's, there's always a trap: is the plot going to be every chapter in a different city? Sure, it worked for Odysseus, but Andy didn't have ten years. So, what I had to do was make sure that each location gave you a new clue or new question about the overall mystery of the story. And to me the mysteries aren't so much about what happened, or whodunnit. It's more about *who are these people?* Andy's trip, like Laura's, is a trip of self-discovery. But I wanted them both to be doing things that informed their choices. It would be really easy for a character like Andy, who has a tendency to sit around and stare at her navel, to just wait for some exterior thing to push her in a direction. Part of her metamorphosis was being able to take the reins and make choices about her life. And that really happens when she starts to learn about Laura's past. That gives her this quest, and to me that's what gives her story momentum. She isn't just going from city to city, she is very deliberate in her actions, trying to get to the bottom of this great mystery that is her mother. And as she gets closer to the truth, she realizes what a liar her mother is. I gave a lot of thought to how that would frame Andy because these revelations could have made her really angry. But that's not who she is. She's a person who's built a life on making mistakes, and, a lot of times, people who are prone to horrendous mistakes get angry and blame other people, but sometimes they're like Andy and they feel like they are flawed, and that makes them more likely to forgive flaws in others.

**Q:** *Your books always start with an opening chapter that ends with a bang. How much of that is because you think it works structurally for readers, and how much is because it's a creative trigger point for you?*

**A:** It's all for me. I never think about my readers when I'm writing. I love it when they're there when I finish writing—that's fantastic—and I like hearing from them and reading their questions, but I never think about them when I'm writing. That first chapter is something to make me interested. It's sort of like, there are two kinds of cat toys: one is battery operated and it moves, and then there are the ones that are static. I've always been drawn to the sparkly, moving things. That pulls me into the book and makes me interested in telling the story.

**Q: What are your favorite books and movies? Are you usually drawn to thrillers, or do you stay away from them when you're writing?**

**A:** I read all kinds of stuff. I can't read when I'm writing because I need to focus on my story and I don't want to suddenly write like someone else. It's very important to me that my writing has a voice and I don't want anything to clutter that up. But when I'm working, I do read magazines and blogs and look at cat pictures; I just can't read books. When I'm free to read, I love historical fiction. I've been reading a lot about the Tudors lately. I've also been reading about reconstruction; I read this really fascinating book called *Masterless Men* about the South during the time of the Civil War. People who look at my list on Goodreads will probably think, "What the hell?" But they will find some of my favorite crime novelists, too—Lisa Gardner, Lisa Unger, Sara Blaedel, Lee Child, the usual suspects. I don't like slasher movies because they scare me. The stupider they are, the more terrified I'll be. You know, the person's standing and talking to someone and then someone else goes up behind them? That freaks me out. But I love *The Silence of the Lambs* and subtle scary movies. I don't like anything with demons and Satan because I was raised to be terrified of those things, and no matter what I do I'm always worried about needing an exorcism. It's in my blood. My favorite movie of all time is called *Clay Pigeons*. It's very dark and funny and fantastic. ▶

### Q: Who's the best (read: worst) villain of all crime literature?

**A:** Oh wow. I'll keep it to contemporary times. I think probably the worst would be the woman from *Misery*—Annie. She's terrifying, and I think that's a real thing to be afraid of. As I became more successful as an author, I thought about the story a lot—when I first read it, I wasn't an author, so I was like, "This is fantastic!" Then I read it again after I was published, and I was like, "F***, this is the most terrifying thing in the world!" I can totally see it happening—not with me. Maybe Lee Child because he can take it.

But the best villain . . . you know, I'm always drawn to Scarlett O'Hara. And I think, worst of all, she was certainly part of the "lost cause" B.S. But as a female character of her time, she was pretty amazing in her badness. She was really crappy to her sisters and a terrible mother, and she made decisions that she thought were right, but she didn't care who they hurt so long as things went her way. The runner-up would be The Misfit from "A Good Man Is Hard to Find" because he gets the best line in literature when he kills the grandmother at the end and says, "She would've been a good woman . . . if it had been somebody there to shoot her every minute of her life." That's so thrilling to read because it's what you're thinking when you get to the end.

### Q: What inspired you to be a writer? Was it always in your mind as an ambition, or did it take time to realize it was a realistic career? What do you think you'd have done if you hadn't become a writer?

**A:** I always wrote, from the age of six. Most of my books were about my two older sisters being mutilated or dying. My dad would give me a quarter for every book I wrote so I was incentivized early on to do this. My sisters were not fans, weirdly. I give it to them—the illustrations were not kind. But I was always writing and telling stories, and I had a fantastic teacher. I was in a private Christian school until sixth grade, and after, in public school, I had some of the most amazing teachers. I was really lucky. They really encouraged me. One of my teachers gave me the best kind of challenge you can get as a writer. She said, "You're good, but you could be better." She made me understand that language can be a tool. It's a very clever way to express your point without people knowing. That's one of the reasons I studied Renaissance literature in what little I did of college, because I was just fascinated by the coded language of the Renaissance poets. On the surface they'd be saying one thing, but underneath they're talking about pubic hair and sex and politics and cheating on their wives. There will always be a ten-year-old boy inside of me that loves a good pun. But if I wasn't a writer, my dream job would probably be working in a watch factory in Switzerland, where I could create all the pieces by hand and put all the gears together. I love solving puzzles. ∾

# Questions for Discussion

1. Andy and Laura have a very close bond, but they also mystify one another. Do you think it's possible to ever fully know a person, particularly your parents? Do you think Laura is a good mother to Andy?

2. *Pieces of Her* explores elements of the Witness Protection Program. What do you think it's like to give up everything? Do you think we can ever truly escape our pasts?

3. Many of the characters in *Pieces of Her* are exceptional—talented, intelligent, charismatic, successful— but also extremely flawed. Do you think the most magnificent people are also the most fragile? Why?

4. *Pieces of Her* shifts between present day and the 1980s, as well as across the United States and Europe. How did these backdrops shape your experience as you read the novel? Do you have any distinct memories of this time you would have liked to see included?

5. Laura and Andy have led radically different lives in many ways, but other characters continue to point out how alike they are. How do Andy and Laura parallel each other?

How do the opportunities they are afforded change the paths they take?

6. Nick is a charismatic and manipulative leader. Why was Jane so drawn to him? Did you sympathize with any of his stances? Have you ever met someone like Nick?

7. When did you realize the connection between Jane and Andy's stories? Did you have any suspicions early on?

8. Think about the power of family bonds in *Pieces of Her*. How do choice, opportunity, and circumstances reveal the strengths or weaknesses of the characters' connections?

9. Mysteries and thrillers often touch on themes of social justice. Did Jane's story give you a stronger perspective of the political and social turning points during the 1980s? What stands out to you the most?

10. What does *Pieces of Her* convey to you about the power of identity? What role do our pasts and relationships play in the formation of our identities? ◠

# Jinx's Carnegie Hall Program

## CARNEGIE HALL
### 1982-1983 SEASON

**CARNEGIE HALL presents**

# The New York Philharmonic & Jinx Queller

*Saturday Evening, March 12, 1983 at 8:00*

Stern Auditorium

WILLIAM STACKPOLE, *Music Director and Conductor*

| | |
|---|---|
| **LUDWIG VAN BEETHOVEN** *(1770-1820)* | **Piano Concerto No. 3 in C Minor op.37 (1800)** <br> Allegro con Brio <br> Largo <br> Rondo Allegro <br><br> JINX QUELLER, *piano* |
| **WOLFGANG AMADEUS MOZART** *(1756-1791)* | **Piano Concerto No. 24, K. 491 (1786)** <br> Allegro <br> Largetto <br> Allegretto <br><br> JINX QUELLER, *piano* |
| **ANTON BRUCKNER** *(1824-1896)* | **Symphony No. 3 in D Minor (1878)** <br> Gemäßigt, misterioso <br> Adagio <br> Scherzo <br><br> Finale |

# More Books by Karin Slaughter

Read on

### THE GOOD DAUGHTER

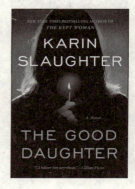

*Two girls are forced into the woods at gunpoint. One runs for her life. One is left behind . . .*

Twenty-eight years ago, Charlotte and Samantha Quinn's happy small-town family life was torn apart by a terrifying attack on their family home. It left their mother dead and their father—Pikeville's notorious defense attorney—devastated. And it left the family fractured beyond repair, consumed by secrets from that terrible night.

Twenty-eight years later, Charlie has followed in her father's footsteps to become a lawyer herself—the ideal good daughter. But when violence comes to Pikeville again, and a shocking tragedy leaves the whole town traumatized, Charlie is plunged into a nightmare. Not only is she the first witness on the scene, but it's a case that unleashes the terrible memories she's spent so long trying to suppress. Because the shocking truth about the crime that destroyed her family nearly thirty years ago won't stay buried forever. ►

**More Books by Karin Slaughter** *(continued)*

*PRETTY GIRLS*

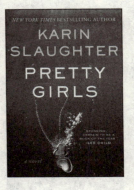

*Sisters. Strangers. Survivors.*

More than twenty years ago, Claire and Lydia's teenage sister Julia vanished without a trace. The two women have not spoken since, and now their lives could not be more different. Claire is the glamorous trophy wife of an Atlanta millionaire. Lydia, a single mother, dates an ex-con and struggles to make ends meet. But neither has recovered from the horror and heartbreak of their shared loss—a devastating wound that's cruelly ripped open when Claire's husband is killed.

The disappearance of a teenage girl and the murder of a middle-aged man, almost a quarter-century apart: what could connect them? Forming a wary truce, the surviving sisters look to the past to find the truth, unearthing the secrets that destroyed their family all those years ago . . . and uncovering the possibility of redemption, and revenge, where they least expect it.

*Husbands and wives. Mothers and daughters. The past and the future. Secrets bind them. And secrets can destroy them.*

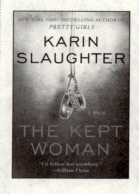

With the discovery of a murder at an abandoned construction site, Will Trent of the Georgia Bureau of Investigation is brought in on a case that becomes much more dangerous when the dead man is identified as an ex-cop. Studying the body, Sara Linton—the GBI's newest medical examiner and Will's lover—realizes that the extensive blood loss didn't belong to the corpse. Sure enough, bloody footprints leading away from the scene indicate there is another victim—a woman—who has vanished . . . and who will die soon if she isn't found.

Will is already compromised because the site belongs to the city's most popular citizen: a wealthy, powerful, and politically connected athlete protected by the world's most expensive lawyers—a man who's already gotten away with rape, despite Will's exhaustive efforts to put him away.

But the worst is yet to come. Evidence soon links Will's troubled past to the case . . . and the consequences will tear through his life with the force of a tornado, wreaking havoc for Will and everyone around him, including his colleagues, family, friends—and even the suspects he pursues.

Discover great authors, exclusive offers, and more at hc.com.